A Most Inconvenient Marriage

Books by Regina Jennings

A Most Inconvenient Marriage
Caught in the Middle
Love in the Balance
Sixty Acres and a Bride

*An Unforeseen Match**

*featured in the novella collection *A Match Made in Texas*

A Most Inconvenient Marriage

REGINA JENNINGS

BETHANYHOUSE
a division of Baker Publishing Group
Minneapolis, Minnesota

© 2014 by Regina Jennings

Published by Bethany House Publishers
11400 Hampshire Avenue South
Bloomington, Minnesota 55438
www.bethanyhouse.com

Bethany House Publishers is a division of
Baker Publishing Group, Grand Rapids, Michigan

Printed in the United States of America

Library of Congress Cataloging-in-Publication Data
Jennings, Regina (Regina Lea)
    A most inconvenient marriage / Regina Jennings.
      pages ; cm
    Summary: "To fulfill a Confederate soldier's dying wish, Civil War nurse Abigail Stuart marries him and agrees to look after his sister in the Missouri Ozarks. But then the real Jeremiah Calhoun appears alive"— Provided by publisher.
    ISBN 978-0-7642-1140-9 (softcover)
    1. Nurses—Fiction. 2. United States—History—Civil War, 1861–1865—Fiction. I. Title.
PS3610.E5614M67 2014
813'.6—dc23   2014029251

Scripture quotations are from the King James Version of the Bible.

Cover by John Hamilton Design

Author is represented by Books & Such Literary Agency

14 15 16 17 18 19 20   7 6 5 4 3 2 1

To my parents,
whose particular variety of inconvenience
has stood the test of time.

CHAPTER 1

February 1865
Gratiot Street Prison
St. Louis, Missouri

"First, you're going to write a good-bye letter to my sweetheart, and then you're going to marry me." The prisoner's smile belied the beads of sweat condensing on his forehead.

Abigail Stuart wrung tepid water out of the rag and mopped his brow. "I will not write your Lady Juliet to tell her that I've replaced her. Your fever must be causing you to hallucinate. Romeo was no fickle lover."

A fly landed on his chin. The prisoner lifted what was left of his arm, forgetting he couldn't reach his mouth with the putrid stump. Abigail shooed the pest away and wished for a blanket to alleviate his chills. Two years of caring for the dying Confederate prisoners had numbed her to the sight of mangled flesh, but she'd never stopped mourning the senseless pain these young men suffered.

"You won't be happy, Miss Abby. Not without a stable full of horses," he said. "And I can give you that. You've got to be sick and tired of this prison."

"My horses are gone. Nursing is all I have left."

The man wet his lips. "Marry me and you won't have to stay here another day. The farm, the stock, the nicest horseflesh in the hills—they'll all be yours. If the last thing I can do with this life . . ."

Dr. Jonson caught Abigail's eye. She'd already tarried too long with her favorite patient, but she wasn't sorry. He'd been kind to her, no matter what color his uniform had been before they'd cut him out of it. She sloshed the rag in the basin. The gangrene had poisoned his blood. She didn't have much time. Neither did he.

"What about your lady? Why not will the farm to her?"

"My sweetheart?" His eyes grew soft beneath the pain. He closed them and inhaled as though filling his lungs with the smell of fresh hay instead of the stench of the medical ward. With his good hand he tapped the thin mat beneath him. "My fiancée can take care of herself. This war won't slow her down. It's my . . . my sister that I worry about. Rachel isn't strong—hasn't been since she took the fever. You're a nurse, and you could help her ma with the farm. It's the perfect solution."

A faint hope stirred in Abigail's chest. Could this be the answer she'd been praying for? "But what if I don't like the Ozarks? What if your family doesn't welcome a Yankee invading their home?"

"Then walk away. What have you lost?"

She took his hand, surprised again by the dry heat in the freezing room. "You don't even know your real name, Romeo. Or has that memory finally been restored, too?"

He wiggled his feet against the end of the cot and shuddered as another chill ravaged his body. Quickly he mastered the pain, and the smile returned.

"My name is Jeremiah Calhoun. Captain Jeremiah Calhoun."

She'd suspected that his memory loss was a convenient occurrence, but like her, he had his reasons for hiding his past. "And what will I tell Lady Juliet?"

"The truth." An ornery grin stretched across his face. "She might be angry, especially when you turn up, tall and fair—everything she's not—but Rachel will be taken care of. That's where my duty lies."

Duty. Abigail knew only too well where misguided duty led. The graves outside the prison were filled with adherents.

"What's it going to be, Miss Abby? Don't leave me in suspense. I haven't got time for a long engagement."

She set the bowl on the stone floor and dried her hands on her apron. The South couldn't hold out much longer. The war would end soon. Abigail had fended off proposals from lonely patients since the siege of Vicksburg, but soon those who survived would be reunited with their families and their loved ones. Soon she would be alone in a world where able-bodied men were scarce and opportunities to work even scarcer. She couldn't go home. She wasn't welcome there anymore. With all the upheaval caused by the war, perhaps she should consider this offer, no matter the risks. And like he said—if it didn't work she hadn't lost anything.

"Captain Calhoun, if you'll allow me to procure a sheet of stationery, I'll return and we can send your love to your intended. That'll give me time to reflect—"

"While you're gone, you might want to freshen up." He winked mischievously. "I expect my bride to look her best."

March 1865
Hart County, Missouri

The stationmaster had said it was eight miles farther, but he hadn't mentioned the steepness of the mountain trails. Still, Abigail enjoyed the exertion in the chilly air, especially after her inactivity on the train. Muscles were meant to be challenged, so Abigail did her best to stretch her limbs in the privacy of the leafy path.

Moisture gathered between the fine riverbank gravel on the road. Water pooled beneath the pressure of her feet and then disappeared as she traveled upward, feeling the exertion in parts of her limbs that ladies didn't mention. The acres of rocky forest contrasted with the smooth pasture and farms—proof of the heroic effort expended to create the few clearings.

She shouldn't be surprised. Her Romeo had persevered like a hero, even if he was wearing the wrong color. He'd accepted the loss of his arm with fortitude, marching the two hundred fifty miles from Westport to St. Louis as a recent amputee, insisting he would soon be well enough to return to his hills and his love. But the infection he'd contracted along the way changed his focus.

By now his fiancée would know of his death. She would have his letter, and his family would have the notice penned by the medical staff. Abigail hadn't allowed them to share news of the marriage, still unsure if she would make use of the gift Jeremiah Calhoun had given her. How hard would it be to hear that your lover had married someone else? Especially if he died before you could give him what for. But Abigail had to consider his sister— the sister whom he had loved enough to jilt his intended, to drop the pretense that he would recover and see to his responsibility. If nothing else, at least she was honoring Jeremiah by checking on his mother and sister. She wouldn't remain if they were well, but where she'd go was still a mystery.

Abigail hadn't truly had a home since Mama remarried. After the wedding, everything from her new colt to her father's oak desk became John Dennison's. And rather than bite her tongue in two, Abigail had expressed her opinion rather forcefully as John sold everything in the stables. But he'd taken his revenge.

Abigail brushed aside the troubling memory. Forget the past. She had no past. She'd only look ahead. A honey locust tree crowded the path, the thorns on its trunk mean enough to please a Roman centurion. Abigail crushed the sides of her jade skirt as she passed, protecting it from damage. Perhaps she should be wearing mourning, but it didn't seem practical to dye her clothing before she decided if she was going to be a widow or not. With no new dresses since she'd left home, she couldn't afford to waste one.

The road leveled and a roughhewn cabin appeared at the back of the next clearing. Smoke curled from the stovepipe, and a dog scrambled from beneath the porch to announce her presence.

She heard raised voices, louder than the dog they were attempting to quiet. A child started crying. Abigail gripped her satchel tighter and sped her steps, eager to leave the chaos behind her.

"Where you going to?"

She skidded to a stop but couldn't find her questioner.

"I'm up here." A grimy face peered down between the naked branches. The boy's words whistled through the gap between his front teeth. "You're new 'bout these parts."

Was his face scratched or just dirty? Abigail couldn't tell. The boy dropped down, not noticing when his bare feet hit the stony path.

"Pa!" he called. "We got company."

"No, I'm not stopping," Abigail said. "My destination is the Calhoun farm."

"The Calhouns'?" A wide-eyed girl with uneven pigtails stepped out of the woods. "Should've known since you're dressed all nice and that."

"Me? Dressed nice?" Abigail looked at her traveling costume, then at the girl's shift. "Thank you, but I can't stop to visit. I have an important—"

"Going to the Calhouns'?" A man stepped out of the cabin, his beard spread across his chest like a napkin at suppertime. "I reckon we can show you the way."

"But it's right along the road, isn't it? The stationmaster said I couldn't get lost."

"No bother." He stuck his head inside the cabin and called, "Irma, I'll be back. Mind the hominy." Pulling a threadbare felt hat off a nail, he bounded off the porch steps with elbows and knees flying like the wooden limberjack dolls the prisoners made. He skidded to a stop before her. "Is that your only bag?"

A mountain man, yes, but with his children climbing up his back and clinging to his hand, Abigail didn't feel threatened. Even the dog ran circles around him, wagging its tail and barking playfully.

"The rest will be delivered tomorrow."

"Oh, sure. Finley's going to fetch them when he brings the post, huh? You wouldn't want to carry your luggage through these hills. Not a fancy lady like you."

And she had worried that her dresses were out of date. She surveyed the ragtag bunch. What if Jeremiah had exaggerated? What if his beautiful horse farm was no more than a cabin and some mules? The butterflies in her stomach turned into crazed birds. She slipped her hand into her pocket and held on to her father's penny. Jeremiah had said his sister needed her. Could Abigail leave her in a battered cabin, just because she was accustomed to a prosperous farm?

"What's your business at the Calhouns'?" With twinkling eyes the man pulled a corncob pipe out of his vest pocket and set it into his mouth.

"I'm coming to visit Mrs. Calhoun. I tended her son when he was a prisoner."

Hostile eyes accosted her from every side.

"Mr. Jeremiah was in prison?"

"You locked him up?"

"Are you a jayhawker?"

At the last word, tension bristled through the youngsters. Even their father eyed her suspiciously.

"I'm not sure what a jayhawker is," Abigail said. "I'm a nurse. It was my duty to care for the Rebel prisoners, so that's what I did."

"There aren't any jayhawkers around now, son," the bearded man said. "All those outlaws joined the Federal Army."

"But she worked for the Yankees, too." The tree climber spat.

"Josiah!" His father grew stern. "You mind your manners with the lady. She was a nurse to help our soldiers. Don't meddle in other folks' doings." Then forgetting his own advice he asked, "Were you with Jeremiah when he died?"

His gentle tone produced feelings of unexpected kinship in Abigail. It pleased her to meet people who admired Jeremiah as much as she did. "Yes, sir, I was. I held his hand as he passed and was there for the burial, as well. I was privileged to know him, even if it was for only a short time."

"Jeremiah was a good man. Don't know what his family will do without him." The rip in the knee of his trousers flapped with every step.

And he was worried about the Calhouns making ends meet?

"How's his sister?" Abigail asked. "He was concerned over her health, right until the end."

He scratched his beard. "Miss Rachel is sickly, so we shouldn't judge."

A sure voice piped up, "She don't like us to come into the house. We've got to leave her bundles at the back porch."

"And we can't whistle when we come up the drive. It 'fects her nerves."

The man nodded. "But she's been dealt a cruel blow. The same rheumatic fever that took her father took her health, and she hasn't been the same since. Lord have pity on poor Mrs. Calhoun."

More pity on the mother than on the afflicted sister? Abigail chewed her lip. What had Jeremiah forgotten to tell her?

The path crested the hill and continued downward until it reached a clearing that stretched over several acres. Bare winter saplings popped up through the split-rail fence that zigzagged toward a graceful stone house nestled in the valley.

Abigail rocked to her toes to get a better view of the farm before her, straining to see the barn. While it was a far cry from the elegant stables of her home, the large rock structure looked sturdy. Big enough to hold a decent herd through the winter. Perhaps Jeremiah had done her well, after all.

The children chirped in excitement, the dog adding to the cacophony until Abigail found sympathy for Miss Rachel's nerves. She stopped where the rail fence gave way to massive stone posts, pieced together like a crazy quilt. "I can hardly miss it from here. Thank you for . . ." but she was too late. The bottoms of grimy feet flashed as her young escorts raced down the drive.

"Them young'uns." In an amazing feat of dexterity the man passed the pipe to the other side of his mouth without touching it. "They sure run fast."

"Indeed."

They followed the children to the two-story house, its white trim defining the door and windows of the rock walls, lending order to the zigzag pattern. The children banged on the front door, and before Abigail could step on the porch, a silver-haired matron emerged.

"Please, children, keep your voices down. You don't want Miss Rachel to hear you."

If she'd thought to see any family resemblance between the woman and Romeo, Abigail was disappointed. The woman had generous features, wide cheekbones, and an ample mouth, unlike the narrow face of the soldier. But hadn't Jeremiah spoken of the woman as *Rachel's mother*? His stepmother, no doubt. Clad in mourning, she held a pair of scissors upraised like a broken parasol, perhaps keeping them out of the children's way. She definitely didn't demonstrate the carefree attitude that Romeo, er, Jeremiah was known for throughout Gratiot Prison.

She squinted up at Abigail, probably trying to place her.

"Mrs. Calhoun." Abigail dipped a faint curtsy. "I hope my visit isn't an inconvenience. I've traveled far to see you."

The woman tilted her head. "Not at all. I rather enjoy unexpected visitors. Are you an acquaintance of the Huckabees?"

Huckabees? They'd never even introduced themselves.

"No, ma'am," Mr. Huckabee said. "We just saw her on the road and thought we'd show her to the right spot. It's the least we can do for our neighbors. Now, before I get back to Mrs. Huckabee and the babies, I might just check on your stock, if you'd like."

"I would. That cow was stingy with her milk today. I don't know how you manage to get so much out of her."

"Confidence, ma'am." And he made a long pulling gesture to demonstrate his technique.

Mrs. Calhoun's chins waggled in mirth as Mr. Huckabee dragged his children off the porch. Abigail thanked him and followed Mrs. Calhoun into a messy parlor. The scent of lemon wax and the roaring fireplace imposed order on an otherwise chaotic setting.

An overturned basket of wrinkled laundry lay scattered across the settee. Ladies' journals balanced precariously on a small round table in the center of the room. Mrs. Calhoun deposited the heavy pair of scissors atop a stack of clippings that threatened to flutter away as she bustled past.

"Have a seat," she said. "I wasn't expecting a guest today, but I'll have some coffee hot in a jiffy."

"That would be delightful." Abigail needed time to collect her thoughts. She removed her hat and coat and hung them over a chair.

She'd finally arrived. Abigail straightened her green velvet cuffs as Mrs. Calhoun exited. What would she say? How could she broach the subject? Should she move the sharp scissors out of her mother-in-law's reach before she told her? Her hand slipped into her pocket and found the solitary penny she cherished. She turned to practice her speech on a collection of bells sitting in a dusty curio cabinet.

"When I met Jeremiah, he was a prisoner," Abigail whispered. "No, that's not right. How about: Jeremiah asked me to take care of his sister, Rachel. It was his last wish that I would make this journey." True, but how to mention his proposal? In all her imagining she hadn't been able to come up with one satisfactory introduction on the topic of her matrimonial state.

"Ma," a voice called from upstairs, "what brought the Huckabee swarm to our door?"

Abigail froze. There was no answer from the kitchen.

"Ma?"

If this was his sister, she obviously wasn't used to being ignored.

Soft footsteps could be heard sliding across the upstairs rug, then descending the stairs. Rachel Calhoun entered, stooped like a much older woman. The joints of her fingers flared an angry red. So Mr. Huckabee was correct about the rheumatic fever.

The girl straightened. "I'm sorry." She flipped her chestnut braid over the shoulder of her house gown, clearly not apologizing for anything. "And who might you be?"

Abigail stepped forward. "Hello, I just arrived—"

"Obviously." The lines about her mouth had settled deep, as if perpetually troubled.

"Yes. I'm a friend of Captain Calhoun. I promised him I would visit."

"A friend of my brother?" Rachel crossed her arms. "Your name?"

"Abigail . . ." she halted. When would she tell them the truth? Was it too early?

At Abigail's hesitation, Rachel sniffed. "Whoever your people are, you must not be proud of them. I might not be high and mighty, but I'm not ashamed of my kin."

Abigail lifted her clenched jaw at the reproach from the mountain girl. She was proud of the Stuart name, even if her mother no longer shared it and the farm she loved no longer bore it. But that door had closed. Besides, if she worked hard enough, maybe someday she could garner respect with a new name.

She took a deep breath and squared her shoulders. She'd found a new name for a new life, and she might as well start using it.

"My name is Calhoun . . . Abigail Calhoun. I'm Jeremiah's wife."

CHAPTER 2

"Jeremiah's wife?"

Abigail watched closely as the younger woman's eyes widened and her pale face turned celery green. Rachel stumbled forward, swinging her hands about, searching for the sofa.

"Let me help you," Abigail said.

Rachel sank into the cushions, heedless of the laundry that slipped to the floor. She reclined full out and covered her face with the crook of her arm.

A weak heart caused by a fever. That's what Jeremiah had said. Abigail's eyes flickered over the woman, assessing her condition. Shallow breaths that were obviously painful, stiff joints, a flair for the dramatic. Perhaps Jeremiah should've warned Abigail that her sister-in-law's most noticeable medical condition was a sharp tongue.

A crash sounded behind her. Mrs. Calhoun had shoved a tray of mugs onto the already crowded table in the center of the room, upending her sewing box and the stack of clippings.

"Did you have a spell? What are you doing downstairs?" She knelt beside her daughter. "Don't wear yourself out, especially after the Huckabees have unsettled your nerves."

"She's a fraud. She's lying," Rachel said. Strong words for such a weak voice.

Mrs. Calhoun cast a nervous glance at Abigail. "Simmer down, Rachel. There's no excuse for rudeness."

"Did you ask her who she is? Did you even get a name from her before you showed her inside? Her with her fine dress and city voice—"

"Don't get riled up. You're endangering your life," her mother said.

Obviously Rachel was now getting enough air to fill her lungs. Abigail tried to reassure the worried woman. "She's going to be fine, Mrs. Calhoun. Since the initial shock has worn off, she's regained her color. I'm a nurse and I don't think she's in imminent danger."

"That's probably a lie, too. You're too young to be a nurse." Rachel kept her arm over her face, probably so Abigail wouldn't be able to mark her return to health.

"I was certified by a Regional Aid Society," Abigail said. "When desperate, qualifications aren't as important, especially for one working with prisoners."

"I . . . I don't understand your quarrel. Why are you arguing?" Mrs. Calhoun turned to Abigail. "Please forgive my daughter. She's feeling poorly."

At least she had some spirit left in her. Abigail would rather work with a difficult patient than one who'd given up.

"Mrs. Calhoun, if you'll seat yourself, I'll share the news that's responsible for Miss Calhoun's distress."

"Shouldn't we help Rachel upstairs first?"

"I have a feeling she'll prefer to hear for herself. It's about your son, Jeremiah." Abigail seated herself. Her stomach rolled as she tried to find the right words.

"Was the letter from the prison wrong?" Mrs. Calhoun dropped onto the simple wooden chair. "Please tell me it was wrong. Tell me that Jeremiah's alive."

A pang of jealousy assailed Abigail. Did her family even remember that she existed? But this was about Jeremiah, so she focused on the woman who obviously valued her children above all else. "I wish that was my message, but it's not. You have the facts from your notification, but I shared his last days. I thought you might like to hear more."

"All we know is that he was captured at Westport and died in prison. That's all they told us."

She could tell them much more, but would they understand her motives? How badly she wanted to help? How badly she wanted a place to belong and a family to love? She hoped they didn't blame her for his unorthodox arrangement. Yet she'd faced unfounded accusations before.

"Jeremiah was wounded before his capture," Abigail said. "They amputated his arm at the field hospital and then marched him to the prison in St. Louis."

"All the way across Missouri?" Mrs. Calhoun fished a crumpled handkerchief from the pile of laundry on the floor. "What he must have suffered."

Mrs. Calhoun's tears prompted a stinging in Abigail's own eyes. How she wished she could've known Jeremiah here, whole, instead of sick in the prison. "But he kept strong. He'd already contracted infection and was in incredible pain, but everyone who met him loved him. Even when they had to carry him into the infirmary, he asked them to stop so he could cheer some dejected soul."

"Oh, Jeremiah," his mother cooed. "See, Rachel. I knew he'd have a change of heart."

From her position, Abigail could see that Rachel wasn't moving, but she was fully alert, listening closely. Abigail tried to steady her voice for what was to come.

"Of all the soldiers I met during the war, your son was my favorite. His first thought was for his fiancée, but when the situation changed and he realized that he would not recover, his concern for his sister eclipsed every other bond." Again the silence of the house pressed heavy as they drank in a last story of one they loved—one from whom they'd get no more news. "When he learned that I was knowledgeable about horses and nursing, Jeremiah asked me to come here to care for Rachel and to keep your farm profitable."

"He arranged that for us?" Mrs. Calhoun shook her head. "We can't pay, you know."

Rachel pulled herself up by the back of the sofa. "She doesn't want pay, Ma. That's not what she's shooting for. She wants everything—the whole farm. If we allow her story to go unchallenged, she will own everything and can evict us out into the wilderness. You know as well as I do that Jeremiah wouldn't marry a stranger."

"Marry?" The handkerchief fluttered to the floor. Mrs. Calhoun's face contorted through an encyclopedia of emotions as she stood. "Are you Jeremiah's wife?"

No matter how little she deserved it, the license had been legally binding. Abigail nodded and glanced at the scissors as she waited for the woman's response, a response that was building, whether of outrage or sorrow Abigail couldn't judge. Mrs. Calhoun's chin trembled and her arms opened.

"My beloved child, welcome home."

Abigail's head spun. All her worries, all her uncertainty, but God was faithful. He'd directed her to a safe place. Jumping to her feet, Abigail fell into the woman's embrace.

"You're not angry?"

"Oh, honey, you stayed by my son through his suffering. Thank the Lord for sending you to Jeremiah's side so he wasn't alone."

Mrs. Calhoun stepped back and took her hands. "I can never repay you."

Rachel groaned. "Ma, Jeremiah wouldn't marry without telling us. Not after the way he carried on about me."

"He didn't have time to notify you," Abigail said. "And he wouldn't have married me if a chance for recovery existed. In fact he'd almost waited too late. He didn't even have time to explain to his fiancée in his last letter. He only shared his love."

"Well, she never took up mourning," Mrs. Calhoun said. "And I suppose it's a blessing that she's been able to carry on. Any day now I expect to hear that Laurel and Dr. Hopkins are engaged."

Laurel? Jeremiah had always called her Juliet. He'd even asked Abigail to address his last letter to her by that name. What would her reaction be? At least Laurel had recovered enough to consider an alternative beau. Hopefully she'd accept Abigail's appearance with as much grace as Mrs. Calhoun had.

Finally looking her in the eyes, Rachel spoke. "You didn't happen to meet any other men of Jeremiah's division, did you? Were many of them captured?"

"I suppose so, but most of the prisoners at Gratiot Street were transferred back east. Jeremiah stayed only because he could go no farther."

Rachel grasped the doily-covered arm of the sofa to steady herself. "But who did he speak of? Did he mention Alan White? Was Alan a patient of yours?"

"Alan White? No, I don't recall anyone by that name."

"Don't fret," Mrs. Calhoun admonished her daughter. "Alan didn't say where he was in that last letter, but he's hardly had time to write again. Especially with the war winding down. You'll hear from him soon."

What unshed tears were stored in the dark circles below Rachel's eyes? She glared, obviously not satisfied with Abigail's tale. "If what you say is true, Jeremiah had nothing to lose, but what about you? Don't you have any family, or suitors, or anybody to care if you never come home? Why would you depend on strangers to take you in rather than friends?"

Abigail walked to the curio cabinet. Ceramic bells, crystal bells, brass . . . her head rang with accusations and defenses. She'd start anew if they'd let her, but there'd be questions about who she was, where she'd come from, why she wasn't welcomed by her family. Well, the truth was messy. Better to clean up the story before they pried any further.

"My father died in a riding accident, and after that my mother . . ." She added her fingerprints to those already smearing the glass curio cabinet. "I miss her. I have no one, so I came west."

There. That was enough. She'd told herself that if they didn't accept her, she could leave at first light. Nothing lost. But now that a glimpse of a home, a family, a farm had been offered, she didn't want to lose it.

"See, Rachel. Abigail has every reason to stay with us." Mrs. Calhoun sat next to her daughter and wrapped an arm around her. To Abigail's surprise, Rachel had the grace to look ashamed.

"I don't want her to cause you any trouble, Ma. You have enough of a burden caring for me. If she doesn't pull her weight—"

She might as well get started. Abigail turned to the ladies. "Before I became a nurse, I lived on a horse farm. I helped my father in every aspect of the business, and I promise I'll work harder for you than anyone ever has. In fact, I'm anxious to take a look around and visit the stock."

Mrs. Calhoun nodded, already deep in her memories. "That'd be fine."

Abigail gazed at the mug of coffee that'd never made it to her hand, but she couldn't wait to reach the barn. She took up her coat.

Mrs. Calhoun stood. "Oh, and Abigail, I know you had a mother you loved, and I don't want to take her place, but I'd be honored if you'd call me Ma. That is, if it ain't presuming too much."

Although the family resemblance wasn't visible in her features, her warmth and kindness had clearly shaped her son's character.

"I'd love to have you as my ma," Abigail said. "You're all the family I have left."

Besides visits from his caregivers, the single shaft of light from above was the only connection he had to the world outside. Soon he'd be set free from this prison, this cave, and he could finally crawl out of hiding. He could finally go home.

Home.

He'd made a mistake and because of it home could change forever. He prayed it wasn't too late to undo what he'd done. When he was free, he'd get it straight and no one would be hurt. He'd take care of everything if, for once, they'd let him.

He sucked the last of the marrow out of the chicken bone, thankful for each morsel that they'd spared him. Oh, that God would give him the strength to see to his duty. He wouldn't quit until his family was safe and their lives were restored, but if he went home alone, nothing would be solved. He'd never be forgiven.

The barn hugged a rise on the south of the house. As no sip of coffee had made it to her lips, Abigail strode to the trough.

She dumped out the water bucket, pumped fresh water in, and drained a full dipper in one thirsty pull. She wiped her mouth with the back of her hand and smacked her lips. Poor breeding? Her mother had taught her how to behave in a drawing room just as her father had taught her how to behave in a barn. Manners consisted of nothing more than the ability to put someone at ease, and she dearly hoped she could ease the troubles here.

After helping herself to another dipper, Abigail was in a better frame of mind to meet the horses. At least they wouldn't behave as poorly as Jeremiah's sister.

The pasture appeared somewhat maintained. Despite the errant saplings, the fence was intact and the barn solid. She found the gate between two stone posts, hinges a bit rusty but still swinging with only a slight protest.

A bay raised his head at the noise. The gray horse perked his ears, too. Abigail shielded her eyes to get a better look and was pleased by what she saw. Deep chests, strong haunches, with delicate feet and heads—promising even from this distance. Then their alert ears picked up the sound of something more interesting than the gate. Rattling a bucket of corn, Mr. Huckabee stepped out of the barn.

"Oh," Abigail breathed as the two horses sped to a graceful canter. If it weren't for the tufts of wet soil flipping up behind them, she could almost believe they were floating above the ground. Jeremiah hadn't exaggerated. She would be proud of these horses.

She latched the gate behind her and approached them cautiously.

"I thought you might want to inspect them closer." The stallion pushed ahead to get first dibs on the bucket, his tail swishing high. "By the way, I'm Calbert Huckabee. Did you get to meet Miss Rachel?"

Remembering that barn manners were different than parlor, Abigail extended her hand, pleased when he took it without pausing. "Yes, I did. And please call me Miss Abigail. Do you mind?" She nodded to the bucket.

"Help yourself."

She plunged her hands into the dusty corn, surprised by the memories the familiar action revived. The rolling kernels, their simple weight and sweet smell reminded her of a happiness that had eluded her since her mother had remarried.

Bringing up brimming handfuls, she stepped away, drawing the stallion after her for a better inspection. The bay seemed to read her intent. His eyes flashed. He tossed his head and pranced to her.

"He's a proud one," she said.

"He should be. He's from Texas, sired by Steel Dust."

"Is that so?" She held her hand flat. The horse's velvety muzzle razed her palm, snorting the familiar scent in her face. "How did I manage without my horses?"

Calbert smiled. "How long are you staying with Mrs. Calhoun?"

"This is my home now." She'd found somewhere new and she'd fight to keep it. Abigail scratched the stallion on the forehead as he nudged the last kernel from between her fingers. "You know these horses well. Are you their groom?"

"Don't know that I'd have any such fancy title as that. I'm busy with my own place most the time, but I try to keep an eye on Mrs. Calhoun. Just being neighborly. I figure I owe Jeremiah that much, God rest his soul. After his Pa died he wore himself out keeping this place going."

But Abigail was already planning the future. One stallion and a gelding—not a fortune, but they were first quality. When she returned to the house, she'd ask to see their pedigrees, not that it mattered. Their breeding was obvious by sight, but she was curious. What familiar names would she see? Could either of these have Stuart bloodlines?

Mr. Huckabee was inspecting her as closely as she'd been watching the horses. "You say you knew Jeremiah?"

Abigail had better become accustomed to telling her unusual story and making it sound as convincing as possible. "I married Captain Calhoun."

Mr. Huckabee snatched his hat off his head and slapped it against his knee. "I knew it! The minute I laid eyes on you I thought, 'There's a lady for Jeremiah. They would've been a fine matched team, for certain.'" He sobered. "If only he'd made it home."

"If he thought he was coming home, he wouldn't have married me."

"What's that?"

Abigail dusted off her hands, then hid them in her coat pockets. "It was a practical arrangement on his end. I didn't know what to expect from his farm, but I'm fully eager to fall in love with this place."

"And you haven't seen the prize pumpkin yet. She's entitled to some time by herself, if you know what I mean." Mr. Huckabee tossed the remaining corn in a trough and turned toward the barn.

Abigail nearly skipped along behind him. The rock walls hugged the warmth from the animals and kept it from stealing outside. A pen of pigs huddled together, and a goat bounded off a table as she walked by. With the shutters closed it felt a bit muggy, yet to Abigail there was nothing unbecoming about stable smells. A whinny drew her eyes before they adjusted to the shade. A gentle face watched her approach, black forelock falling across a yellow-dun hide. Love at first sight.

"Her name is Josephine Bonaparte. Lancaster out there is her sire." Mr. Huckabee continued to describe her gait, her intelligence, but Abigail didn't need to hear an appraisal. She was convinced.

"She's in season, I gather." Abigail scratched her cheek. "Has she been bred before?"

"No, ma'am. Laurel's pa bought a stallion for her, though. He was going to be a wedding present for Jeremiah and Laurel when he came back from the war."

Laurel, her husband's fiancée. Abigail saw her face reflected in Josephine's gentle eye. The horse blinked knowingly and nudged her hand. Abigail smiled. She'd lost her horses back home, but maybe God had blessed her with this opportunity. Talking to Laurel would be awkward, but she had to be told. Procrastinating only impeded progress, and right now the progress Abigail was most concerned with was filling the pasture with horses. That was the best way she could help her new ma and Rachel.

Romeo was counting on her.

"How far away is this stallion?" Josephine nibbled at a blond lock that had escaped Abigail's coif.

"Just across the river, about a mile from the ford."

"Would it be possible to take Josephine to visit tomorrow?"

Mr. Huckabee pulled at his beard. "I've just been waiting for permission."

---------------∞---------------

The next morning, Abigail sat at the table inhaling the rich scent of the coffee warming the ceramic mug. She hadn't worn her riding habit since leaving Ohio. The wool skirt and jacket felt perfect for the crisp March air. She only waited to see if Ma Calhoun needed her before setting out on her quest. The previous day her prayers had been vague, aimed at finding direction in a swirling mist of possibilities. Now she had concrete requests and hoped God didn't mind her being specific.

She prayed that Napoleon, Laurel's horse, would be no taller than sixteen hands high, that he would be agile and good-natured. She prayed that the Wallaces would waive the stud fee, although she would take her nurse's earnings with her as a precaution. She prayed that Laurel wouldn't have a strong reaction to her presence—to her existence—and that Rachel's health and temperament would both improve. She prayed that her own mother would see through John's false accusations and come running to find her, although how she was to track her to Hart County, Missouri, Abigail had no clue. Since her mother hadn't answered her first letter, Abigail didn't feel up to writing again. Still, she prayed that someday they'd be reconciled. Then, with quick thanks for Ma Calhoun, Abigail finished her morning petitions.

"Do you always rise this early?" Ma shuffled into the kitchen, still in her night robe. Pins trained her white hair into curls around her face.

"I'm sorry if I woke you. I thought taking the downstairs bedroom would keep you from hearing me."

"Keep it. Jeremiah would want you to have his room." She took a chair at the table and arranged the salt shaker and the sugar bowl until they were an equal distance from the butter dish. "You know, I hope you don't judge Rachel too harshly. I'm not blind to her faults, but if opposing her could shorten her life . . . well, I'd rather have an ill-tempered daughter than no children at all."

Abigail tried to understand Ma's position, but the closest she could come was *I'd rather have an ill-tempered husband than no husband at all.* And with that statement, she could not agree.

"She hasn't always been like this," Ma continued. "The fever changed her. It changed us all. And the longer she goes without hearing from Alan, the quicker her decline."

Abigail reached for the coffeepot and filled a second mug for Ma Calhoun. "Who is Alan?"

"Alan is Rachel's beau, at least I think I can say that now. Jeremiah wouldn't let us call him that, even if everyone knew it." She took the mug from Abigail. "When Mr. Calhoun died, Jeremiah took on all his father's responsibilities. He was too young, really, but he did the best he could. Not only did he have to work the farm, but he had Rachel to fret over, too, and he didn't want something to happen to her while she was in his care. Alan came around about the time the other girls Rachel's age started courting. If I had to wager, I'd say Alan was enchanted by Rachel's frailty. He'd do anything for her, and she blossomed under his attention, but it wasn't enough. Jeremiah didn't want them courting until Rachel was well, so Alan wasn't allowed to visit Rachel once Jeremiah realized his intentions."

"That doesn't sound like Jeremiah. I admit I didn't know him well, but I can't imagine him wanting to keep them apart."

Mrs. Calhoun patted her arm. "I'm blessed to hear that. When he and Alan joined the cavalry, Rachel and I prayed Alan would convince him to reconsider. Rachel's life has held such little happiness, the prospect of being denied Alan's love was more than she could bear. Her last letter from Alan was grim, and she's finding it harder to hold on to hope."

"Jeremiah didn't allow her to accept Alan, but he married a complete stranger? No wonder she doesn't like me."

Ma raised white eyebrows. "If only she and Jeremiah would've reconciled before he left for the Missouri State Guard. It's guilt that plagues her, and she doesn't know what to do with it."

"I've done nothing wrong." Rachel stood in the doorway holding a slender pipe between her fingers. "Jeremiah was the one who was wrong, strutting around, demanding his own way. He's the one who should have been ashamed." With defiance she pulled a long draw from the pipe.

Mrs. Calhoun bowed her head. "If Alan would've stayed here, he would've been forced to fight for the Federals, and you know he wouldn't have done that. You'd be waiting for him either way, so you might as well wait with a cheerful heart. Alan won't be pleased to find you dishonoring your brother's memory."

And what would Alan think of the tobacco pipe she was puffing on? Abigail had only heard of pipe-smoking women in caricatures ridiculing poor Southerners. Never did she imagine she would have a sister-in-law with the habit.

Rachel slowly released a stream of smoke directly into Abigail's face. "What's wrong? You didn't bring your own tobaccy?"

Abigail swallowed down a cough. "What does your doctor say about your pipe?"

"Dr. Hopkins?" She laughed. "As long as Dr. Hopkins is shining up to Laurel, he tiptoes around here. He doesn't want any trouble with the family."

Ah yes. They'd mentioned that Jeremiah's fiancée had been seeing a doctor, but he was Rachel's doctor? That was uncomfortable. Rachel blew another ribbon of smoke. Then again, maybe Rachel preferred uncomfortable.

"Well, the sun is up." Abigail set her mug down. "I'm taking Josephine to the Wallace farm this morning. No sense in wasting time. We need to start adding to our herd."

"*Our* herd? You're already taking the credit for them?" Rachel asked.

"And the responsibility. Those animals are good stock, but they're an investment that will lose value if they aren't producing. You can't keep selling them off without replenishing the herd. Now, let me get you a cup of coffee."

Abigail rose, pulled out a chair, and turned to get another mug. She was proud that her hands were steady even though her heart pounded. She wanted to earn Rachel's trust and friendship, but she could tell that Rachel wouldn't like anyone she didn't respect.

"I suppose you'll tell Laurel who you are." Ma's cup clattered on the table. "There's really no way around it. Poor girl. I never thought she and Jeremiah suited each other, but they were so in love I didn't have the courage to oppose them. It'll be a blow."

"Ma, if Jeremiah really married this woman, how can you say he loved Laurel? You need to hoe your rows straight."

"Jeremiah did what he thought was best for us. Marrying Abigail had nothing to do with his feelings for Laurel."

Jeremiah loved Laurel. Alan loved Rachel. Abigail was the only one unspoken for. She looped her finger into the crook of the mug handle and thought about the hundreds of men who'd passed through the prison hospital, some entering eternity before they could be identified. If God had made a partner for her, what were the chances that he was still alive? Could her perfect match have suffered on a bed in her ward and she missed the chance to say good-bye—or even hello?

She'd always championed lost causes. Now she might be one herself.

CHAPTER 3

With no sidesaddle available, Abigail kept tugging at her riding habit to keep it from bunching up above her ankles. Might as well smoke a pipe while she was at it, and be a true hill woman. She ducked as they passed beneath a low cedar. The horse's tail swished. Josephine trotted up the steep trail as surefooted as a mountain goat.

"Has she ever raced?" Abigail asked over her shoulder.

"No," Calbert Huckabee said. "She was barely broke before Jeremiah left. I've ridden her now and then but haven't worked her like she needed. She flies across the pasture, though." The mule Calbert rode nipped at Josephine and earned a sideways kick. "That's Hiram Wallace's field ahead. You might as well see what she can do."

Abigail wouldn't wait for a second offer. As soon as they reached the clearing, she secured her feet in the stirrups, getting a feel for the unusual posture, and gave an encouraging, "Yaw!"

That was all it took.

With a twitch of the ears, Josephine was off. So sudden was

her start, so quickly did she reach a full gallop that Abigail had to remind herself to loosen the reins, and once she did, Josephine found another exhilarating burst. Abigail's body swayed with the hooves thundering across the uneven field. To smile was to risk catching bugs in her teeth, but she couldn't keep from grinning.

Abigail flexed her fingers over the reins. Had it really been since Chillicothe that she'd ridden? How had she borne it? So perceptive was Josephine that by the time Abigail thought about slowing, she'd already fallen into a canter. Abigail was pleased with the horse, and it increased her determination to have more just like her. Josephine should be the matriarch of many fine steeds, and it was up to Abigail to see it happen.

And only that goal could've brought her to the Wallaces'. Now that Abigail had found a course worth mastering, it'd be best to take her hurdles head-on when she was expecting them. Like Jeremiah's fiancée. If Abigail didn't meet Laurel soon, Rachel would send word to her, and Laurel deserved a more delicate disclosure.

Calbert took the reins while Abigail went to the door, but before she could knock, a gentleman appeared from around the clapboard house.

"No use beating on the door. We're outside." The man's bald spot had pinked in the cold wind. He stepped into the shelter of the porch. His pleated dress shirt looked out of place with canvas pants and suspenders, but times were tough.

"Hiram, this is Mrs. Abigail Calhoun." Calbert scratched his beard. "She's got business to discuss with you."

"A pleasure to meet you." He produced a handkerchief from a back pocket to clean his hands. "I figured you came from the Calhouns' place when I saw you riding Josephine. Mrs. Calhoun and Rachel are well, I hope?"

"Yes, sir. They send their greetings."

"Greetings shared and troubles bared. That's what neighbors are for. Now what can I do for you?"

Abigail looked to Calbert. She hadn't planned on getting to business so quickly, but from the look of Mr. Wallace, he was eager to return to his tasks.

Calbert spoke up. "It's high time we make use of this good breeding pair we got ourselves. Miss Abigail is looking after Mrs. Calhoun's interest, and we believe that every season Josephine doesn't produce a foal is a crying shame."

He smiled. "I agree. What sort of partnership are you offering?"

Abigail exhaled. Finally she was on familiar ground. "I'd like to inspect Napoleon first."

"Of course. But you'll find nothing wanting. He's a fine specimen and has sired some beautiful colts."

Admittedly, the people in Hart County spent more on their horses than their clothing. She hadn't expected to find such good stock here, and while Abigail knew how to haggle, she'd never denigrate an animal to get the price down. If Napoleon was as stunning as they promised, she wouldn't pretend to be disappointed.

"After an inspection, I'd be willing to offer half ownership in the foal. Josephine is untested and we'd hate to waste our money—"

"I have no interest in half a horse. It'd be a year before it's born, and it'd be a wonder if you keep her that long, seeing how the law in these parts has no interest in watching out for livestock. I'm afraid I need the payment up front."

It'd been worth the try, but she expected as much. They were strangers, after all, and that's why she'd brought her savings.

A rustling drew Abigail's attention to a well-worn path that wound behind the house. A young woman emerged with a basket of pinecones in her hand. From beneath her straw bonnet, hair as dark as poppy seeds peeked out. Her brows painted stark lines above cornflower blue eyes that noticed the horse immediately. "Father, isn't that Josephine?"

Her skin glowed from her expressive face all the way to dainty fingers that emerged from an unraveling sweater, making Abigail feel pale and ungainly in contrast. No wonder Jeremiah had been smitten.

"Yes, dear. This is Mrs. Calhoun, who has come to stay with her family."

"I'm afraid we haven't met. I'm Laurel." She secured the basket in the crook of her arm and tilted her head to smile up at Abigail. "Pretty dress. You must be from Springfield."

"Further east, I'm afraid." Abigail's eyes darted to Calbert. His beard slid up and down his chest with his nod. Waiting wouldn't make it easier. "I confess I've dreaded our meeting because of the tidings I bear."

Creases appeared on Laurel's forehead. "Bad news for me?" She stepped closer to her father. "What about?"

Laurel's troubled eyes did nothing to ease Abigail's disquiet. She could only pray that Laurel was more understanding than Rachel. "I met Captain Calhoun, your fiancée, after he was injured at Westport. He spoke of you constantly—no praise was too high, no comparison worthy."

Laurel ducked her head and pulled her sweater tighter. "Well, he never did do things by half. He didn't . . . well, I hope he didn't suffer, did he?"

"He bore it well. He was brave, cheerful, always thinking of others even when it became clear he was dying. He was a great favorite among the men for his antics to keep their spirits up."

"Jeremiah?" Hiram frowned. "Jeremiah's never been one to cut capers."

"War changes people, sir. It causes people to act in ways you can't predict." Abigail owed Laurel a personal explanation. After this revelation the news would travel on its own legs. She took a deep breath. "What I'm about to tell you is difficult. He loved you, Miss Wallace. If you'll consider the sentiments he expressed in his last letter—"

"Please, don't." Laurel's eyes darted to her father, then back to Abigail. "I know it'll be painful getting over his death, but Jeremiah wouldn't want me to mourn indefinitely."

Indefinitely? It'd only been a month. Then Abigail remembered the sparking doctor.

"Jeremiah would approve of you moving on and would hope you'd understand his own practicality. When Jeremiah realized his death was imminent, he wanted to guarantee his sister and Mrs. Calhoun would be cared for. Knowing that I'm a nurse and that I was raised on a horse farm, he asked me to come here. And to ensure that legally I could make decisions for the Calhoun farm"—she looked from father to daughter—"he made me his wife."

Laurel's mouth dropped open. "His wife? All this time I worried that—" She clutched at her midsection. "Are you sure? Jeremiah isn't . . . wasn't the type of man to change his mind easily."

"He didn't change, not at all. This was purely a matter of convenience. If it's any comfort, we were never even alone together. He was faithful to you until the end."

Her basket slid off her arm and toppled to the ground. "I . . . I don't know what I'm supposed to say. I'd assumed his last moments were spent thinking of me."

No longer able to bear the hurt on Laurel's face, Abigail

studied the pine cones spilled at her feet. "They were. You and Rachel were all he cared about. I'm only here to honor his wishes."

"I thought you must be a cousin of some sort." Hiram slid his hands into his pockets. "But a dead man's wife only brings strife. Can you imagine how humiliated Laurel will be when everyone finds out that Jeremiah married you?"

"I'll explain the situation as often as you'd like," Abigail said. "I have no desire to present myself as something I'm not."

"But far as I'm concerned, the horse deal is void. Those horses were to be wedding gifts—"

"Father." Laurel secured an ebony lock behind her ear. "Don't be hasty. We might not like the situation, but harassing Mrs."— she swallowed—"Mrs. Calhoun accomplishes nothing. If Jeremiah would have married me, you'd have the upkeep of both farms on your hands, so perhaps it's for the best. Besides, we could use the money."

She should've known that Jeremiah's Juliet was a woman of valor. Hadn't he told her so?

"I'd appreciate the assistance," Abigail said. "I'm prepared to pay and leave Josephine today."

Hiram grumbled through the negotiations. Laurel remained subdued, but given the circumstances, Abigail thought she'd conducted herself heroically. She owed the young woman for not making her task any more difficult and would look for every opportunity to thank her.

After Abigail inspected Napoleon, they haggled a price and soon reached an agreement. Josephine would stay at the Wallace ranch for a few weeks. The fee was the same, whether she foaled or not, and Abigail handed over the velvet drawstring bag of her earnings, knowing how little remained in the bureau drawer back at the farm.

"Thank you, Mrs. Calhoun." Hiram passed the bag into his

daughter's hands. "I hope a year from now you have a healthy, pristine foal, but even more than that I hope your tale does nothing to tarnish Laurel's memories of Jeremiah."

Abigail nodded. As long as she had his farm, she'd leave the memories for Laurel.

April 1865
St. Louis, Missouri

The stench seeped from the wooden floors and brick walls of the third-floor prison hospital even though most of the patients had gone. Where they ultimately rested, the man didn't want to imagine. He had enough trouble keeping up with those he was responsible for. Miles traveled, records searched, soldiers questioned, and he was no closer to an answer than at Westport when he last saw him.

The nurse offered a chair. He refused, though the effort cost him. Putting the war behind him would be difficult when he bore the painful reminders of his involvement, but unless he wanted his mind to be as unsound as his body, he couldn't dwell on all that had happened.

"Here's the register, sir. I looked for the dates you requested, but I didn't find the name." The nurse didn't wear a uniform, but then again, neither did he. She held the book out to him, and noticing his situation she flattened it open on the desk. "Truthfully, our records got behind after '64. Still, if you'd like to have a look yourself "—her ragged fingernail pointed to the correct line—"start here and work your way down."

Whether the nurse stayed or left, the man didn't notice. The names, stacked one on top of the other like corpses bound for a communal grave, burned into his memory.

"Sherman, Matthew. Smythe, Thaddeus. Pettey, Oliver."

There was no order, no reason. He was not allowed the mercy of being able to bypass any of the names—several familiar, a few dear. No, he had to look at each one and endure the memories.

"Stevens, Edwin. Grisham, Clement. Calhoun, Jeremiah."

The pit of his stomach grew cold. He blinked and bent closer to touch the register where the blotched ink spelled out the horrendous mistake. "Calhoun, Jeremiah. Died February 23, 1865."

His hand trembled. He fell against the desk, causing it to screech across the floor. The nurse appeared instantly.

"Are you ill? Let me help you to a chair."

He waved her away, his eyes fastened to the register.

Jeremiah Calhoun wasn't the name he sought. It was a shock, but more important than a faulty record was finding the man he'd wronged.

He prayed that he wasn't too late.

Hart County, Missouri
Two Weeks Later

Abigail read the rejection in Varina Helspeth's sneer before she spoke.

"I don't care if she did marry Jeremiah, I don't want no Yankee woman looking after my son."

The woman's face was as plain as an empty paper sack and just as flat. A fine line of whiskers dusted her top lip. Abigail thought her mouth would sooner splinter than curve into a smile.

Dr. Hopkins picked up his medical bag from her front step. "Come on, Mrs. Calhoun. They don't need our services here." He dropped his hat atop his thick shock of hair and spun his lanky frame.

Another rejection. Abigail didn't blame the woman. If her own mother didn't trust her, why should a complete stranger?

She had one foot on the bare dirt path when Varina grunted. "But you have to help him, Doctor. We have to get the shot out of his back."

"I don't work without my nurse. If you don't need her help, you don't need mine."

Let her son die or allow Abigail in the house? The length of time it took the woman to decide proved once again how hated outsiders were in these woods.

Without a word, Varina disappeared into the house, leaving Abigail and Dr. Hopkins outside. Was that a no? As if reading her thoughts, Dr. Hopkins leaned down and whispered, "She left the door open. You won't get more of an invitation than that."

With a smile she followed the sharp-chinned doctor inside.

The young man's wounds weren't serious. He'd been peppered with bird shot in an innocent hunting accident. The injury would heal quickly if it was kept clean. Seeing that the Helspeths' cabin was on the same mountain as the Calhouns', it only made sense for Abigail to check his progress and leave Hopkins free for his more important daily duties—holding down the porch swing at the Wallace place, for example.

"Have Calbert ride with you," Dr. Hopkins suggested as they departed. "There are dangerous men lurking about. Our troubles started before the war began, and they aren't ended just because it's over."

It wasn't difficult to believe the foreboding woods held hidden dangers. Even graced with the breathtaking dogwoods and cheery redbuds, their dark crevices covered secrets. If honest, hard-working people would snub her to her face, what were the outlaws capable of?

Abigail shuddered. She didn't need an imagination to know

what evils men would commit—she'd seen them, both in battle wounds and in the care of the prisoners she'd worked with.

"Did you serve with Jeremiah?" Abigail asked as the horses picked their way back to the Calhoun side of the mountain.

"Yes, ma'am." Hopkins had the creaky voice of a much older man. "We joined the Missouri State Guard to protect our state from foreign invaders, but General Fremont declared us traitors. No surrenders, no prisoners. Men merely hung as common outlaws if captured in battle. Little by little as we found opportunity, our divisions enrolled with the Confederate Army, so we'd be treated as proper soldiers. In '62 Jeremiah signed under Major General Price in the Army of the West. I stayed with Colonel McBride as he went to Arkansas."

"But you've been home—" Too late Abigail realized how her words could be heard as an accusation. "I don't mean to pry."

His chin rose. "I have nothing to be ashamed of. I provided medical care with the army until '64, when General McBride requested my services for himself. He'd been unwell and was headed further south, hoping warmer weather would rid him of the pneumonia that had afflicted him. By the time he died, I knew my chances of finding a unit to join were slim with Arkansas under Union control, so I decided to go home and help the families left behind."

Abigail couldn't help but like the earnest young man who obviously cared more for healing than conquering.

He continued. "Naturally I had no intention of falling in love with Laurel. It's bothered me that I was enjoying her company while Jeremiah fought . . . and died. But you're here now, and I thank you. Evidently even Jeremiah believed that four years was too long to wait."

He tugged his hat a bit lower on his head. At least someone was grateful for her—two people, counting Ma Calhoun. She didn't have the heart to tell the doctor that Jeremiah never stopped loving Laurel. If she'd learned anything recently, it was that people often preferred not to know the whole truth, and that suited her just fine.

CHAPTER 4

May 1865

Life at the Calhoun farm was settling into a pleasant routine. Before Abigail's arrival, Rachel's dependence on her mother meant that the housework had been abandoned, but Abigail soon had it set aright. Although the simple furnishings couldn't compare to those of Abigail's childhood home, she took pride in the cozy, tidy rooms. And every day after she completed her household chores and finished rounds with Dr. Hopkins, Abigail spent her afternoons grooming, feeding, and exercising the horses. In the beginning, they resisted being put through their paces, but they soon accepted their daily routine. If only Rachel would adjust to her care, as well.

Rachel. Abigail tossed a bucket of oats into the trough. If her sister-in-law possessed the strength of an able-bodied woman, she'd be a nuisance indeed. But to be fair, if she weren't sick she wouldn't have been allowed to carry on so. Abigail balanced the bucket on the top rail of the fence and wiped her hands on her cotton everyday dress. If only she could find a way to break through Rachel's harsh façade. Judging the severity of her symptoms, one more bout of the fever would be the end of her. Had Rachel considered the memories she'd be leaving behind?

The horses were fed, but Ma wouldn't have supper ready for another hour at least. The sun skimmed the tops of the trees at the back of the pasture. Another area she hadn't explored. Not wanting to disrupt the horses' dinner at the trough, Abigail set out on foot, pausing to inspect a thresher set against the fence, rusty with idleness.

Yes, they would need to plow up a field and get some barley in soon. One foal a year wasn't enough to live on. The farm was capable of producing more crops than Ma had scratched out during the war.

Abigail snapped off a head of Queen Anne's lace as she made her way up the ridge. Stopping where it crested, she looked down on the valley below. She hadn't realized that the road she walked in on curved around the back of the property. Not that she was surprised. The Ozark wagon trails wormed through the hollows as crookedly as a greedy quartermaster. Twirling the stem of Queen Anne's lace, she made her way down the steep hill, cautious of the loose rocks that tumbled before her.

No wonder this area hadn't been cleared. It was too sharp to ride on, too sheer to farm. Its only benefit was that it provided a protective barrier between the road and the farm. Unless those bushwhackers and jayhawkers she kept hearing about rode billy goats, they wouldn't sneak up on the house from the back.

Taking advantage of her height and the privacy, Abigail hitched up her skirt and scaled the split-rail fence, sliding the last few feet down to the road that cut through the narrow valley. If she figured correctly, the walk around to the front gate wasn't far—easier to tackle than trudging over the ridge on the rough side. Besides, she could inspect the fence more carefully and see if there were any gaps or more farm equipment rusting outside the barn.

In the valley the late afternoon sun was too weak to throw honest-to-goodness shadows. Instead, everything appeared hazy, making it unclear where undergrowth ended and where darkness began. Abigail caught herself straining to peer into deep crevices, wondering if they were truly caves or merely overhangs. There could be any number of eyes watching from the craggy dens—animals or men. She remembered Dr. Hopkins's warning. She shouldn't stray too far from home.

The road swerved around a boulder. The passage narrowed, a dangerous turn for a buggy. Abigail was just thinking how she'd have to remember to slow here when she stepped into the sight of a man standing in the road.

With one hand on his pommel and one hand grasping the back of his saddle, he froze when he saw her. The horse shifted toward him, and he did an odd hop backwards to keep from being bumped. Turning back to his horse he tried to pull himself up by the pommel without putting his foot in the stirrup. Uncomfortable with the off-center weight, the horse stumbled to the side again, causing him to slide back down.

He landed easily on one foot, but the other never touched the ground. Obviously he was favoring it. Abigail saw his difficulty. His leg had drawn up short and wouldn't hold his weight. The horse would have to stand still for him to mount.

Was he dangerous? Possibly, but as of yet the fabled bushwhackers and jayhawkers sounded more like the bogeymen of her youth. This man showed no interest in her, wasn't mounted, and definitely couldn't run. She approached cautiously, compassion overriding her fear.

"I'll hold her for you." She smiled to ease his embarrassment.

He dipped his head, only showing her the top of his hat. "If she'd stand still I could do it myself. I just wanted to test my leg before I got home. My family doesn't know . . ."

Abigail snagged the reins and rubbed the nag's nose. How many of her patients were still on the road home, heading to a future fraught with similar difficulties? "Your horse looks tired—like she's traveled hard. No doubt you could both use a stretch after being on the road all day." Once she had control of the horse, she nodded to him. This attempt was successful, graceful even. His chest filled once he was in place, the embarrassment of his condition vanishing on horseback. Had she not seen his struggle, she would've never guessed that he'd dealt with any weakness—besides pride, perhaps.

"Thank you for your help." Only seated would he face her, his strong features direct and honest, if not necessarily patient. His dark brows framed piercing eyes. His nose—well, if she was being kind she'd call it senatorial.

He shook the reins, reminding her to release them and stop staring at him. She felt her face warm. Had she been in the mountains so long she'd forgotten how to act around a gentleman? Without a word she stepped aside, allowing him to move forward. After a few steps he turned.

"It's getting dark. How far a piece do you have to go?"

Abigail touched her hair, suddenly wishing she had it up properly instead of hanging down in a braid. "Not far at all. This is my home." She gestured to the mountain wall on her left.

He looked around as if to assure himself of his surroundings, and then his penetrating gaze settled on her again.

This time his voice was rough. "Do the Calhouns not live here anymore?"

"They do. Are you a neighbor?"

His laugh was mirthless. "I'm no neighbor. I'm Jeremiah Calhoun, and I'd like to know what claim you have on my farm."

———⊷∞⊶———

He'd never met her before, that was certain. Jeremiah wouldn't have forgotten the willowy blonde frowning at him. She kept staring, but this time instead of gazing at his face, she looked at his hands. Squaring her shoulders she seemed to come to a conclusion.

"You are a liar." Her voice echoed off the stony bluff. "Jeremiah Calhoun is dead."

Jeremiah's throat tightened. Ever since he'd seen his name listed with the casualties in the prison register, he'd wondered who would be surprised by his appearance, but still the words made the hair on his arms stand on end.

"My family might think that, but they'll be plumb excited to hear they were wrong."

"The gall!" Her lean body shook as she marched closer. Her eyes narrowed into blue crescents. "You dare toy with a grieving family? You'll immediately be exposed as a charlatan. I knew Jeremiah for only a few weeks, but it's clear that you are not him."

Jeremiah's gratitude for her assistance vanished. "I don't need a stranger to tell me who I am."

"I'm not a stranger, just ask Ma. Everyone knows me, even Laurel."

His heart skipped a beat. He hadn't heard her name spoken since he'd lost Alan.

"Laurel." Was it irreverent that he breathed the word like a prayer? Every dawn brought the question of whether he'd live to see nightfall. Every evening ended with the question if he'd live to see his love again. "You've seen Laurel?" But he stopped himself. He'd wasted enough time on this woman who stood with her hands on her hips, her nostrils flared like a horse's smelling fire.

"Thanks for your help," he said, "but my family's waiting."

With a mighty huff, she marched off the road, gathered her skirts, and hopped the fence. Petticoats flashed—fancier petticoats than any he'd ever seen, not that he'd spent much time noticing such things. It wasn't until she'd climbed halfway up the bluff that he realized his mouth was hanging open. She would beat him to the house if he didn't get to moving.

He spurred the nag for a last short jaunt and tried to forget her. He was home. Of all the devastation he had seen, of all the waste of human life, limb, and property, Jeremiah had feared the worst for his own estate. Stories of bushwhackers razing homesteads and ambushing innocents had reached him. But now, as he rode through the gates of his farm, an indescribable weight was removed. Besides some unwelcome saplings, normal wear on the barn, and an irate woman trudging up the back hill, everything looked as he'd left it.

Jeremiah eased himself to the ground, pulled out his crutch, and hopped his way up the porch. While he knew he'd get a warm welcome from his mother, he dreaded seeing his sister. How many letters had he begun, only to crumple the paper and toss it into the fire? He was sorry she was sick, sorry she couldn't carry on like other young ladies her age, but he was still convinced she had no business getting married.

But maybe Alan had beat him home. For all he knew Alan and Rachel might be happily married already.

He heard footsteps approaching the door and then nothing. Was Rachel looking out her window, wondering whose old horse stood at the post? Was his mother trying to sneak to the parlor so she could catch sight of their visitor? He banged on the door again. "Ma, open the door. It's me—Jeremiah."

A scream pierced the air. The door shook as she fumbled with the lock and cursed the key, the knob, and anything else that stood between her and her only son.

With the light at her back, Jeremiah couldn't see her face, but from her swift launch into his arms, he assumed that the years had been kinder to his mother than to him.

"Jeremiah! Jeremiah! It's a miracle." Tears rolled, making her face a wet mess. "You're alive. Praise God!" She kissed him on both cheeks, patted him, hugged him, and kissed him again.

He wrapped his arms around her shoulders and held her, pleased to have caused happiness for once. Pleased to have a promising beginning.

"I thought I'd never make it back alive," he said.

"Well, I'm not letting you leave again." Her arms tightened around him. "I won't let you out of my sight."

Jeremiah almost laughed. "I suspect Laurel will have other plans. How is she?"

His mother's smile faltered. She wiped her face and stepped back. Hesitated. "Laurel is well. She will be surprised to see you, of course . . . and so will Rachel."

"Will she?" His mother had yet to notice the crutch hanging from his arm or how he was using her to keep from keeling over. "The last letter I received from her was none too civil. I hope her outlook has improved."

"She needs grace, just like the rest of us. You've been gone for four years. It might take some time to get reacquainted."

"I doubt he's changed at all." Rachel stepped outdoors.

Jeremiah straightened, ready to wrap her up in a hug if she'd allow it. How he ached to put their differences behind them, but she came no closer.

"Is Alan here? Have you heard from him?" he asked.

"He's not with you?"

At that moment Jeremiah would've given anything—his farm, his life, his other leg—to have his best friend at his side. "I tried, Rachel. I've been searching all over for him. That's why it took me so long to get home."

Whatever life had flickered in her eyes was extinguished. Her arms dropped to her side, only then showing how bony she'd become. "So you'll manage to keep Alan and me apart for a bit longer while you have a joyful reunion with Abigail?"

Abigail? Their mother stepped between them. "Both my children home safe. If only your father . . . but let's be content to celebrate Jeremiah's return. All my family finally gathered under one roof."

"Speaking of family," Jeremiah said, "I met a woman coming out of the grove. A lunatic from the sound of her. I suppose she's your guest, but please keep her away from me. All I want tonight is a hot meal and a good night's sleep."

Rachel raised an eyebrow. "She wouldn't begrudge you that as long as you don't snore. She's staying in your room, after all."

Her smug look hadn't changed since he was nine years old and she caught him stealing sugar cubes, but this time he was innocent.

"There are other rooms."

"But your wife will expect to share yours."

"My wife?" Jeremiah thrust his crutch to the floor. What were they talking about? Was this Rachel's doing?

"Oh, dear! What happened to your leg?" His ma clutched his arm.

But he didn't want to talk about his leg. "I don't know who that woman is, but I'm marrying Laurel, not some stranger."

"Abigail is a nice girl, Jeremiah," his mother said. "She's been very helpful."

"And according to her, you're already hitched," Rachel said.

They had to be fooling. But no, Rachel's smirk had all the markings of the genuine article. And this Abigail woman was almost upon them, cutting through the lawn from behind the house. In vain he thought back to every woman he'd met since leaving, but with her tall frame and slender neck she would've been difficult to forget no matter what the circumstances. That left only one possibility.

And she'd called *him* a liar.

All eyes turned as she approached the porch.

"I'm sorry, Ma," she said. "I tried to stop him. I'll summon Calbert and we'll be rid of him directly."

"Ma?! You call her Ma?" Jeremiah asked.

Rachel smiled. "Why would you get Calbert, Abigail dear?"

Abigail paused. Clearly she didn't trust Rachel, but she seemed to be searching for a sign from his mother. Could she really be confused?

"As you can see, miss, my family is satisfied with my return," he said.

"You don't recognize Abigail?" His mother's face turned as gray as her hair. "But she was with you at the prison."

"This isn't the man I knew. Jeremiah injured his arm, not his leg. This isn't your son."

His arms tensed. His hands squeezed into fists.

"Consider, Jeremiah, before you say anything harsh." His mother's hand lay gently on his arm. "It could be an honest mistake."

Judging from Rachel's unladylike snort, they agreed on at least one thing.

The woman took the lantern from Rachel and thrust it in

his face. "I know you want to believe he's returned, but look at him. He's an impostor."

Here he was on his own porch, being run off like a stray dog. Jeremiah shoved the lantern away. "Don't you think my own mother knows me?"

His mother frowned. "Oh, dear. There's going to be trouble. Why don't we go inside?"

"I'll be there," he growled, "as soon as I see to the horse."

"I see to the horses here." The woman took the reins, gentle with the mare even though she bristled like a porcupine. Shooting him a last confused look, she trudged to the barn.

By thunder, did she think him incapable of walking, too? Stupid leg. Jeremiah turned to his mother, who rubbed her brow.

"There's got to be a logical explanation," she said.

Rachel piped up. "There is. She lied to steal our farm. Motive enough."

"Don't be so quick to judge. Abigail is my guest until we figure this out. Besides, can't we just be happy that Jeremiah came home? Let's not ruin it by turning out an innocent young woman."

He wouldn't be able to deal with her as long as his sympathetic mother was a witness. "I'll get this sorted." Jeremiah stumped across the drive to the barn.

Despite the annoyance, it was good to be home. Good to be giving orders instead of taking them. Good to stand in an open field and not worry about having his head split in two by a bullet. Good to have control over his life.

Sort of.

He stepped into the familiar barn, immediately struck by the empty stalls and pens. Of course. Ma would've sold off or butchered some stock. Her letters had described how they'd scrimped to survive, but still the missing animals shocked him.

The woman had hung the lantern on the hook and had taken up the brush. How she could have missed his approach when he was bristling like a razorback boar, he couldn't fathom. He hadn't tried to be quiet, but there she stood, deep in thought while brushing that dreadful bag of bones that had carried him home.

. She looked the part. Pretty enough to pull off a heist, confident enough to think she could get away with it. Even now she was probably concocting a story or devising a plan to bamboozle him. His mother might be easy to fool, but he wasn't. Good thing he came home when he did.

"Planning to steal my horse?"

She didn't look up. Her calm strokes continued uninterrupted. "If so, I wouldn't take this one, although she's not without value." She combed her long fingers through the mane. "Combine her girth with Lancaster's strength, and you'd get a good pulling horse. She wouldn't produce a Saturday racer, but people need to pull up rocks and tree stumps more than winning a bet."

Jeremiah blinked. She knew horses. Whatever her strategy, he hadn't expected that approach.

She turned and unabashedly stared at his hands with eyes too cunning for her gentle face. "A man in prison little resembles the man on the street. I wouldn't expect to recognize Jeremiah Calhoun dressed, groomed, and presentable, but I would expect him to recognize me. And I'd expect him to be missing an arm."

"I'm sorry. Would you like me to lop one off for you? If I'd known that I'd ruin your game, I would've been more considerate and stayed dead like I was supposed to."

Her lips pursed. "This isn't a game. I came because of my promise to a dying man. He told me about his sister, Rachel, and his horse farm. He sent me here. If it wasn't you, then who was it?"

"Fortunately, I'm not the least bit curious. Nice story. I applaud your efforts, but it's over. Perhaps you can follow the Union troops out west and find another victim to—"

The woman took the lantern and marched out of the barn into the darkening evening. The lights from the rock house across the span of yard winked at him. His home. How he wanted to just rest—forget supper, forget catching up—to just lie down somewhere safe for a night. But he had one more obstacle to remove before his home was secure.

"Where are you going?" he called to her back.

"To my room."

"That's not your room. It's mine." Jeremiah hobbled to catch her.

"I have nowhere else to go, and I'm tired. I got up early to go to the Wallaces' this morning, and—"

"The Wallaces'?" Jeremiah stumbled. "What were you doing there?"

She didn't slow down. The raw end of the crutch had a tendency to slide on gravel, but Jeremiah had to risk it to catch her.

Her words were as brisk as her steps. "I had to talk to Dr. Hopkins about one of his cases, and I knew I could find him there."

Dr. Hopkins at the Wallaces'? Was Hiram sick? Before he could ask, she continued.

"I really like Laurel, by the way. We're getting on splendidly."

Jeremiah stopped again. The woman should be horsewhipped. He gritted his teeth. The thought of Laurel believing her lies liked to kill him. He wouldn't allow this impostor to stay a moment longer than necessary.

He watched her stride toward the house, jealous of her ability to cover ground. Well, she wouldn't walk all over him. For years he'd dreamt of the moment when he'd return to claim Laurel for his own. He wasn't about to let a tricky Yankee get in his way.

Abigail slammed the bedroom door behind her and fell against it. Who was he? She unbuttoned her collar, fighting for air. According to Ma and Rachel, the man whose voice she could hear lecturing her through the door was Jeremiah. But whom had she married? Who was Romeo?

Her head throbbed. How many times had the descriptions of judgmental Jeremiah failed to correspond with jovial Romeo? The man's hazel eyes, his square jaw, even the hawkish nose were family traits she now recognized. How could she have ignored all the inconsistencies?

Only after she heard Ma's gentle voice trying to control her son did Abigail relinquish her post at the door.

If anyone was at fault, it was she. She tried to imagine herself in his situation, returning home after four years, injured, weary, only to be called a liar and told he was supposed to be dead. Abigail sank onto the bed and covered her face. What a welcome she'd given him. As if Ma and Rachel didn't recognize their own son and brother! She had to make things right. She owed him an apology.

Abigail poured herself a glass of water from the pitcher on her nightstand. The water sloshed as she fought to steady her hands. If he was Jeremiah, then she had no right to be there. The horses, the farm, the cozy rock house—she'd never see any of it again. And what about Ma? How could Abigail abandon her adopted family? Leaving her home the first time had ripped her heart in two. She couldn't do it again. Not when she'd finally found people who needed her. Surely she could reason with Captain Calhoun. Surely she could prove to him that she was an asset.

From the tone of his voice outside the door, he hadn't relinquished his rights to his bedroom yet. She set down the glass and opened the door to find a glowering man still pleading with his mother to expel her.

"Captain Calhoun," she said. "May I have a word with you?"

His eyes pierced her. "Don't make me regret it."

Abigail stepped back into the room to allow him entrance. He rapped the doorframe with his crutch.

"You are not my wife. Don't think that I'll be hornswoggled into saving your reputation. I wouldn't hesitate to have you run out of town."

"This isn't a trick. Anything said in the parlor can be heard upstairs, and I'd like a private word if you don't mind."

Jeremiah looked to his mother for permission. Abigail rolled her eyes. As if she had designs on his virtue. Honestly.

Evidently Ma thought he was safe, for he entered. His eyes scanned the room greedily. Realizing he hadn't seen his room for years, Abigail gave him a moment to take it in. He nodded as if pleased to find it as he remembered, until his eyes caught her emerald taffeta wrapper hanging on a hook. With that his pleasure vanished.

"Captain Calhoun, I want to apologize. I no longer doubt your word that you are Jeremiah."

"There's progress."

"But we owe it to your family to figure out who sent me. The man I married at Gratiot Street gave me specific instructions—"

"Really, miss . . . what is your proper name?"

"Everyone here calls me Mrs. Calhoun, but I suppose you should call me Abigail."

He looked like he'd just as soon put on skirts and perform "The Merry Widow Waltz."

"How long have you been here?"

"Two months."

"You've had two months to go about telling your tale, spinning your windies, telling everyone you're my wife?"

"I don't know if I've met everyone—"

He threw his hat on the dresser. "If you've lived here for two months, then word's got out. How are you going to fix this mess?"

He had every right to be angry, she reminded herself. She couldn't blame him, although she could wish he wasn't standing so close, glowering at her. Abigail tried to take a step back, but her knees were already pressed against her bed.

His bed.

And even as tall as she was, her eyes only came up to his mouth. A rather nice mouth, if it wasn't so busy frowning at her.

"I understand how confusing this must be for you," she said. "I'm confused, too. I don't know how I could've made such a mistake, but maybe there's an explanation. The Jeremiah Calhoun I met claimed to have a head injury and didn't give us his name until the very end. We thought he was bluffing, but maybe we were wrong. Maybe his memories got confused. I can't explain it. All I can say is that I mean you and your family no harm. We'll figure this out soon."

"But you're sticking to your story? You're not hiding anything?"

Abigail would never tell anyone about her stepfather's accusations or her mother's betrayal—no use in stirring up more suspicion. Maybe that qualified as hiding something, so she settled with saying, "I'm telling you the truth." So far.

He picked up the timepiece off the nightstand and turned it over in his hands. With his head bowed he reminded her of a little boy examining a treasure. "I'm so tired. Tired of fighting. Tired of enemies. I wanted to come home and find some peace, but if there's none to be found, then I'll keep striving. Fighting might be all I'm fit for anymore."

"The war is over, sir."

"Is it? Are my family and farm safe?" He narrowed his eyes and did a perfunctory account of her from head to toe. "Mother said you're welcome to sleep in her room—at least for one night. Maybe tomorrow I'll have the energy to throw you out properly."

Abigail recognized a hint of satisfaction in his last words. He stumped past her and collapsed on the bed while she gathered her nightclothes from the wardrobe. By the time she'd removed her robe from the hook, he was snoring softly.

"Only one night?" Abigail folded her clothes over her arm. She'd determined to stay on this farm, but the appearance of the real Jeremiah Calhoun had thrown her plans awry. Regardless, she had invested in his property, and she wouldn't leave empty-handed. Tomorrow they'd talk and perhaps she could work out a deal with him. But if Captain Calhoun planned to run her off, he'd better be prepared for one last battle.

Chapter 5

Home. He'd thought of it for years while digging trenches, sleeping in his saddle and eating wormy hardtack. Home where his loved ones waited on him. Home where he could bend his efforts toward healing, strive to mend instead of destroy. But now he was here, and he didn't know what to do. With his bad leg curled up, Jeremiah sat on the stone steps leading up to the house and watched the sun rise over the ridge.

The Lord is my rock, and my fortress . . . my strength, in whom I will trust. And he'd need a heap of strength now that he was a cripple. Was God's offer of help still good even if Jeremiah had much to account for?

He had blood on his hands, but God allowed for soldiers. The Old Testament was full of them. Only problem was he hadn't been fighting pagan Canaanites or blasphemous Romans. How exactly did God judge between His children?

And then there was Rachel and Alan, although God didn't need to chastise him for that. Jeremiah already felt whipped, and just in case he was too easy on himself, it looked like Rachel would continue with the punishment.

So whether or not he and God were good, he couldn't guess. All he could do was to thank Him for getting him home and for taking care of his mother, his sister, and Laurel while he was gone. And pray that they heard from Alan soon.

As far as his tasks, planting was behind. His mother had set a garden, but much smaller than they'd had before the war. Would he be able to plow the field? Reckon he had no choice. Rachel couldn't, and Jeremiah couldn't imagine his mother behind the plow. Where was Alan when he needed him?

Where *was* Alan?

A shadow in the trees moved. Likely a deer, but would he ever stop feeling the urge to shout an alarm when he saw someone approach? The codger broke through the trees, took one look at Jeremiah, and then stumbled backwards.

Jeremiah smiled. "Come on, Calbert. You ain't seeing a ghost."

Calbert snatched his hat off and scratched his head. "Somehow I knew you'd be back. I just couldn't imagine that you were really gone for good." He lumbered up the drive while Jeremiah got his crutch situated in time to give the man the bear hug he'd come after. Ever since Jeremiah's father's death, Calbert Huckabee had stepped into the void and done his best to see that none of Jeremiah's raisings was neglected. Jeremiah owed him much, and as he considered the farm it was obvious that Calbert had continued his care while Jeremiah was gone.

"The place doesn't look half bad," Jeremiah said, "and I know it's on account of you."

Still smiling up at him with shining eyes, Calbert waved away his praise. "Your ma kept it middlin'. She just needed a hand now and then."

"Like the milking every morning? I should've known Ma didn't do that."

"No, it's been Abigail recently. She's a much better hand than your ma or your sister. Hard worker, too."

If she was such a hard worker, why didn't she earn herself a farm instead of trying to trick him out of his? "Calbert, I know nothing about that woman. I've never seen her before, and I sure as shooting didn't marry her."

Calbert scratched his chest. "Abigail wouldn't lie. I've spent a fair piece of time with her. . . . Well, it wouldn't do any good to argue with you, I suppose. Still, you might want to reconsider your stance. You could do a lot worse." Calbert noticed his leg, then looked away quickly. "I didn't mean anything by that."

Jeremiah tightened his grip on his crutch. "I know you didn't."

"Well, I was just headed to the barn. Tell Abigail I'm started on the chores."

"Thanks again for everything, Calbert. Ma couldn't have made it without you." Jeremiah took the two steps to the porch, cursing his crutch, and hobbled to the door. By the light of day, he could see the stacks of his mother's journal clippings, her bell collection, and the spinning wheel all in their place. Perhaps less dust than he remembered, but memories tended to shift, given enough time.

"It's not like Jeremiah to sleep so late." He heard Rachel through the kitchen door. "You didn't keep him up last night did you, Abigail, claiming a wife's privilege?"

His stomach did an odd little flop.

"Such a base imagination, Rachel." Abigail's voice was tight. "I'm astonished at you."

His mouth twisted. At least this Abigail was willing to stand up to Rachel. Then again, if she'd bowed up to him, who would she back down from?

"Are you looking for me, Rachel?" He let the door swing closed behind him and held out an arm to greet his mother's embrace. Abigail turned from cooking at the stove, her blue dress brighter than anything else in the drab kitchen . . . besides her eyes. He'd better just focus on his mother.

"I'm never going to stop hugging you." Ma sniffled.

"I'll give you a few days, Ma. After that you can't keep crying on my shirt." But he didn't mean it. Let her shed the tears that seemed caught in his heart, and maybe he'd feel better, too.

As if reading his mind, Abigail's eyes softened. Her head tilted and her lips spread into a smile. Maybe she did really care for his mother—how could you not love the tenderhearted woman? Or maybe she was the consummate actress. And a liar. And definitely not his wife.

With a last squeeze, Jeremiah released Ma.

"Now sit a spell and tell us about this awful war," she said. "The last I heard you were fighting near Marshall, and after that nothing. I suppose that's when you got your leg hurt?"

Jeremiah swung his leg out and eased into a chair. "I'm hungry, Ma. I don't really feel like talking about all that just now." And he probably never would.

She smiled at him and patted his cheek. "Sit down, then, and help yourself to Abigail's cooking. You did yourself good when you married her."

"Ma," he warned as he accepted the plate of eggs and sausage. His mouth watered at the spicy scent. With the edge of his fork he burst open the sausage and watched the grease drip onto the plate. At the first bite he closed his eyes. Heaven.

And when he opened them, there stood that beautiful angel who'd made it possible. Jeremiah nearly choked at his weakness. Esau, selling his birthright for a bowl of pottage. He could sympathize with the man.

Taking another bite he plowed ahead. "How many bags did

you bring, miss? Can you carry them back to the train station, or will you need to borrow the wagon?"

"Jeremiah!" His ma slapped his arm. "Abigail isn't going anywhere."

He shoveled in some egg. "Yes she is. I'm sorry that things haven't worked like she'd hoped, but she can't take advantage of us anymore."

Now the angel crackled with indignation. "I haven't taken advantage of anyone. You should've seen this place before I got here. Ask Ma. No lady ever worked harder. But if I do go, you should know that I'll not leave empty-handed." She waved a sharp, two-pronged fork in his direction. "Last night you were too tired to talk, but we will discuss the matter of my colt."

"Exactly which colt would that be?"

"The one I paid for. The one Josephine is carrying."

"Josephine's been bred?" he sputtered. "By who?"

"By Napoleon. I paid Hiram for his services with my own money."

"You bred her without my permission?"

"As your widow, I didn't need your permission."

"But you aren't—" He tightened his lips. Did his farm somehow attract unreasonable females, or did they become that way after they arrived? "I don't have time for this. I've got to get to Laurel before she hears about me from someone else." He scraped the last forkful of eggs from the plate.

"You can't go to the Wallaces' without a warning." His mother passed him the bread basket. "You need to prepare Laurel. Poor girl thinks you're dead."

"Then it's time to turn her mourning into dancing," he said between bites.

What was Ma's worry? Didn't she understand how much he and Laurel had missed each other?

"Let him go." Rachel pressed her napkin to her lips. "Jeremiah doesn't need our advice."

Then Abigail chimed in. "You should listen to your mother. She only wants to protect you."

"Protect me from Laurel? She wouldn't squish a spider." He drained his coffee cup and thunked it on the table. Didn't these women realize the dangers he'd faced? Didn't they understand the men he'd had under his command? Why did they think they could tell him what to do?

Using his crutch for balance, Jeremiah stood and departed. After four years of war, he didn't need them looking out for him. The sooner he saw Laurel, the sooner he could start living again.

Jeremiah saddled the old mare he'd come in on. Laurel wouldn't be impressed with his mount, but he hoped the fact that he still had a pulse would make up for his simple arrival. Jeremiah wished now that he'd written. After his old leg got shot up, he just couldn't bring himself to write home. He didn't know what kind of life he'd have, if any. Besides, the family that hid him had no business risking their lives for a letter. An envelope written in a strange hand might cause the local postmaster to ask uncomfortable questions about their guest. And he hadn't been their only visitor.

Jeremiah slapped his thigh, letting the sharp jolt remind him he wasn't dreaming. He was really riding to the place he'd longed for. He'd imagined it so often that he feared he'd wake and find himself on a mat in a dark cellar again. He filled his lungs with the clean morning air, catching the sharp scent of cedar. Never again. He'd face whatever came, but never again would he hide from trouble.

Riding the familiar trail reminded him of the autumn days when he and Alan took the crops to market. They'd put on their Sunday clothes, comb in some hair tonic, and go to dazzle their neighbors' daughters with their charm and wit. He'd stolen kisses behind the post office and brokered deals over a barrel lid. Then he and Alan would share tales of their adventures all the way home.

Life had been so simple, and the only part that remained unchanged was Laurel.

The road to town curled up to the Wallace farm. Smoke puffed lazily from the chimney of the white clapboard house. What would Laurel think of his leg? He'd picked out his nicest britches that morning, but they couldn't hide his crutch. He reined the horse toward the barn. He could manage on the ground and on horseback, but the in-between time still troubled him something awful. Better to dismount when no one was watching.

He looped the old nag's reins over the fence. Laughter lit on his ears like the daintiest butterfly. He cleared his throat, smoothed down his hair, and started toward the tantalizing sound.

Laurel stepped out of her front door. She stood, smile as wide as a sycamore trunk, with her hands on her hips. The ruffle on her pink-and-white skirt fluttered in the wind. He could almost smell the scent of her rose perfume drifting to him. Jeremiah halted, waiting for her to respond to his presence, but she spun around with a laugh and ran back into the house.

Had she gone to tell her pa? Poor girl was probably out of her mind. At least she'd laughed, so he'd not frightened her. Jeremiah continued to the front steps. Couldn't guess how he might act under the circumstances, so he shouldn't judge.

The front door stood ajar and Laurel couldn't have gone far. She might be suffering vapors just around the corner. He wasn't going to wait any longer to find out.

Jeremiah pushed the door open.

Laurel squealed, just out of sight. "No fair. You were supposed to hide it while I was out."

Jeremiah frowned. Had she not seen him? He glanced down at his suit, his boots, his hated crutch. He wasn't invisible, was he?

"It's hidden. You still haven't taken the prize." A man's voice. Now Jeremiah's frown deepened until it was like to furrow his jaw.

"I'll find it." She laughed as Jeremiah stepped through the parlor doorway.

Dr. Hopkins stood with his hands hidden behind his back. His cheeks fell when he saw Jeremiah, and his eyes bugged out like they were being pulled by fishing hooks. Laurel couldn't see Jeremiah on account of her being too busy reaching around the doctor, almost as if she were hugging him.

Immediately she drew back. "What's wrong?" Then she turned slowly, following the doctor's horrified stare.

"Jeremiah? It can't be." Instead of rushing toward him, Laurel clutched the doctor's arm. Instead of turning white with shock, she blushed. Instead of lighting up with happy surprise, she looked to the ground.

Maybe he should've listened to his mother and sent word ahead of time.

"You're alive?" She looked to the doctor again, gave a half smile, and then finally acted like she ought.

She fainted dead away.

He knelt at her side and cradled his beloved Laurel in his arms. Finally his homecoming was shaping up the way he'd expected. If only that pesky doctor would make himself scarce. What business did he have pushing his way into their reunion?

"She only fainted. She doesn't need a doctor."

"I'll be the judge of that."

Laurel stirred. Both men ducked forward, crashing their foreheads together.

"Don't you know anyone else ailing?" Jeremiah asked.

"Jeremiah?" Laurel touched his face.

"I'm here, sugar."

She smiled softly . . . before her jet-black eyebrows drew together over snapping eyes. "You are *not* here, Jeremiah Calhoun. You are dead. Dead, and don't you try to prove otherwise." She slugged him in the chest.

He laughed. "I'm very much alive, Laurel, and thinking of you is what kept me that way."

"Well, I've been thinking of you as deceased, so you shouldn't be too all-fired up expecting me to . . . to . . ." Her eyes widened. "I just remembered. You're married. You married Abigail." She slugged him again and pushed out of his arms, falling to the floor. "You didn't have time to write me, but you had time to get hitched to some nurse?"

"I'm not married. That's a misunderstanding."

"So you claim . . . just as you claim to be alive. I-I don't know what to believe." She pressed her hand to her forehead and turned to the doctor. "Newton, I feel faint again. I might need your assistance."

In Jeremiah's uninformed opinion, a doctor should know not to snatch one recovering from a fainting spell away so quickly.

"It's been a dreadful shock, my dear. I'll get you a glass of water."

"Dreadful? Me being alive is dreadful?" Jeremiah pulled himself up on his crutch, too angry to take issue with the pitying look it got from Laurel. "And did you call her *your dear*?"

"Please, Jeremiah," Laurel begged. "I don't mean to be cruel, but seeing you again wasn't expected. You've been assumed dead for months. When the prison in St. Louis sent the notice to your family, we knew it for a fact. And then Abigail—"

"Oh yes. Abigail. Well, I don't know her."

Laurel raised an eyebrow.

"I swear. She's a complete stranger."

"But the point of the matter is that I thought you were dead. And while I'm very, very glad to see you alive . . ." Her eyes darted to the doctor again.

"Jeremiah," he said. "Miss Wallace appreciates you coming to share your news, but maybe it'd be better to give her some time to consider."

"Consider what?" When had she taken the doctor on as watchdog? Jeremiah never knew Hopkins to be an interfering type of fellow.

Then, like a chimney tumbling down on him, awareness crushed Jeremiah. Dr. Hopkins and Laurel—

"How could you?"

Laurel wrung her hands. "Please, Jeremiah. You've been gone so long."

"Not long enough to forget you."

"What was I supposed to do? You were dead and then Abigail came and said that you'd married."

"And you believed her? Don't you know me better than that, Laurel? I would never—"

"That's enough." Hopkins stepped in front of Laurel. "I understand how you must feel, but you have to stop. After she's had time to consider, then you can talk. Until then, please leave her alone."

Jeremiah looked down on the scrawny man and felt another of his few remaining supports crumbling away. He turned to Laurel. "Is that what you want?"

Her chin quivered. She couldn't meet his eyes. In fact, she

could look no higher than his permanently crippled leg. "I'm glad to see you, Jeremiah, but please go, just for now."

He blinked as though she'd thrown sand in his eyes. He'd expected to gaze at her, to memorize every detail of her dress, her smile, compare the real Laurel to the dream picture he'd carted around. He hadn't thought that his study would end so soon.

Jeremiah limped out alone, wishing he could shatter his crutch against the wall and march off without it. He pulled himself into the saddle, no longer caring who saw his awkward efforts. After he'd been shot, he had wondered what kind of life he'd have. If it weren't for knowing that Laurel waited, would he have tried so hard to survive? But maybe she was only surprised. Who knew what kind of pressure the doctor had put on her? He spurred the horse into a trot. She'd come back to him once she had her wits about her. Once she got used to idea that he was home, nevermore to leave, she'd figure it straight. And he'd do all he could to help her along.

CHAPTER 6

Ma hadn't asked Abigail to wash Jeremiah's clothes, but after his long journey, goodness knew they'd offend a skunk. While he was off sparking Laurel, Abigail ducked into the room to gather his dirty laundry piled in the corner. Fully grateful for the laundry basket that kept her from hugging the clothing against herself, Abigail headed toward the cauldron with water already steaming.

The road from the house dipped slightly before rising again and disappearing into the woods. Out of those woods stepped two barefoot urchins—Calbert's children on one of their frequent visits. They spotted her immediately and, after a whispered conference, set out toward her. Before coming here, Abigail had never seen such dirty children. They looked more like grubworms than humans, and she suspected that the deprivations of war weren't completely responsible for their condition.

They came to stand by her basket, the girl digging her grimy toe into the soft soil.

"Good morning, Josiah and Betsy," Abigail said. "What are you up to?"

"Nothing, ma'am." But Abigail didn't miss the warning Josiah shot his sister. "We just thought we'd be neighborly and see what you'uns are doing."

Abigail motioned around her. "Laundry."

Betsy pointed to the basket of Jeremiah's clothes next to her. "These clean or dirty?"

"Dirty, of course. Just look at how brown the cuffs are."

"They goodness me," Betsy exclaimed as she rifled through them. "Ma would call these good enough for Sabbath."

The boy knelt for his own inspection. "Mrs. Calhoun must be just as finicky as Miss Rachel if she means for you to wash these."

Abigail bit her lip. From the way they were standing, these two were right pleased at their accomplishment, but what had they done? More than likely the basket would answer her question.

The top shirt looked harmless enough. With a quick movement Abigail snatched it off the pile to expose a black and yellow garter snake.

Her hand flew to her throat as she jumped back. The children squealed in laughter at her performance.

"Shame on you!" Abigail tried to scold. "Scaring me like that!"

Josiah held his side with one hand and pointed with the other. "You should've seen your face. Your eyes got as big as walnuts."

Betsy's little nose wrinkled. "It was funny, ma'am. I hope you're not holding a grudge over it."

"I most certainly am. Just think what might have happened had I picked up this whole load at once."

"Aw, that little snake wouldn't hurt you," Josiah said.

Suppressing a smile had never been more work. Abigail knelt at the basket's rim. "If I didn't find him, then I could've thrown the poor thing into the boiling water. You wouldn't want your snake hurt, would you?"

Before the children knew what was happening, she snatched up the snake and threw him toward the mischievous pair. With shrieks, they ducked and covered their heads.

"Your eyes got as big as walnuts." Abigail laughed.

New respect twinkled in Josiah's eyes. "You're a rum one, young Mrs. Calhoun. You are that."

Across the way, the barn door closed. Abigail pulled a tendril of hair out of her face to watch Jeremiah exit. At breakfast she'd noticed that he'd cleaned up since last night. He'd made use of the going-to-meeting clothes that she'd spotted in his bureau, and his broad shoulders looked capable of handling any crisis. Fatten him up a bit and he'd cut a fine figure, but then he leaned into his crutch and the effect faded. Abigail's pulse slowed. In that moment she wanted nothing more than to see him whole, to make him the man he'd been before. Although she'd always been a sucker for lost causes, there might be hope for him. Because of inadequate nutrition and lack of sanitation, she'd never been able to see Dr. Jonson's techniques work at the prison, but now she had a chance. If only Jeremiah would allow it.

Jeremiah caught her staring. Barely noticing the two children still frightened of him and of his resurrection, he clomped toward her.

"Children, your father is in the barn. You might want to go to him," Abigail said.

But they were rooted to the spot. The boy's eyes shone at Jeremiah. "Captain Calhoun, we're glad you're home. And I might as well say you got yourself a humdinger of a wife. She ain't even afraid of snakes."

Jeremiah's jaw jutted forward. "She ain't my wife, Josiah. She mistook me for someone else."

"She don't know her own husband?" Betsy laughed. "No one's that addled. Besides, she's living with you, ain't she? If she ain't your wife, then don't tell Ma, 'cause she don't tolerate such goings-on."

His brow seemed to lower until it rested on his nose. Maybe an exaggeration, but Abigail had to look twice to clarify.

"Your ma is a good woman, and you should heed her, but Miss . . . er—"

"Miss Stuart," Abigail supplied.

"Miss Stuart is a guest of my ma's, and she won't be staying long."

The youngster looked to her for a reply. "I'll be here until my colt is born. After that, we'll see what God has willed."

Jeremiah's jaw tightened at the contradiction. "While the children will undoubtedly miss you, it'd probably be best to go before they get any more attached."

Abigail motioned Betsy closer and cheerfully wrapped an arm around the child. "Oh, we've already bonded, Captain Calhoun. I count Josiah and Betsy as some of my dearest friends."

"That's right." Betsy's grin was as crooked as her pigtails. "We love Mrs. Calhoun—especially the younger one."

"Come on," Josiah said. "Let's find Pa and leave Miss Abigail to do her husband's laundry."

With a last grin, they ran as if hound dogs were nipping at their heels, obviously forgetting that Jeremiah couldn't catch them even if he'd wanted.

The steam from the cauldron sent sweat running down Abigail's spine. She plucked at her shirtwaist to peel it from her sticky body, then picked up a pair of Jeremiah's trousers and dropped them into the mix, trying to think of a topic besides her departure.

"How was Laurel?" she asked.

"It's time for you to go." He took his weight off his crutch and stood straight. "I'll get the money together for a ticket, traveling expenses, whatever you want. It's going to take work to get everything back to where it was before the war, and you're definitely a distraction."

"You can't go back," she said. "The war changed everything. Doesn't it make more sense to let me help you around here?"

He raised an eyebrow. "What about your family? Don't you have someone who'd take you in?"

Another line of sweat ran down Abigail's back. How had she thought she could mislead people with a clean conscience? If this man knew why she wasn't welcomed at home, he'd never let her stay.

"There's no one." Not after their fight.

"Not an aunt? A brother? A distant cousin?" His sharp gaze warned her that he wasn't easily fooled.

"No one." Abigail tried to meet his eyes but failed. She had family, but they might as well be dead. "I could stay with Laurel."

"Stay away from Laurel." He loosened his simple cravat. "Look, I don't want to be crude, but how am I supposed to court a lady when a woman claiming to be my wife is living under my roof? Betsy's ma won't be the only one to think it ain't fitting." Jeremiah's face had turned the same shade of pink as hers, and he wasn't standing over a boiling cauldron of laundry.

With the wooden paddle, Abigail pushed the trousers beneath the water, grunting with the effort. "I can't leave without my colt."

"As for that, first off, Josephine is mine, so at the most you might own half the colt. Secondly, if I was charging you room and board for the last two months—"

She gasped. "You wouldn't dare! If anything, you owe me for the work I've put in here."

"But now I'm home and you aren't needed."

The water boiled, sending slow white bubbles popping up at her. Not needed. Would she always be the one on the periphery—locked out, chased away?

He leaned in closer, trying to catch her gaze, and his voice gentled. "Look, I don't know who you are or why you're here, but I can't be held responsible for whatever promises another Jeremiah Calhoun made you. Go back to St. Louis and look at the register again. Maybe another Calhoun was mistakenly identified as being with my division. Check if you'd like, but you'll find that I had nothing to do with it. I'm innocent."

Abigail pulled the paddle out of the cauldron and planted the end into the rocky ground. "I'm not asking for your permission to stay, Jeremiah Calhoun. I came here and found a family that needs me. I've invested in this farm, and I'm not leaving my investment behind. If you kick me out, I'm taking the horse with me. Take me to court and see what they say."

"Nice try, but there's no fair court hereabouts. No man who fought the Federals is allowed to be on a jury or vote."

"Then we'll let the Union sympathizers decide the case, if that's what you want. My service should bolster my testimony."

His jaw hardened. "I fought a war to keep invaders off my land. Some treaty in Washington City might say I lost, but I haven't surrendered this farm."

His shoulder muscles strained against his raggedy suit coat. Abigail told herself that it was his determination that she admired, not his sturdy build. But shouldn't she of all people understand what it felt like to have an intruder invade the family? She took a long breath.

"I'm not asking for your farm. I'm merely asking that my investment be returned. I'd leave if I could, but I won't throw away my savings."

"Once Josephine has her colt, I could sell it and send the amount to you," he said.

Was he really that desperate to get away from her? But Ma wanted her to stay. She still had Ma . . . and her promise to look after Rachel. Besides, the arrogant man really did need her. Maybe he could use a reminder.

She handed him the paddle. "That'd require a lot of trust, wouldn't it? To just leave and believe that you'd send me anything, especially the correct amount? But then again, if you plan to keep this place up without me, you should have some practice. So, go on and finish this load of laundry. The wringer is on the back porch. I'm going inside to see about supper."

If he'd missed some stains, his family better keep their complaints to themselves. Jeremiah had never done the washing before in his life, and this was fixing to be the first and the last time combined. Holding the clothespins in his mouth like he'd seen his ma do, he shook out the dripping sheet. Why bother with a wringer? The sun would dry it soon enough. Getting the heavy sheet over the line wasn't easy balancing with a crutch under one arm, but he managed. Then pinned up his pants—a fancy trick that required three pins per pant leg—wool held a lot of water.

Jeremiah had just tossed a tablecloth over the line when his world fell apart, or at least the clothesline did. The clean clothes tumbled to the ground, ruining his labor.

Have mercy. They needed to be washed again—preferably by someone else. Of course Rachel couldn't. She kept his mother scurrying about at her beck and call with no free time on her hands. They needed more help, especially with the house chores.

He needed . . . well, he needed Laurel to just go on and marry him, but she wasn't keen on the idea. Not yet.

How many months until Josephine foaled? Nine? If he let that beguiling woman stay until February, could he keep her in her place? Still looking at the crumpled clothes getting muddied on the ground, Jeremiah gritted his teeth. His ma, Rachel, Laurel, and Abigail—no man since Solomon had been so beset by troublesome females.

"Jeremiah?" Jeremiah looked up to find a friend of his father's ambling toward him, agile as a goat. "We thought you's dead."

He remembered to remove the clothespins from his mouth before answering. "A common misunderstanding."

Caesar Parrow hitched his pants up his bony hips and nodded. "Wish I was wrong more often. Just had to come see for myself."

Caesar had also joined with the Missouri State Guard but had been placed under a different division when they enlisted with the Confederate forces. He'd spent much of the war in the artillery, which explained his lack of hearing.

"Glad to see you made it home," Jeremiah bellowed.

"Home don't mean nothing, does it? We're like to get killed yet." The man moseyed closer, frowning at the duds scattered in the grass. "You doing washing, boy?"

It was Jeremiah's turn to be hard of hearing. He stepped over the soggy clothes to his guest. "Have you had any trouble up your way?"

Caesar nodded. "Strange tracks. Dogs barking at night. No-account soldiers from both sides are taking their time getting home."

Jeremiah's heart skipped a beat when a man broke through the trees on a scrawny mule. It was the postmaster, his mail pouch bulging with deliveries.

"Well, I'll be. Jeremiah Calhoun. Didn't think we'd see you again." He dismounted and nodded at each of the men.

"You shouldn't count me out too soon, Finley." Jeremiah's spine stiffened. Never did like the shifty man.

"Well, when your wife says she saw you buried, I ought to believe her." Finley handed Caesar a creased envelope.

"Aww, Mrs. Calhoun?" Caesar stuffed the envelope into his half-buttoned shirt. "I met her when I got burned smithing. She's uncommon pretty, she is."

Jeremiah shook his head. "Miss Stuart and I are not married. She's only here for a few months."

Caesar smiled. "Let her live with you for a few months, and you'll be full sorry to see her go."

The two men wheezed their amusement. Jeremiah counted to ten. Then counted again. "I haven't decided whether or not to let her stay that long, but she has no family. Nowhere to go. What am I supposed to do?"

Finley stroked his beard. "No family, you say? Don't Yankees know how to take care of their own?"

"I didn't realize she was an orphan." Caesar removed his floppy hat and scratched his head. "That makes me right sad for her."

"Especially with her husband pretending he don't know her." Finley's bottom lip drooped in a pout.

Hilarious. These men thought they were hilarious.

Jeremiah gathered the wet clothes and dumped them back into the wash cauldron. She had to go. Perhaps laundry was a chore he could learn to love.

———— ❧ ————

Nothing made Abigail feel more like a nurse than carrying a tray of food. She ascended the narrow staircase, her blue skirt brushing the wall on both sides, and knocked on Rachel's door.

"Who is it?" Rachel asked.

"I brought your dinner."

A grunt, not necessarily permission, but acknowledgment nonetheless, so Abigail entered. With her stocking feet propped up on the footstool before her, Rachel fanned the air with her mother's journal.

Abigail took one sniff and frowned. "You may be able to whisk the tobacco smoke out of the room, but not out of your lungs." She deposited the tray on the bed and pulled the still-warm pipe from beneath the pillow. "This could start a fire."

"Have we got any mail?" Rachel's eyes watered from the smoke. A red rash crept above her collar. No wonder she hadn't made it downstairs. The same rheumatism that flared up on her skin would inflame her joints, as well.

"Mr. Finley didn't come to the house, so probably not." Abigail emptied the bowl of the pipe into a damp flower pot and stashed it into her pocket. "How are you feeling?"

Rachel eyeballed the pocket. Her lips pressed to white. "Fine, I suppose. The rheumatism is in my knee today, and I'm dizzy when I rise, but what else do I expect?"

"Especially when you're depriving yourself of clean air." Abigail lifted Rachel's hand from the arm of the chair. She pressed her thumb against the back of her wrist and then checked her fingernails.

"Dr. Hopkins does that, too." Rachel narrowed her eyes. "What are you looking for?"

"Honestly, I don't know much about your condition. The prisoners kept us busy with battlefield injuries, pneumonia, and dysentery, but Dr. Hopkins informed me of your bout with rheumatic fever and the progression. Just as your joints swell up and cause your pain, so do your heart valves. These black spots under your nails are hemorrhages that have traveled from there."

"And every time the fever comes back, it's worse. I already knew that. Please tell me your nursing instructions involved more than chatting with Hopkins."

Pain and fear brought out the worst in people, yet as poorly as Rachel behaved, Abigail recognized some things admirable in the woman—determination, a grim humor—things that drew Abigail to her. Although she would tend Rachel no matter how Rachel treated her, she longed for even a small sign of respect.

Rachel reached over and picked up the jar of preserves. Her neck tensed as she struggled to open it. Abigail smiled. Like her brother, Rachel needed her, but she wouldn't admit it. Abigail turned as if to leave.

"You forgot to open the jelly," Rachel called out.

"I beg your pardon?" Abigail lingered in the doorway. "Do you have a request?"

Rachel held out the jar. "You forgot to open the jelly. Ma always opens it."

"Your mother. What a gem! And I'm pleased to help if you'll but ask."

Rachel's chest expanded and her mouth turned a healthy shade of pink. She clunked down the jar, picked up her dry toast, and tore a vicious bite from it. Maybe they wouldn't be friends, but Rachel wouldn't find Abigail as malleable as her ma. Abigail couldn't help but chuckle as she left, but she hadn't expected to find someone waiting at the foot of the stairs.

"Laurel?"

With a finger to her lips, Laurel motioned Abigail to follow her into the parlor.

"I saw Jeremiah out front, so I slipped around back." The wool fringe on her shawl swung as she paced the room.

"He's still washing?" Abigail could tell the girl was distraught. Poor thing. She must have had quite a shock. "Have a seat, Laurel. You don't look well. Do you want me to get Ma?"

"No." She cast a glance out the window. "He came to see me this morning, and the encounter didn't please him."

"He does have high expectations."

She snorted as delicately as Abigail had ever heard. "What about *my* expectations? He's supposed to be dead."

"I told him the same thing."

Laurel's fine black eyebrows knitted together. "And married! You told me he was married."

"Turns out I didn't marry Jeremiah Calhoun after all. I'm not sure who I married, but if he weren't already dead I'd have hot words for him."

Laurel put a hand to her forehead and seemed to wilt. "What am I going to do? I never stopped caring for Jeremiah, but he'd been gone forever, and then Newton treated me so nice, and then I thought Jeremiah wasn't coming back, and then Newton started calling, and then Mrs. Calhoun got a letter from the army saying Jeremiah had died, and then . . ."

Poor lady. Two men in love with her and she had to choose one. Abigail couldn't begin to imagine what that would be like. Unfortunately.

"So you wouldn't have even spoken to Dr. Hopkins, but you thought you were free?"

"I didn't choose him over Jeremiah. Jeremiah was dead. But now I'm not sure I'm willing to let Newton go." She picked up one of Ma's knitting needles and tapped the point against her finger. "I'm not the same girl he knew before. I'm different. We'd be starting from scratch."

"But don't you owe him that chance?" Why was she helping him? Heaven knew she owed him nothing.

"What will Newton think?"

"That you're sensible and thoughtful. That you want to know your heart before you give it away."

"You're right. Jeremiah deserves a chance, but he needs to understand that getting yourself declared deceased does come with consequences. We can't pretend that he never left or that the last months didn't happen." Laurel sighed. "Thank you, Abigail. I didn't expect to come to you for advice on your dead husband." Her eyes rolled in mock horror. "Our lot in life is a strange one, but before I go I suppose I should visit Rachel. Do you think she'd mind?"

Abigail gestured to the staircase by way of answer and followed Laurel up.

"Laurel?" Rachel's forehead creased in genuine puzzlement. "What are you doing here?"

"I kept meaning to drop by sooner, but you know how busy planting season is."

How smoothly Laurel could make an excuse. How quickly Rachel blew it away.

"I wondered if you'd feel more friendly now that Jeremiah's home."

Laurel had the grace to blush. She fiddled with Rachel's keepsakes on her dresser. Abigail had just gathered Rachel's supper dishes when Laurel opened a pocket-sized picture case. The golden frame of the interior caught the sunlight as she eased the hinges open. A flash of light beamed onto Abigail.

"You haven't heard from Alan, have you?" Laurel's dark braid swung forward as she bent over the picture.

"Not a word after his last letter."

A strange foreboding made Abigail's skin pucker. The dishes rattled as she dropped the tray onto the dressing table and approached Laurel. She peered over her shoulder at the leather-covered case in the girl's hands.

"Such a handsome man," Laurel said, "and so merry. We'll pray he's on his way home even now."

The soldier in the picture held a saber, while his pistol was tucked into his belt. His thick mustache curled handsomely above a kind mouth that didn't look accustomed to remaining stern, even for the length of a daguerreotype exposure. His eyes begged Abigail not to look away. Stay until she understood his message. Stay until she recognized—

Abigail covered her mouth.

"What is it?" Rachel frowned at Abigail, then drew Laurel near to peer at the picture. "What's the matter?"

Abigail's tongue swelled up, and her throat stuck shut like an empty sausage casing. She shook her head. Romeo never mentioned his love's true name. Only at the end did he mention he had a sister. Abigail clasped her hands together and closed her eyes. She was willing to wager that Romeo's love for Rachel was anything but brotherly.

And Rachel's missing beau would never come home.

CHAPTER 7

"He probably reminds her of her fella back home." Laurel's eyes misted as she latched the picture closed. "I should've guessed you'd lost a loved one, too. Didn't everyone?"

Abigail forced her lips into a smile. She nodded and picked up the tray.

Alan White. The name didn't want to stick to the image she'd seen. Jeremiah Calhoun fit better. Romeo, better still.

But why would he marry her? Was he trying to break Rachel's heart?

Somehow she made it to the kitchen, her thoughts jumbled. Malice couldn't have been his aim. She wouldn't believe it of him. If he truly loved Rachel, why would he pose as her brother? The faucet dripped. Abigail caught the droplets in her palm. They sparkled as they followed the creases of her skin to pool in the hollow of her hand.

Love. Perhaps he hadn't lied about his motivation. He'd wanted Rachel to be cared for, but he was dying. If he'd married Abigail as Alan White, what would he have profited? Instead he took on Jeremiah's identity—Jeremiah, whom he'd probably seen shot and believed to be dead. As Jeremiah's wife she'd be tied to the property, tied to the farm, and obligated to look after Rachel.

Abigail cranked down on the pump handle. Poor, poor Romeo. He never got to be with his Juliet, but his last thoughts were of her.

But how would Rachel respond when she learned Alan wasn't returning and that his last moments had been spent binding his life to Abigail?

"Oh, Romeo . . . Alan . . . whatever your name was," Abigail whispered to the window. "Your plan would have worked beautifully if Jeremiah had stayed dead."

"What's that?"

Abigail spun. Jeremiah balled his hand into a fist. His voice quavered. "Your plan would have worked if I stayed dead?" He pointed to the door. "Get out."

"That's not what I meant."

"I didn't want to accuse you right out, but I had my suspicions. Your story didn't make sense from the beginning, and I'm done waiting for you to concoct a better tale. You're finished here." He closed the distance between them, leaving the back door as Abigail's only way of escape.

She stopped him with a hand on his chest. "I know who the soldier was. I know who married me."

He caught her wrist in a powerful grip. "I'll gather up your things and throw them outside to you."

"I'm sure now. It all makes sense." Her fingers splayed on his shirt.

"Don't stand under the window. You might get hit."

"Alan. Rachel's beau. Your friend Alan."

His eyes flashed dangerously between anger and vulnerability as he weighed whether he'd let her speak again. Beneath her palm, his heart pounded. "You're lying."

"I just saw his photograph in Rachel's room. That's the soldier

I was assigned to at Gratiot Prison. He called himself Romeo and told me stories of Juliet, his fiancée, back in Hart County." As she spoke, the pieces fell together with more certainty. "It wasn't until after he realized his case was fatal that he gave me the name Jeremiah Calhoun. He told me that he was willing to abandon his fiancée in order to see that his sister was taken care of. Who else would go to such lengths to protect Rachel?"

"Why should I believe you?"

"What do I have to gain? I only want to know the truth."

He searched her face as though not wanting it to be true. Finally, he could deny it no longer. "Romeo. Star-crossed lovers." Jeremiah's grip on her wrist lessened and then dropped altogether. "Alan was the one who lost his arm . . . and then died?"

"I was with him when he passed. I paid for a burial and a headstone out of my wages. In St. Louis there's a tombstone with your name . . ."

He swayed toward her. Again her hand went to his chest, but this time to steady him.

"I searched for him," he said. "Rachel won't believe me, but I did. I could've made it home months earlier, but I didn't want to return without him."

He covered her hand with his own, obviously lost in thoughts too bleak to share. But he needed someone to share them with, didn't he?

"Jeremiah?" Laurel had glided into the room unheard.

Abigail snatched away her hand as Jeremiah straightened, and the pain in his eyes turned into something more hopeful.

She had come to him. There Laurel stood in all her dewy freshness, smack dab in his kitchen. Her dark, black-rimmed eyes drew him to a time before the world had been set aslant. She had come to find him, and that was a miracle worth celebrating.

He didn't want to move, standing as motionless as a skittish buck. "I'm glad you're here." It didn't matter why. Just the chance to see her again was bullion worth hoarding.

"I'd like to talk to you."

Still dazed, he followed Laurel into the parlor, wishing he could spill his heart to her and tell her his awful news, but Rachel had to hear first. His stomach twisted as he forced thoughts of Alan behind him. If anyone could comfort him through the times ahead, it'd be Laurel. He needed her with him, now and forever.

She walked slowly, probably worried that he couldn't keep up. What wouldn't Jeremiah give to never see the hated crutch again? A lifetime of hunting? Every horse in his stable? Unfortunately, he didn't have much to bargain with. He sat on the sofa next to her. A mite crowded, but she'd never complained before. She tucked her skirt beneath her, leaving a definite canal between them.

"I don't think you're going to like what I have to say." She fiddled with a wooden button on her dress.

Jeremiah braced himself. Whatever she had to say couldn't be worse than what he'd heard already. "Go on."

"While you were away and I thought you were dead, I might have fallen in love with Dr. Hopkins."

Jeremiah winced. "But you don't know if you love him?"

She picked at her fingernails. "That's the problem. If you hadn't returned, my feelings would've been certain. Now you're here." She took a deep breath and peeked up through her thick eyelashes. "I don't want to tell him good-bye, but I'm happy you're back."

He'd heard clearer declarations of love from hound dogs, but knowing the conversation with Rachel that loomed, Jeremiah was desperate for some encouragement. He leaned forward, resting his arms on his knees.

"I was gone a long spell, so I guess it's understandable that you'd be confused, but you're doing the right thing in coming here. We'll get this set straight."

Her chin lifted. "I'm not sure I want it set straight. That's what I'm saying. I was content to be Newton's girl, and I might be yet. I don't mind you coming around, but please don't rile your feelings up. If you have any doubts about me, then you're free to go. I won't hold you to any promises."

As if she had the right to cancel a promise he'd made. "I want to marry you. If I have to win you again, I will." She turned her rosebud lips up toward him. Normally he'd think about kissing them, but he had more serious matters on his mind. "When you become my wife, I want you to know there's no one else. Take your time and think it over. You'll begin to see clearly again."

And she would. God had been good to keep her from marrying when she'd learned of his disappearance. He'd kept her safe for Jeremiah and brought Jeremiah home in one piece, even if not all of those pieces functioned properly. Compared to everything else he'd gone through and what still lay ahead, waiting on Laurel was the least of his worries.

Taking a wet rag, Abigail scrubbed at a scuff on the kitchen wallpaper. The only way out was through the parlor, and she'd rather not interrupt Laurel and Jeremiah. Still reeling from her discovery, Abigail crouched as the tiny floral print blurred before her eyes. All this time Rachel had been waiting, watching, listening for any sign that Alan would return. All this time he was lying in a grave, and Abigail had seen him buried.

How tragic to wait and not know. Did her mother spend more than a passing thought on her? Probably not. She'd allowed her new husband to run Abigail off, after all. Besides, her mother had all but forgotten her while they still lived under the same roof. Unlike Abigail, who loved fiercely and forever, her mother had decided she no longer needed her daughter.

"Abigail, could you come here, please?"

It was Jeremiah. Abigail stood, tossed the rag into the sink, and located the penny in her pocket.

Ma was helping Rachel to the sofa as Jeremiah tapped his crutch impatiently.

"My, it's so late. We need to get the evening chores done—"

"Ma, have a seat," he said. "We've got something to tell you."

Abigail's heart hammered. She hugged her arms around her stomach, knowing she would be called upon to testify. With solemn eyes Jeremiah directed her to the rocker.

"What happened?" The dark pools beneath Rachel's eyes looked like bruises. "Did you hear from Alan?"

"Rachel"—his sister bristled at his voice—"Abigail figured something out today that might be hard to believe, even harder to accept."

Rachel's lip curled. Her eyes narrowed. "So Abigail has uncovered secret information that pertains to me? How fascinating."

There was no placating her, but Abigail recognized the sarcasm as Rachel's only defense.

"Had I known, I would've told you immediately," Abigail said, "but it wasn't until I saw Alan's picture in your room that I figured it out. After Alan White was injured at Westport he was captured. They brought him to the prison where I worked."

Rachel leaned forward, her eyes alight. "He was injured and captured? Well, if he's in prison that would explain why he hasn't made it home."

Abigail looked to Jeremiah. Sadness etched his face, but he nodded for her to continue.

"When he was captured he refused to give his identity. We called him Romeo because he spoke only of his love back home."

Mrs. Calhoun sniffed and took Rachel's hand, but Rachel shook her off. "And?"

"He lost his arm in the battle, and by the time he came to us, he was beyond our abilities. The doctors did their best, but gangrene set in." Rachel's face hardened. Abigail continued. "He knew the end was coming. That's when he told me his name was Jeremiah Calhoun. He asked me to marry him so I could care for his sister. He promised me the farm if I'd look after you."

Rachel sprang to her feet, wobbling forward to clutch the center table. "You have no conscience. First you claim to be Jeremiah's wife, and when you're caught in that lie, you tarnish the name of my . . . of the only man . . ." She swayed. Jeremiah took her by the shoulders and guided her back to the sofa.

She jabbed her finger toward Abigail. "Do you see what she is? She's a Lucifer, accusing, twisting a knife in our most guarded hurts. She'll change her story again when Alan comes home. She can't stay here—"

"She's staying."

Jeremiah said that? Abigail bit her lip and studied her hands, unable to watch the anger on Rachel's face any longer.

"She's staying because we need her," he said. "She'll leave after the colt is born. And I don't think she's lying. What would she gain by saying she married Alan?"

"She would hurt me."

Ma wiped the tears from her cheek. "Rachel, Abigail doesn't want to hurt you. Just think of all the good she's done for us."

Still kneeling beside Rachel's couch, Jeremiah took her hand. "I'm sorry, Rachel. Alan was my best friend, but I don't pretend to miss him as much as you do. If I had it to do over again, I wouldn't have got between you. I wouldn't have discouraged him."

Rachel pulled her hand free. With dry eyes and a face of stone she turned from her brother. "Some friend. Some brother. If this is true then there's no way for you to fix it. You stole my last chance for happiness, and I don't think I'll live long enough to forgive you."

Jeremiah flinched. But with the same stubbornness Abigail had come to recognize as his family's legacy, his mouth hardened.

"I said I was sorry and there's nothing else I can say. You won't hear me speak of him again. If you need me, I'll be here, taking care of my family. That's all I wanted to do in the first place." And he trudged to the door, his crutch clicking against the wood floor.

CHAPTER 8

June 1865

He'd heard that hard work caused a woman's beauty to fade, that bearing a heavy burden dulled her youth until she became stooped, wrinkled, and grew as brown as a pecan.

So far hard work hadn't hurt Abigail any.

It'd been two weeks since Jeremiah had made his decision to let Abigail stay, and he'd had ample opportunity to regret it. Every time the blond braid she wrapped around her head like a Swedish crown caught the sun, every time she bent over the oven, every time she dozed in the rocker exhausted from a hard day in the field, Jeremiah reminded himself that she wasn't staying. She didn't belong at his farm.

Of all the inconvenient women, why had Alan sent this one his way? Had Alan spared a thought for the tangle he'd created for him? If so, had his friend smiled at the conundrum? Jeremiah buckled the low sled to the horse's harness. He'd said he wouldn't speak of Alan, but that didn't mean he couldn't think of him. And now at least he could stop imagining Alan dying alone in a field churned with death. Better that Alan's last days were spent with a compassionate, competent nurse at his side—one he evidently trusted to do right by Rachel, impossible though it seemed.

And that's why Alan had sent Abigail. Because she was the perfect nurse for Rachel. Tough enough to take her abuse while patient enough to care about her, and also right handy when it came to the farm. He sighed. He'd just finished the spring planting and it was already June. Too much time had passed without a chance to make it back to the Wallaces' and commence courting in earnest. Besides, tales of missing cattle, noises in the night, and strange tracks still found their way through the forest to him. Everyone was staying near their hearth. Only problem was that his hearth had a beautiful woman sitting at it.

Jeremiah hawed to the horse. The old nag leaned into the harness and pulled the load of split rails to the fence where Abigail waited. Her collar flapped open where the first two buttons had sprung loose, exposing her glistening neck. Jeremiah swiped his forehead with his sleeve. Funny how sweat looked like something fancy on her, all shiny like Christmas ornaments. Why would God tempt him so?

Then again, maybe there was a benefit. He'd promised Abigail board for eight more months. After Josephine had her colt, he'd have to show Abigail the door, but kicking her out would be like putting the tea back into the leaves. That is to say, impossible where his mother was concerned. If he was ever to be shut of her, he needed to find a place for her to go. The most likely solution was to get her married off. As far as that matter, her appearance didn't hurt her none.

"You gonna stay on that horse all day, or are you going to climb down and help me?" she asked with a grin.

Good thing she was pretty. Abigail spoke directly even when a little wandering might be appreciated.

Jeremiah slung his poor leg over the saddle and put what weight he could on it until he could get his good foot on the ground. He jammed his crutch into his underarm before she had time to comment and met her at the back of the sled. She bent at the waist and grasped a rail with both hands. He could only use one, but was equal to the task. Slowly, so as not to lose his grip, he hobbled to the fence and helped her lift the rail into place. He wished Abigail didn't have to walk backwards, but he couldn't manage with his crutch.

"Is your leg going to get any better?" she asked.

"It's a sight better than it was last winter."

"I know you got shot at Westport, but what happened then? You didn't come to one of our hospitals, or we would've had a record, and I would've never married you."

His head snapped up. She corrected, "Married Alan, rather."

Unlike his mother and Laurel, Abigail had an inkling of the horrors of war. He didn't need to tell her everything, but she could take the truth. Jeremiah carried another rail before he answered.

"My horse got hit and when it went down I got caught beneath. I was crawling out when the back of my leg got shot."

"Your hamstrings?"

He nodded. "Passed through from left to right. We were in retreat by then, but I couldn't run and I had no horse, so I did what I could with the rest of my ammunition and then I hid." He'd always wonder if he'd done right by hiding. Something about it seemed cowardly, but on the other hand, surrendering as a prisoner wasn't particularly brave, either.

Abigail dusted her hands off after placing the rail. "What about Alan?"

"He stopped for me. I knew I'd go no farther that day, but he had to make it out. I owed Rachel that." At Rachel's name, he looked toward the stone house nestled in the valley. Dissatisfaction twisted his gut, and he turned back toward the field, leaning against the partially finished fence. "I fell. I told him to go on. He refused, so I let on like I was finished. Gut shot. Told him I had my pistol, to let me die fighting."

Abigail came to his side. She stood next to him and surveyed the wilderness past the fence.

"But Alan didn't leave you behind. He told me that his best friend was hit during the retreat and a Minie ball hit him in the arm as he came back around to find you."

"He was shot looking for me?" He searched her eyes, as if Alan could speak to him through her, but all he saw reflected in the clear blue was sympathy.

"Where did you go?" she asked.

Alan lost his arm, lost his life looking for Jeremiah. If only Jeremiah could forget their discussion on the porch behind them—the one when Alan asked permission to call on Rachel and Jeremiah refused him. He didn't deserve a friend like Alan, and he no longer had one.

"I got away from the battlefield and made it to the edge of a pasture before I gave out. They should've found me there, but the farmer spotted me first and brought me inside."

"Confederate sympathizers?" she said.

"No. Quakers, who refused to take a side. They doctored me up and hid me out of Christian charity."

"And the soldiers didn't look for you there?"

"They did, but those Quakers had practice hiding folks. They'd been part of the underground railroad."

"And they helped you, a Confederate soldier?"

"I was fighting for my freedom just the same as the slaves they helped."

Her mouth twisted and a sharp eyebrow rose. She stepped

back and took no pains to hide the fact that she was staring at his leg.

"So you healed, but your movement was inhibited during your convalescence?"

"I couldn't get out and walk, if that's what you mean."

She nodded as she circled him, staring at his hindquarters in a most unladylike manner. Jeremiah felt his ears grow warm.

"You know, those Quakers might inspire me to do some Christian charity, as well," she said.

"I'm glad you added *Christian*, 'cause I can't imagine what you have in mind."

"The doctor I assisted was Swedish. Dr. Jonson trained for years at Dr. Pehr Ling's academy in Stockholm. His ambition was to improve healing through exercise and massage."

"This doesn't sound promising."

"Poor Dr. Jonson didn't get to see much progress. The prisoners we tended weren't given much by way of nourishment or medicine, and many died from the lack of both. And yet, since physical manipulation doesn't require a budget and the prisoners had nothing else with which to occupy themselves, he was able to perfect the techniques he'd studied. If Dr. Jonson were here, I'm confident he could improve your leg. Perhaps get you off the crutch entirely."

His heart skipped a beat. As much as Jeremiah hated to admit it, it wasn't only his chores that kept him from going back to Laurel. He remembered too well her disappointment at his injury. How could he compete with Dr. Hopkins when he couldn't even walk? But he shouldn't get his hopes up.

"They let him practice this quackery on people?"

"On prisoners. True, I wasn't allowed around the more able-bodied prisoners, but the doctor did report that the difference between those who participated and those who didn't was remarkable."

He tried to straighten the hurt limb, but the best he could do was to sweep the toe of his boot against the ground. Impossible. It was too late to fix. All he'd accomplish would be to make himself look like a fool. "I think I can manage without the experiments."

She twisted her mouth to the side. "Then by all means, manage. That cripple leg won't slow you down. Not by much, anyway."

She waited for him at the pile of rails, holding her end until he could clump over.

"I'll work twice as long and twice as hard if I need to." He scooped beneath two rails, lifting the double load easily.

Abigail walked stiff-legged, holding the beams low. Her breath chopped, but the strain didn't keep her quiet. "Yes, I'm sure Laurel will want you to work from dawn to dusk. Every woman wants a husband who's too busy to spend time with her."

Jeremiah dropped the rails. With a squeak Abigail hopped back as she lost her grip, and they crashed at her feet.

"Don't talk to me about Laurel." What was wrong with this woman? His men had respected him. "In case you haven't noticed, I've been busy around here. I have to work to save my farm. I can't just find a lonely soldier and weasel my way into a family."

Her jaw clenched. Her fists rested on her nicely rounded hips. "Do you honestly think I tricked Alan? That I used some womanly persuasion on him?"

He swallowed, unsure he could resist her womanly persuasion. "Why you? Why did he send you here when he could've sent any number of people?"

"Maybe because I wanted to help him, just like I want to help you. Does there have to be another motive?"

Everyone had motives, didn't they? "It's unnatural. That's all."

She raised an eyebrow. "Then keep searching, Captain. Refuse my help until you figure out why I'm here. In the meantime, why don't you finish up alone?" She spun away and marched to the house.

Infuriating. As if he hadn't had enough of Yankees coming to his territory and bossing him around. Hadn't he gone to war over the matter?

And he'd lost.

Jeremiah wobbled as he bent to grab a rail. With his first step backwards it slid out of his hand. The second time he found better purchase and pulled it all the way to the fence—a drawn-out affair with stumbling and sweating. Then he had to balance one end on the fence while he hobbled to the other side and lifted it. He could work twice as long and still couldn't make up for two good legs beneath him.

He'd come home prepared to throw himself on God's mercy and pray he could survive with his injury, but what if he didn't need to be injured after all? Everyone would benefit if he were healed. Laurel, his family, his farm. Being able-bodied would make his goals possible. Maybe Abigail's remedy was God's answer?

But he wouldn't let that uppity nurse line him out. She'd have to realize who was boss. And if she couldn't help, he'd have to let on like it didn't matter. He couldn't put too much hope in her. He'd been disappointed too many times already.

Abigail's spoon clicked against her bowl. The ceiling creaked above her head. Ma glanced up, waited, then took another bite of stew.

Rachel hadn't felt like coming down. Ever since learning of Alan's death, she'd withdrawn even further into herself, and worrying over her was taking its toll on Ma, too.

Abigail drained the milk from her cup. She'd go up after dinner and visit with Rachel. Abigail would enjoy hearing more about Alan, and perhaps talking about him would ease Rachel's pain, although she wouldn't be surprised if Rachel would shut her out.

Jeremiah hadn't spoken to her yet, either, come to think of it. He hadn't mentioned how he fared with the fence since she'd left. Abigail might as well have brought a book to the table for as much company as he and Ma provided. He looked up and caught her watching him. She looked away, snatched her napkin, and wiped her mouth, trying to act natural, but it did no good. Unable to ignore his glower any longer, she met his gaze straight on. For a heartbeat his hazel eyes captured hers, seeming to ask something of her, but she didn't understand the question. He grunted and bowed his head over his stew again.

Nothing left in her bowl, Abigail took another slice of the bread, just to keep her hands busy. He, too, took to the bread basket but found it empty. One look at his sharp cheekbones and she remembered how injury wasted away at a man.

"Here." She offered him her slice, only a bite missing. "I've had enough."

Again he searched her face. "Are you sure?"

She nodded.

"Thank you." He took it from her hand and crumbled it into his bowl to mop up the juices.

Ma roused herself. "I'll clean up. Are you going back to the field?" she asked Abigail.

"I thought I'd check on Rachel." Abigail rose to put together a tray for her.

Ma tugged her sleeves down from around her elbows. "Maybe it'd be better if I went. I know it's not your fault, Abigail, but she's having trouble understanding why Alan married you."

Abigail's hands stilled. Couldn't Rachel understand that she and Alan were trying to help her? But that would require rational thought—something Rachel seemed unwilling to attempt. "I'll wait until tonight to check her swelling," Abigail said. "You go on up and I'll get the dishes."

Ma took Rachel's tray and swept out the door as Abigail busied herself at the sink. She'd find something to work on, but she wasn't going to volunteer her time to Jeremiah. Not until he admitted that he needed her help. How long was he going to sit there, anyway? Hadn't he finished that last piece of bread by now?

He cleared his throat. "Abigail?" The uncertainty in his voice sent a flutter through her stomach. Goodness, he'd be a dangerous man if he occasionally acted halfway Christian.

She turned. Under his right arm dirt clumped on his shirt, probably from lugging the rails without her. He followed her gaze and made to brush it off.

"Were you serious about my leg getting better? If not, then tell me now because I don't want—"

"I'm serious." Abigail sat down across from him. Was he giving her a chance? If she could heal his leg, then there'd be no way he'd ever ask her to leave. "Besides some hard work, it wouldn't cost anything to try."

He lifted his face. "I'm not afraid of work."

"Neither am I."

Whatever uncertainty he'd allowed her to see vanished.

He leaned back, crossing his arms over his chest. "Exactly what do you have in mind? I don't know how you can doctor me without being inappropriate."

Inappropriate? Like the thorough appraisal he gave her that morning? But this sounded like a promise to do better. "You might feel uncomfortable, but I assure you, I'm no sheltered miss. My time serving your fellow men at arms exposed me to sights that would turn a butcher's stomach."

His eyes lost their focus, reminding Abigail that he'd witnessed atrocities of his own—perhaps committed them against her countrymen. He pulled his crutch from the wall and stood. "Tomorrow then? And where? The barn?"

"I'll meet you there after breakfast."

"And you can't be telling anyone about this."

"I wouldn't dare."

He walked to the door. With his head bowed he added, "That fence work is going slow."

"I'm sorry to hear it." She rose from her chair and picked up the dish towel. "I told your mother I'd tidy up in here."

He turned. "Do you need any help? I could give you a hand, and then when we're done maybe you could come back outside . . ."

She hoped he understood her smile to be happiness and not gloating. "That'd be marvelous."

CHAPTER 9

"I'm going to the barn, now." Jeremiah's cheeks sported a flush that Abigail hadn't noticed before. "You don't need anything, do you, Ma?"

Ma sipped her morning coffee and turned the page of her ladies' journal. "Me? Naw. If I do, I know where to find you."

He shifted in his chair and almost dragged the tablecloth off with him. "But I'd hate for you to bother. Besides, I don't want to be disturbed once I get my chores going."

Abigail bit her lip. Gathering the empty breakfast plates, she had to hide the smile that threatened to break through. Jeremiah wasn't kidding when he said he didn't want anyone to know about their project. Well, she could understand. What passed for normal in a prison hospital would be shocking in civilian life, and the paces she'd put him through weren't even considered normal in a hospital. Not yet, according to Dr. Jonson. She hoped it wasn't too late to help Jeremiah. Her experience, limited as it was, dealt with fresh injuries. Could Dr. Ling's methods work on muscle that had already mended?

"I'll go on up to Rachel," Ma said. "Perhaps reading *Frank Leslie's Monthly* to her will brighten her morning."

Jeremiah had already fled, although whether from eagerness to get started or embarrassment, Abigail couldn't guess, but as soon as the kitchen was tidied she took the short walk to the barn.

He'd already opened the high window, but even with the cheerful light flooding in, Jeremiah looked a bit green as he peeked at her from over a stall.

"Are you sure this is necessary? If Laurel finds out—"

"She wants you healed. If we're successful I don't think she'll complain about the method."

He nodded, then straightening his shoulders he came out from the stall.

Abigail's jaw dropped. "Where are your britches?"

Jeremiah's nostrils flared. He tugged his shirttails as far over his drawers as they'd reach. "You said . . . you said it wasn't inappropriate. That you'd seen everything."

She couldn't squelch a giggle. "But that doesn't mean I want to see more." Abigail covered her mouth and spun away, right across the tongue of the wagon and onto the floor. The landing knocked the air out of her, but she continued to shake with laughter. She propped herself up on her elbows and tried to catch her breath.

"And I thought you'd be mad that I kept my drawers on," he said. Was that a touch of humor from the grim Captain Calhoun? He'd darted back into the stall, almost smiling at her from over the divider. "I'm glad I'd already sworn you to secrecy. Now toss me my trousers. They're hanging on the plow."

But before Abigail could move footsteps sounded at the door.

She scrambled to her feet. With a finger to his lips, Jeremiah ducked just as the door opened and Calbert entered.

"Abigail?" Calbert scanned the barn. "Where's Jeremiah? Have you seen him?"

She'd seen quite a bit of him, actually. "Yes, but he seems to have disappeared. Can I relay a message for you?"

His chin slid sideways. "Are you feeling up to snuff? Looks like you've been rolling around on the ground."

"Oh my. I just tripped over the wagon tongue." She brushed the straw off her skirt. "Very careless of me."

"There's usually a rag of sorts in here if you need it to clean up."

But the only piece of cloth Abigail could see was Jeremiah's britches hanging from the plow.

"It's fine. I'll get dirtier before the day's through. You don't need to worry about—"

"Where did that rag go?" He rustled through a bucket full of tools while the light from the upper window seemed to illuminate the convicting article of clothing. "I know it's here somewhere."

Abigail darted between him and the plow. "Really, I'm fine. I'll keep a lookout for it, though. Let you know if it turns up."

He craned his neck to see past her. "Is that it behind you?"

Abigail snatched the trousers and balled them up in her arms. "I've got it. Thank you."

Calbert stared pointedly at the suspender loops that swung out of her grasp. His bushy eyebrow waggled like a caterpillar. What could she say? She met his gaze directly. If he wanted to ask a question, he might as well do it now.

He shrugged. "I came to ask if you could come with me. Bushwhackers shot Mr. Rankin over on Fulton's Bald. Doc Hopkins is out to Pine Gap today. They need you."

"But what if the outlaws are still out there?"

"I'm watching for them." He stared down at the trousers. "Not much gets past my notice, Mrs. Calhoun."

"Calbert, I thought I'd explained the situation. Just call me Abigail."

"Whatever you say, ma'am. I'll wait on the porch and give you a few minutes to say good-bye . . . if you see Jeremiah, that is."

What a disaster. Just when he'd let down his guard and started to enjoy her company, things got complicated again. Jeremiah had a fair idea of what Calbert suspected and didn't know how he'd ever explain to the man.

His britches flew over the wall of the stall and landed on his head. "Listening to you will be the biggest mistake of my life," he said as he pulled his trousers on.

"Do you know the Rankin family?" Abigail asked.

He bowed his head, and not just so he could see the buttons as he did them up. "Yes. They're Union, so you should get along right enough. He can't have been home much longer than I've been. He outlives the war and then gets attacked after peace is proclaimed." He pulled his suspenders over his shoulders. "Peace? Peace is a foreign idea here, I'm afraid."

"But it wasn't always. Surely after a while—"

"You don't know."

By the time he stepped out of the stall, her humor had faded. Well, so had his. Maybe someday there'd be a place where happiness didn't feel like pouring salt on a wound. That day wasn't today.

She finished saddling Josephine. He checked the straps on the old leather tack, said a quick prayer for the Rankin family, for Abigail's safety, and for his own, because he was going looking for the people who'd done this . . . crippled leg and all.

Clouds had rolled in over the mountains, trapping the heat and adding humidity. Abigail caught a line of sweat rolling down her neck and thanked God once again that Calbert had the grace to pretend the barn encounter never happened. They would have enough controversy to handle once they reached the Rankins' cabin.

"I hope they'll let me help," she said.

"Of course they will. Word is getting around about how you helped Varina's family," Calbert answered. "They're starting to trust you."

Abigail's lungs squeezed painfully. This mountain man thought more of her than her own mother did. Another reason she was determined to stay here and never go home. She gripped the horn of her saddle. "I'm still an outsider. I appeared claiming that Jeremiah was dead and I'm his wife, then he showed up and set the record straight. They have to suspect me."

Before Calbert could argue further they arrived at the Rankins' cabin. A knock on the rough door brought instant results.

The raw-boned youth had a scrape on his cheek, marring his scraggly attempt at a beard. His blond lashes rimmed red eyes that were desperately trying to disguise his sorrow. "Pa said we couldn't trust you to bring good help."

Calbert jerked his pipe out of his mouth and pointed it at the boy. "She worked for the Federal Army, and if that ain't good enough for you, I don't know what is."

The boy looked over his shoulder into the cabin. He swallowed and turned back to them. "We sent for Dr. Hopkins and he's as secesh as anyone, but Pa don't want a lady playacting on him. He'd rather die with dignity."

If only she could persuade the boy—not for her own pride

but for his father's life. "Is it that bad, then?" she asked. "I want to help, and while I'm not as good as Dr. Hopkins, I do have some medical training."

The youth pulled the door closed behind him and with lowered voice said, "It's bad. He's in terrible pain and running hot. His breathing is all rattle-like. Some blood coming up, but not much."

"Does it look like he was shot in the lungs?"

"Yes, ma'am." He turned at his name being called from inside and cracked the door open. "I'm sending her away."

Calbert scratched his head. "It's a tough decision, son. Disobey your pa or take away his best chance at a miracle."

"Help is right here," she said. "If I can save his life . . ."

Abigail prayed as the boy weighed his decision. She'd known rejection—expected it even—but she didn't want someone else to suffer because she'd been deemed unworthy.

"Come on in," he said at last. "If Pa survives, surely he'll forgive me."

Calbert motioned her ahead, and she rushed past him, praying that the delay hadn't cost Mr. Rankin his life.

※

Sometimes he hated being right. Jeremiah had set out on the slim chance that he might see something pertaining to Rankin's attack, and there it was. A plume of smoke on the back side of the mountain. He adjusted the pistol riding in his belt and wished once again he had two legs to fight on. But this was his home, and it was his duty to face the dangers that threatened it. Chicanery was afoot, but once the land was cleared of outliers, the womenfolk would be able to travel safely. Abigail could wander away from the house more, which would be good. Too much time with her made him tetchy, and goodness knew the last thing his house needed was another crabby apple rotting inside.

Before he reached the ridge, Jeremiah could smell the fire, and it wasn't no cook fire. His nose wrinkled at the familiar odor. A moonshine still. On his property. He followed the scent to a crevice hidden by thick bushes. He made a wide pass around the area first, looking for anyone hunkered down next to the awkward copper contraption, but it seemed recently abandoned. The fire beneath the boiler blazed and the mash bubbled, but no one sat with it.

Jeremiah dismounted, furious at the proof that a stranger was using his land. They'd probably run off just as they saw him coming. He clumped to the still and, swinging his crutch, knocked it to its side. A few more hits and the copper chamber busted, leaking out the sickly sweet-smelling mash.

He'd scared someone away, but the one who shot Rankin might be headed back there even now, and Jeremiah would be waiting for him. He tied Lancaster to the nearest tree and crept to the cave that overlooked the tight clearing. There could be someone hiding in there, he supposed, but once he slid behind the thick cedar that grew up against the opening, he saw it was empty.

Or next to empty. Nestled between the limestone gills of the cave, a fire had been laid out, but if it weren't for the presence of the still, Jeremiah would have no reason to believe anyone had been there for years.

This spot had been a favorite hideout when he was small. He knew every lump and hollow of it. He squeezed into his favorite cubbyhole, much smaller than he remembered. True, if a shooting broke out, he'd be trapped, but it wasn't as if he could run anyway. The shelf hid him from view, made a nice sniper's nest if it weren't for the dripping water. Still, it was a right smart place to lie in wait for someone to show himself.

Once in place, he loosened his gun and stretched out, or tried to, but that lame leg of his remained tented up.

If only. If only he could get his strength back. If only the hills were safe for decent folks. If only Laurel would settle down and marry him. If only Rachel were healed. Those were his foremost prayers. Beyond that he supposed he could spare a prayer for the Yankee nurse, that whatever problems she'd left behind would be solved. He'd sensed trouble in her terse attitude and vague answers. He'd pray that, seeing how she was a kindly person and hard worker, she'd find someone who'd do right by her. Otherwise he might find himself more worried about her than was seemly.

Minutes passed. A quarter of an hour. Plenty of time for him to imagine his future—horses to sell, fields full of orchard grass and red clover, golden-haired children playing on the porch.

Jeremiah scrunched his nose. Golden? How in thunder could he and Laurel have blond children? He rubbed his eyes. He'd been sitting there so long, he couldn't even daydream worth a hoot.

No one was there and probably no one was coming. Only after listening closely did Jeremiah leave his hiding place. He couldn't outrun a child, but his senses had been honed over the years so that nothing escaped his notice. Somehow rustling leaves, the birds, and even the scent of the dirt told him that no one was near. He parted the bushes and ducked under the growth to find Lancaster patiently awaiting his return.

"Nothing, huh?" he asked his old friend. "No one messed with you?"

Lancaster blinked slowly at him, a droll expression on his face. Stepping around the busted still, Jeremiah untied the reins and slid his crutch across Lancaster's withers. If he kept working, soon he'd be able to lift himself in the stirrup. No more scrambling up like a boy climbing wet rocks.

He grasped the saddle horn and Lancaster stumbled sideways.

"Not you, too. I expect that old nag to be unsteady, but you can hold me."

Jeremiah pulled again. This time Lancaster took two steps forward, leaving Jeremiah hopping to keep up with him.

"Whoa, boy." What was wrong with the horse? Suddenly Lancaster's stomach tightened and his back stretched. Lancaster's head dropped and he released a satisfying belch. Only then did Jeremiah fully appreciate the condition of the still.

The copper pot had been nosed away from the fire and emptied. The stones, which had been splashed with mash, were now licked clean. Jeremiah turned to stare at his horse. Lancaster, like any guilty boy, kept his head down.

Sugar, cornmeal, yeast—no wonder the animal couldn't resist lapping it up. But how to get him home? Once he stepped out of these bushes, Jeremiah was a target. He couldn't hobble down the mountain leading an intoxicated equine.

"I don't care how bad you feel, you've got to carry me home." Jeremiah stopped short of the "let this be a lesson to you" lecture his own pa had delivered him the first time he'd found a still. Instead, he dragged Lancaster to a tree trunk. He wrapped the reins around it for leverage. This time Lancaster kept his hooves beneath him as Jeremiah mounted. Jeremiah wanted to ease downhill, walk slowly and quietly, but the mountain was too steep. Lancaster stiffened his legs and tried to resist, but his inebriated condition left him no match for gravity. Stumbling and skidding, the horse crashed through branches, picking up speed as they descended. Jeremiah tugged on the reins, but Lancaster couldn't help himself. It was all Jeremiah could do to duck branches and stay in the saddle.

Fortunately there weren't any bad guys to see them as they barreled out of their hiding place, but they would've been a tough shot the way they were weaving from side to side.

Giving up on sneaking anywhere, Jeremiah would settle on making it home. Poor Lancaster. The mash had so impaired his sight that he would've run himself smack dab into a tree if Jeremiah had let him. Of course he didn't, but a tug on a rein that should've corrected his path instead sent him careening toward another obstacle, swaying first one way, then the other.

If they did run into trouble, Jeremiah dearly hoped they'd just shoot the horse.

The ground leveled. Lancaster stopped to pant. Jeremiah pried his knuckles off the reins. Never in the cavalry had he experienced such a harrowing charge. More gently now, he urged Lancaster forward. His head drooped and he lagged as if pushing himself each step. And who should be there to note their arrival but Abigail and Calbert walking out of the barn. She halted midstep to stare. Her voice carried to Calbert, his mother, everyone to witness his disgrace.

"Come on, Lancaster. Try to get home without embarrassing us both."

But Lancaster had done give out. He sank on his haunches and sat like a mule.

Now even his mother had made it outside. Abigail was running toward him, Calbert hurrying just behind.

"Get up, you worthless piece of horsehide," he mumbled. "Come on, get up."

With a heave and another burp, Lancaster rose to his unsteady feet. Abigail swung the barn gate open for him.

"What happened? Is he shot?"

Ma scurried toward him. "Shot? You're shot?"

"No one's shot." Jeremiah tried to direct Lancaster into the barn, but Abigail caught his bridle and started her own inspection.

"What's that smell?" She leaned close to his side. Jeremiah held motionless as her upturned nose twitched. "Whiskey? You haven't been drinking, have you?"

His mother cried out and covered her mouth. Calbert removed his hat and scratched his head, looking like he wanted a place to hide.

"No, I haven't been drinking. It's this miserable horse. I found a still up on the ridge, and he helped himself to the sour mash while I took a look around."

"The horse is tipsy?" Calbert asked. "If that don't beat all."

"You should try riding a skunked horse down a mountain," Jeremiah said.

"The way he's belching, I think he might want some fresh air. Let me unsaddle him and get him to water." Noticing the slight pout to her lips, Jeremiah had to guess that Abigail's visit hadn't gone as planned. With one last stroke she led the horse to the barn.

"Don't be scaring me like that, Jeremiah. I thought you were hurt." Ma lifted the hem of her black skirt and ambled back to the house.

"A still, you say?" Calbert squinted toward the mountain. "Did you see anyone?"

"No, but someone had been keeping the fire until they saw me coming up." Jeremiah looked over his shoulder. "How's Rankin?"

Calbert shook his head. "By the time we got there, he was too far gone. We stayed until his last breath."

"And Abigail?"

"She's taking it hard. They didn't want to let her help and after they did, he died anyway." Calbert dusted his knee. "I'd best get home. Don't want Mrs. Huckabee to be alone with the babies if there's a killer out."

Calbert climbed aboard his mule as Jeremiah made his way back to the barn and found Abigail combing her fingers through Lancaster's mane.

"Calbert told me about Rankin," he said. "I'm sorry."

"I did everything I could. No one could've saved him." Her fingers glided over the horse's neck. Lancaster stood transfixed.

"I'm sure they realize that. They have no reason to question your skill."

"They will now. And it doesn't help any that you've already denounced me."

"Me? I've never said anything to the Rankins about your nursing."

Forgetting the horse, she spun to face him. "But just you being here calls my honesty into question, especially after I told everyone I'm your wife and you said that we'd never met."

A familiar warmth crept over him—the same warmth that appeared every time the subject of their marriage came up. "I have to tell the truth. We aren't married."

"I know, but it's very inconvenient."

"You have no idea." He shifted his crutch before his underarm got sore. Losing a patient would hurt. Almost like losing one of your men. Next thing you knew, you were questioning your abilities, your calling. He'd been there, and the only way to get over it was to move on until you reached another victory.

"Come on," he said. "Our morning appointment was interrupted, but there's no reason we can't start now."

"Really?" The slightest smile from her could coax a badger out of his sett. "I would like that."

"So what do I do?"

She found Calbert's missing rag and brushed the goat droppings off the old table. "This table will work. Move it so only the narrow end is against the wall."

Not easy while holding the crutch, but possible. He grasped the end of the table and swung it away from the stone wall. Then with two swinging moves of his crutch, he was at the head. He lifted and pushed it into place, leaving enough room for Abigail to make her way around it.

She inspected the table, paying particular attention to a wobbly leg. "I don't imagine it'll overturn. Climb on up."

Was he really going through with this? He had to remember that besides encouraging Abigail, his true motivation was Laurel. She deserved a husband who could walk and work, who could help her up and down stairs instead of needing assistance himself. If submitting to Abigail's insane theories could help him win Laurel, then it was worth it.

Tossing the crutch aside, Jeremiah lifted himself and slid onto the table until his back was against the wall as Abigail directed.

"Straighten both legs as much as you can."

"That's the problem, isn't it?" One leg lay flat. The other had enough space beneath his knee for a raccoon to pass. "It won't stretch."

"It doesn't want to stretch," Abigail said. "Our job is to make it."

He had tried. Didn't she realize how hard he'd tried? Evidently not. Taking a milking stool, she placed it near the table and stepped up to sit at his side.

Too close for his conscience. He scooted to the far edge to keep space between them, but she stopped him.

"I'm trying to get close to you. Don't run off."

He could feel his face growing warm. "What if Calbert comes back? He'll know for sure something funny's going on."

"Don't worry, by the time I'm done you'll hurt so bad, you'll despise me."

Jeremiah swallowed. "Let's hope."

Twisting so she faced him, Abigail placed one hand beneath his knee and one above it. "I'm going to put some weight here. Tell me when it hurts."

He watched her long fingers against his trouser leg. He was trying to help her forget the death of a patient, but how far was he willing to go? A woman really shouldn't act so familiar. It could give a man the wrong idea, but then pain shot up his back. He gritted his teeth and forgot any attraction she held.

"I'm going to hold it here for a ten count," she said. "Try to release the muscles."

He grunted.

"Breathe, Jeremiah. Unclench your fists. You're fighting the pain."

"But I'm winning." His back felt clammy against his shirt. Sweating without even moving. She let go.

"I told you to tell me when it hurt." She reached her hand beneath his leg and touched his hamstring.

He grabbed her wrist as his pulse sped. There were limits—for her own safety as well as his. "Don't you get frisky."

She glared at him. "I wouldn't dream of it."

Unfortunately, his dreams most likely would contain some part of this encounter. A lock of blond hair brushed against his sleeve, the curl catching and separating on his rough homespun shirt. He closed his eyes as she probed the back side of his leg. "Please get back to the hurting part," he rasped.

She kneaded the hard knot of his scar. "Feel that? That Minie ball tore all this muscle when it passed through. It grew back together just like God intended, but it drew up short."

"Considering my foot barely reaches the floor, I'd say I guessed as much." He didn't know where to look, not with her sitting so close.

Reaching to his ankle she slid his foot forward until it resisted. This time she leaned the underside of her arm against his knee. The warmth of her body washed through his pant leg.

"Thank you for letting me do this," she said. "I'd like to think I accomplished something positive today . . . besides making you uncomfortable."

With her hands all over him he was beyond uncomfortable. He'd welcome pain if it chased away temptations. But more than the pain was the fear that his muscle would tear. He could imagine it snapping, detaching, and recoiling like a broken spring. His elbows tightened against his torso, his back arched.

"It hurts." The words made him feel defeated, like he was giving in.

"Good. Stop fighting it. Breathe." She continued to lean on his leg, but put a hand on his chest. "Release this. Let it rest. Your shoulders. Make them soft."

She ran her hand across his arms, her light touch sending chills down his spine. Good thing Laurel never touched him like this. It was hard enough to ignore this stranger. Better to focus on his leg, which, to his surprise, had lowered a hair more. A new wave of pain caused his gut to tighten, but with effort he willed his body to submit.

"I bet you didn't do this to Alan. Else he wouldn't have married you."

She finished the count, then rose off him. "I couldn't rehabilitate a limb that was gone. You have more to work with."

He drew his knee up and shook out the burning. "I don't know what I expected, but that wasn't it."

Abigail smiled and patted his leg in a gesture that was surprisingly comforting, considering his confusion seconds ago.

He pulled his left leg up to bend it at the same angle and compared the two, the strong versus the withered. If he could straighten the leg, he could strengthen it. Maybe there was hope after all.

"Let's do it again," he said.

CHAPTER 10

Abigail pulled off her slat bonnet and fanned herself as she walked to the house. Having already put the horses through their morning exercises, she turned her attention again toward her patients—two of them now. Truly she hadn't expected Captain Calhoun to submit to her instructions with such dedication. Yesterday it'd taken her a quarter of an hour to convince him that there was a limit to what they could accomplish in one appointment. Thankfully he'd finally believed her, or else they'd still be in that barn—and then what would Calbert think?

Abigail grinned. As if she'd have her head turned by Jeremiah Calhoun. During the war she'd worked with handsomer patients than him—fresh-faced boys with rakish grins pouring on the Southern charm even as their lives ebbed away, men whose classical features would've inspired Renaissance sculptors. This backwoods Missouri boy couldn't hold a candle to them. Not with his square jaw, his aquiline nose, and his . . . well, there was something about his eyes. She slowed as she approached the house. What was it that made them unsatisfactory? Perhaps because they found everything more interesting than they did her. Why, even yesterday when she'd been helping him out of the goodness of her heart, he'd rather close his eyes in boredom than acknowledge her.

Just as well. His indifference protected her. Abigail had learned to guard her heart at the prison. Too many men died. Caring grew costly. But she'd never been in a situation like this—one patient over a course of months, living together with his family. A weaker woman might mistake concern for affection.

From the stairwell, Abigail heard Rachel's voice. "Why do you read those papers, Ma? Don't they make you sad over what you're missing out on?"

"Of course not, dear. The journals are only to 'broaden my horizons,' as it says on the cover."

"Well, I understand wishing you had a different life."

Ma stashed the ladies' paper on the table next to her just as Abigail entered the room. A cloud of smoke curtained Rachel. With two fingers Rachel removed her pipe and blew a slow, steady draught directly in Abigail's direction.

"Do you think you're hurting me by making yourself sicker?" Abigail asked.

"It's not about you. I'm doing what makes me happy."

Ma fanned the cloud away. "You don't think it's bad for her, do you? I thought if it relieved her rheumatism, it couldn't hurt."

"Her achy joints won't kill her," Abigail said. "Lack of oxygen and stress on the heart will." But sharing that information only distressed Ma. Best to get her out and her mind on something more productive. "I thought you might enjoy working in your garden while it's still cool outside."

Ma tucked a strand of white hair behind her ear and pushed out of her chair. "That's a fine idea. No reason to wait until it's scorching."

Rachel's eyes darted from Abigail to her mother, as if trying to make a decision. "Go on, Ma," she said at last. "I can sit by myself."

"No need for that. Abigail will stay with you."

"That's what I was afraid of." Rachel's thin mouth twitched, almost smiling at her own ill temper.

"She'll be just fine." Abigail sat beside Rachel's bed as Ma departed. "Or we could go outside. Nothing's preventing you from leaving the house. I'll make you a pallet in the shade if you'd like a change of scenery."

"Will you let me smoke outside?"

Abigail shook her head and extended her hand. With a generous amount of muttering Rachel passed the pipe to her. "If you have something to say, we'd might as well get it over with."

Abigail opened the window to lessen the effects of the tobacco smoke. The warm breeze tossed the flowered curtains against her arms. "I wanted to talk about Alan, actually. I knew him for only a few weeks and I miss him. I wish you'd tell me more about him."

Rachel placed a hand to her chest. Her breathing sped, shallow pants that measured her displeasure by half gulps. "Those memories are mine. Maybe I don't want to share them, especially with you."

The woman sitting before her was nothing more than a scared, bullying child controlling the only part of her life left to her, but Abigail wouldn't shy away from Rachel's displeasure like Ma did.

"We all have fond memories of Alan," Abigail said, "and I'd think you would want to share them. He was a good man and deserves a remembrance."

"Talking about him won't bring him back. It won't help him one bit."

Abigail picked up Ma's journal and folded it neatly. "No,

once someone passes it's too late. Which is why we shouldn't wait to express our love, our admiration . . . and our forgiveness."

Rachel humphed. "You're a nurse, not a minister. Why don't you get me well instead of poking around where you're not welcome?"

Abigail leaned forward. "I can't get you well, Rachel. The fever has damaged your heart. I'll do what I can to ease the inflammation and protect you from another onslaught, but the next round could be your last. Please don't leave your mother and brother remembering only how angry you were. Nothing hurts like a hostile farewell."

And Abigail should know. Had she understood the cost of her banishment, she would've fought harder to clear her name.

"If you truly understood what a fine man Alan was, then you'd understand why I can't forgive Jeremiah for sending him to his death."

"You hold Jeremiah responsible?" Abigail asked. "Alan didn't. He was devastated that he lost his friend at Westport. Of course he didn't name Jeremiah, but every story revolved around either his friend or his Juliet."

"Stop." Rachel swung her feet over the side of the bed. Her eyes shot daggers at Abigail. "I told you I don't want to talk about him. You took my beau, and now you're trying to weasel your way into my home. I see through your maneuvering. Your story about being Mrs. Calhoun didn't stick, but that doesn't mean you aren't looking for another chance to make it true. Catching Jeremiah would mean you get this farm, and that's what you've been after all along."

Catching Jeremiah? Was there no end to Rachel's outlandish claims? Abigail held her gaze just long enough to prove she wasn't intimidated. "Alan sent me here, and I'll stay until my work is done. And I can promise you I have no designs on your brother."

With a disbelieving huff, Rachel fell back onto her pillow. Abigail stood and straightened the quilt tangled beneath her, still ittitated by the idea. She'd been desperate enough to marry a stranger the first time, and her circumstances hadn't improved since then. Yet marrying a dying man was a far cry from being bound forever to an opinionated, disruptive force like Jeremiah. There were worse fates than being a widow.

She didn't know what she would do, but she could say with certainty what she wouldn't. The sooner Jeremiah won Laurel back, the sooner everyone would be at ease.

Bending at the waist with Josephine's hoof supported against her thigh, Abigail ran the hoof pick alongside the horse's frog, knocking loose the mud from the day's ride. While she wasn't giving up on Rachel, Abigail needed this time with the horses. Working with them reminded her of her father . . . and reminded her of a time when she was valued.

When her father died, Abigail determined she'd look after her mother and make certain they'd never lack. She woke early and oversaw the grooms, not afraid to pitch in and shovel, feed, or saddle if necessary. When buyers visited she helped her mother provide a fitting reception and then dealt with them professionally, just as her father had taught her. Even her older brothers, by then working their own farms, were impressed. Constantly her mother sang her praises to their friends, so pleased that her daughter could manage the large operation on her own, but when John Dennison came calling, her mother no longer needed her.

Abigail took up the brush and swept loose the remaining

debris caught in the horseshoe. John was the thief. He stole her mother from her. He stole her farm and her horses, and when she challenged him, he claimed she had taken his gold pocket watch. Ridiculous. No one would believe it—except her mother.

When John threatened to banish her if she didn't return it, her mother stood silent. Furious, Abigail had stomped upstairs, threw her clothes into a traveling case, and left, thinking they'd track her to town and beg her to return. But they didn't. Well, she could be just as stubborn. She wouldn't go back if they didn't want her.

As she picked through Josephine's last hoof, Jeremiah entered. Looking up, Abigail blew a wisp of hair out of her face. "I'll be done here in a second." She didn't bother asking if he needed something. Obviously he wasn't looking for her company.

He lifted the end of the oak table and swung it into position against the wall of the barn. Jeremiah hopped into place and scooted his back against the wall.

"This old leg feels worse today than it has for a while."

"You shouldn't push yourself so hard." She ran the brush over the bottom of the hoof, flicking the dirt and leaves free.

"Doing nothing hasn't worked. Might as well try your methods."

Abigail lowered Josephine's leg and set her tools aside. "I suppose you're my next patient?" She brushed off her hands and pushed the bittersweet memories of her family behind her. If she didn't earn a home here, she had nowhere to go. She'd let her first home go too easily. She wouldn't give up this one without a fight.

After leading Josephine to her stall, Abigail climbed up on the table beside Jeremiah and fitted her mind into a professional reference. However much he frustrated her, however deeply their lives were temporarily intertwined, he fit a category that removed barriers and forbade emotion. He was her patient. What would Rachel think about their secret meetings in the barn? Would she insist they were part of Abigail's scheme to seduce Jeremiah? If so, she didn't know Abigail at all. True, Jeremiah was handsome and had a vibrancy that was impossible to ignore, but Abigail wasn't the type to insist on attention. She'd rather do her job and be judged by her performance than try to beguile someone into a favorable response. She wanted him to admit she was an asset, not be blinded by infatuation. Empty flattery had never healed any of her patients. Competency and efficiency did.

Although, with his clean soap and fresh laundry he smelled a lot better than any man she'd ever helped before. Tenderly she probed the back side of his leg, encountering the hardened mass deep beneath the skin.

"Let's loosen you up first."

He cleared his throat and looked away as she massaged his leg. Obviously he still wasn't comfortable with her this close. Maybe once they got to know each other better, the awkwardness would fade.

Or maybe not.

She slid his foot forward, then leaned her arm against his knee. "Tell me when I'm pushing hard enough."

"I'm trying to set my mind on something else." He leaned against the wall, tilted his head back, and closed his eyes. "But all I can think about is how you're torturing me."

"Think about Laurel." Abigail released the pressure. "Tell me how you met."

She briskly jostled his leg, shaking it loose before returning him to the stretch.

"We grew up on the same mountain, all the way back to when she was a barefoot gal running around in short skirts." He grimaced, and then through clenched teeth he continued.

"Pretty little thing. We reached an understanding before I left for the war."

"Engaged?" Abigail asked

"Purt near. Her pa thought her a bit young, so we decided to settle the matter when I returned."

Four years ago Laurel would've been quite young. She still seemed immature to Abigail, but it wasn't her place to notice. "Waiting was probably best for both of you."

He squirmed and the muscles in his neck tightened. If only he could stop fighting against the pain. She reached up and brushed her fingers along his neck. His eyes opened and he jumped away as if she'd touched him with a hot poker.

"What's that for?"

Abigail straightened. "You need to relax. If you're in that much pain, then we should slow down."

A flush crept up his neck. "You spooked me. That's all."

"Try to remember this is only medical, Captain Calhoun."

The corner of his mouth tilted up. "How would you feel if I had my hands all over you?"

A bolt of lightning jolted through Abigail. Too well could she picture herself seated at the table with him leaning over her, his strong arms wrapped beneath her. She snatched her hands away. A thud sounded outside the high window. Giggling and quick steps brought Jeremiah to his knees atop the table. He pulled himself up to the window.

"It's the Huckabee kids." He rearranged his collar. "They moved a barrel beneath the window and were snooping on us."

Abigail paced from the stone wall to the stall. "I'm employing techniques for which Dr. Ling of Sweden has become world renowned. There's nothing to be embarrassed over." But she was.

"Those ornery young'uns will make the most of their story."

How many men had she washed, cleaned, performed the most humiliating chores for when they couldn't do it themselves? Working together was not a crime. She would not cower before the flimsy threat of a rumor. They must focus on their goal. And she mustn't think about his hands.

"Back to work, then," she said. "Getting your leg straight is a priority, but we also need to strengthen it."

"Now you're talking. I want to be able to pull like a draft horse."

"Then sit on the ground over here." Finally on a safe topic, Abigail's mind clicked along the steps she wanted to accomplish before the morning got too late and they were missed. She grabbed the corner of a heavy feed sack, gripping the scratchy burlap as it rasped against her hands, and tugged it in place before him.

"Bend your leg up as close to your body as you can get it."

He drew his bad leg to his chest, best he could. With a final heave Abigail pushed the bag over, and it dropped on his toes.

His eyebrows rose. "You gonna bury me?"

"Jury's still out." She stooped to move the milking stool, making the way clear. "Push that sack of feed with your bad leg. Just stretch it out as far as you can."

His mouth firmed and determination flared in his eyes. His foot indented the tight sack, but it didn't budge. He took a deep breath and pushed again. Nothing moved.

"I'll look for a lighter sack." Abigail started past him, but he caught her ankle with an iron grip.

His shoulders curved forward, his eyes bore ahead, channeling all his strength toward the feed sack. The determination she so admired was on full display. His hand tightened on her ankle, but he didn't seem to notice. He strained his leg, then again. And again. The sack rocked with each pulse until it slid an inch. He kept at it until it went another, slower than a grapevine grows, until his leg was extended to its farthest possible length.

His eyes glowed fiercely. He grunted with a sense of accomplishment and gave her ankle a squeeze, his fingers brushing just above where her boot ended. Then his eyebrows jumped, his hand shot away, and he tucked it under himself as if he could hide it. He didn't raise his head. Didn't say a word.

Abigail backed away, suddenly wishing for a large dipper of water to splash down her burning throat. She couldn't work with him if she continued to have such unladylike thoughts. On the other hand, how could she stop when he was making progress?

She'd never had this problem before.

With her toe she pointed to the feed sack. "Scoot forward and do it again. Stop when you reach the wall. I'm going now. Going to the ash hopper to collect lye."

He didn't stop her, which was a good thing. She might need some time before they worked together again. Some time to remind herself that he was her patient . . . and that her patient was in love with another woman.

Jeremiah didn't remember learning to walk the first time, but this time wasn't a lick of fun. His muscles hurt. His awkward jabs frustrated him. Why couldn't his leg just obey? Why'd it have to act so contrary?

Pushing the bag away from the wall, Jeremiah was just fixing to start the other way when he heard his name called.

"Jeremiah! Jeremiah, come to the house." The choppy words proof that Ma was running.

He grabbed his crutch and pulled himself up. "What's a matter?"

Ma pulled a wisp of white hair out of her face. "Varina Helspeth is here and she's raising a ruckus. You have to help me."

Varina? What had they done to set the woman off? But he didn't have to be within cannon range of the house before he could hear her hollering about something.

"Don't play all innocent with me. You mentioned that horse every time you came up to see my boy. You admired it something fierce."

Jeremiah opened the door. Abigail's normally fair complexion had lost even more color. She plunged her hands into her pockets and murmured, "I was merely being nice. I didn't see any other livestock to compliment you on, so I tried to find something kind to say about the nag."

From Varina's flat nose to her chin, the only thing that stuck out was her mustache. "Well, my nag is gone and I think you had something to do with it. No one else has been up to our place."

"Hello, Mrs. Helspeth. Have a seat," Jeremiah said, but Varina didn't spare him a glance.

"I want my horse back and this woman knows where it is."

Abigail's blond eyelashes fluttered down. "Truly, I've never stolen a thing, no matter what everyone says."

Everyone? Jeremiah's ears perked. Had he missed something?

"What else is gone?" he asked.

"Isn't a horse enough?" Varina huffed. "What else needs to disappear? My cabin?"

The charge was ridiculous, but Jeremiah understood Varina's anger and fear of outsiders. Hadn't he accused Abigail, too?

"I haven't seen your horse," he said, "but besides the fact that Abigail noticed the animal, do you have any reason to think she's a horse thief?"

Varina gnawed on her bottom lip. "Someone took it. She's the only new person in these parts."

"Only one you've met. We can't know who is lurking about nowadays. I'll tell you what, if Abigail has a horse hidden here, I'm bound to find it. If I do, I'll turn her over to you and the law. What happens next will be out of my hands. Does that satisfy?"

Abigail clasped her hands before her, looking like some kind of Swedish martyr. Varina narrowed her eyes and studied her. "I reckon I ought give her the benefit of the doubt. After all, she doctored my boy."

"That's mighty fine of you." Jeremiah went to the door and held it open. "And I promise, if I see or hear of anything, I'll let you know. You have my word."

With a last withering glance, Varina made her departure. As the door clicked shut Ma sank into the sofa and Rachel called out from upstairs, "Should've seen that coming." But Abigail didn't move an inch.

What had brought on the accusation, and why had Abigail stopped defending herself? Instead of fuming, she had cowered. Why?

Jeremiah took her arm and propelled her to the kitchen. She stopped where he left her and didn't move again until he'd pushed a cup of water into her hand. "It's going to be all right," he said.

Were those tears she was blinking back? "You believe me? You think I'm innocent?"

"Of course."

"And you aren't going to run me off?" She set her cup on the table.

"Did you steal her horse?"

"No." She sniffed.

"Then that's all I need to know."

"Just like that? That's all it takes for you to believe me?" Her face went all blotchy.

Something was awry with her response. "How'd Varina get you so upset?" he asked. "When I got mad at you, you laughed in my face. You called me a liar."

"I thought you were upset because I called you my husband." She smiled even as her voice cracked.

Smiling and crying at the same time? Women! But as always, mention of the husband talk irked him. "Still, I was mad and you stood up to me. So why do you care what Varina thinks?"

"I'm not crying because of Varina, you imbecile. I'm crying because of you." She dabbed at unspilt tears, her confidence restored.

He crossed his arms. "It's my fault again. I can't win."

Her face broke into a grin. With a last swipe at her eyes, she turned to the basin where a pile of potatoes wanted peeling.

"Go on," she said. "You've got work to do." And she hummed as she picked up the paring knife.

He scratched his head. All women were a puzzlement, but this one . . . well, there were pieces of her puzzle she was hiding, and he aimed to find out why.

CHAPTER 11

July 1865

Abigail sat on the porch with a bowl of fresh green beans on her lap and watched as Jeremiah gathered the livestock into the barn for the night. After a month of their morning exercises, he could steady himself on his bad leg. His heel came just short of reaching the ground, but he was making progress, and with each ounce of progress his impatience grew a pound.

And so did her regard for him.

She snapped another bean, drawing a breath of the fresh earthy scent. Despite what Jeremiah thought, her emotions hadn't arisen from Varina's accusation. Varina's opinion had no sway over Abigail. Instead, her tears had come from Jeremiah's defense. Even though her decision to stay had inconvenienced him, Jeremiah had sided with her over a neighbor.

He left his crutch resting against the fence, choosing instead to balance himself on the gate as he closed and latched it. Abigail smiled. A more determined patient she'd never had. If only Rachel cared half as much.

As if on cue, the door behind her opened. Ma motioned

Rachel out before her. "Well, isn't it a nice night? I told Rachel she'd be more comfortable out here than in that hot upstairs. She'd enjoy the airish evening temperatures."

Abigail abandoned her rocker for Rachel and moved to the steps. "I don't mind," she answered to Ma's protests. Ma took the old chair that rested against the wall behind her where she could keep an eye on them all.

They sat in peaceable silence, listening to the bullfrogs down at the river, watching the lightning bugs dazzle the deep, dark woods. The kind of night she wished could last forever.

With the last chicken in the coop and the last hog in the pen, Jeremiah made his way to them, a stalwart figure against the moonlight, if it weren't for the one flawed limb.

He lowered himself to the step next to her and just sat. Abigail threaded her fingers through her bowl, feeling for longer beans to snap, but couldn't keep working with the same focus. Not when the night seemed so alive—buzzing, humming, croaking. Here they sat near their tiny refuge built against all the critters that ran, crawled, and flew out there. They called this their land, but the overpowering screeches of the cicadas challenged that assertion.

"What was your home like?" Ma asked from her seat by the wall.

Abigail's chin dipped. Home. She didn't have a home anymore. Nowhere that would claim her. "We have hills, too, but they are tamer than this. They invite you to explore instead of erecting impossible barriers to keep you out."

Jeremiah picked a piece of clover and spun it between his fingers. If he noticed how she avoided a personal answer, he didn't mention it. "That's why we love these mountains. They're barriers to discourage people from entering."

"But it didn't work." Rachel's skirt rustled against the rocker. "We minded our own business, but violence still found us."

133

Abigail wasn't looking for a fight, but neither could she allow them to malign the men from her home who'd given their lives to preserve the Union. Their sacrifice should be honored. "Those soldiers didn't want to fight you, but what choice did they have when your region was in rebellion to the federal government?"

"Rebellion?" Jeremiah spoke the word carefully. "Is it rebellion to protect your house? To keep your family safe? Jayhawkers raised havoc through here, claiming it was because of some action in Kansas, but none of my folks raided Kansas." He shook his head. "When the war started, those same men were made official soldiers, and defending my property against them would make me a bushwhacker—a common highwayman—to be hung on sight. No trial, no truce, no courtesies afforded to prisoners of war."

Ma's chair scooted forward. "Then they made a proclamation that every able-bodied man was to report to Springfield to serve. Those people who claimed to believe in freedom told our sons to report or be shot."

Jeremiah tossed the clover away. "Miles from here, there might be noble men with fine motives, but somehow that honor was spread thin by the time it reached these mountains."

Abigail had a hard time reconciling their bitterness with the stirring speeches she'd heard about freedom and God's will. Since she'd arrived in the Ozarks she hadn't seen any evidence of the slavery these people were supposedly fighting to protect. She didn't like this feeling of uncertainty. Easier to think one side was good and pure and vilify everyone who opposed them.

"There, there." Ma reached forward to pat her on the shoulder. "We don't mean to blame you, not when you were busy taking care of our wounded men."

Jeremiah tensed next to her at the mention of Alan, but here was one sorrow they held in common.

"I met many fine men," she said, "and all were devastated that the conflict was so costly."

"What you must've seen," said Ma. "So much suffering."

Abigail felt a lump forming in her throat. "They joined so confident, thinking they were invincible, only to have their lives cut short."

Rachel strained her words between clenched teeth. "It's not just soldiers who live with certain death. Their war is over and they can live now. They've been pardoned."

And no such pardon was coming for Rachel. Her fate was certain.

A possum waddled across the field, its gray humped back swaying in the bright light of the full moon. Abigail closed her eyes and thought of Romeo. What would he want her to say to his Juliet? She prayed for guidance as she spoke.

"I've been at the bedside of many who died, Rachel, including Alan. Do you know what I've observed? When death approaches, we weak humans finally drop our pretenses. We see more clearly what God had placed us on earth for. Maybe our purpose was to fight, maybe it was to proclaim truth, or to protect, but no one passes without trying to complete his task. Preparing for death is part of living. The tragedy is that we wait so late to begin."

Abigail had meant to encourage Rachel, but now she wondered about her own purpose. Had coming here been God's plan all along? What about her family? If she were to die tonight, would she feel she'd left anything undone? Should she try to reach her mother again? Her conscience pricked at her.

"I'm going to bed." Rachel stood, her breath coming shallow. "Enough of your cheer for one night."

Ma rose without a word and followed her in, the door clicking shut behind them.

Abigail stood and set the bowl of beans on the empty chair.

The dark forest beckoned her—a much better place to ponder than caught inside the stifling stone walls. "I'm going on a stroll," she said.

Jeremiah stood. "Not by yourself, you aren't."

Drawn to the leafy roof of the forest, she sauntered with him at her side.

"I didn't think anyone else ever thought like that," he said. "I mean, really ponder what God gave you breath for. Most of our suffering means nothing. What are we striving for? To make ourselves more comfortable? To add prestige or honor to our reputation? But then you find something—a cause, a person—worth dying for, and you realize that's the best gift God can give you, because until you know what you'd die for, you don't know what you're living for."

His efforts to use his bad leg slowed him. Abigail paused so he could stay next to her. "To hear you talk, to see what it's like here, makes me wonder how we can know a worthy cause," she said. "How much has been excused in the name of justice?"

Now in the trees, Abigail stopped. She held her hand out waiting . . . waiting . . . and then with a quick scoop, caught a lightning bug. Through her fingers it blinked patiently.

"Thank you," he said.

She looked up. His eyes caught hers and held them as he'd never dared before. "You're from the North. You knew people who fought against me, but thank you for not believing that we all wanted this."

Abigail stammered, shaken by his honesty, by his sincerity. "I never considered what it must be like for you. I mean, I'm not sorry that emancipation occurred. That needed to happen. It's just a pity that it cost so much . . . on both sides."

The lightning bug floated out of her open hand and landed

on Jeremiah's shirt. Its small bulb illuminated a circle above his heart.

"After I was shot, those Quakers hid me in a cellar hidden by a trap door. It took weeks before I realized that the colored people caring for me weren't the farmer's slaves but runaways he was helping escape."

"The underground railroad?"

"I hadn't really been around colored folk before, but there I was, depending on them for my life. And to hear them talk about their hopes for freedom and their families, well, I understood. I had the same hopes. It just doesn't make sense that the same people who wanted to help them had to destroy my life to do it."

This was his plea, his defense. She could tell he desperately wanted her to understand that he hadn't meant the harm he'd caused. He hadn't wanted to kill, but bound by his sense of duty he had no choice. Now she stood here, a representative of every daughter, mother, and wife who'd lost their loved ones, and Captain Calhoun wanted her to know he wished he hadn't been involved.

Abigail caught the lightning bug, her fingers brushing against his chest. "I don't judge you, Jeremiah. Only you know your intentions, but even if they were wrong, God is merciful. He offers grace even when our hearts have deceived us."

The trapped lightning bug shone through her fingers, reflecting its gentle fire off Jeremiah's face and illuminating his anguish. "I promised my family that I'd protect them. How could that be wrong?"

"And I promised a man I'd take care of his sister, even though fulfilling that promise has brought havoc to the family I wanted to help."

"We need you." He took her hand and held it open, allowing the firefly to walk unrestrained. The pulsing light glowed on their entwined fingers. "I can't imagine where we'd be without you." His eyes rested on her lips.

Alarms sounded in her heart. He wasn't safe. He wasn't hers. But he must have heard the warnings, too.

Jeremiah turned toward the house. Abigail followed his gaze to the moonlit rock structure. The crazy-quilt stonework gleamed in the light of a lone lantern that had been left on the porch for them.

"I've got a promise to keep, as well." He dropped her hand and straightened his shoulders. "Tomorrow I'm having dinner with the Wallaces. I'm beholden to more than just my own family."

Laurel. It was only right he should think of her. They both needed the reminder of what they were working to accomplish. "You're leaving for the noon meal? Then we need to get our chores done early."

"And the most important chore is to work on this leg. Once I can walk, I'll be better able to keep my promises . . . all of them."

And not one of those promises had been made to her.

<hr/>

Ground taken in war had to be held, guarded, protected. Advance, retreat, regroup, and advance again. Sometimes blood was spilt over the same few feet repeatedly, but here he could make progress. Here, Jeremiah would hold on like the snapping turtles that wouldn't let go until lightning struck.

These were his thoughts as he bore down on the sack of feed, shoving it before him. Sweat trickled down his brow until it soaked into his collarless shirt. Finally his foot moved with purpose. His leg still wobbled like a newborn colt's when he put weight on it, but he'd taken it prisoner. It would serve him and he wouldn't let it go again.

If only he could tame his desires with the same force of will. He thought he knew himself. He thought he could share his time with Abigail and leave his emotions and attraction for Laurel. Evidently he was wrong, and *why* had him flummoxed. He knew everything about Laurel—barring the few years they'd been separated. On the other hand, Abigail's past was blurry. No one could verify her story. No one could bridge her vague descriptions of her past with where she was now. Yet the unknown only whetted his curiosity and made him want to know everything.

He jumped when the door swung open.

"It's only me." Abigail's cheeks pinked from the July morning's heat. With thick kitchen rags, she carried the copper kettle from the stove.

Jeremiah's heart sank as he once again noticed her slender form. Why'd she have to be so beautiful? Why couldn't she be built like a Shorthorn cow?

"What's the kettle for?" he asked.

"Thought we'd try something new." Loose straw on the barn floor stirred as she passed. With her forearm she swept bits of straw and dust off the table to make room for the kettle and a bowl she carried beneath her arm.

Jeremiah rolled to his knees and stood. With a half hop he reached the table and pulled himself up.

"I reckon you want me here?"

"Yes, sir. Let's see how far we can get that leg today." Gathering her skirt, she climbed up next to him.

Jeremiah's chest tightened. He knew what to expect. He knew that her attentions meant no more than when she brushed Josephine's growing belly. Less even. When she cared for Josephine, she sang a sweet little lullaby. No singing occurred while she had her hands on him. Her actions were kind, her intentions generous, but whether he was man, woman, or beast made no matter to her.

And that's how he preferred it.

So when she slid her hand beneath his knee and found the knot of muscle, he could honestly say that her nearness had no bearing on his feelings for Laurel. The smell of lavender water in her hair only reminded him that he needed a wife like a fiddle needed strings. Nothing personal in the attraction at all.

"You're not breathing." She caught her bottom lip between white teeth. "Am I hurting you?"

He swallowed. His mouth opened, but nothing came out. Jeremiah looked away.

She straightened and tented his knee to release the pressure. "Should I stop?" Her warm hand scuffed against his chin as she gripped it and turned his face to her. "Cat got your tongue?"

No, it was definitely in there and about to make him choke. He cleared his throat. "You caught me woolgathering."

She nodded. All business. "Going to Laurel's today, aren't you? No wonder you're diverted. We can quit. I'm sure you're anxious—"

"No. This is the most important part of my day. I mean . . . only because I want to walk. Not because, well, time with my mother and sister are more important, of course." He was jabbering like a fool.

"Of course." Her eyebrow cocked. "Well, I brought a warm compress. I thought I'd apply it to your injury and see if we could get it to loosen any further today. You'll need a dry pair of pants when we're finished."

"I think I can manage." This conversation must end before any recollection of his long drawers occurred.

"Then roll over." She took the thick folded rag and dropped it into the ceramic bowl. Jeremiah lay on his stomach and watched the steam curl up as she tipped the kettle over the bowl. He swung his heels toward his backside and back again, noticing how far he had to go before he'd have the full range of motion. She wrung the rag out, then slapped it heavily against his leg. The heat soaked through his pant leg, easing the tension he'd worked up. He expelled the breath he didn't realize he'd been holding.

"That feels good and I don't mind saying it."

She took his boot heel and drew it further toward him. The stretch was satisfying. She hummed as she eased his foot down to the table and let his own weight pull it straighter. Jeremiah wrapped his palms around the legs of the table. He must've lain like this when the Quaker farmer checked for the bullet fragments and packed his wound. Mercifully, he didn't remember it. Someday when he looked back on this injury he'd much rather remember lying here with the warmth soaking through layers of flesh that hadn't felt anything but pain for months now. He'd rather remember the anticipation of seeing Laurel again, of the beautiful summer morning . . .

And the singing.

By thunder, she was singing. Wasn't that supposed to be reserved for the horses? Even his pain couldn't cover his growing awareness of her. He turned his head the other way while she changed out the rag for a hotter one. What was he going to do? How could he live with her under his roof without going mad? How many months before that colt was born?

But as he groused he felt his toe brush the table. He lifted his head. "Was that my foot?"

Her song stopped. "It sure was."

"My toe touched the table?" He dropped his head down, relief making him dizzy. "Do it again."

With a last kneading motion on his hamstring she eased his

heel forward. He willed his body to relax. His toe tapped the wooden plank, and he smiled. Almost straight. Almost healed. Almost free. "Not much longer before we can quit, and I won't have to come in here with you again."

Her hands stilled. Wordlessly, she released him and the rag disappeared.

Jeremiah sat up. When had he grown so rude? "I don't mean that I'm not grateful." How could he explain what their time alone was doing to him? He didn't want to admit it, even to himself. "I'm excited that I might walk again. That's what I mean. The sooner I can leave this crutch—"

"The sooner you can get everything back like it was before the war." Her light lashes fluttered against her cheek. "I know. No use explaining."

Water sloshed as she poured the remains into a trough. Her normally crisp movements lagged. "Do you want me to bring you out some dry laundry?"

"Naw. I'm headed to the field. It'll dry soon enough." And the sooner he could get out of this awkward situation, the better. He held the barn door open for Abigail and heard snickering. The perpetrators were easily spotted. Young Josiah and Betsy peeked around the well at him.

Wonderful. Another opportunity for him to be misunderstood. "What are you laughing at?" Jeremiah shot a quick look at Abigail, but her face was as impassive as a mask.

"You." Betsy twisted the dirty hem of her short dress. "We wondered what Miss Abigail was giving you a spanking for."

"A spanking?" Abigail's eyes stretched wide. "No, Betsy. I was not spanking Captain Calhoun."

"You had him laid out like to take a switching," Josiah said, "and then we figured he deserved it if'n he done wet his pants."

The breeze chilled Jeremiah's legs. "You are lucky I can't

catch you. Once Miss Abigail has me fixed up, I'm going to chase you down and—"

But with squeals of laughter they flew down the drive, their dirty feet flashing, and disappeared into the forest.

He couldn't help but chuckle at their orneriness, but Abigail moped like she'd lost her best friend. He chicken-winged her with his elbow. "Hey, don't look so worried. Your work with me is almost done. Then you can spend some time teaching those two some manners."

Abigail's brow furrowed. "It's dangerous out here. Their Ma should keep a better eye on them."

"They certainly are keeping a good eye on us." Her cheeks went rosy at his remark. Well, dandy. Maybe she understood his discomfort after all.

CHAPTER 12

Jeremiah couldn't take his eyes off Laurel as she flitted around the kitchen, a flurry of skirts, a shimmer of ebony hair, a flash of a strawberry-sweet smile. With the smell of fresh-baked bread and Laurel's musical voice, he'd finally found a place where he could keep thoughts of Abigail at bay. If only Dr. Hopkins's frog-ugly face didn't get in the way. With every pass Laurel made from the stove to the table, Hopkins's pointy chin and enraged eyes interrupted Jeremiah's view. He might be unhappy, but they needed to reach an understanding about where things were headed. The good doctor was fixing to be replaced.

"I think that's all." Laurel slid a plate of biscuits on the table between the two men and wiped her forehead with the back of her hand.

Jeremiah stood to pull her stool out for her, but no sooner than he reached, Hopkins lurched for it. The table moved, causing Jeremiah to question his balance. He steadied himself against it.

Laurel looked at his hand gripping the table and bit her lip as she sank into her seat, sadness tinting her eyes. Jeremiah's chest burned as he glared at Hopkins. His crutch might come in handy when he decided to beat some manners into the doctor.

"I'm sorry your pa isn't here." Hopkins passed Laurel a bowl of pinto beans. "We were getting on so well last night. He's really difficult to get to know, but now that he's warmed up to me, I don't think I've ever had a closer friend."

Jeremiah dipped a spoon of sorghum onto his biscuit. The golden threads stretched and thinned. "Is that so? I've known Hiram since I was a boy, so I don't guess I've ever thought of him like a stranger would. He's always been a second pa to me."

Laurel smiled. His heart skipped a beat. "Ever since your pa died, he's tried to look out for you, Jeremiah."

"What an unwelcome burden." The doctor tore a piece of chicken off the bone.

Laurel's eyes sparkled. Like a falling leaf, her hand landed on Hopkins's arm. "Oh, Newton, you tickle me something fierce." He ducked his head toward her and winked. Jeremiah stabbed his piece of chicken with his knife. What he needed was a diversion. Something to drag the doctor's thoughts away from Laurel.

"How's your doctoring going?"

"I . . . uh, it's going well. Quite well, actually."

"I'd imagine. What with the lack of food and medicine, you probably stay busy looking after sick folk. Then if the bushwhackers would shoot someone now and then, you might be able buy yourself another pair of shoes."

Hopkins lowered his tin cup. "How's your sister, Jeremiah? Your ma was right grateful for my help before you came home."

Jeremiah's neck twitched. Why'd he have to drag Rachel into the conversation? Thinking about Rachel took the spark out of Jeremiah's sparking.

"She's no better. That's a fact. But nobody gave us any hope that she ever would be."

Now Laurel leaned toward his end of the table. "Poor Jeremiah. How hard it must be to see her suffer."

This wasn't the place. He shrugged. "You know how it is. She can't forgive me for not letting her marry Alan. She'll go to her grave hating me."

A few minutes passed in silence before anyone felt compelled to speak again.

"That nurse has been living with you for quite a while." Hopkins sipped water from his tin cup.

"Oh yes. Abigail!" Laurel clapped her hands. "She is such a dear. The second I met her I knew she was the kind of person I could share my deepest, darkest secrets with. I've been meaning to show her the best places to gather berries and nuts. Do tell her to come any time."

"She stays so busy upstairs with Rachel and visiting other folks, I don't see much of her. It's like she's hardly there." Sometimes he could go a whole hour without seeing her.

Hopkins scratched his chin. "Now correct me if I'm wrong, but aren't we talking about your wife, Jeremiah? The beautiful woman who claims to be married to you?"

"You think she's beautiful?" Jeremiah raised an eyebrow. "I'm surprised to hear you say so."

Laurel shook her head. She snatched the empty biscuit plate and pulled the heavy crock of beans to her. "Why don't you two go outside and see who can spit watermelon seeds the farthest? That's all the good you're worth today, the both of you."

Jeremiah stood. Two steps to the sink, but he couldn't make it. Not yet. And he wouldn't stumble again in front of her. He crammed his crutch under his arm and carried his plate away. "I guess I'd better be getting home. Calbert and I are shoeing the horses today."

"How's Josephine?" Laurel twirled her braid around her finger. He could imagine its silky weight in his hand.

"Missing Napoleon something terrible," he rasped.

Laurel was so dainty. He could wrap his arms around her and almost make her disappear. Her cheeks flushed and Jeremiah stood close enough to feel their heat.

"Newton?" She stepped sideways to peer around Jeremiah. "Newton, why don't you see if Jeremiah needs any help with his horse?"

Jeremiah stumbled backwards. "I don't need any help with that horse or any horse."

"Hopkins is a doctor," Laurel said. "He's used to helping the infirmed."

The infirmed? Is that what she thought of him? Jeremiah's plate clattered into the sink. "I can take care of myself," he said and then leaned close. Desperation gruffed his voice. "I could take care of you, too, if you'd let me, Abigail."

Her head snapped up. Hopkins choked on a laugh. Jeremiah frowned. "What?"

"You called Laurel Abigail." Hopkins beamed a toothy grin.

"I did not." Only a dunce would . . .

But Laurel looked at him like she'd found a booger in the sugar bowl. He'd made a mistake and he couldn't blame this mess on the Yankees, unless you counted one Yankee nurse.

"Well, if I did say it, it was an honest mistake. No one could compare the two of you."

But Laurel had closed up tighter than a bloom for the night. The day was wasted.

His pride screamed at him to throw his crutch aside and stomp away, but he mastered his frustration long enough to get on his horse and make himself scarce. Jeremiah wouldn't let Hopkins best him at anything, whether horseshoes, coon hunting, or arm wrestling. He definitely wouldn't let him win this contest. Given time, Laurel would come around. She was just too tenderhearted where Hopkins was concerned. Once she mulled over the choice, she'd choose Jeremiah, hands down, guaranteed.

But how in creation did Abigail's name find its way onto his lips? As if it weren't bad enough that she'd spent months posing as his wife, now he was whispering her name to his sweetheart. People were going to get suspicious.

Something had to change. He couldn't send Abigail away, but he couldn't take the strain of having her near. He was about to snap.

When Ma entered the room, Abigail set aside the sock she was darning to find a vase for the roses Rachel had requested. She'd seen the red blooms at the stack of boulders Ma called the thinking place but didn't realize they ever took cuttings from the bush. Once the roses were in water, Abigail buried her nose in the petals. "Why do you keep these beautiful flowers so far from the house?"

Ma tossed her bonnet on the sofa. "I don't know. They just seem more special if you have to travel a piece to see them, I guess. If they were here by the porch, I wouldn't appreciate them near as much."

Similar to working every day with a kind, decent woman at your side, and then traipsing off to visit someone who didn't care? A thorn nicked Abigail's finger.

"How's Rachel?" Ma asked.

"She spent the morning resting and suffered no ill from your being gone." Abigail wiped the drop of blood from her finger onto her apron.

"Praise the Lord. I have no right to complain, but sometimes

I need to get out of that room." Ma stopped before the mirror to tidy her thick silver hair. "You just don't know, dearie, how it upsets her when she doesn't get her way."

"Oh, I think I have a good idea, but catering to her whims hasn't helped her. You can't do anything for her physical state, but you might ruin her spiritual state, as well."

Ma nodded. As usual, she accepted Abigail's words without question, but she'd easily dismiss them as soon as Rachel grumbled.

Abigail sent Ma up to meet her fate, removed her apron, and hurried out of the house. At the edge of the stone porch, Abigail stretched her hands above her head and arched her back. One could imagine how a crimped body could crimp a spirit. She prayed the ugly habits Rachel had fallen into would be broken before it was too late.

Abigail caught sight of a rider moving through the trees. She leaned in tight against the porch beam to watch Jeremiah approach unobserved. He sat tall in the saddle, cutting a striking figure on Lancaster. His white shirt hugged his shoulders, then billowed loose as it covered his slim torso, which, thank goodness, had been spared any harm during the war. His bad leg was still discernible by its length and the thinner muscles in the thigh, but the difference wasn't immediately obvious.

And the only reason she looked was because she needed to measure his progress, right? And while she observed him, she supposed that if his scowl was any indication, his visit with Laurel hadn't been a success. Well, he might as well get it off his chest before suppertime. Ma sure didn't need more disruption under her roof.

Abigail tucked in the stray locks that'd escaped from the braids pinned across her head. She'd act like she was only there to help him groom the horse, and maybe he'd feel like unburdening himself while they worked. If not, then surely Calbert could pull it out of him when he came to do the smithing.

Jeremiah was pulling the girth through the buckle on the saddle when she entered the barn, but he didn't look up. His crutch lay far from him, thrown in a pile of hay. Not a good omen. "Can I help you?" he said.

"I came to help you, actually."

His eyes flamed. "Why would I need your help?"

Abigail stopped in her tracks. She'd already locked horns with one member of the family that morning. Did she have to best another? "You have in the past and told me so just last night."

"Well, I'm getting stronger every day."

The cinch belt swung free. He slid the saddle off of Lancaster's back and the weight threw him a tad off balance, but Abigail noticed his bad leg held him steady. Soon he'd have no need for the crutch. Or her.

He tossed the saddle across the stall divider, removed the blanket, and took up a brush. Abigail ran her hand down Lancaster's opposite shoulder, surprised at the dampness. While the horse wasn't winded, Jeremiah must have ridden hard for home.

Taking a brush, Abigail joined him in his task, keeping the horse's body between them. Something about skin fascinated her. The twitch of the muscle, the ripple that could be harnessed either for speed or for strength. One only had to will it, and arms, legs, flanks, and hooves obeyed. She'd never tire of the marvel of it—whether human or beast.

She ran her hand down Lancaster's neck, feeling the play of the muscle beneath her fingers. After all the time she'd spent working on Jeremiah's hurt leg, she'd never fully taken stock of his healthy one. She should've done that before she started his treatment, and a visual examination wasn't sufficient. How could she achieve symmetry with no knowledge of what his muscles felt like uninjured? She ducked beneath Lancaster's head and peered down at Jeremiah. His trousers might be threadbare, but they hung as loose as a turkey's wattle. No question which leg was thicker, but she'd need to feel them to know how far the hurt one had atrophied.

He stopped brushing the horse. She lifted her face to meet his eyes. Stern. Angry. Impassioned over some wrong. Abigail smoothed her hair behind her ear. Maybe she should go back to the house.

"Can't keep from staring, can you?" He held his arms out. His white shirt billowed above his trim waist. "Go on and get your fill. Wonder at my injury whilst you can. I won't be crippled for long."

His crooked smile had an edge to it. A challenge.

Abigail never was one to back down from a challenge.

"How's Laurel?"

He tossed his brush on the table and dusted his hands. "Laurel is a daisy. Too politic for her own good, but she'll set old Hopkins straight soon enough."

Abigail took Lancaster's bridle and led him toward his empty stall. "Did she talk about him?"

"She didn't have to. He ate dinner with us."

Her mouth dropped open, and she stopped fumbling with the bridle. "He did? And she knew you were coming?"

He took the bridle from her hands. "Her father wasn't home. She probably wanted to make sure we were chaperoned." He smacked Lancaster on the rump, sending the horse trotting inside.

Was Jeremiah this delusional? She stepped aside so he could fasten the stall door. "Well, Hopkins is the perfect chaperone because there's no one more suited to keep the two of you apart."

"Caution, there, miss." He spun on his good heel. His chin

rose. "You can't keep your hands off me, so I must be somewhat of a temptation."

"Are you accusing me of impropriety? I'll not be added to your inaccurate list of women who find you irresistible." How dare he! She tried to stomp past him, but he stepped into her path.

"I'm not imagining Laurel's affection, if that's what you're getting after. She'd do anything for me."

"Besides leave her beau, you mean?" Abigail crossed her arms across her chest. Why couldn't she just play along? What was it to her if he preferred to be deceived? But it wasn't in her nature to see folly and not expose it. Especially when the man strutted around so cocksure, unable to admit his shortcomings.

"You know, I feel sorry for you." Jeremiah stretched his arm across the walkway to hang the bridle on the stall divider. "It must be lonely to be so far from home and not have a sweetheart. Or maybe you do. I'm not quite sure what to believe about you."

Her hands went to her hips before she remembered how his gaze would follow them there. She raised her chin to meet his arrogant level. "If a man did love me, I wouldn't make him dance around like a fool while I carried on with another fellow."

"Stop!" He stepped closer, stirring up the scent of clean straw. "This war cost me my leg, my best friend, and nearly cost me my farm. I will not fail again. I've already lost too much."

Was this really about Laurel, or was she merely a symbol? A victory to be counted? His dark hair stuck to his damp forehead. His face flushed. Poor Jeremiah. He didn't want to hear the truth. And what if he failed? How would he cope?

His eyes narrowed. "I don't need your pity. I'm not some feeble invalid. My wife will have no regrets, and if you don't believe me, then . . ."

Abigail watched his chest rise with every ragged breath. Jeremiah's stare wandered to her lips, and his face wiped clean of anger.

"No," he whispered. "I shouldn't."

But then he did.

With an arm around her waist Jeremiah pulled Abigail to him, his breath catching at her nearness. Day and night, thoughts of her teased him, clouding what should have been clear. He'd fought valiantly, but every soldier lost a battle now and then.

About time she got an inkling of what he was warring against. He held her tight, her supple body squirming against his, setting every nerve on fire. One kiss. That's all he wanted. One to show her she couldn't taunt him without consequences. He took her mouth, her muffled protests vibrating throughout his body, but immediately his desire to teach her a lesson was overcome by his need for her. With a sob in his own throat, he realized it wasn't about the taste of her sweet lips or the heady scent of her skin. It was about her—Abigail—and how much he relied on her. He wasn't teaching her a lesson. He was pleading with her not to turn him away. Not to reject him. And she didn't. She stopped struggling as he stroked the milky whiteness of her neck down to her collarbone. Her lips softened—allowing him, inviting him.

His hand traveled down her back, delighting in every plane, every curve. He touched her without restraint, just as she'd touched him day after day, and he was intoxicated with the freedom.

He needed Abigail to care about him. Needed her respect.

Respect.

Jeremiah's hands stilled. What had he done?

Slowly he set her on her feet and drew away, unable to meet her questioning gaze. The room turned deathly silent as he found his words.

"I'm sorry," he mumbled, taking the coward's escape. Her chest strained against her cotton work dress, her breath coming in quick bursts now. He shoved his hands into his pockets. "I didn't mean to do that."

He was lying. He meant it with every ounce of his body and soul, if souls could be weighed, but the passion of one sultry afternoon couldn't undo years of planning. A weak moment. That's all it was.

Abigail clenched her fists as she pieced together his meaning. Her voice shook. "You used me. Laurel wouldn't have you, so you . . . you . . ." She drew back and slapped him full on the cheek. By the time his sight cleared, she had her finger in his face, jabbing with every word. "I have stood by you and helped you at every turn, haven't I? And then you dishonor me? I am not a substitute, Jeremiah Calhoun. I am not standing by to accept attentions others have rejected. Do you understand me?"

His cheek stung, but not nearly as much as his conscience. How had the strength of their friendship turned into something that could hurt them? "I understand, ma'am. It won't happen again."

How he wanted to smooth the thick hair he'd loosened, but he had to keep his distance. He'd given in to temptation once. He couldn't afford to do it again.

Abigail stalked to the pasture and whistled. Josephine neighed in response and trotted forward.

"Where are you going?" he asked.

"I'm going for a ride."

"By yourself?"

"Don't try to stop me."

So he didn't. Instead, he watched her saddle Josephine. "Don't forget the foal she's carrying," he said.

"How could I forget?" Abigail threw the blanket over the horse's back. "It's the only reason I'm still here."

Chapter 13

Jeremiah wouldn't stop her, but he wouldn't let her go alone. Not with the possibility of men loitering on the property. He wadded a handful of coarse hair from Lancaster's mane and stroked his velvet neck. With all the worries that plagued him, he had to go and make one more. He'd kissed Abigail—Abigail!—and his brain might as well be pickled in brine after that. He waved the flies from Lancaster's eyes and slipped the bridle into his mouth and over his ears.

What had made him grab ahold of Abigail in the first place? He remembered an argument. Something about Laurel. His jaw ground tight. Laurel was the least of his worries. First he had to figure out what to do with the hurricane that Abigail had kicked up in his bones. Not since he was a youth had he kissed a girl, but this was no childish game. Something very adult had passed between them, and he hadn't meant for it to turn out like that. What he'd thought—if he could claim to have been thinking at all—was that she'd stop her yammering. From the hundreds of ways he could've quieted her, he'd chosen the most expedient, but he hadn't expected to react as he had, and he hadn't expected her to react, either.

But he had no time for confusion. No time for naïvete. He was a healthy man. She was a more than passable woman—a woman whose blood ran hotter than he'd suspected. For his part, the tenderness that caught him off guard was nothing more than the natural response God had given His creation to propagate the human race. On this occasion, his baser instincts had gotten the best of him. Simple as that. It settled his soul to have an excuse for his turmoil.

Once she'd put a fair distance between them, he loped around the far side of the clearing. She spotted him, turning to watch often, her blond hair blowing in her face, but he didn't give an account for himself. He didn't want to talk to her. They were both looking for the same thing—solitude—and once they reached the woods, he'd drop away and leave her to her own company.

Whenever he felt again the warmth of Abigail in his arms, he'd have to remember he'd promised himself to another woman. When he thought of her sweet lips responding—and she had responded, most definitely—he was safe knowing she'd never allow it again.

Abigail turned off the bare wagon tracks of the road and broke through the brush to forge up the side of the mountain.

Without thinking, Jeremiah reined Lancaster back toward the farm to catch a deer trail that cut through the valley. Once she got to the top, she'd spot the river, and nine chances out of ten, that's where she'd head. It was a good quiet place to think.

And they both had some thinking to do.

------⟨∞⟩------

Abigail saw him turn off and normally she would've joined him, but not now. Maybe never again. She'd rather face a firing squad than Jeremiah.

He'd been taunting her. Ridiculing her. And what had she done in return? She'd laid her heart bare.

The horse scrambled up the rocky surface. Abigail leaned forward, her burning face nearly buried in Josephine's mane, urging her up and up. Of course he didn't mean it. He loved Laurel. Not her. And now what could she do? Avoid him? Impossible. Pretend that she was toying with his affections, same as he was hers? She shivered. She may be able to hide the truth about her family, but she wasn't that good of a liar.

She paused at the crest. It was challenging country. Harsh, jagged, and for the most part not worth the taming. It'd take generations to clear these hills, and then what would they find? Only more rock. This beauty demanded to be appreciated for itself, not for the way it could serve you.

Carefully Josephine descended, stepping over fallen limbs and stones until she found a path leading down to the river. The horse surged ahead once she gained clear ground. Abigail rode on, nerves raw, shocked by his betrayal. He'd taken her friendship and profaned it. If he'd made a sincere declaration of affection . . . well, he hadn't and he never would.

The trail joined the river, really more of a wide, shallow creek. Minnows darted above the rocky bottom. So clear. Must be spring fed, which meant cold. Maybe taking a quick plunge would cool her toasty skin and erase the memory of his caresses. Maybe not. Her shadow passed over the pool, and the minnows streaked away. She wished she could disappear just as effortlessly, but she had nowhere to go. Despite his boorish behavior, she was trapped.

And just across the river rode Jeremiah. Where had he come from? She clenched her jaw. Didn't he understand she wanted to be alone? Could he not give her some time to compose herself, or would he claim it merely coincidence that he was riding the same direction, at the same speed, on the same river? Opposite sides of course. His horse showed no signs of being winded, which meant he'd cut through some pass to meet her there. As familiar with the gullies and hollows as a gopher with his tunnels.

They both rode forward, neither acknowledging the other. Surely he had better things to do than follow her. And then it hit her. He wasn't worried about her safety. He was guarding his property.

Her chest tightened. He didn't trust her after all. Were his kind words after Varina's accusation empty?

A snap, and Josephine lost her footing. Abigail clutched at her mane as Josephine plunged, then reared. Bucking, thrashing. A flash of metal and Abigail's blood boiled. A snare? Caught on the horse's fetlock was a mean, metal trap. Josephine jerked the anchor out of the ground, but the jaws held tight.

Abigail jumped off her horse, still gripping the reins. Just as she slid down, the horse pitched again and threw her off balance. She landed poorly, causing a sharp pain to bolt from her ankle to her knee. Terrific. Already they had a shortage of healthy limbs. They didn't need to lose another one.

Murmuring soothing, calming noises even as she fumed, Abigail hobbled to Josephine's side. One quick look across the river told her that Jeremiah had disappeared again. Lot of help he was.

Grimacing at the sharp metal teeth digging into Josephine's fetlock, Abigail bunched her skirt around her hands and dug them in between the jaws. Pulling with all her might, she separated them an inch, but it would take more, and with a throbbing ankle her balance was off. She went to her knees and behind her an unfamiliar voice put goose bumps on her teeth.

"What do we have here?"

For a moment she thought Jeremiah had come to help, but

instead she found herself looking up at a man on the bluff above her. His unbuttoned coat resembled the butternut uniform of a southern militia, but his boots and hat were Federal.

"Is this your trap? You buried a trap on the trail?!" Her voice pitched.

His eyes glinted as he descended. "What better place to catch someone?"

A chill ran down her spine. This was no accident. Abigail stood, but she couldn't outrun him. With eager steps he descended, his glee more evident as her fear grew.

But before he reached her, Jeremiah thundered into sight. He swung between her and the man, forcing him back a step.

"What do you think you're doing?" he growled at the man.

"Just having a talk with the lady. None of your concern." The man fell back another yard and sized Jeremiah up. "Why don't you stay on your horse and let me help her? You wouldn't want to hurt that crippled leg any further."

Her ankle twinged with every step, but it was probably only a sprain. It'd heal quickly—if she survived this encounter. Abigail tightened the cloth around her hands, crammed them into the trap, and pulled again. The teeth cut through her skirt and broke the skin on her fingers.

"I'm not worried about my leg none," Jeremiah said. "What's your business here?"

"Just passing through. Don't mean any harm." Even his voice had changed. Neighborly, now, but Jeremiah didn't sound fooled.

"You wouldn't know anything about a moonshine still set up on my property, would you?"

Josephine's eyes rolled, the whites flashing. Abigail was scared, but nothing like her poor horse. She ignored the searing pain and held the trap open until Josephine pulled her leg free.

"Moonshine?" The man grunted. "That's your property? My apologies. I thought that was Fowler's land."

Abigail surveyed Josephine's leg. Deep scratches gashed her bone, but the tendon looked intact. With bloodied hands she pulled herself back into the saddle, surprised to see Jeremiah still shielding her.

"You know Fowler?" Jeremiah spared a quick glance at her, then surveyed Josephine's injury. With a nod of his head he motioned her toward home. Abigail didn't need to be told twice.

"Come on, girl," she urged. Her skin crawled at the stranger's voice behind her, but as much as she wanted to flee, she wouldn't force a run on a hurt leg and a pregnancy. She'd reached the crest of the ridge that overlooked the farm when she heard Jeremiah catching up with her. Maybe racing Josephine wasn't a bad idea after all, but she held her at a steady pace, no matter how badly she wanted to avoid him.

"Do you know him?" She couldn't bring herself to look at Jeremiah, instead focusing her attention on controlling their pace.

"I know his type, and I don't like it. I might have dug at him harder, but if he challenged me I'd have to admit I didn't have a revolver. I shouldn't have left the farm in such a hurry."

"I didn't ask for your company." Abigail sat even straighter in the saddle.

"You'll have to forgive me," he said. "Again."

She lifted her chin, hoping that the gesture communicated the appropriate level of disdain. He might have saved her life, but it was his fault she was out there in the first place.

They'd gained the clearing now. Blood from her fingers slicked the reins, and her tightening boot gave evidence of swelling in her ankle. Between her, Jeremiah, and Rachel, they might as well open a hospital ward on the Calhouns' farm. Maybe they could keep Dr. Hopkins so busy Laurel would have to take another look at Jeremiah. Then again, Abigail liked Laurel. Should she wish such a curse on her?

As they reached the barn, Jeremiah jumped down and dragged Lancaster inside. Abigail dismounted gingerly and limped to the water pump, shoving a bucket beneath it. The jagged cuts on her hands couldn't compete with the hurt in her heart, but both would have to wait until the horse was cared for. Ripping a piece off her already tattered gown, she padded her palm, grasped the pump handle, and shoved it through its motions, gritting her teeth with every pump.

"Let me do that." Jeremiah bumped her out of the way, only then seeing her bloodied hands. He stopped. Fine creases appeared around his eyes. "Did the trap do that?"

"I was in a hurry." And she didn't regret the stinging pain. Not when it meant saving Josephine.

When she bent to retrieve the filled bucket Jeremiah stopped her. "Put your hands in the stream."

Remembering how their last argument ended, she complied. The first splash of the icy water burned. She jerked away, but he caught her hand.

"Don't touch me." She pulled against his grip.

"You need help."

"Not from you." The pulse in Abigail's wrist throbbed against Jeremiah's stern grip, but he didn't release her. He turned her wrist over and pried open her hand.

"You are my responsibility. We'll care for you first, then worry about the horse." Gently he ran his thumb over the cut, knocking loose any debris, then immersed her hands again in the stream. Whether she was shaking from the stinging water or his touch, she couldn't tell. Abigail looked away as he bent to inspect the injury.

He nodded his satisfaction and released her. She propped her hurt foot on the trough and fumbled with the shredded skirt for another clean strip to bandage her hands with. With a look that could cauterize an artery, Jeremiah swooped down, snagged the bottom ruffle, and tore it clean off.

She thought she'd faint.

Taking one end of the cloth between his teeth, he ripped it into bandages. She couldn't swallow, not until he held her hands again.

"I understand how you feel," he said. "But after all you've done for me, don't you dare tell me I can't do this for you."

It was humbling to have someone else doctor her, especially when she'd been in the man's arms an hour earlier, acting like a complete wanton.

Knowing the sooner he was finished, the sooner she could work on Josephine's leg, she submitted until he tied a tight square knot and released her. She stumbled backwards, desperate to get some space between them.

He propped his fists against his waist. "Now, about your other injury . . ."

Whatever blood was left in her body drained from her face into her throbbing ankle. "You aren't touching my . . . anywhere else."

His neck reddened. "I wasn't going to. All I meant was if you can't walk, I can help you."

Well, that was certainly ironic. Abigail tugged on her collar. "It's only turned. I can walk it out."

But first to look after Josephine. Turning her attention to her task, Abigail knelt and ran her hand down the horse's forearm to her knee, so the touch wouldn't surprise the skittish mare. The teeth of the trap had dug painfully into her fetlock but had mercifully missed the tendons. While there might be chips of bone that could cause her trouble, all signs pointed to a complete recovery.

"Who would do this to a horse?" Abigail gently pulled back scraped hide to clean the cuts as best she could.

"Maybe the same man who killed Rankin and stole Varina's horse." Jeremiah scanned the woods surrounding his farm. "Make sure you stay close to the house."

Abigail sighed. Just when she most wanted to get away from this man, he was short-leashing her. He'd better behave himself, or he might find her more dangerous than anyone else he'd crossed today.

No longer could Abigail blame Rachel for the crackling tension in the house. Fearing that the lone man was a dangerous bushwhacker, Ma kept a constant vigil at the windows all day while Jeremiah worked outside alone—and he was alone because Abigail refused to put herself in his path again. Her sore ankle wouldn't serve as an excuse for long, but she'd be firm. She'd come to the Ozarks to tend Rachel, and she'd neglected her station. Although no remedies she knew of could cure the woman, Abigail wanted to prepare Rachel for a peaceful farewell. She'd walked to the doors of death with more men than any reverend, and she knew a thing or two about the regrets that often met them there.

Not that one had to die before they became acquainted with regrets. She dumped the dough out of the wooden bowl and onto the table. On the long evenings of half light after the chores were done, Abigail had ample time to wonder if she could've done anything different. Perhaps when John sold her horses, she could've held her temper. But would it have mattered? Was he just looking for an excuse to run her off? What if she'd refused to leave? Would her mother have listened? Then again, she'd written home before and didn't get a reply. All that was left was for her to make the best of her situation.

A situation that was getting worse. Even through her pretended indifference, Rachel had noticed the tension between Abigail and Jeremiah that evening, and Ma had asked if either of them were coming down with something. Abigail's medical training led her to suspect a case of regretful osculation—a horrible condition that left one feeling resentful and irrational. Hopefully she'd soon recover and be inoculated from further bouts. Until then, she blamed her moodiness on her bandaged hands.

Tenderly she glided the wooden rolling pin over the mound, leaning her shoulders into her work until the dough spread flat on the table. Dusting more flour, she flipped it over and rolled it from the other side, an awkward endeavor considering Jeremiah's bandages resembled mittens. According to Ma, pumpkin pie was Rachel's favorite. Abigail hoped Rachel appreciated her gesture.

"If she's sweet on him, why ain't she sitting by him on the porch?"

Abigail's rolling halted at Betsy Huckabee's whispered question. She leaned toward the open window to catch Josiah's next words. "They must've gotten cross at each other. Pa said Jeremiah went to see Miss Laurel today."

"Poor Miss Abigail. No wonder she's staying clear of him."

Oh, the stories they were concocting. Ever since they'd snooped on her in the barn, Abigail had determined to better them. They weren't the only ones who could pull a caper. She cast about the kitchen looking for something to surprise them with. A jug of water out the window? Too obvious. A sudden *Boo*? Not scary enough. And then she realized the answer was at her fingertips.

Quickly Abigail gouged out two holes in the pie crust. Dragging her fingers downward she created drooping triangles, and then a horizontal gash where the mouth should be. She smoothed her hair back, although it didn't matter. She'd be filthy, but it'd be worth it. Peeling the crust from the table she draped it over her head, arranging the eye holes and mouth appropriately. If done correctly she'd look like the ghoul of every child's nightmare, flesh melting off the bones, eyes and mouth distorted. Even her bandaged hands looked like something from the crypt.

Hobbling to the window, Abigail sighed dramatically. The rustling beneath the window stopped as she began her performance, surprised by the ease with which the emotion gushed forth.

"Poor, poor me. Now that Captain Calhoun has seen my true appearance, how will I ever earn his love? No one can look at me without horror." She'd rather he not look at her at all, but she wasn't going to let the little pranksters get away again.

The whispering commenced. "Shh. She's in there. What did she say?" The peony bush rustled against the rock wall.

"If only the fairy hadn't cursed me." Abigail flattened her back against the wall, thinking it better not to mention Captain Calhoun again. "If only I hadn't promised her my youth in exchange for the love potion." The cool breeze floated in, but her face didn't feel it through the layer of dough. They argued in whispers until she heard them reach their final compromise.

"We'll both look."

Their bare feet padded up the wall as they hoisted themselves up. Abigail waited until she saw grimy fingers clutching at the sill, then sprang forward, thrusting her dough-covered face toward theirs.

"AHHHH!!"

Through the holes in her pastry mask Abigail saw their

mouths stretch wide, their eyes bug, and their breathing stop. Clenching the windowsill, Betsy screamed at a pitch that'd make a dog hurt. Josiah gave a startled squeal, then dropped to the ground. He grabbed his little sister by the waist and tried to drag her away, but her fingers refused to release the sill.

"C'mon Betsy. Let go! We got to run! Let go!" he pleaded.

Abigail stretched her bandaged hands toward the girl. "Now that you've seen my true face, I can never let you escape."

"Let go, Betsy." He jerked her hands free and with a thud she landed on top of him.

"Her face," Betsy cried. "What happened to her face?"

Credit her with one victory for the day. Abigail grinned beneath her shroud. Who would've thought that a simple pie crust could be so terrifying? But her foes hadn't fled the field. Josiah's head popped back into the window.

With his head slightly askew he watched her through narrowed eyes. "What is that?" he lisped between his gapped teeth, while Betsy waited a safe distance away.

Didn't take the boy long to find his courage. Or to figure out her trick for that matter. Abigail pinched off a piece from her chin and poked it into her mouth. "Melting flesh. Delicious!"

The boy flashed her an ornery smile. "Maybe we's even, but I don't like to be even. 'Specially when Betsy's gonna keep us awake all night with nightmares."

"Be careful." Abigail hollowed her voice. "You might be the one with nightmares next time."

Josiah wrinkled his freckled nose at her and dropped out of sight. The warmth of her skin had melted the dough to it. It wouldn't be easy to peel off, but Betsy and Josiah were delighted. Their laughter faded with their quick footsteps racing home to make their plans.

But other footsteps approached and the uneven gait couldn't

be mistaken for any other. The kitchen door flew open and Jeremiah entered.

"I heard screams—"

One look at her face and he skidded to a stop. His crutch hit the rag rug and slid out from under him, but he caught himself on his bad leg and the doorframe. His mouth opened. He pointed. Blinked. Pointed again.

Feeling brave beneath her mask, Abigail twirled an errant lock of hair around her bandaged finger. The dough clung and moved like a second, albeit looser, skin. "Is something amiss?"

"Are you trying to scare the living daylights out of me?" He looked nervously behind himself before allowing the kitchen door to close. "What is this? Some kind of beauty treatment?"

Starting at her chin, Abigail rolled the dough up, wishing he wasn't watching so closely.

"The Huckabee kids were spying in the window. They'll think twice before they do that again." The dough peeled off her face but clumped to her hair.

"I'll think twice before I eat another of your pies." Jeremiah reached for a messy lock, but with a frown let his hand drop obediently to his side. "Is this a family recipe?"

Her chest tightened at the question. She shrugged and looked at the floor.

"Where exactly do you come from, again?"

Her neck tensed. Why would he ask that? "Ohio."

"Can you be any more specific?"

"Outside of Chillicothe. Why?"

He took the dough out of her hand and dropped it in the slop bucket with a thud. "I really don't know much about you, do I?"

Usually when a man showed an interest in a lady, he had romance in mind, but somehow, even after a knee-wobbling kiss, Abigail doubted that was his aim.

"Why bother? I'm leaving next spring, and you'll never see me again." The way he stared, she was certain she still had dough on her face. She rubbed her nose.

He cleared his throat. "When I go to Pine Gap in a few days, I'd like to take Laurel. I think it'd be best for everyone involved if I spent more time with her."

Abigail forced herself to face him. Why should she feel slighted? Jeremiah had never hidden his intentions to marry Laurel. "That's a wonderful idea," she managed finally.

"But I can't go on my own. Hiram will insist on her being chaperoned, and Ma doesn't want to go. That leaves you."

Last choice again. "Do you think after your behavior in the barn that I'd want to be alone with you?"

He might as well put her beneath a magnifying glass the way he studied her. "I have questions I want answered about the man we met today. I'm hoping to run into him or someone who knows him. Besides, you never know who you might meet on market day."

Was he trying to play matchmaker? Abigail scolded herself. She couldn't allow her feelings to be hurt. Besides, what did it matter what this hillbilly thought of her? His opinion wasn't worth a Confederate dollar.

CHAPTER 14

The clear morning gave promise of a beautiful journey ahead. Jeremiah broke his fried egg with his fork and scooped up the runny yolk with his toast. He dashed pepper on top, enjoying the biting scent, and practically hummed as he devoured it. Breakfast had been a disappointment lately. While the food tasted fine, the mood had felt flat. Not that there was usually any conversation at breakfast, but he had always left the kitchen feeling optimistic, looking forward to the day ahead.

Maybe it was his time working with Abigail that he'd looked forward to. He dared a glance toward the tall woman. Dressed as she was in a fancy pink getup, he found it hard to believe she lived in his house. Why would a city lady like her help him? Well, she wasn't anymore. Ever since he'd gone and smooched her, she'd come nearer to sitting on a beehive than being in the same room with him.

Which was why she wouldn't help him through his exercises anymore. Which was why breakfast wasn't the cheerful event it used to be. Which was why Jeremiah was itching to go to town with Laurel.

He shoveled in his last bite of egg. The part about needing a chaperone was as true as Ole Blue's nose, but maybe seeing how pretty Abigail was would remind Laurel that she wasn't the only choice around. She shouldn't pass up a fella that other gals would give their eyeteeth for.

They needed an early setout if they were going to get the best trades. His saddlebags were already loaded with bags of shelled beans, padded jars of honey, and some beets. They hadn't raised anything uncommon, but neither did they need anything. Just some extry that might mean some nice lace for Ma or new shoe soles for him in case his didn't last until tanning season.

He met Abigail's gaze. Barely disguised impatience. That's about all she gave him now. Well, it was his own fault. He missed her friendship and was working toward gaining it back, but it wasn't easy when she kept him at a distance.

"You be careful, Jeremiah." His mother said as he stood. "Don't forget there's a dangerous man in those woods."

"That's why I'm going to town, Ma. And I'm not likely to let my guard down." He swooped in to kiss her forehead. "Not while Laurel's with me."

His mother patted his cheek. "That's exactly when you're most likely to be distracted."

Abigail cleared her throat. As if he'd forgotten her. He straightened. "Let's go."

She followed him to the barn without saying a word. He gestured to the gelding, and she set to saddling it while he went to work on Lancaster. Did she notice that he didn't need his crutch here in the barn? With his leg nearly straightened, he could now take enough weight on it to stand steady, even while handling the heavy tack.

She didn't notice.

With a swift hop, Abigail sat astride the big horse. From her satchel, she pulled out gloves. Their existence surprised him out of his silence. "Where'd you get those?"

"I've had them all along."

"I've never seen them."

"I've never ridden to town before." With a tug to pull them smooth, she clucked to the horse and directed him out of the barn. The dress was new, too. Proof that she'd taken particular care with her appearance. And why shouldn't she? Maybe if she caught the eye of some old bachelor or widower in town, she could go on and leave. It'd be for the best.

He got in the saddle, easiest time yet, and loosened his pistol in his belt. Nobody better get in his way when he was heading to Laurel. She wouldn't spend another day by the window wondering where he was. And he wouldn't share that sentiment with Abigail, for likely Abigail would question whether she ever had.

Abigail didn't know her. She didn't understand how it was for a girl like Laurel, whose blood ran thin and swift in the summer but could barely move in the winter, almost hibernating like the little creatures she loved. Laurel's decisions were based on instinct. All she needed was a steady hand, and that's what Jeremiah offered. They'd be good for each other.

Not a word was said the entire journey over the mountain, and the closer Jeremiah got to the Wallaces' farm, the less aware he was of his riding companion. The chickens scattered as they approached the door and the wagon parked before it. Laurel stepped outside and pulled on a poke bonnet. She tied the thick ribbon beneath her chin.

"Good morning, Jeremiah. Good morning, Abigail." Her bright eyes sparkled.

"I'll take my horse to the barn if you don't think he and

Napoleon will bicker." Jeremiah nodded as Hiram joined his daughter on the porch.

"Leave him in the barn. He'll come to no harm," Hiram said. "And since we have two bags of cotton, I hoped you'd be agreeable to driving the wagon."

"Absolutely." Plowing, hoeing, all those tasks that took two good legs were coming along slowly, but driving a wagon he could do.

"And I didn't realize you were bringing Miss Abigail. I'd already sent out for another escort."

"That's unnecessary. I'd planned so that your daughter would be properly—"

"No matter. Newton is already stabling his horse."

"Newton?" His stomach dropped. Laurel refused to look him in the eyes. Lancaster snorted, sensing his frustration.

Newton ambled out of the barn. "Good morning, Mrs. Calhoun."

Jeremiah turned in his saddle to glare at Abigail. She smiled, obviously tickled by his discomfort. "Good morning, Dr. Hopkins. I hear you'll be accompanying us this morning."

"Yes, ma'am. And it looks like it's going to be a fine morning for a trip to town."

He hitched up his straight-legged trousers and climbed right up to the wagon bench.

"You can't ride in the wagon," Jeremiah sputtered. "There's only room for three on the bench."

"I thought I'd save you the trouble of getting off your horse." Newton tilted his hat back to smile at Jeremiah.

He wouldn't be replaced so easily. "I'm riding in the wagon. I asked Laurel's pa if I could take her to town, and by george, I'm taking her to town."

"Then I'll be right here, too."

"But you can't leave a lady on horseback." Suddenly finding a use for Abigail, Jeremiah motioned toward her. "Surely you don't expect Abigail to ride just so you can sit in the wagon?"

"Why don't you give up your seat for her?" Newton asked.

"Really, boys," Laurel said. "The way you're carrying on gives me half a mind to stay home. How could either of you expect Abigail to ride—"

"I'm riding." Abigail stretched her long fingers in their fitted gloves and lifted her reins. "I won't ride in a wagon when I can be on a horse."

Well, that was just dandy. The day had already soured. Jeremiah urged Lancaster to the barn. He'd find some way to get Laurel alone before they returned, but it wouldn't be easy—not when Newton Hopkins guarded her like she was his pet bone.

———————◇———————

Served him right. Jeremiah Calhoun pushed people around like chess pieces, all pawns sacrificed in the pursuit of the enemy's queen. Abigail enjoyed seeing him taste his own medicine while crowded in the wagon with little Laurel smashed between him and Hopkins. Riding behind them, Abigail had a perfect view, but with her favorite dress pushed up around her calves, she must stay behind them, or they'd get more of a view than they bargained for.

Two suitors. A blessing or a curse? Laurel seemed embarrassed by the situation, but Abigail didn't think her cruel. She'd tried to reject Jeremiah, and when he persisted, Laurel had agreed to give him a chance. How could anyone fault her for wanting to be sure of her heart? If Jeremiah would bow out, Abigail suspected that Laurel would embrace his decision enthusiastically or, more likely, embrace Dr. Hopkins. On the other hand, if Dr.

Hopkins bowed out, would Laurel be just as content? Abigail thought it possible.

No, Laurel couldn't be faulted. Any hurt that Jeremiah incurred was the result of his stubborn pursuit. It'd take a much stronger woman to reject Jeremiah when he was determined. Even she'd weakened when he'd turned his attentions . . .

Abigail cleared her throat. Better to thank her stars that he had another victim to trap. Otherwise she might find herself being hounded by the arrogant cad. She wouldn't wish that on anyone, but if Laurel kept another innocent woman from trouble, then God bless her.

She rode all morning, dallying behind the wagon, preferring to listen to the birdsong rather than the occasional caustic conversation ahead. The longer she stayed in the mountains, the harder it was to imagine leaving them. God hadn't forsaken her but had led her to a nurturing home where she'd be loved. Now, if she could only convince the rest of the family that she belonged.

The valleys they traveled through remained cool despite the strength of the late-morning sun. The rugged green mountains, so foreboding at first acquaintance, had grown familiar. The gelding's hooves slid occasionally on the loose rocks dotting the hills, but he gamely carried on up and over the mountains.

They stopped at a spring to let the horses drink. Laurel hopped from the wagon to kneel at the spring's edge and scoop the cold water to her mouth. Abigail dismounted, but before she could join Laurel, Jeremiah intercepted her.

He took her by the arm and propelled her away from the others. "Are you tired?"

She wanted to slap him again, just for the memories his touch resurrected. "Me? Not in the least."

"If you get tired, I'll spell you." His hand dropped from her arm. "I really thought that louse would've relented by now."

So he was only being nice? Abigail smoothed her muslin bodice. "Not going well, is it?"

"I spent the first two miles avoiding Hopkins's questions about you spanking me in the barn."

She choked down a shocked giggle. "The Huckabee kids?"

"Naturally." He looked over his shoulder at the couple by the wagon. "But please ride closer to me. I don't want you to get picked off by a bushwhacker."

"You don't?" Abigail raised an eyebrow.

"Well, you are riding my horse."

She caught a splinter of his smile and chuckled. After everyone had a drink, they loaded up and soon were pulling around a bend into the small community of Pine Gap. Evidently one store, a post office, and a dozen or so dogs was enough to be considered a town. Well, that wasn't exactly accurate. Through the trees she could make out houses dotting the hillside, and beneath the framework of new construction, rough pews were being assembled for a church building. If Abigail's sense of direction served her correctly, the train station was probably just over the ridge, but from the isolated setting, you'd never know it.

Jeremiah found a shady spot, which wasn't difficult considering the forest surrounding the little clearing was merely waiting to reclaim the land that'd been stolen from it. Mules, horses, carts, and wagons boxed in the buildings, with people wandering from wagon to wagon, seeing what they might barter.

Abigail looped the horse's reins around a wagon spoke and pulled them firm. A few tufts of grass poked out between the rocks, and there was hay scattered about, dropped from farmers coming to exchange their pasture's produce for some people food. It was enough to keep the horse satisfied for the afternoon.

Jeremiah and Dr. Hopkins jostled to take Laurel's arm. Abigail adjusted her lace collar. Since they were occupied, she'd have to go around by herself. Although not shy, Abigail hesitated. Was she imagining the cold stares? Or had these people formed their opinions of her already?

Jangling the coins in her pocket, she headed toward a rack of lace displayed over the back of a wagon bed. A toothless granny licked her lips. "Where you from?" she asked, bright eyes peering from a face withered like a dried apple.

"Me? I'm from Ohio. I'm staying with Mrs. Calhoun."

The woman spit a brown stream into the gravel. "You don't say! The Calhouns?" Her head drew back. Abigail followed her gaze to a displeased Jeremiah bearing down on her.

"What do you think you're doing?" he asked.

"I'm making friends. Even considering purchasing a new lace collar."

"Come on." He spun around and marched toward the wagon where Dr. Hopkins and Laurel were sharing a stick of horehound candy.

"We just got here." Abigail hopped a few steps to catch up as he hurried away, barely relying on his crutch at all.

"You can't go to that wagon. We don't trade with them. The McLouds are Union sympathizers."

Abigail planted her feet. Jeremiah had traveled the length of a six-horse pulling team before realizing she wasn't with him.

"Union sympathizers? What if they were full-out Union supporters? A soldier or nurse, for instance?"

"They were. Their son fought for General Lyon at Springfield. They've done enough damage, and now so have you. How can I pay any attention to Laurel when I have to keep you out of trouble?"

Laurel sure didn't look like she lacked for attention with Dr.

Hopkins leaning toward her like a lovesick puppy. She waved gleefully, her bonnet hanging by its ribbons around her neck and a daisy stuck behind her ear.

"The war is over, and I disagree with this division," Abigail said.

"Fine. Varina's by the post office if you want to jump into the fire."

Abigail bit her lip. "It wouldn't hurt me to inquire after her horse."

"You'd do that?" Jeremiah frowned. "I wouldn't suggest—"

"But it might clear the air. At least she should know I don't hold a grudge." Abigail took out before she lost her nerve. She wanted Jeremiah's trust in her to be justified. She wanted the issue settled so he could see that he'd been right to defend her. She turned the corner of the tiny post office and nearly ran straight over Varina.

"What do you want?" At Varina's startle the crate of chicks beneath her chirped in alarm.

"I just wondered if you'd found your horse." Abigail smiled at the jowly woman knitting next to Varina. Her mother perhaps? With the back of her hand, the woman wiped a stream of tobacco from her mouth and continued knitting.

"I didn't misplace the horse." Varina's thin whiskers twitched like a mouse's. "It's gone."

"I realize that. I just thought maybe you'd caught someone with it. I'd hoped, anyway."

"I haven't." The squeaking chicks quieted. Varina continued to stare, without interest but perhaps without malice.

Abigail picked at the neat tucks adorning the waist of her bodice. "Well, please let me know if you do. I'd be relieved on your account."

She'd done her best. As she made her way toward the hitching post, she heard the old woman ask, "Who was that?"

Varina answered, "She's a friend of the Calhouns. Decent nurse, if you're in need of one."

A small victory, but she'd take it. With a quick prayer of thanks Abigail approached a crowd that was gathered around an arena of sort. Maybe she'd be welcome there. A gray-haired man stood on a makeshift platform consisting of raw lumber nailed over three large barrels.

The man's words shot out like a volley from sharpshooters. Sometimes singing, sometimes yelping, the auctioneer's cadence brought whoops and hollers from the crowd. Straining over the shoulder of a man clad only in his flannels, floppy hat, and trousers, Abigail caught sight of a gaggle of geese. Bids flew until the geese found a new home. Money exchanged hands and two handsome mules were brought forward to be the next items for sale.

Abigail drifted away until she spotted a woman with sewing notions. Thimbles, needles, and scissors brought Ma to mind. If Abigail was correct about Rachel's prognosis, Ma may soon have many hours to sit silent and wish for time to speed by. New needles would probably be appreciated.

She approached the little table next to the woman. Her eyes narrowed as she took in the handiwork on Abigail's dress. "That's fine stitching," she said finally. "Someone from around here make it?"

"No. I brought it with me."

The woman leaned forward. "You talk funny." She traced her fingers over the handle of a Bowie knife strapped to her side like a holster.

"I'm from the East."

A man appeared out of nowhere. Or that's what Abigail thought when he sat up in the back of a wagon and pulled at his beard. "Northeast or South?"

Where was Jeremiah when she needed him? Now might be a good time to see his scowling face. "I'm a guest of the Calhouns." And that's all she said. If those credentials wouldn't hold, then she had nothing better to offer.

"Is that so?" The man climbed out of the wagon, exposing a pair of britches patched on the backside. "Are the Calhouns here?"

"Jeremiah is." She motioned toward the unhappy man holding a bag of cotton on his shoulder. He tried to ignore her summons, but when the man split the air with his whistle, Jeremiah dropped the cotton next to Laurel, bent to make his excuses, and stalked to them.

"Peter." Jeremiah's mouth flattened in a grim line. "Is there a problem?"

"This Yankee gal claims to know you."

Before she could protest over the man's doubting her word, Jeremiah held up a hand silencing her.

"She does. Miss Stuart is a nurse and she's caring for my sister."

"A nurse, you say?" Abigail's skin crawled at the way he leered at her. "And where would you be meeting a Yankee nurse?"

Jeremiah's chest expanded. "I reckon that's none of your business."

The man sized him up. "Perhaps not. Does make me curious though. Especially when you disappeared after Westport, but here you are alive. I'd think you'd be eager to clear your name and explain the difference between you and a deserter."

Abigail gasped. Jeremiah stepped toe-to-toe with the man. "I don't owe you an explanation, but I'm not ashamed of my service for my state. I was injured during the battle, as you might have noticed, and was unable to keep up with the retreat. I got stranded behind enemy lines."

"And there was no way to rejoin your troops. What a pity."
A sneer crossed his bristly face.

"Let's go." Once again Jeremiah dragged her away. "It was
a mistake bringing you."

"The problem isn't me. It's you . . . all of you. Half the town
won't talk to the other half. People on your own side question
your loyalty. You can't get along with anyone past your own
mountain. You can't even get along with people in your own
house."

"That's enough." The veins in his temple bulged. "You're
not eager to go home, either, so before you point your finger at
me, you might take a look in the mirror."

"That's different."

"Is it? Don't think I haven't noticed your aversion to talking
about your past. You want to keep secrets? Fine. Until then, I
have a lady who is missing my company."

Abigail stepped back. What did he know? He suspected something. Cautiously she continued. "Aren't we here to get some
help with the man who set the traps? Why aren't you asking
about him?"

"Chances are, he's kin to someone, so it'd be foolhardy to
announce I'm hunting him. Out here information comes forth
bit by bit. You can't rush people, and you can't make them
talk. So please don't wave me down again. You aren't exactly
helping my case."

She shrugged one shoulder. "I'll do my best to carry on without you."

He turned toward Laurel and Hopkins. "Everyone else seems
to be coping just fine," he said and stalked off.

Nowhere to go, nothing to do, but now the small gatherings
made sense. Once the hostile glances that flew from group to
group had been translated for her, she realized she was traipsing

through a dangerous no-man's-land still under dispute. The wagons represented stakes in the ground. Territory had been established, and the only neutral area appeared to be the auction taking place just uphill of the general store.

Abigail brushed past the curious stares, wondering at the hostility. If they hated their neighbors so, why did they all stay there? Stubborn might describe more than the mules of Missouri.

Barefoot children darted between the adults, chasing grasshoppers, begging for a treat from the store, tattling on siblings. Yelps sounded over the crowd as men bid on the steer being led around the circle. The bids slowed, the auctioneer's cadence repeated, repeated, repeated until he yelled, "*Sold!*" and smacked a peach crate with his elaborate gavel.

The owner of the steer led it outside the ring to the winning bidder. Abigail watched as the new owner passed a gold piece to him. They shook hands and then parted, going to their opposite sides of the road, presumably to glare at each other again once their business had been completed. Abigail shooed a persistent fly away. At least they could trade animals without a blood feud breaking out.

The auctioneer called for the next offering, and the crowd parted. A thin young man wearing the blue trousers of the Federals led a horse into the ring, and Abigail's heart stopped.

Impossible. Unbidden, her hand sought the penny she always carried.

Never in her grandest dreams had she expected to see one of her father's horses again. Abigail pushed past a stately oldtimer and a grizzly trapper and stumbled into the ring with the chestnut mare. Together, she and her father had chosen this horse's parents, delivered her, and began her training once she'd grown, but her father hadn't lived long enough to see it completed. Pulling her hand out of her pocket, Abigail ran it along the cheek of the mare. It pushed its nose into her hand. A swish of the tail. The knowing spark in her giant liquid eyes. Ladymare recognized her. Abigail's voice quavered. "You came to me, didn't you? Even hidden here in this Philistine land you found me."

"Is there a problem, ma'am?" The auctioneer mopped his brow with his bandanna.

"This is my horse. You can look on her belly. She has a scar on her underside."

"Now, looky here." The young soldier stepped forward. "This horse was commissioned to me back in Ohio. If you're calling me a—"

"I'm not calling you anything." Abigail pressed her cheek against the horse's neck. "She was sold to the army, not stolen. I'm just surprised to see her so far from home."

"Then if there are no objections, we're going to sell this animal."

Sell her? Abigail took quick inventory of her condition. Ladymare's hips jutted out, evidence of poor provisions, much like the soldier who had brought her. To look at her, no one would suspect her smooth gait, and even more valuable, the bloodline that she'd pass on during the many fruitful years she still had in her.

She couldn't let her go. This horse represented her father's and her grandfather's toils and dreams. They'd carefully planned and chosen their stock to produce this horse. She wasn't about to let her get away.

The soldier led the horse around the circle. Men stepped forward to inspect her as he opened her mouth to display her teeth.

Abigail darted through the crowd, forgetting any shred of dignity as she raced for the wagon, but Jeremiah wasn't there.

The log where he'd sat with Laurel and Dr. Hopkins was empty. She bounded up the steps to the tiny store and burst inside. Hopkins jumped.

"Where's Jeremiah? I have to see him." Her hands braced against each side of the doorframe. "Hurry. I don't have time."

Dr. Hopkins pounded his fist against a barrel top. "He and Laurel disappeared and if you find him, you better tell me. I've got a thing or two to say—"

She didn't wait for him to finish, running outside instead. She didn't have the money to buy Ladymare, but she wouldn't let her disappear. She wouldn't let her go to some farmer and be bred by a donkey. She wouldn't waste the best bloodlines in Chillicothe on some bag of bones. At the very least, Jeremiah should have her. He'd appreciate her. Lancaster would make the perfect sire, and thus her bloodlines would be preserved.

But how could she stop the sale?

One more scan of the area, but no Jeremiah. Well, she wished him luck with Laurel, but she couldn't wait on him to return. He knew horses. He'd understand.

She reached Jeremiah's gelding and ripped his reins free from the wagon wheel. "Come on, come on," she urged as she pulled him toward the crowd. The auction had already begun. Ladymare's ears perked when Abigail neared. The auctioneer stopped.

"Do you have a bid?"

Feeling every cold stare, Abigail straightened her shoulders. "I'm sorry, but I don't have any money. All I have is this horse to offer in trade."

The soldier frowned. "I don't want another horse. I need the cash money."

The auctioneer tapped his gavel lightly. "Do you want to sell your horse first?"

But what if it didn't work out the way she wanted? What if she lost Jeremiah's horse and still couldn't afford Ladymare?

"No, I need to trade straight up. Is anyone willing to be a go-between?"

Stony faces met her question. Murmurs rumbled behind hands. Was no one going to help her?

The crowd parted and Dr. Hopkins stepped forward. "Come on, you'uns. This lady needs help. This here horse is Calhoun's. You know it's good stock. You know it's a working horse, well trained. Someone here can use this horse."

With his hands in his pockets he strolled around the circle, his gaze challenging those he thought could help. He hailed a man at the back. Abigail's eyes widened in recognition. "Mr. Parrow, even if you don't need a horse, I know you can trade up on this gelding. He's worth two of the mare."

Caesar Parrow. Abigail remembered tending him for a burn. The man slung his sack over his shoulder and took the gelding by the chin. He cracked his mouth open, then nodded. "I'll bid on the mare, but if I win, we trade even."

Abigail nodded. Caesar blurted his bid, picking up where the last bidder left off. Abigail waited breathlessly as bidders dropped out, leaving only the trapper and one other. Finally, with a dip of his chin, the man stepped back into the crowd.

"Last chance on this fine mare. Going . . . going . . . *gone!*"

The gavel fell. The air whooshed out of the soldier. "That's more than I expected to get for her."

Caesar gave him the required gold as he unbuckled the saddle from Ladymare's back. "I wouldn't have paid so much for her, but I got this fine horse. He's a high-dollar specimen if I ever seen one."

Abigail helped switch out the saddles and bridles, her hand shaking with uncontainable excitement. She ruffled Ladymare's mane with every pass. A treasure, unexpected, unforeseen, but truly a gift from God when she least expected it. Even if she left the mare behind with Jeremiah, seeing her again soothed her heart. Knowing that she was in capable hands gave Abigail a sense of continuity. Her father's legacy would live here, blended with the sure feet and endurance of the Calhouns' stock.

It was more than she'd hoped for.

CHAPTER 15

He'd hoped for more.

While sitting on the log watching Hopkins entertain Laurel, Jeremiah dearly wished for a plague or an epidemic to break out that would keep the man too busy for socializing. When finally a dysentery sufferer appeared and insisted on Hopkins's undiluted attention, Jeremiah spirited Laurel away. Taking her by the hand, he dragged her, giggling, into the forest and through a dale, barely relying on his crutch. He stumbled, but she threw her arms around his waist to steady him, marking the first time he was thankful for his injury.

Once again she was his wood sprite, her laughter trilling through the forest as he gathered a bouquet of wildflowers for her. Once again they were young, with no thought of hardships or sorrow, assuming the sun would remain high overhead forever, and they'd never get tired, or old, or hungry.

He picked wild strawberries as she demonstrated the latest dance steps, and he wondered who he missed more—Laurel or the Jeremiah he used to know. The strawberries mushed in his mouth. Already past their prime, they coated his tongue with an unpleasant flavor. Only with Laurel was he ever this carefree, but his carefree days were over. Would she understand the burdens he shouldered? Had she changed?

Sensing his darker thoughts, Laurel dropped to her knees beside him and spread her skirt primly.

"We should be getting back. Newton won't be happy."

Trouble etched across her little face. How she hated to cause pain. Maybe that's why he loved her so.

He smiled his consent. Laurel took his hand in both of hers and pulled him to his feet. The sun had moved, after all. The worries hadn't disappeared. They'd merely bide their time, waiting for him to shoulder them again.

Their steps sped as they neared town, both anxious to forget all they'd lost. Laurel's skirt caught on a blackberry bush and ripped in her haste to pull free from its grasp.

"We should finish our trading, then head home," Jeremiah said. "Don't want to be out after dark."

"I'll see how Newton's fared." She measured the two sides of her ripped skirt against each other and frowned.

They reached the wagon, but neither Newton nor Abigail was anywhere to be seen. His horse was gone, too. Jeremiah scratched his chin. Had Hopkins and Abigail headed home without them? What if the two of them formed an attachment?

When he saw them approach he could almost believe they had, and it didn't leave him as satisfied as he'd expected. Abigail beamed like she'd just discovered a whole troop of injured men needing her assistance, and Newton looked as smug as a blacksmith in a horseshoe throwing contest.

Laurel rushed to meet the doctor. She looped her arm through Hopkins's and batted her eyes. Any anger Hopkins felt at her disappearance had to disappear at such a welcome. Any comfort Jeremiah had found melted at the same rate.

And then there was Abigail. Once he got over her goofy smile, he noticed the horse she led behind her. The thin nag had more spirit than flesh. Perhaps she'd been a beauty at one time, but like the rest of them, the war had stolen years from her.

"Where'd you get the horse?" He couldn't help but notice the way Laurel leaned into Hopkins's side. Much like she'd walked with him just moments ago.

"This is my horse. From home. Can you believe it?"

His attention snapped back to her. "What? You know this horse?"

"It's a miracle, Jeremiah. She's from the Stuart stables and came all this way with a Federal private. He was selling her as a mere farm horse. Had no idea what a treasure he had."

Jeremiah stepped to the side. She had good lines. Her eyes were intelligent and her feet looked nimble enough, but her dimensions were difficult to appreciate, as thin as she was.

"She might look decent if she thickens up. Hopefully a farmer will treat her good."

Done with his appraisal he turned to reclaim his spot at Laurel's side when Abigail stopped him.

"A farmer didn't buy her, Jeremiah. I did."

"You bought her? You shouldn't ever carry that much gold. . . . Wait a minute. Where'd you get money?"

"I didn't have any money . . . or not enough anyway. I traded her for the gelding."

"You did what? My gelding? You gave away my horse?"

Abigail glanced over her shoulder at the crowd, stepped closer, and lowered her voice. "I didn't give him away. I traded him, and it was a good trade. How is a gelding going to help you fill your stables?" Her words sped, quiet and pleading. "And Lancaster is Josephine's sire, so that's no help. You need Ladymare."

But that was his call. Not hers. No one disposed of his property without his permission. He leaned down, getting as close to her face as was prudent and yelled. "You. Traded. My. Horse?"

Her face went white. "Stay away from me, Jeremiah Calhoun. I don't care how mad you are, you better not kiss me again."

"You kissed her?"

Jeremiah spun to see Laurel with one hand pressed to her bosom. "Jeremiah, if that's how you feel—"

"That is *not* how I feel!"

Hopkins placed his arm around Laurel's shoulders. "I think I'd better take you home, dear. You've endured enough today."

Sweat beaded on Jeremiah's forehead. "I'm not going anywhere. Not until I get my horse back."

Ever helpful, Hopkins tried to steer Laurel to the wagon, but she broke loose. Wringing her hands, she looked up at him with those doe eyes.

"Really, Jeremiah, if you have feelings for Abigail, I understand."

"The only feelings I have for Abigail at this moment are murderous anger and frustration. I can explain the kiss. It was . . . well, I can't explain, but ask her. It was a mistake."

Abigail crossed her arms. "The only mistake I made was being alone with you. If I'd had any inkling that you were going to kiss me—"

"Oh, stop it!" Jeremiah pounded his crutch into the ground. "You liked it and don't even pretend you didn't!"

"We're going now." Hopkins's smile was as big as a watermelon slice. He lifted Laurel into the wagon, and she didn't protest this time, keeping her head ducked and avoiding the two of them altogether.

Jeremiah stomped toward the auction, then turned on Abigail. "You'd better catch them or else you're on foot."

"I'm not leaving Ladymare. She's all I have of home. I can't lose her."

"If you're so fond of home, why don't you go there?"

Her head snapped up. "That horse is all I have left of my life. You have your family, your farm, Laurel . . . more or less. I have nothing."

"Well, you don't have this horse, either. You had no right." But he was wasting breath arguing with the bull-headed woman. Jeremiah took the reins and dragged the mare to the gathering. No sign of his gelding. He turned to holler for Abigail but she was right on his heels.

"Who'd you trade with?" he asked.

She pulled on her ear. "It's complicated. A soldier had Ladymare, but he wanted specie. No one wanted your horse until Hopkins talked Caesar Parrow into—"

"Hopkins?" His jaw tightened.

"Now that I think of it," her mouth twisted, "perhaps he wasn't merely being helpful."

"Perhaps not." Jeremiah scanned the gathering for Caesar. To her credit, she was searching, too, although to what end, he couldn't imagine.

The gavel fell on the last bid. The tight circle broke apart as buyers and sellers wandered back to their clusters of kin. Mr. Ballentine, the auctioneer, hopped off of his rickety platform and saluted Jeremiah with a hand to his forehead—the habit not yet broken in the few months since the war had ended.

"Captain Calhoun. Never thought I'd see you again." Ballentine draped his arm over his youngest son, who'd come to stand at his side.

"Hey, Ballentine. You can stop with all that captain nonsense. I ain't captain of nothing no more."

"But I was more than uncommonly pleased to hear you'd survived. We thought we'd lost you at Westport."

Jeremiah's neck stiffened. Was Ballentine digging at him?

But if Ballentine had any questions, he'd ask them flat out. No prissy stepping around for the man.

"I managed to hide from the Yankees after I was shot."

"And Alan? What ever happened to him?"

He sensed rather than heard Abigail step closer. Ballentine noticed, too. He dipped his head in acknowledgment of her presence but waited for Jeremiah to speak.

"He was captured. Died in the prison hospital."

Ballentine ducked his head. He shuffled through the dirt. "That's a sore shame. Didn't know Alan for long, but he was a fine man."

"Yes, he was." As if Jeremiah needed the reminder.

With a gentle push, Ballentine directed his son Wyatt toward the empty platform.

"Go on and load up our gear, boy." And then to Jeremiah, he said, "It'd be nice to have a permanent auction house here. But that's not what you came to talk about."

Jeremiah waited for the boy to depart. "You sold my horse today," he said.

"Sure did. A nice little piece of switchery, but the Rawlins boy paid my commission, so I've got no bone to pick."

The Rawlins were Union. Not likely to help him unravel this tricky trade. But maybe with Ballentine's help . . .

"I'd like to get my horse back. He was sold without my say-so."

Ballentine shot a quick glance at Abigail. His brows lowered. "A deal's a deal, Jeremiah. You know that."

"But it was my horse and I didn't make the deal."

"But if you give your horse—"

"He was stolen."

A soft gasp from behind him. Well, what did she expect? That he'd just let her get away with the theft?

Ballentine raised an eyebrow. "Those are serious charges, friend. If someone truly stole your horse, then yes, I'd be honor bound to get it back for you, but in this case the law isn't on your side. Your wife has as much right to your property as you do."

Jeremiah sucked in a half a barrel of dust in one breath. He threw a baleful look at Abigail, but she had already turned away from him, arms crossed and chin up.

"This woman is not my wife."

"She's not? I heard some Yankee nurse showed up to take care of Rachel and that you—"

"It's a tangle, but we've got it unknotted." He motioned to the irate woman. "Tell him, Abigail."

Slowly she turned toward him. She fluttered her eyes upward, looking for all the world like innocence decked in pink ribbon. "You are breaking my heart, dear husband."

Jeremiah's jaw dropped. "You've got to be kidding me." He held pleading hands out to Ballentine, but the man's eyes crinkled in amusement.

"I think you two need to come to a more convenient understanding. But my work here is finished. Have a safe trip home, Jeremiah . . . and you, too, Mrs. Calhoun."

The afternoon sun baked the rocky ground at his feet. No breeze stirred the muggy air, but day was slipping away. He took another look at the bony horse whose reins he held. The animal met his gaze with patience, challenging him to declare her unfit. But still, she wasn't his choice, and Abigail had no right.

Once again she'd interfered with his plans.

Abigail had really hated taking his horse—especially since he'd been kind enough to defend her against horse-thieving claims. There'd be a high price to pay—that she expected—but she'd do what she could to make it up to him. Within reason, of course.

He pulled Ladymare down the hill, walking well, considering the uneven ground. Soon they reached the bottom of the clearing, and the forest swallowed them into its narrow throat.

"Do you think we'll catch Laurel and Hopkins?" Abigail trotted a few steps to catch up with him.

"Hopkins will make good time if it means leaving me behind."

She trailed her fingers through the flowering Gaura at the edge of the path. "I hoped you'd be pleased with the trade instead of angry."

"You're an educated woman. Isn't there a stronger word than angry?"

Abigail snapped off the head of a black-eyed Susan. "Let's see, how did I feel after you assaulted me in the barn? Furious? Is that the word you're looking for?"

His mouth twisted with wry humor. "I've shot at men who've done me less harm."

They continued up the mountain in silence. Jeremiah's day of squiring Laurel hadn't turned out as he'd wanted, and Abigail had done nothing to improve his mood. She felt guilty but couldn't be sorry over the trade. Finding Ladymare just made her whole trip to Missouri worthwhile. If she knew where any of their other stock was, she'd travel twice as far to retrieve them. Her dreams of restoring the Stuart stables suddenly didn't seem so improbable.

"And before you gloat," Jeremiah said, "don't think for an instant that I'm giving you this horse."

Another obstacle. "I'd rather you have her than someone who doesn't recognize her worth."

"And you think I do?" His eyebrows formed question marks.

Abigail hoped her smile was dazzling. "I have faith in you, Jeremiah. You'll come around."

"You mean you'll wear me down. That's what you're really saying."

She thought it wise not to answer that charge.

"Did you find out anything about the man who trapped Josephine?" she asked.

"It sounds like we're the only ones who've seen him . . . and lived."

"And if you hadn't been there . . ." Abigail shuddered. Her shoulder bumped against his arm before she straightened her path.

"Jeremiah, that auctioneer said something about Alan that surprised me. He said he hadn't known him long. Didn't Alan live here?"

Jeremiah brushed through the limbs that crowded the narrow path. "His family is from northwest of here, just along the Kansas border. He left home before the war when the jayhawkers came over from Kansas and stirred up trouble."

"The jayhawkers stirred it up or the bushwhackers?"

He snorted. "Alan didn't raid Kansas, if that's what you mean. His ma wanted him out of harm's way, so she sent him to Springfield to look for work. I met him on a dock at the train station and offered him a job, back when we could afford to hire a hand or two. Those were different times."

"So that's when he and Rachel fell in love."

"I don't know that I'd call it love." One look at his stubborn face and it was obvious that even he doubted the truth of his statement.

"So they didn't love each other? Then it's a good thing, Jeremiah Calhoun, that you kept them apart. Otherwise, Rachel would've been fooled into thinking she was happy before he went off and died."

Her quick steps scattered pebbles before her. Sometimes there's no easy answer. Sometimes a person has no good options, but when they choose poorly they should acknowledge their mistake. Not Jeremiah. He would never admit he was wrong.

"I was wrong."

Abigail almost tripped. She stopped. Ladymare halted at her side. "What's that?"

"You're going to make me say it again? Fine!" He waved a hand to the sky calling for a witness. "I was wrong. I thought the war would be over quickly and Alan would return home. That once he got away from our farm he'd forget Rachel. I thought that having children would kill her."

"And it very well could've," Abigail admitted.

"But she's going to die anyway, so instead of giving her a few happy years, I only extended her loneliness. I can't help but think how much simpler life would be for everyone if Alan had survived instead of me. Hopkins and Laurel would be happy. Rachel would be happy. And you . . . you'd probably be somewhere in Kentucky trying to wrangle a horse farm there." He stared off between the trees ahead. "I should've been the one to die, not Alan. Rachel has every right to hate me."

Evening was coming on quickly, and they had yet to reach the creek they'd passed at midpoint, but the walk was doing them good, both physically and spiritually.

"And you have every reason to hate me," Abigail said. "I invaded your house, made decisions over your property, and frustrated your sister to no end. And although I've tried, I've not been any help reconciling you and Laurel. I understand why you're anxious to get rid of me."

Jeremiah's eyes snapped to hers. "You are a heap of trouble, no denying it, but I don't discredit how you worked my leg over. That was pure charity."

196

Abigail's heart skipped a beat. "Josiah and Betsy might disagree on how pure it was."

His eyebrow hopped. "Those two are as quiet as Indian scouts. I wish I could've seen them screaming when you surprised them with the dough face." He actually smiled. "This isn't so bad. You know, I was dreading the ride home with Hopkins. His conversation is duller than a widow woman's ax."

The longer they traveled, the more weight Jeremiah was putting on the crutch, and they had a long way to go before they reached home.

"You can ride the horse," Abigail said. "I don't mind walking."

"I might have to take you up on that offer. I'm getting plumb wore out."

Abigail stepped over to him and held out her hand. He lazily considered for a moment before handing her the reins and mounting.

"Much better than the first time I saw you," she said.

"Go on. Toot your own horn." He settled into the saddle, then almost under his breath added, "There's room for you, too, if this bag of bones can carry both of us."

"That bag of bones can carry both of us all day and all night."

He extended his hand down to her. "Then climb on up. We'll see if your boasts about the impressive Stuart stables are true."

Abigail peered up at him. Was he safe? Suddenly the thought of riding behind him, arms wrapped around his waist seemed a very foolish one. She felt her face warming.

"No, thank you. Maybe once I'm winded, but for now I'd prefer to walk."

From the way he watched her, she knew he'd discerned her objection.

"We can take turns," he said. "I'll let you ride uphill on the next rise. Of course, we'll lose the sun behind the mountain before we get to the Wallaces'. Once it's dark—"

He straightened. Ladymare's ears perked and stretched forward. Jeremiah laid his hand on Abigail's shoulder, stilling her. Silently he swung from left to right, scanning the thick forest and undergrowth. He loosened his pistol from his belt. "Get up," he whispered.

Up where? But Abigail didn't have time to answer before three men came around the rock pass. They pulled their horses to a stop. She waited for Jeremiah to greet them, but then a chill ran up her spine. The man in the middle was the one who'd caught her in the trap, and judging from the sneer on his mouth, he recognized them, too.

"If it ain't our cripple friend and his lady." He stood in his stirrups before plopping back into his saddle. "I never got a chance to introduce you to my friends."

Her hair stood on end. The deferential tone from their last encounter had disappeared. The man now had them outnumbered, and Abigail knew too much about the world to expect mercy.

Jeremiah's hand tightened on her shoulder, then he thrust her toward the rear and tried to angle in front of her. Abigail leaned in close to Ladymare as much out of range as possible, but Jeremiah had no option. He sat tall, facing the three men without a hint of fear. "You're awfully brave to still be in these woods. Arkansas might be a healthier place for you."

"Too bad you won't have a chance to follow your own advice. Now, get down off that horse, and we'll see if we're feeling generous or not."

"That's the problem," Jeremiah said. "It's this blamed leg. I can't get down without help." A quick look told Abigail that he'd deliberately pulled his foot up short out of the stirrup.

He had a plan. She didn't know what it was, but she was fairly certain she wanted to be ready.

"What do you expect us to do? Carry you off like a baby?"

Slowly Jeremiah rode to them. Abigail inched toward the side of the path and the green refuge, but she was noticed. "Stay where you are," the mean one ordered. Jeremiah was easing closer to them when Abigail saw a way to help.

"I have a gun," she called. "But I'll throw it down, if you want. Here, let me get it." Her heart hammered as she flipped up her pink skirt and braced her boot against a large rock on the side of the trail. Rolling her skirt up to her knee, she looked to see if her efforts were in vain. While she'd definitely distracted the three men, Jeremiah was turned in his saddle staring as well. He swallowed hard. She widened her eyes at him and he blinked to attention. He'd better hurry and do something, because she only had so much limb left to expose before she'd have to admit there was no gun.

"Oh, it's on the other side." Her laugh fell flat, but it was enough to give Jeremiah the opening he needed. With lightning quickness he shoved his bad foot into the side of the closest horse and gave a mighty shove. The horse shied into the horse next to it, creating an opening for Jeremiah to bolt between them. In a flash he disappeared. Abigail dove behind the rock, but no one had shot at her, not yet. No, they were too busy turning around in the narrow pathway to pursue Jeremiah. Amid scalding oaths and orders the grim man took after her while the other two reversed course. Abigail searched the steep hill above her. Not enough cover, but it might be enough to keep her alive.

She scrambled up the hillside, getting a good head start before the outlaw spotted her, but unless there was something just over the hill, she'd have nowhere to hide. She'd just neared the ridge when she heard limbs breaking and hooves thundering. Jeremiah flew over the ridge, crashing through the dry branches between them. He reached down and grabbed her arm in a bruising grip. She jumped, pushing off as hard as she could, still not clearing Ladymare's back, but with his help she managed to throw one leg over the horse's rump. Clawing at Jeremiah's shoulder, wadding his shirt in desperate hands, Abigail wiggled her way up. Somehow, although leaning precariously, Jeremiah managed to keep his seat and muscle her into a riding position behind him. Abigail buried her face into his back and held on for all she was worth as they raced along the top of the mountain.

He'd come back for her. But then again, she wasn't surprised. Jeremiah did his duty whether he wanted to or not.

A gunshot blasted as bark flew from a tree trunk next to them, but Ladymare kept running, weaving through the trees nimbly. Abigail thanked God that she hadn't lost her sure feet and that her war experience hadn't left her gun-shy.

Once they headed down the hill they picked up speed, but with three horses now in pursuit their odds weren't good. Their lead couldn't last—not carrying both of their weight.

Abigail couldn't see where they were going. All she knew were the lean muscles of the man she held and the tiring horse beneath her.

"Be ready to run," Jeremiah said. "When we get around this bend, jump and go for the ledge."

"What about Ladymare?"

He didn't answer.

The trail made a blind corner, and true to his prediction, layers of rock jutted out bare from the mountain. Both of them slid off the horse before she came to a stop. Jeremiah jerked the reins through the crook of a limb and pointed toward the outcroppings. Abigail ran two steps, then returned to his side. He threw his arm over her shoulder, forgetting his crutch, and they ran together to the wall of stone. Jeremiah shoved her toward a thick bramble.

"Crawl," he said.

She ducked her head, cautious not to damage the bush that would hide them, and wormed back until she met the rock wall of the mountain. Jeremiah came in right behind her. Working their way beneath a ledge, they found a dark cove overlooking the trail.

Abigail's body began to shake. Those men would've killed them. They still might if they found them. She grabbed Jeremiah's collar and pulled his ear to her lips. "Can you shoot them from here?"

"No. Not with my pistol."

Her heart pounded as she surveyed the valley, growing dark with the waning of the sun. "Then what are we doing? They'll take the horse."

"If they come up here, I'll kill as many of them as I can, but otherwise they can have the horse."

"What?" Abigail jolted up and cracked her head against the rocky ceiling. In a heartbeat Jeremiah's arms were around her, his hand over her mouth.

"Shh!" He pulled her against him, crushing her head against his chest. "I'll die protecting you if it comes to that, but I'd rather live to fight with you another day."

He was giving them her horse? Ladymare? She considered biting him, but for once she thought better of it. She lay still, as still as she could with the tremors that racked her body. Jeremiah loosened his grip, allowing Abigail a view of the scene below. Through the bushes she watched the horsemen as they cautiously approached Ladymare. Abigail clutched a fistful of Jeremiah's shirt and held it against her mouth. With guns raised they scanned the shadowy cliffs, seeming to peer directly at them, but after a whispered conference, the bushwhackers pulled Ladymare's reins free and led her away.

Abigail's eyes filled with tears. Her beloved dreams once again torn from her hands. Her chin rubbed against the cotton of his shirt as she whispered, "I remember when she was born. My father gave me a new copper penny to celebrate. That was the last gift he ever gave me. Today, when I found her, I thought maybe everything would be put right. That something good had survived from my family."

He brushed her hair away from her face. The last light of evening reflected off his eyes. It wasn't the first time she'd worked this close to him, but that was before. Now she knew what it could feel like to be loved by him. She had to keep her distance, whether through sarcasm or anger. Otherwise he'd invade the places in her heart where he didn't belong, vulnerable places that were better off sealed.

She dug her fingernails into her palms and forced her emotions down. "What are we going to do?"

Still close enough that she could feel his breath against her cheek, he whispered, "I'm going to hunt those men down and get her back. They mustn't be allowed to lurk about and pick us apart, man by man."

"Who's going to help us?"

"Us? Why is it that you're the only one I can count on?" He tipped her chin up. "I wish you trusted me enough to tell me how you ended up in St. Louis."

The sudden declaration caught her off guard. She looked deep into his eyes and wanted to tell him—wanted someone to share her burden, but she was too ashamed to admit she was unloved, even by her own mother.

"We should go now before it gets any darker," she said.

He didn't answer right away. Probably still wondering what horrendous secrets she held. "No, we stay here tonight."

"What?" Abigail tried to sit up again, and again met the same rock jutting out above her. "But why? They got the horse. That's what they want." She rubbed her skull.

"That's not all they want. Not after your little performance."

She would've crossed her arms over her chest, but there wasn't room between them. "I was trying to distract them. And it would've worked if you had taken the opportunity instead of gawking at me, too."

He cleared his throat. "You should've warned me."

"Well, I'm warning you now. We can't stay here."

"You have one of two choices. You can spend the night with those men who are right now sitting in the overlooks and passes, waiting for us to try to sneak past, or you can stay safe here with me."

"Safe with you?" She scowled at him. "I'm not so sure."

"I'm not the one strutting around town telling everyone we're married."

"We might as well be if we stay here."

"Oh, the sacrifices I'm making to save your hide." He stretched his free arm up and tucked his hand behind his head. She felt his chest expand against her.

The bushes rattled at the foot of the ledge. Leaves dropped onto the damp, loose soil beneath. Jeremiah raised his head. Both remained breathless, until a squirrel burrowed out of the brush. Jeremiah stomped his boot and sent it scurrying away.

"Nice kick on the horse, by the way." Abigail felt around, trying to find a flat place on the rocks away from him. She'd resolved to keep her distance. Pretty sure spending the night alone in a cave while horizontal wasn't wise.

"Only pretended that he was a giant feed sack. That's what my nurse taught me."

She reached down in the darkness to straighten her skirts around her ankles. "This was my nicest dress. It's going to be ruined."

"Well, it looked very—" He grunted. "You shouldn't fish for compliments. Just go to sleep."

"How can I sleep like this?" She tapped his arm pillowed beneath her head. "You don't find this awkward?"

"Extremely." His voice was husky. "Which is why I don't want to keep up the chitchat for the rest of the night."

No, although conversation would at least keep his warm lips busy. She sighed. "I see your point. So I'll pretend to sleep until I really do, and we'll both forget the improper situation we've found ourselves in."

But something told Abigail that she'd remember this night for the rest of her life.

CHAPTER 16

A mockingbird landed on the elm branch and brushed the morning dew off the leaves as it bounced. Its songs stirred Jeremiah to clarity, although he'd never completely given in to sleep. By the light and by his growling stomach he judged morning to be well under way. He looked at the lady cuddled against him. Her cheeks were flushed, but surely not by the cool air. They'd stayed snug all night. True, she'd occasionally startled him by mumbling gibberish—words of horses, pocket watches, her father, and even his name once. Jeremiah had nearly jumped out of his skin when she'd rolled and thrown an arm over his chest, but he soon settled back down and occupied himself by enjoying the silkiness of her blond locks.

The strand of hair glided between his fingers. Her eyes fluttered. Her lips moved silently, and he remembered again the bliss at taking them. It'd never happen again, but any more lonesome nights like the previous one, and his resolve would be tested. He dearly wished to care for someone, to lavish love on a worthy woman like Abigail, but she wasn't his and he had no right to act as if she were.

Rumbling wheels echoed through the valley. Branches cracked as a wagon made its way down the mountain path. Taking advantage of a last excuse, Jeremiah laid his fingers against her lips. With gentle strokes he outlined the full curve, even though the warmth in his belly warned him to stop. He waited breathless until she opened her eyes. Placing his finger to his own lips, he then gestured to the conveyance below as it made its appearance around the bend.

Slowly she seemed to realize their situation. Again she tried to move away, and again she had nowhere to go. Her brow troubled with creases.

Tearing his eyes away, he found the wagon again and recognized it as Wallace's. Sure enough, holding the reins was Hiram with Hopkins and Calbert riding shotgun, diligently scanning both sides of the pass.

Jeremiah whistled. Calbert held up his hand, and Hiram halted the team. Calbert returned the call, and slowly Jeremiah squeezed past Abigail, worming his way beneath the brush to finally stand in the open.

"We're up here." He waved and the men lowered their guns.

"Wondered what became of you." Calbert continued to gauge the mountainside for danger.

"We were waylaid. Stole my horse, in fact."

"Your horse or Abigail's horse?"

That Hopkins. Couldn't leave well enough alone.

Jeremiah turned to take Abigail's hand. He lifted her out of the brambles and set her down to dust off her skirt. Jeremiah could see Hiram's mouth move, even though he couldn't hear the words. Hopkins's shoulders bounced in mirth, and Calbert shook his head ominously.

"We had to hide." Jeremiah explained. "We figured they'd be camping right over the ridge, waiting for us to come out."

"And that's exactly what they done." Calbert pulled on his

beard. "We saw their camp just over the way. Must have flown the coop when they heard us coming."

"We're glad you did." Abigail picked her way down the hill. Jeremiah nearly swallowed his tongue. Her tousled hair gave her a decidedly unholy halo. And blast it, if that old Calbert didn't read his guilt from a hundred yards away. Jeremiah took two steps forward before realizing he didn't have his crutch.

"Well, I'll be," Calbert drawled. "Whatever happened last night must've done you some good."

Abigail spun and gaped. "Jeremiah! I had no idea you were doing so well."

"I'm not exactly, but they stole my crutch. Hand me that stick, would you?"

She bent, then extended the knobby branch toward him. Too little to replace his crutch, but if he could do with a cane, then glory hallelujah! Jeremiah pulled himself into the back of the wagon with Calbert and Hopkins while Abigail sat on the bench next to Hiram. "Keep alert. There were three of them, and they are downright nasty."

"It's time we stopped hiding," Calbert said. "Seems like it's them that should be doing the hiding."

Hopkins scanned the ridge above them, thick with trees. "And I'm tired of riding from patient to patient, watching over my shoulder. If you've got an idea, count me in."

Jeremiah thought again of Abigail's horse being led away. Of the trap. Of Varina and Mr. Rankin. His shoulders tightened. Enough was enough. "Consider it started."

Tired of being the prey, they were going hunting. Jeremiah hefted the last bushel of sweet corn into the wagon. A few days to get their work set by was what they agreed on, and then Hiram, Calbert, and even Dr. Hopkins would meet to flush out the raiders from the mountains. Sorrow weighed heavily on him with the thought of killing again, and killing there would be if they succeeded. No outlier horse thieves would surrender, not when they knew what awaited them at sentencing. Jeremiah couldn't fool himself into believing this task would be accomplished without bloodshed. Whether it was his blood or theirs, he knew the price such justice cost.

The Bible said that the Lord was a man of war. God offered strength for such ventures, and Jeremiah wasn't shy in asking for His help, but he did have to wonder how long before he could beat his sword into a plowshare. How long did he have to fight before he could become a man of peace? When would his home be a place of rest instead of another field to defend?

Fastening the tailgate, Jeremiah limped to the seat in time to see Abigail leave the house with the slop bucket—one shoulder tilted high and an arm thrown out straight from her side for balance. She never complained. And the physical work wasn't the worst. Rachel's acidic attitude wore at the woman. Even Jeremiah could see how discouraged Abigail looked after tending his sister. At a flick of the reins, the old mare rocked the wagon out of its deep ruts toward the barn. Hard to believe a nice woman like Abigail didn't have anywhere she'd rather be. Even if she had no home, surely she could find nicer folk than his family.

But did he want her to?

He slowed the horse until Abigail had dumped the bucket into the trough and left the barnyard. Not since that kiss had they worked together in the barn. Not since the night in the cave had they had a conversation alone. He missed her. How he wished he could share his frustrations and concerns with her.

If only he could let Abigail know what her friendship meant to him without giving her the wrong idea. But getting near her was like crossing the creek on slippery stones. He was bound to slip and fall head over heels . . .

Laurel and Hopkins had nearly reached him before he noticed them walking up the trail. Laurel plucked a violet from her hair and tossed it behind her while Hopkins swung his doctoring bag merrily. "Howdy, Jeremiah."

Jeremiah clucked to the horse and pulled up to meet them. "We don't ride until tomorrow."

"I know." Hopkins's smile disappeared as though the gravity of the coming task had settled on him. "I'm making rounds before then and thought I might ought to check on Rachel."

"Much obliged." And he meant it. If something happened to him, Jeremiah wanted to know he'd done all he could before he died. "Ma's in the house. Just knock."

Hopkins tugged on his old vest and took long steps to the house.

Laurel hung back, eyeing the bushels. "You need help unloading?"

Jeremiah shrugged. "I wouldn't turn down an offer."

She ducked her head as she skipped ahead of him to swing the barn door open. He directed the horse into the barn beneath the trapdoor to the loft. Laurel climbed the ladder in a flurry of tattered petticoats and scuffed boots. The trapdoor crashed open, and she smiled down at him.

Usually her smile could warm a chick out of its egg, but today it only caused guilt. He hated this uncertainty. He hated this double-mindedness. A man was supposed to decide once, and then it was settled. How had he gotten so confused?

Climbing into the back of the wagon, Jeremiah lifted the first bushel to her waiting arms. "I didn't mean to put you to work."

"Newton told me I shouldn't be in the room until he finished Rachel's examination."

Rachel. More guilt.

Laurel's ebony hair swung down on either side of her rosy face. "I'm so worried about tomorrow, Jeremiah. Will it be terribly dangerous?"

"You know the type of men we're going after."

She disappeared as the bushel thudded on the loft floor above him, then returned with tears in her eyes. "If anything happened to you . . . or Newton . . . I'd be so sad. Once before I thought I'd lost you. I couldn't bear it again."

The first time Jeremiah had ridden into danger he hadn't understood the stakes. He heard only the cheers, not the cautions. Now he knew the consequences, and so did Laurel. She had matured, after all.

She stretched her arms down for another load, but when Jeremiah lifted a basket to her, she covered his hands with her own. "Do you remember the last time you left?" she asked. "I cried every day, but then the days turned to months and the months to years."

Her chin trembled. She took the basket from him and put it aside.

"Your promises were all that kept me going," Jeremiah said. "When I was shot, when I lost Alan, I knew I had nothing to come home to . . . nothing but you." Her brown arms extended past her faded sleeves. He reached up to take the hand she offered.

"And still I haven't given you the answer you want." Her eyelashes fluttered to her cheek. "I do love you, Jeremiah. I've just got to get my mind around it. Will you give me a little more time? Please? Will you wait on me?"

Would he wait? He'd told Alan no. He'd told Rachel no.

Here was someone else asking for a chance at love. Would he ruin this relationship, too?

She glowed with hope. Laurel, who'd never harm a soul, reaching down to him as if she could snatch him up away from all the pain and trouble. He couldn't reject her. He'd turned away too many friends already.

"Yes. I'll wait for you. You take your time."

For he wasn't going anywhere. And in the meantime, he'd keep on working and praying that he could protect the people he loved.

"I'm glad you sent for me." Dr. Hopkins gulped the coffee down before returning the mug to Abigail. "Her temperature is slightly elevated. Her heart murmur is more pronounced, and she's dizzy if she stands. Another attack will kill her."

"That's what I thought, too." Abigail set the mug in the basin, then glanced through the doorway to assure they were not overheard. "If she were one of my soldiers, I'd suggest she write her letters home, but I'm not sure what to do in this situation."

Dr. Hopkins's fine brow lifted. "I'd say she has some peace to make before she goes."

But would she? Rachel had known for years that she would die young, but she hadn't made any effort to set her family at ease. "What did you tell her?"

"That her prognosis wasn't good. That every fever will be more dangerous than the one before. She reacted flippantly, as I expected. She said she'd been promised a short life for years, yet it'd already lasted longer than she wanted."

With her fingernail, Abigail picked at a crack in the ceramic mug. Scores of earnest faces came to mind—men who'd fought for each last breath. Men who'd left behind families. And yet, no matter what Rachel's attitude, she would still die. Maybe her anger was her defense against becoming too fond of the world. Either way, Abigail had a duty to this family to let Rachel go in peace . . . and hopefully leave peace behind.

"Thank you for coming and for not mentioning to Ma that I summoned you. I didn't want her to be distraught, especially with Jeremiah setting out tomorrow."

"And you wanted to borrow my expertise one last time in case I didn't return," the doctor said.

"The future is uncertain, Doctor. No one knows that better than we do."

He tapped the table and smiled roguishly. "Why doesn't he marry you and get it over with? We all know he's going to, sooner or later."

"What? I'm not getting married." Abigail's mouth went dry at the jest. She didn't want anyone to think she was after Jeremiah. Her hands suddenly had nowhere to rest but swept nonexistent dust from the table.

"No cause for embarrassment, Miss Abigail. He'll come around, but not soon enough for me."

"Shame on you," she choked out. "Wistful thinking doesn't make it so."

"Are you wistful?"

"I'm speaking of you." She hoped her face reflected the horror of his suggestion instead of her unease at the thought. "I understand your predicament, but leave me out of it."

A throat cleared. They turned to see Jeremiah and Laurel standing inside the door.

Laurel bloomed under Newton's gaze. "Are you finished with Rachel?"

"I am, and considering the day we have before us tomorrow,

I'd better be on my way." He clasped the leather handles of his physician's bag. "Tomorrow morning, Jeremiah?"

"We'll meet at Calbert's at daybreak."

"I'll be there. And Abigail, I trust my patient in your capable hands. As for that other issue . . . please take whatever measures you think necessary."

Her face warmed. Dr. Hopkins and Laurel departed, leaving her alone in the kitchen with Jeremiah.

She removed the coffeepot from the stove top and burned her finger in the process. "Rachel isn't doing well. Her heart can't go on much longer."

The lines around his eyes deepened. "How long?"

"Much depends on the fever she's fighting off, but her heart is already struggling. The end could come suddenly, or she could linger. Either way, it doesn't look like she'll ever improve. I've been trying to prepare her. She can't leave with things the way they are."

The sinews of his arm strummed as he flexed his hand. "I've tried to speak to her, too. She doesn't want to hear my apology."

How it hurt her to hear the sorrow in his voice. Just as she would've during his exercise, Abigail laid her hand on those tense muscles in an effort to soothe them. "But never close the door. As long as she has breath, she can change."

His lips parted. He studied her hand. "Abigail. I don't know what's going to happen in the morning, and I don't want to leave anything unsettled between us." He covered her hand, his warmth coursing up her veins. "If I die tomorrow, you will stay here, won't you? Even after Rachel passes and the colt's born, you'd be a comfort to Ma."

She closed her eyes. This was home. She'd known that even before Jeremiah returned, but there were still complications. "And if you don't die? Am I still welcome?"

213

He blinked. "And stay here with me?" He frowned. "That would depend. There's Laurel's opinion to consider."

Abigail stiffened. Perhaps she should be content with his admission, but it wasn't enough. Whether it was Newton's observation or her own growing desires, something compelled her forward. "What if Laurel isn't agreeable?"

"Well, she'd have no reason to send you away. You get along with her—better than with Rachel. Besides, it's my place. She'd have to listen to me."

Abigail pulled her hand free and turned to the window. "Jeremiah Almighty, imposing his will on everyone within his reach." The scene blurred before her eyes. She already had a home where she'd been tolerated. She thought she'd found something more.

"What's wrong with you?" Jeremiah asked.

"You've wanted to send me away as soon as the colt was born, and now you can't fathom why Laurel would have a single objection to me staying. Whatever mood strikes you—stay, don't stay. Be my enemy; be my friend. Kiss me; don't touch me. We're all supposed to fall in line with the captain's orders."

"Abigail."

She sensed his nearness and feared turning around. He was too close. She was too emotional.

"I apologize again," he said. "I haven't treated you fairly, but there are limits to what I can offer."

And she knew then that she could never be content with less than his all. Abigail rubbed the penny in her pocket. She had her dignity. She wouldn't make a fool of herself. She'd already said too much.

"I'm praying for your safe return." She forced a playfulness she didn't feel and turned to him. "And I'm praying you find no excuse to bring Hopkins to harm."

The lines on his face vanished. "I wouldn't hurt him. I need him to help me get my horse back."

"Your horse?"

One corner of his mouth rose in a tentative grin. "You should see her. The best blood west of the Mississippi."

CHAPTER 17

They probably wouldn't find the outlaws, much less get into a shootout with them. Jeremiah flopped onto his back and scratched at his belly. His windowless room beneath the stairs was cozy in the winter, but on sleepless nights like this one it could feel like a cave. Or a coffin.

Jeremiah sat up. He'd made a mistake. Somehow yesterday he'd messed up. Something had put him on the wrong path, and he couldn't peg it down. What was causing his unease? What had he forgotten? He'd loaded his guns and had supplies set by for his saddlebags. Lancaster was fit and ready to ride. And while Jeremiah couldn't run, he could mount up or stand and shoot without aid, thanks to Abigail.

Abigail. Jeremiah got to his feet and paced the tiny room. He'd wanted her to be happy with his offer last night. Wasn't that what she'd been angling after, a permanent place to live? So it should be settled. She'd stay here to help his ma if something happened to him. If he returned, well then, maybe she didn't have to leave, after all. Not since Alan had there been someone so likely to listen and understand him. He'd learned such friendships were hard to come by. You'd better wrap the reins around your fists and hold on when you found one. Of course there'd always be the threat of another man taking an interest in her. She was comely enough. Definitely no lack where looks were concerned. To be honest, a man might do a lot worse than to claim her for his own. Assuming the man didn't have Laurel Wallace waiting on him, of course.

The niggling of doubt intensified. Whatever hook was stuck in his gill had Laurel's name on it. The conversation he'd had with Laurel felt right. He hadn't made the same blunder he'd made with Rachel and Alan by closing a door on a friend. So why did it now feel like a mistake? Why, when he was possibly facing death, did he feel like he'd wronged Abigail?

The rooster crowed. The long night had finally ended. Pulling his cotton shirt over his head he marveled once again at the permanency of something as simple as a bedroom where a person's soul could be molded and shaped again and again.

Light gleamed from the crack beneath the kitchen door. He startled at the sound of footsteps on the stairs, but it was only Rachel. Leaning heavily against the railing and holding a candle in a shaking hand, she eased tender feet down to the first floor.

Rachel had come downstairs to greet him? He barely managed to hide his surprise. "Good morning."

The pallor pasted on her face reminded him of Abigail's dough mask. She wet her lips, her chest rising with the exertion of one who'd run a mile uphill. "Be careful," she said at last.

"Rachel, what are you doing down here?" Ma hurried across the room, took her arm, and pushed her toward the horsehair chair. "You shouldn't be up this early."

Abigail stood behind Ma. Her face freshly scrubbed and pink.

"Let me have my say before I give out." Rachel squared her shoulders to him. "If something should happen to you and you don't make it back . . ." She wiped her lips with the back of her hand. "If you, by some miracle, meet up with Alan in the great beyond, tell him that you were wrong and that I still love him."

A hint of satisfaction flitted across her face. Ma gasped and Abigail's downturned mouth showed her disapproval.

Jeremiah's skin puckered. "I'll pass on any message you have, and I don't need to make any excuses to Alan. He understood my concern for you, even if you never could."

Rachel trembled, whether from anger or from exhaustion, he couldn't guess. "That's all I had to say. I'm going to my room."

"Let me help you." Ma kissed Jeremiah on the cheek. "I'm not saying good-bye, because you're coming back and that's all there is to it." She wrapped an arm around Rachel's bony body and, with a heave, lifted her a few inches with every step.

Abigail remained planted in the kitchen doorway. "We put together a parcel of food for you." Her thick braid lay flat between her shoulder blades as he followed her into the kitchen, still unable to believe he didn't need assistance walking. The burlap bag rasped against the table and then swung free as she extended the strap to him.

Her puffy eyes gave evidence of a night poorly spent. Had she lost sleep over him, too?

"Jeremiah, last night I decided something." She ran her braid between her fingers. "Seeing how I have no home, no family, and seeing how much I enjoy your companionship, I've decided that when you're finished running these men away, we're getting married."

His suddenly nerveless fingers dropped the burlap bag to the floor. Abigail didn't flinch. Had she gone loony? He knew she had nerve, but to propose? Something wasn't right.

"The last I heard you didn't want to be alone with me, so how in the world did you decide we need to get hitched?"

"Well, Laurel doesn't want you. She's had ample opportunity to say she does. Besides, you know down deep that we're better suited. You yourself said that you'd rather talk to me. That I'm more likely to share your opinions—"

"I said that to you?" He'd thought it, sure, but how did she know?

Abigail stepped forward, her blue eyes fixed on his. "And what about that kiss? That was true. That was your heart. Neither of us has been able to stop thinking about it. That night we spent hiding under the ledge, when I slept in your arms, all you could think about was kissing me again." She reached up and threaded her fingers through his hair, brushing it back and catching it at the nape. His mouth went dry. He wanted to close his eyes, enjoy her touch, but he was too busy drinking in the sight of her. "Maybe I'm being forward, but I say let's make it official. Get the parson here so we can quit pretending to ignore each other and—"

A banging at the kitchen door interrupted her. Heart pounding, Jeremiah stepped backwards, but she followed him, not letting any space between them. He had to answer the door, but he couldn't help remembering how silky that braid felt unbound.

"Jeremiah!" It was his ma. "Jeremiah, you need to wake up."

"I am awake, Ma."

Abigail frowned. Her proposal astounded him, but he had to admit she made a compelling argument.

"I think about kissing you every minute of the day," he whispered, "but I thought you were angry—"

"Jeremiah," Ma called. "It's nearly daybreak. You've got to get on the road."

Jeremiah rolled over and sat up. Where had Abigail gone? He looked around his room. With shaking hands he lit the tallow candle, but no woman was hiding there. She was gone and he wasn't dressed and in the kitchen. And he was late. Jeremiah sprang out of bed and pulled on his shirt. He had to find Abigail. He wanted to know everything. Why had she tried to keep secrets from him? When had she decided that she loved him? His heart was full with the possibilities. He stopped with one leg in his trousers. But what had she said? Had he imagined the whole thing? Couldn't be. No, it was too real.

He toppled out of his room, still pulling his suspenders over his shoulders. His ma waited for him in the parlor, twisting her hands. Abigail worried her braid, trailing it between her fingers.

"Where's Rachel?" he asked.

Ma frowned. "She's to bed. I didn't wake her."

The stairway was dark and empty. So she hadn't asked him to say howdy to Alan after he died? Not that he'd expected anything less from her.

"Now, give me a kiss, and I'll go get dressed for the day," his ma said. "You be careful. Hopefully you can scare them off without a shootout."

"And get Ladymare back," Abigail added.

His head tingled at the sight of her. With her rosy cheeks and soft eyes she looked exactly as she had in his dream. But then again, did she look different from any other morning? He kissed his ma just as Abigail leaned against the kitchen doorframe.

"We put together a parcel of food for you."

His hair stood on end. Hadn't she said that, too, or was his dream changing to match the circumstances? What if it wasn't a dream but a premonition?

He followed her, hobbling through the muffled ticking of the parlor clock and the muted birdsong. His hearing fuzzed. Only Abigail's voice cut through the haze.

"Jeremiah, last night I decided something."

The trap door of his chest broke open and his heart fell into his boot. This couldn't happen, could it? He held up his hand. "You don't need to say anything else. I know already." Premonition. He called it.

Her eyes narrowed. "You do? Well, then, do you accept?"

Seemed like her last proposal was more winsome. She sounded almost impatient this time, but he still hadn't thought of a good answer. How could he marry someone who was hiding the truth from him? He ran his hand through his hair. "Look, I've thought of that kiss every day, but you were so mad I didn't think you'd ever consider—"

Her chin dropped. "What are you talking about? What's this have to do with Ladymare?"

There was her blond braid, just like the first time, but she sure wasn't walking into his arms. "The horse conversation will have to wait until we settle the marriage question."

Her eyes bulged. "Marriage? Are you asking me to marry you?" The noise coming from her beautiful face sounded akin to a snort.

"Of course not." He straightened his shirt. "You were asking me."

"Me!? You conceited . . . No, I wasn't. I wasn't thinking about that at all, but evidently you were."

"Forget I said anything. It was a mistake." He jammed his hands into his pockets. Hadn't he spent a sleepless night worrying about getting something wrong? "I must've been thinking of Laurel."

"Did Laurel ask you to marry her?"

Any other woman would've kindly let a man escape. Why did she have to follow every rabbit to the burrow and dig it out?

"You have vittles for me?"

She grabbed the burlap sack and threw it at him. "What I

was going to tell you is that I might offer a trade. Instead of me waiting around until February for the colt to be born, I could take Ladymare. You'd have the colt that you and Laurel planned on all along, and I'd have a grown horse I could ride away and be gone from here. I was also going to tell you to be careful today, but I changed my mind. Some birdshot might improve your intelligence."

"You'd leave already?" February. He'd counted on six more months before she left. Anything could happen in six months. "But I don't have your horse."

"You will shortly."

He shook the sack. She couldn't leave. They were just getting comfortable, weren't they? "I told you if something happened to me . . ." But the disgust on her face stopped him. Yeah, something about that had irked her. There was nothing left to do beyond thanking her for the food and stomping out. He'd find more sympathy with the bushwhackers.

------◦∞◦------

What could she do with his lying eyes? When they spoke to her, they contradicted his words. Abigail stood firm until he pushed through the kitchen door. Then she fell into a chair, thudded her elbows on the table, and sank her head into her hands.

He'd told her to stay, but he was unsure. She told him she'd leave, and he looked stricken. What was the truth?

She said a silent prayer of thanks that she'd thought of the horse trade last night. Without that counter, how could she have denied that she wanted to marry him? And how had he recognized her thoughts when they'd only recently made themselves known to her? Slowly her admiration of him had grown. He might talk rough, but he never failed to act with compassion—dropping back to check on her when they rode to market, sacrificing himself so she could escape, defending her against Varina's accusations. Jeremiah grumbled often, but his toil for others showed his heart. And his heart would never be hers.

It was time to give up. Time to give this lost cause to the Lord and see what He would do with it. Would God work a miracle, or would He comfort her through her disappointment? Either way, she had to face reality.

Jeremiah knew her. They'd spent many hours alone working with his leg, working with the horses, hiding from outlaws, and discussing the farm. If he didn't love her already, there was nothing else she could do. She was who she was, and she wasn't Laurel.

Quickly, before she lost the courage, she'd write her mother again. After her mother failed to respond to her last and only letter, Abigail had promised herself that she'd never again submit herself to the painful waiting for a reply and not receiving one. The sting of rejection hadn't numbed an iota, but what choice did she have? If there was a chance that her mother would welcome her back, she had to try. She couldn't stay here.

In a way, Jeremiah's misunderstanding had been a mercy. It'd given him a chance to consider marriage to her, and he'd decided against it. Now she knew. She'd be happy for him and Laurel, but she couldn't be happy living under the same roof.

Jeremiah and Hopkins rode along the north side of Fowler's land, ears perked for any sound that rang false through the trees. Calbert and Hiram had spurred off to the south side more than an hour ago. From the looks of it, they would meet near Fowler's homestead, and if there was anyone caught in the cave betwixt them, they were in for a hot battle.

Hopkins held up his hand. Jeremiah tugged on the reins and rose in the saddle, wondering yet again at how nice it was to feel both feet in the stirrups. Hopkins cocked his head. A razorback burst through the undergrowth with her scruffy piglets following behind. Hopkins's horse shied, but Jeremiah's mount stomped, chasing the aggressive sow away.

Reluctant admiration flickered in Hopkins's eyes. Jeremiah nodded toward the trail and they continued, two roosters scratching after the same hen. As much as he hated to admit it, Hopkins, with his school learning and highfalutin ways, was here riding next to him, which was more than he could say for many of the mountaineers. They excelled at minding their own affairs, but when one needed help, they were just as likely to hole up in their hollows and let you be. If it weren't for Laurel . . .

Rustling ahead of them brought him out of his reverie. He and Hopkins approached the cave from the low ground on the north while Calbert and Hiram would come in above them. Frequent use had widened the trail here. The limbs didn't catch at his sleeve, proof that visitors had been common recently. A dark figure appeared above the cave. Between the evergreens, Calbert's flopping hat floated as he and Hiram tried to locate the younger men.

"I guess this is it," Jeremiah whispered to Hopkins.

"Do you think they're in there?"

"We're fixing to find out."

CHAPTER 18

The wooden pail bumped against Abigail's knee as she toted the slops from the kitchen to the barn. She'd composed the letter and, to a lesser degree, composed herself before Ma had come down for the morning. The postmaster should be by soon. She'd get it posted and pray that John and her mother would accept her plea, or at least that they'd clear the way for her to apply to her brothers for help instead of insisting that she'd wronged them.

She could feel the key to the padlock in her pocket clicking against her penny and tugging down at her skirt's waistband. No doubt the horses would be restless in their stalls, not understanding why they were being stabled on such a beautiful day. And the tomcat wasn't happy about being locked out after a night of carousing. He slunk across the green as angry mockingbirds dove and pecked.

"Did you get too close to the nest?" she asked the indignant cat as he crouched, striped belly to the ground. She emptied the slop bucket into the sty, to the delight of the greedy pigs. The tomcat rubbed against her skirts, nearly tripping her on her way to the barn door. She stopped to run her hand over his arching back. Already she could wax nostalgic about this place, and she hadn't left yet.

She dropped the bucket and inserted the key into the heavy padlock. One twist and the lock sprang. She slid it off the staple, pulled the metal hasp free, and shoved the door open. Abigail reached down to pick up the bucket and froze.

Footprints.

Definitely a man's and they were not Jeremiah's. They approached from the woods, leaving a dark path, and then appeared in the bare rocky soil of the barnyard. She turned the heavy padlock over in her hands. No damage she could see, but that didn't mean they wouldn't be more successful next time.

Goose bumps puckered her arms. Someone was watching. From the deep shadows of the forest, drying leaves rustled and a branch swayed. Abigail stepped behind the barn door, shielding herself. She pressed her eye to the gap around the hinge and surveyed the woods. Nothing that she could see, but someone had been there . . . was still there.

Her jaw set. They wouldn't take another horse from the Calhouns. Praying that no one attacked while her back was turned, Abigail jerked two bridles down from their pegs. Quickly she tugged them onto Josephine and Jeremiah's old war mare, buckling loosely with shaking fingers and keeping an eye on the door. There was only one place more secure than the barn, one place they could better defend.

She dumped three scoopfuls of oats into the slop bucket and threaded her arm through the rope handle. Then she climbed the stall gate, threw her leg over Josephine's expanding back, and grabbed the reins of the other mare.

She didn't have far to go. If they gave chase, she'd turn the mare loose and pray that Josephine could outrun the poachers in her condition, but hopefully they could make their short trek safely.

Taking one last deep breath, Abigail urged Josephine forward, expecting to see a rider burst from the woods, but all was still. The horses trotted easily to the porch, then stopped.

Abigail slid off Josephine and coaxed her forward. "Come on up, girl. You won't get in trouble."

Josephine sniffed the rock floor of the porch. Ducking her head, Josephine stepped daintily up the steps and the mare obediently followed. Abigail had to set the bucket of oats down to open the front door, but then held it beneath Josephine's nose to entice her across the threshold.

"Good girl. Come on. It's tighter quarters than you're used to, but you'll be safe here."

"Oh. My. Stars." Ma stood on the staircase, her needlework trailing on the ground. She filled her mouth with air and puffed out her cheeks, no doubt biting back words no lady should know.

"The horses aren't safe in the barn." Abigail pulled them to the staircase and then walked around to close and bolt the door behind them.

"We can't have animals in the house." Ma stepped between Josephine and her bell collection in the whatnot cabinet. "They'll destroy it."

"Ma, these horses are worth more to you than anything in this house. Unless you and Rachel want to leave the house unprotected and guard the barn, this is our only option."

The mare's nostrils flared as she caught scent of the bucket of oats. Her ears went back and she whinnied.

"Is there a horse in the house?" Rachel called from upstairs.

"You are going to do Rachel irreversible harm," Ma whispered. "She cannot take the strain."

"I won't take them upstairs." Abigail lifted the bucket to the mare, who dipped her head and snorted appreciatively.

"And you're feeding them in here?"

"They're hungry."

"Mother!" Abigail noted that Rachel's voice hadn't come any closer—a sign that she hadn't felt like getting out of bed, even to witness Abigail's folly. "What's happening?"

"Don't concern yourself, dear. Abigail and I will have it settled soon." Then to Abigail, "You have to keep them out of the way. They mustn't be in the kitchen or on my parlor rug."

Abigail squirmed her mouth to one side. They couldn't go upstairs, but if they weren't in the parlor or the kitchen, that left only one option.

"Jeremiah's room?"

Ma pressed her hand to her forehead. "He will kill you."

"Not if I save his horses, he won't." Abigail shifted the weight of the heavy bucket so Josephine could get her share. "Even if the men were to breach the door, they might not find them the way they're hid behind the stairs."

Ma didn't move but repeated her earlier objection.

"Jeremiah won't be happy."

Abigail shrugged. "Let his wrath fall on me, then. It usually does."

Stepping backwards she coaxed the horses to follow the oat bucket into the narrow hall behind the stairwell. She pushed the door open, hoping the room was as bare as she remembered. The bed hadn't changed, still tidy and pushed against the wall. His pitcher and basin would need to be removed before Josephine nosed it off the bureau and broke it. Besides a comb, a few coins, and an extra pair of wool socks, nothing was in harm's way.

Gathering his belongings, Abigail opened the top drawer of his bureau, the one that had so briefly been hers, and placed everything inside. When this drawer had held her duds, she'd still thought of herself as Mrs. Jeremiah Calhoun. Absently Abigail caressed the two worn shirts. She already knew the drawer below held his one Sunday suit and spare necktie. What she wouldn't give to see him in a fine wool jacket and tailored trousers. How fun it would be to spoil him with nice things when he was so used to doing without.

But she'd done the best she could for him. Whether or not her mother answered her letter, she knew her time here was almost over.

With a last caress on the collar, she closed the rough drawer. What was it about these hills that made one long for the impossible?

Warm ashes stirred as Jeremiah stomped past. No one was there, but they hadn't been gone long. While he hoped they'd moved on for good, more probably they'd found a new place to hunker down, maybe even closer to home.

Calbert eased around the corner, rifle drawn.

"They're gone." Jeremiah slid his pistol into his belt.

"There are fresh tracks above," Calbert said. "We're for following."

Hopkins nodded. "Let's go."

They mounted and fell in behind the older men. From the looks of the tracks, the group had grown. Somewhere, they'd picked up a donkey or two. Hopefully those were stolen like Ladymare and didn't represent additions to their gang. The last thing they needed was more men to fight.

The late afternoon sun slanted down at them by the time they broke out of the trees at Sutler's Stream.

"They crossed here." Calbert gestured to the gravel bar. "The slope yonder is churned up something considerable."

"Are we still on Fowler's land?" Hiram asked.

"Pretty close to his cabin." Jeremiah urged Lancaster across the stream. "Too close for him to claim he knows nothing about them."

Up the hill, dogs barked. The sound seemed to come from the same direction as the curl of smoke that snaked through the trees. Jeremiah squinted into sunlight. If the interlopers had been harbored here, Mr. Fowler had much to answer for. He hoped they could converse peacefully. Jeremiah prayed he hadn't survived the War Between the States, only to be shot dead because of a feud.

Leaves rustled. Hopkins drew his gun quick as lightning. Jeremiah felt the cold handle of his own pistol before a fox darted across their path.

"Guess I'm a little jumpy." Hopkins wrinkled his nose. "I know the Fowlers don't cotton to uninvited visitors."

As if they'd ever invited anyone on their property besides kin. But sure enough, the tracks were still clear, following the trace that traversed their mountain.

"You think we should just ride up to the cabin?" Hiram asked. "It might be safer to send a message that we'd like a word with him."

Jeremiah ground his teeth. He'd figured on having this settled one way or another by sunset. He didn't relish putting the confrontation off another day. He turned to Hiram just in time to see the trunk of cedar next to him explode into splinters.

He landed, both feet on the ground, running, pulling Lancaster behind a boulder before he had time to feel the nicks in his face and neck. Ducking, he saw Hiram, Calbert, and Hopkins all taking cover, even though no further shots were fired.

From across the pass, Hopkins turned a white, sweat-drenched face to him. Scared, but the man hadn't lost his senses. He held up one finger. Yes. One shot. Didn't feel like the work of the outlaws they'd been tracking.

"Fowler?" Jeremiah's voice echoed against the rocks.

"Who's asking?"

Hopkins nodded his support as Jeremiah raised his pistol above his head and let it hang from his thumb.

"You know good and well who's asking. You saw me clear enough to draw a bead on me."

Silence. Jeremiah rose slowly. He stepped from around the boulder, praying his leg didn't buckle and get him killed for making a sudden move. "We're tracking bushwhackers."

"That's rich, Calhoun." The voice floated disembodied down to them. "Last I heard you and the bushwhackers were one and the same."

A familiar burning flared in his chest. "I was not a bushwhacker. You know I joined the army proper."

"Any army that takes up arms against their countrymen isn't a proper army. It's an army of traitors."

"Would you say the same of George Washington? You call him a patriot—"

"Jeremiah!" Calbert warned as he left his hiding place behind. "Look, Fowler, we aren't here to debate. We're tracking some men who crossed here earlier. Good chance they're the ones who've been causing mischief around here."

Fowler emerged from the forest wall like a specter. A giant of a man, he looked like he could grow even bigger eating nothing but nettles. "Get off my land."

"Mr. Rankin was a Fed. You don't care to avenge—"

Calbert grasped his arm. "Come on. This trail isn't going to lead us anywhere."

But Jeremiah wasn't through. "What about your neighbors? Those men have killed. They are murderers, Fowler."

"What proof do you have?"

"Three men chased me down, stole my horse coming home from Pine Gap. Before that they set a steel trap on my property and caught another mare of mine in it. Ask yourself where they're getting their herd. Ask Varina to describe her horse, if you don't believe me."

The giant swung his jaw to one side. "I heard you out. You go on now and I'll check into it."

"But we're here now," Jeremiah protested. "How do we know you aren't going to warn them and let them get away?"

Fowler's sharp brow lowered. "I reckon we'll just have to trust each other, huh? Now get."

Ridiculous. Too busy brooding to notice Hopkins's inspection, Jeremiah stalked back to his horse, mounted, and headed to cross the stream as quickly as possible. "What he did just then was criminal. Aiding bandits—"

"But if you take on Fowler, you take on all his kin," Calbert said. "Innocent people would get hurt on both sides. Let's give him a chance."

If it had been anyone else, Jeremiah would've suspected they were being cowardly, but Calbert was merely stating the obvious. Fowler hadn't attacked him or stolen his horse. If he didn't know what those men were up to, he couldn't be held responsible. But now he knew.

The tension began to ebb as they realized no confrontation awaited them. Not today. And perhaps Fowler would find the evidence they sought. They stopped at the next spring to fill their canteens and munch on the vittles riding in their sacks.

"I've got to say, Jeremiah, I'm impressed with your recovery." Hopkins took a crunchy bite of a green apple. "Someday you must tell me what remedies you used."

Jeremiah swigged the cold spring water in his canteen. "It

wasn't any remedies. Abigail just worked the old leg over until it got limbered up."

"She manipulated your leg?" Hopkins lowered his apple and leaned forward. "Tell me more."

Jeremiah straightened his leg. He enjoyed the feeling of strength that had returned but didn't relish the speculation in Hopkins's eyes. Funny how being with Hopkins made him want to win Laurel, but when Hopkins wasn't around, he spent a lot more time thinking about Abigail.

He cleared his throat. "Abigail assured me there wasn't nothing improper."

Hopkins lifted an eyebrow. "Abigail may have been innocent of any untoward thoughts, but I doubt you were." He laughed at his own joke. "Don't worry. I'm interested for purely scientific reasons. Perhaps she'd be willing to perform the same maneuvers on me, just so I could better understand."

Trouble boiled in Jeremiah's heart, bubbling slowly like hot sorghum. The thought of Abigail sharing her time with Hopkins set his world akilter. "She wouldn't do that."

"She wouldn't? Whyever not? Abigail has an interest in healing people. If she could perform the procedure on you, then she should be able to work with any man, woman—"

"But not you." Jeremiah screwed the cap on the canteen with unnecessary force. Calbert and Hiram chuckled at the exchange. Well, he couldn't help it if there was tension between him and Hopkins. They'd both set their sights on the same prize. Someone would win and someone would lose. He didn't intend to ever lose again, even if it cost him . . .

Jeremiah stood. His legs were stiff but they worked well enough to carry him away from the spring. He bumped into a tree trunk and stopped as the thought finally found words. Winning Laurel would cost him. If he kept fighting this battle for her, kept trying to beat the doctor, he would forfeit the one woman who understood him, the woman he most cherished. He would lose Abigail.

How long had he loved Abigail? Some part of his imagination—the part unshackled by his stubbornness—had tried to show him. His dream that morning had pushed his heart where he hadn't allowed it to go. Abigail as his wife? But instead of offering, he'd hesitated, still unsure of what she had hidden.

Jeremiah roughed his hand across the scaly bark of the pine tree. She had secrets, but if he couldn't weather them, then he had no right to her affection. Abigail was shielding an injury, and Jeremiah knew how that felt.

He also knew how much he appreciated Abigail's listening to his hurts. Although he'd bungled every encounter so far, surely he could pass this test.

Once Jeremiah had a goal, he could hardly think of anything else, and at that moment the most important task of his life was to tell Abigail of his discovery. He loved her. Whatever she needed from him—understanding, patience, a sympathetic ear—he was ready to give. If only she'd let him.

Chapter 19

Although the sun had dipped behind the mountain ridge, Abigail could still count on half an hour of daylight. She rubbed her burning eyes, willing the image of the barn to fade from her corneas. All day at watch and no sign of the men lurking about. Laying the rifle across her lap, she stretched her arms above her head. Jeremiah should've returned by now. He wouldn't leave them alone at night, not by choice. What was happening out there in the woods? How she envied them for getting to face their adversaries. She'd prefer anything to this anxious waiting.

A horse whinnied, the noise echoing off the walls. Abigail suppressed a smile. Jeremiah needed to come home safely, else he'd never know that she'd stabled horses in his room. Initially she felt guilty, knowing that well-fed horses would foul the room in a matter of hours, but as the day progressed she had time to appreciate the humor.

Where did he find the nerve to assume she wanted to marry him? The cad. He might be dead set on pining after someone who didn't give two rats for him, but that didn't mean she suffered the same ailment. No, she didn't care what he thought. She couldn't afford to.

"Abigail!" Rachel called from upstairs.

Abigail bolted to her feet and ran to the stairwell.

"What is it?"

"Someone is here. Two people just ran across the field to the back side of the house."

A stone formed in her stomach. So she wanted to face her adversaries? Here was her chance. Abigail wiped her hand on her skirt before swinging the rifle stock into her grip. The shutters were pulled to, but she eased past them just the same.

"Should I come down?" Ma whispered, but Abigail couldn't answer, not when she heard a rustling just outside the kitchen door.

Could it be Jeremiah? No. He wouldn't sneak around to the back door. She placed her hand on the knob and leaned her ear against the wooden panel.

A giggle. Her eyes narrowed and she pressed even closer. Definitely not men. It sounded more like . . .

She pulled open the shutters and stuck her head out to meet Josiah and Betsy's startled expressions.

"What are you doing?" Refusing to wait for an answer, she deposited the rifle on the counter, threw open the door, grabbed fistfuls of their clothing, and dragged them inside.

"You're pinching me," Josiah cried.

"What are on your feet? Are those your father's shoes?" Abigail asked.

Betsy beamed at her brother. "Isn't he clever? He made those big footprints this morning by the barn. You should've seen how scared you looked when you saw them."

Josiah smiled through his grimace. Abigail shook him. "You made those marks? That was a prank?"

"I told you we'd get you back. I never did think you'd put the horses in the house, though," he guffawed. "What's Mr. Jeremiah going to say?"

Abigail released him, fearing she might wallop him if he didn't get out of reach. Suddenly hiding Josephine and the mare in Jeremiah's room didn't sound so heroic. And to make matters worse, she heard someone approaching the front of the house.

"You two better get home." With a little shove she pushed them away from the house. "You don't want to be here when Jeremiah sees his room."

They sped away, Josiah barely hampered by shoes too large. Abigail saw them safely to the trees, then locked the door and prepared to take her medicine. From the fluttering and carrying on in the front of the house, she could tell that Jeremiah had arrived home without harm. She skimmed her hands over her hair and went to join them.

Jeremiah seemed to have been watching for her. Over his mother's head and her repeated questions about his welfare, he beckoned Abigail closer.

He didn't know about his room. He wouldn't look at her with that bizarre expectant look if he did. Abigail approached cautiously. Stable smells assaulted her. She squeezed her hands before her.

"Abigail." More intense than ever, his eyes fixed on hers, begging her not to look away.

"Jeremiah." Had something happened? Had he a message to impart that he couldn't share before his mother and Rachel? His worn face made her ashamed that she'd secretly exulted in the mess she'd made of his room. If only she could clean it before he found out.

"I'm sorry, but we didn't find Ladymare. The bushwhackers were gone by the time we found their hideout. Fowler promises that he'll let us know if they're on his land, but hopefully we won't hear from them again."

So Ladymare was gone? She smiled bravely. "I'm glad no one got hurt."

"Do you smell that, Jeremiah?" Rachel had finally made it downstairs. Her ruddy face looked even worse in the crimson evening light. "Those smells aren't coming from the stable."

His nose wrinkled. "My boots are clean. I didn't track in—" He jerked his head to look past the staircase at the closed door to his room. "Ma?"

Ma wadded her apron in shaking hands. "Those men were snooping around the barn this morning. We knew we couldn't guard the barn and the house, so we—"

He darted past her. Rachel called out, "It wasn't Ma. Ma tried to stop her."

No sound, which scared Abigail worse than the hollering she'd expected.

He turned, his face hard, his nostrils flared. "Have you seen this?" Josephine stuck her head out the door and nuzzled his hand. "Of all the monkeyshines," he muttered.

"What'd you do to make Abigail mad?" Rachel asked.

Besides accuse her of proposing to him? "It wasn't revenge," Abigail said, "although I did smile when I thought—"

Jeremiah's eyebrows shot up.

When would she learn to keep her mouth shut? "I'll get a shovel." With her chin tucked, Abigail sped to the barn. The clinks of bridles from behind let her know that Jeremiah had the horses. She fished the key out of her pocket while he caught up. He held the lock tilted so the last light could fall on the keyhole. Their fingers brushed as she tried to jam the key in.

"Steady," he said.

But it was his fault her hands were shaking.

She pushed the door open wide so the horses could pass. She'd do her best to make amends.

"Ma said there were men here today," he said. "Were they the same that took Ladymare?"

Abigail twisted her toe in the dirt. "This morning I found boot prints at the door—fresh prints and not yours. I guess I panicked. I dragged the horses inside, and since they couldn't go upstairs and they couldn't get near your mother's bell collection or her rugs or—"

"And my room was the closest thing to a stable you could think of." Was he mad or weary? She couldn't tell.

"My biggest regret is bringing them inside in the first place. Turns out Josiah and Betsy left those tracks. I caught them with Calbert's boots, traipsing around leaving prints to scare me."

Jeremiah shook his head. "Their pa better get a handle on those young'uns."

"Are you angry?"

"I'll get over it." His eyes flickered down. "But I wouldn't turn down an offer of help on the cleanup."

Abigail grabbed a bucket and the shovel. "Absolutely. And I'll stay up to sit watch if you'd like."

"I don't reckon it's necessary. It'd probably be best if we went to bed tonight." He suddenly cleared his throat, possibly choking on an inhaled piece of straw, and turned a red face away as he fastened the stalls.

He was certainly pensive. Maybe he'd gone to visit Laurel on the way home. Had she given him something to consider? Not that it mattered. Finley had Abigail's letter and her missive was on its way.

They carried the buckets and shovels to the house. Abigail skidded to a stop when they reached his room. Horse manure garnished the floor from his bed to the dresser. A large dark spot stained the blanket on his bed, looking like it'd soaked through.

"They really grounded it into the floor, didn't they?" Abigail scratched her nose.

"You could've at least spread straw down."

"I thought bushwhackers were chasing me. Straw wasn't a priority."

He grunted in reply as he stepped over the piles. "There's only one way I'm forgiving you for this." He turned to face her, his eyes coaxing her to trust him. "While we muck out this room, I want you to tell me about your family."

Abigail's toes curled inside her boots. "I'd prefer to keep that story to myself."

"And I'd prefer not to shovel manure out of my bedroom, but coming clean takes some work." He scraped the shovel along the floor. The load dropped into the bucket with a plop.

How much could she tell him? Would she survive the humiliation of her own family's accusation?

Stepping carefully, she came to his bed and removed his pillowcase. She dropped the pillow on the dresser and gathered the soiled bedclothes. Whether from the odor of the sheets or her own unease, Abigail felt certain she would gag. She carried the linens into the hallway and dropped them.

"Whenever you're ready," Jeremiah called from inside the room.

He wasn't giving her a choice.

She dragged herself to the room, and he motioned for her to begin.

"My father was the most important person in my world." It wasn't right that she'd gone so long without paying honor to the one who deserved it. Her words quickened. "He treated me like a partner. He asked for my opinion on the horses we purchased, on which to breed, on how much to sell them for—not that he needed my advice. All I knew was what he'd taught me, and he made me feel so important. So smart." Her jaw tightened. "He died when I was sixteen. I was lost, but I took over where Papa left off. He'd taught me well and we continued to prosper. My older brothers told Mama how lucky she was to have me. They knew."

He waited. The shadow of his broad shoulders filled the small room. So rarely did she see him idle, patient. He was always striving, moving, trying to gain, but now he was still. "And your mother?"

The nausea returned. "We need to empty the tick. It's soaked through," she said.

He wrinkled his nose. "Those horses were more accurate than the Yankee artillery. Let's get it outside."

He leaned the shovel against the wall and grasped the opposite end. Together they wrestled the straw tick outdoors. Dirt and straw flew when they dropped it. Abigail hurried inside to the kitchen, thankful that Ma and Rachel were upstairs. Breathlessly she pumped a bucketful of water, added a dollop of lye, and found the scrub brush. By the time she reached the room, Jeremiah was already there.

"I lost my pa, too," he said. "I know how painful the memories can be, but please tell me about your ma. When did she pass?"

Abigail's hands began to shake. The bucket dropped to the floor with a splash. "I . . . I never said she died exactly—"

His eyes widened. The look of betrayal on his face was worse than any accusation. "You lied to me?"

"I didn't lie."

He turned his face away.

"Jeremiah, I didn't lie. Ma mistook what I said and I never

241

corrected her. I should have, but I didn't know how. Not after she told you."

With his hands on his hips, he tilted his head toward the ceiling. Abigail had told herself that she didn't care what he thought of her. She'd never been more wrong.

"So your mother is alive and living in . . ."

"Ohio."

"Yes. Ohio." His jaw clenched. She'd seen him struggle before. Abigail knew the signs that Jeremiah was in pain, but she'd never felt so responsible. Finally he let out a sigh before turning to face her. "There has to be more to the story. The Abigail I know wouldn't leave her widowed mother during a war."

Her throat tightened. "Not by choice." She fell to her knees, plunged the brush into the bucket, and jerked it out, sloshing water everywhere. With both hands on the brush she scrubbed with all her might, working up the nerve to begin. "Two years after Father's death, Mama married a man—John Dennison. Other than my youngest brother, all my siblings were already married. They told me to be happy for Mama, but they didn't have to live with the man." She spun the brush in the water and attacked the floor again. "They didn't have to see him in Papa's chair, holding Mama's hand. They ignored his campaign to erase every memory of my father." She shot a sideways glance to see his reaction.

"Keep going." His face smoothed, making it unreadable.

"He acted nice enough on the surface. I know I irritated him with my attitude, but because of Mama he didn't say anything. Then the war came. My younger brother joined the army, and it was just me and them. I couldn't bear it. The two of them would've been happier without me. I knew that. But that was no reason for him to do what he did."

Jeremiah's body stiffened. "What happened?"

He crackled with tension. Abigail didn't know what to do with him. One wrong word and he might ride all the way to Ohio and attack John. She chose her words carefully.

"I'd sold off a few of our stock. Men were leaving for the war and horses were in great demand, but I wanted to hold some back. Prices were sure to rise. Then one day, a major and his men rode up our drive. They were looking for horses. I told them we had nothing to sell. They asked to speak to my father." Her mouth twisted. "Those horses were mine. I'm the one who'd chosen them, cared for them, doctored them through illness and foaling."

She didn't have the nerve to look toward Jeremiah. What would he think? Would he chide her for her foolishness, or could he, as a man who'd fought for his own property, understand her outrage?

"He sold them?"

"Not just the ones I wanted to hold back, but he emptied the stables. Our breed stock, bloodlines my family had nurtured for years, were sent as cannon fodder. He wasted my father's legacy. Generations of horses were lost that day. And if Ladymare is gone . . ."

Jeremiah's head bowed. He rubbed his knuckles absently. "And for that you ran away."

"Only overnight. I went to my brother's house, but he wouldn't listen to me. He had his own property and was too caught up in the war to care. I went back home the next morning, but John accused me of stealing a pocket watch of his. Imagine. He sells all my horses and then has the gall to call me a thief. He said I couldn't live there until I apologized."

"What did your mother say?"

"She wouldn't speak up for me. She stood by and let him . . ." The words stuck in Abigail's throat. She shook her head in an effort to dislodge them. "I couldn't even go to my brother's, not without Mama's support, so I decided I'd go west. Join a wagon train as a governess, a companion, or anything. I got as far as St. Louis when I saw the opportunity to work as a nurse. Papa always said I had a healing touch with the horses, so I thought it was fitting."

"How could your mother do that to you? How could she not know you better than that?" Jeremiah's chest stretched with a sigh. "I wish you would've trusted me enough to tell me up front. If anyone could understand how you felt about your horses and your farm, it would be me."

The shackles around Abigail's heart broke. He didn't condemn her. She sloshed her brush into the bucket again.

"I wrote to Mother when I got to St. Louis, but I received no response. Then I tried again just today."

"Today?" he almost barked. "What caused you to write today?"

However understanding he'd been about her family, she didn't want him to understand this.

"I don't think I'll be staying here much longer."

Jeremiah leaned the shovel against the wall. "Because of our talk this morning?"

Abigail kept her head bowed over her bucket. Better to remain silent than admit her love for him and the pain of it.

"I see." The floorboards creaked beneath his feet. "I treated you as rough as a cob this morning, Abigail, but if you'll allow it, I'd like to make amends. Why don't we finish here and wash up first? There are certain things a man doesn't want to declare over a bucketful of manure."

Another offer of room and board? She should be grateful, but his generosity stung. "Depending on what you have to say, a bucket of manure might be appropriate," she muttered and dropped her brush into the bucket.

She wasn't coming down. Jeremiah blew out the last lamp and pulled off his shirt. Abigail had gone upstairs to wash, barely acknowledging his request that she return when she was done. He hadn't wanted to wait until morning to speak, but the silence upstairs told him that she'd already gone to bed. He eased his tired body onto the pallet on the floor and pulled a quilt up around his shoulders. Until they washed his tick and got clean straw he'd bed down in the parlor and give the room some time to air out.

He was still shocked to think of Abigail with a large extended family back in Ohio when he'd always pictured her alone in the world. Knowing her as he did, he wasn't surprised that once she'd left home she wanted to forget the whole situation. Indecision wasn't one of her weaknesses.

Yet he must encourage her to mend the rift. He cared about Abigail—cared a lot—and knew how painful trouble in the family was. He'd do whatever he could to fix it, but to his mind, the real issue had already been settled. Her relationship with her family might be uncertain, but he had no more doubts about her relationship with him. And that was something he wanted to speak to her about as soon as she'd let him.

Bare feet padded down the wooden staircase. Jeremiah's senses sharpened. From his pallet he watched Abigail glide through the parlor. She wasn't coming to see him. Instead she disappeared into the kitchen. Water splashed into a pot. If she was sleepwalking they'd have one giant mess on their hands.

What was she doing? Was she up like this every night, or was he dreaming again? And did she wear that fancy green wrapper every night?

Wide awake now and curious, Jeremiah reached for his shirt.

Whatever she was doing, it was more than a trip to the outhouse. He pulled the cool cotton over his head, slid his arms into the sleeves, and stood. Good thing he hadn't lost his trousers for the night. He stuffed half his shirt tails in, then gave up and stumbled into the kitchen.

Abigail nearly jumped out of her skin. Her chest rose and fell as she struggled to catch her breath. "I was watching out the window, thinking about those bushwhackers . . ." She shook her head. "You startled me."

The shiny material of the wrapper looked out of place in the humble kitchen. Besides her ruined pink gown, Jeremiah had never seen Abigail dressed in anything so fine. He glanced down at his rumpled cotton shirt hanging loose and frowned. "I gave up on you coming downstairs and went to bed. Sorry."

Only by the glow of the stove was he able to see her troubled expression. "I thought you'd already gone to sleep. I didn't want to wake you."

She turned to the stove and stirred the pot with a wooden spoon. The piney scent sharpened his senses.

"Do you usually boil juniper berries at midnight?" he asked.

"If you didn't know that, you must be a heavy sleeper." Her mouth tipped. "But of course you are. The day you came home from the war, you were snoring before I left the room."

The beautiful stranger who'd barged into his life. How long ago that seemed. Her hair hung between her shoulder blades, still damp from its recent washing. The shiny green wrapper was cinched tight around her waist, hugging her curves. How he longed to take her in his arms and just tell her how it was going to be. But how was it going to be? His head spun with anticipation. He was about to find out.

"What's the tea for?"

She watched the pot as if it might sprout legs and walk off.

"For Rachel. She has trouble sleeping at night, which is no wonder since she's inactive during the day. The tea calms her and eases her joint pain." The warmth of the stove pinked her cheeks.

"I'm amazed at your care for her. She's my sister, and still I struggle."

She shrugged. "I try to see the person in there God sees. The person Christ died for. And I hope someone would see me the same way."

"What do you see in me?" he asked.

Her head bowed. "From the time I came around the bend and you were trying to climb on your horse, I saw your determination. I knew I didn't want you for an enemy."

"But that's what I became."

The stirring paused. She tilted her head toward him. Her smooth skin shimmered in the light. "Are you still?"

"Definitely not," he said. Her high lace collar brushed against her face. Summoning his courage, Jeremiah reached to run a finger along her jaw. Abigail's lips parted. He swallowed. "My first impression of you was of danger. I knew how hard I'd have to fight my attraction to you, and with the claim you were making on my farm, I didn't trust you. It was a battle I couldn't afford to lose."

She lowered her eyes as he traced her chin. "About the letter . . . I don't know why I even mailed it. Mother never answered the first time, but I know I won't feel whole until it's settled. Even if I don't go home, I want to hear from her again."

"Don't go home."

The tea sizzled in the pot. Abigail remained motionless. "Why should I stay?"

CHAPTER 20

The crushed berries spun in the hot water, the piney steam dampened the wooden spoon, but it was his gaze that made her burn from the inside. He took her by the wrist and turned her from her task.

"Abigail, when I came home and found you here, I was afraid to let you stay. But I needed you. I couldn't handle the horses, the farm, and Rachel without your help. The decision to let you stay was selfish on my part. You were convenient and I was only thinking of myself."

The neck of his shirt was open, exposing his pulse just above his collar bone. Her eyes traveled from her wrist, up past his scruffy chin to his strong mouth, but she couldn't go any further. The spoon clattered out of her grasp and onto the floor. She needed her hands empty—maybe to hold him or maybe to slap him silly if his latest offers were as hollow as those of that morning.

"Staying here was practical on my part, too," she said. "You don't owe me an apology for that."

"But things have changed, haven't they? I can walk now. I

don't need a hired hand in the fields or the stable, and yet . . ."
He took her empty hand and threaded his fingers between hers.
"And yet I need you."

His palm pressed to hers, skin to skin, nothing between them.

"I don't want to do this without you, Abigail. I can't imagine
this place without your courage, your beauty, your spunk. I can't
imagine me without you. Please give me a chance. Don't leave."

Earnest. Intense. Persuasive. Her reservations were crumbling
with every word. But she wouldn't give her heart to someone
who didn't want all of it.

"I need to know exactly where I stand with you, Jeremiah."
She studied her fingers entwined through his. "No more
confusion."

"I'm ashamed of what happened in the barn that day." His
deep voice fit perfectly with the midnight sounds outside. "I
kissed you before my heart was convinced. I promise I'll never
do that again."

She looked up. "You'll never kiss me?" She barely squeaked
out her question.

"No." He released her hand to cup her cheek and tease an earlobe. "I won't kiss you until I'm certain I love you, and only you."

Slowly he pulled her to him. This time he couldn't claim to be
the victim of a rash impulse, not when he so deliberately took her
into his arms. Their foreheads touched and their noses bumped.
He nuzzled his cheek against hers, waiting for what she didn't
know. But then with the slightest turn, his mouth sought hers.
The gentlest of touches. And then more. Much more. Murmurs
of love, not anger. Warmth that made her shiver. Patience and
the mystery that somehow his tender caresses made her pulse
race even more than the fiery time before.

"Be mine, Abigail. Please." His thumb caressed her cheek.
Skimmed over her swollen lips. "I'm lost without you."

If it weren't for his warm hands on her, she might have floated away. "I think I've always been yours. I belonged to Jeremiah Calhoun before I even knew him."

The tea bubbled and hissed. Or maybe she could only now hear it.

Reluctantly she pulled out of his grasp and stared at the pot of berries, still uncomprehending. He loved her? Jeremiah Calhoun loved her? What took him so long?

"Rachel will wonder what's become of me." Her voice sounded hollow and far away.

"Is that all you have to say?" His eyes smiled.

"What do you expect? I can't write sonnets in the middle of the night."

"Let's go up and tell Rachel together. We could wake Ma up, too, but I doubt she'll be surprised."

Abigail's eyes widened. "You aren't going to tell everyone, are you? What will people think after we've lived together for so long?"

"They'll think the same thing I do—that it's about time."

<hr />

She wouldn't see him until breakfast. He'd be out milking and feeding the animals, so she had a few moments to prepare. Rolling up her sleeves, Abigail pushed into the kitchen bright with morning's first light. In the middle of the table lay an unruly bouquet of late-blooming calico aster bundled by twine and a scrap of paper.

Abby,
If last night was a dream, please tell me, but I pray it
wasn't.

Jeremiah

She pressed the paper to her smiling lips and settled the fluttering in her stomach. Her memories hadn't evaporated with the darkness. Here was something solid, something definite. Unfolding the paper, she checked the names once again. Yes, it was to her and from him. No mistake. And she was one hundred percent sure this time that the man truly was Jeremiah Calhoun.

She slid the note into her pocket with her father's coin. If Jeremiah liked to write love letters, she'd have to find a good hiding place. Not much privacy sharing a room with his mother.

Abigail filled a canning jar with water and did her best to arrange the flowers before starting the bacon. Once breakfast was sizzling, she broke off a bloom-covered stem and threaded it through a buttonhole in her blouse. Ma noticed the flowers on the table immediately.

"Good morning, Abigail. That's a pretty bouquet."

"Isn't it? I found it this morning."

"Did you, now?" Her eyes softened. "That Jeremiah. Such a thoughtful lad. Always thinking of his mother."

Abigail ducked her head over the skillet and thanked God for those who always assumed the best.

"I hope you weren't up late last night." Ma took dishes from the drying rack and placed them on the shelves. "I didn't hear you come up."

Jeremiah wasn't the only one who slept heavily. Or snored. "Not too late, but don't worry. It was time well spent."

His shadow appeared at the back window before the door opened. The chilly morning gave his complexion a rosy tint, but his eyes lit up at the flower at her throat. "Good morning, Abigail."

"Good morning." How could she live in his house when the very sound of his voice made her dizzy? "Would you like some juniper tea for breakfast?"

The door clicked closed behind him. He came to her side and extended his hands toward the warm stove, his shoulder bumping hers. "You bet. Especially if it comes with that special sweetener you add."

His mother swatted at his arm. "You a tea sipper? If it weren't for the flowers you left me, I'd scold you for your nonsense."

His eyes widened. Abigail winked and carried the plate of hot cakes to the table.

"Anything for you, Ma." He held out her chair, then performed the same duty for Abigail.

"We might make a gentleman out of him yet." Ma tucked her napkin into her collar, a move directly in opposition to every etiquette lesson Abigail knew.

"I prefer him the way he is."

Jeremiah's fork froze. His teasing smirk replaced by wonder as he gazed at her. "Can you help me in the barn today?"

Abigail could feel her face warming. "I could. I mean . . . what do you need? Do you think it's . . . prudent?"

"Definitely not." He chewed his food while continuing to stare at her with an intensity that made her pulse race. "On second thought, maybe I should see if Calbert can give a day's labor. We need to get the harvest in. You wouldn't mind helping us with that, would you?"

"I can sit with Rachel," Ma said. "We should get the vegetables in the cellar while the weather holds."

———

Within the hour Calbert had returned with Jeremiah and the news that Mr. Fowler had visited them that morning. Whether or not his guests had stolen horses, he couldn't or wouldn't say, but he did assure Calbert that he'd told them of the accusations against them. When they'd heard who was out looking for them, they'd decided it best to pack up and move out.

"So Fowler told them we were hunting them?"

"He did." Calbert removed his hat to scratch at the bushy growth sprouting wild. "I'd rather not be named, but if they left without fuss, maybe they weren't the ones who killed Rankin, after all."

"I almost hope they were," Abigail said. "I'd rather have them gone than worry about another murderer."

"It was them," Jeremiah said. "We need to get word to the sheriff. He might do his job for once and go after them."

"Either way, they're gone and I'm relieved." Calbert pulled his hat down low on his forehead. "I've got better things to do than fret over them . . . like get your greens in. Let's get busy."

Soon the three of them were picking okra, pulling beans, and digging up sweet potatoes. Between serious conversations over the bushwhackers, Calbert would break into song as he forked through the sweet potato hills. Jeremiah's tenor would join him with ridiculous enthusiasm that had Abigail giggling. Never had she seen him so carefree. She paused to watch him, shirt sticking to his back, as he heaved another bushel of sweet potatoes into the wagon. No crutch. No cane. And none of the sorrow that had lurked over him. True, Rachel was still sick and marauders might lurk, but for just a moment they had a touch of pure joy. She wouldn't worry about her family, she wouldn't worry about Ladymare. She had a good man who loved her, and she couldn't help but love him, too.

She rose from her knees and dusted off her skirt. Stepping over the rows of beans, she found the water tin and drained the cool liquid down her throat. Taking another dipperful she approached Jeremiah.

He watched her every step. She extended the dipper to him, and he caught her fingers around it, refusing to let her loose.

"Are you happy?" he asked.

How she wanted to touch that smiling face. "I've never been happier."

Jeremiah shot a quick glance toward Calbert at the other end of the garden. "Why do you want to keep us a secret?"

She stepped closer. "I don't know. Maybe because it's so perfect. It feels more special that only we know."

His hand tightened over hers. "Look at me. I wouldn't recognize myself in the mirror, I've changed so much. Everything is different. No one will miss it."

His eyes sparkled with a life they hadn't had before. The determination had always been there, but now it was combined with the hope that there might be joy someday to mix with their endurance.

"I'm so thankful." And she truly was. God must've directed Alan's plan, because there was no way Alan could've foreseen how perfectly she and Jeremiah complemented each other.

Jeremiah had nothing better to do than stand like a fencepost and gaze into Abigail's eyes, but she finally released the dipper and returned to her bushel of beans. Throwing his shovel over his shoulder, he ambled to Calbert and dug in beside him.

"What do you think about that tomfoolery Alan pulled with Miss Abigail?" Jeremiah asked. "Is that something she should undo?"

"You talking about the marriage?" Calbert slowed. "The man she married is dead, but Jeremiah Calhoun ain't. You might want to get that cleared. Miss Laurel wouldn't appreciate having to wait on an annulment when she finally makes up her mind."

Across the field Abigail shifted quickly and swatted at an

insect that'd come too close. Jeremiah smiled. "On the other hand, in the eyes of the law I might be abiding in holy matrimony with Abigail already."

Calbert smiled so big his beard pulled up three inches. "That's something to ponder, I reckon, but don't think you'll rob Miss Abigail of a trip before the parson on such a flimsy excuse."

"I wouldn't dare, but it bothers me to think there's a paper somewhere stating we're hitched already." How long would it take to have it annulled and then reissued? And what would be the point? The date might be wrong, but the names were correct.

Calbert nodded like the sage he was. "You should've just called her wife the first day you rode home. As it is, I'll wager you don't waste much time. You'll probably be married before the end of the month."

Jeremiah filled his lungs with the fresh morning air, cool and crisp. By the end of the month? To have Abigail as his partner? At his side forever?

He turned back to his work. He hadn't thought ahead to what marriage to Abigail would look like. She already cooked for him, did his washing, kept him company, and felt like part of his family, but besides the intimate, physical aspects of marriage, he would have someone he could share his heart with. Jeremiah had spent years protecting his mother from life's harsh realities and hiding any vulnerability from Rachel. Abigail represented a safe place to share his dreams, his fears, his future. Hadn't she already proven herself? Hadn't she already walked him through the darkest days of his life? And from his knowledge of her home situation, he guessed that she needed a partner as desperately as he did.

By the end of the month? Jeremiah plunged his hands into

the soil and yanked up some sweet potatoes. The possibility was intriguing.

No longer bent over his hill, Calbert studied the road.

"What is it?" Jeremiah asked.

"Wagon coming fast." Calbert instinctively reached for the rifle that remained nearby.

"Abigail," Jeremiah called. "Go to the house."

She rose, but before she could scatter, Laurel's wagon burst pell-mell out of the forest. Her bonnet hung by its ribbons, her skirts blowing up to her knees. One look at her face and Jeremiah realized something was wrong. He hooted and she reined the wagon toward the garden, not slowing until she'd reached its edge.

"Come with me," she panted, tears rolling down her cheeks. "Both of you. Pa needs you."

A quick glance at Calbert told Jeremiah that the man would look after his ma and Rachel. He gripped Abigail by her sleeve and helped her to the bench seat before climbing up and taking the reins from Laurel.

Laurel collapsed against Abigail. "Pa got shot. You have to help him. He's in a bad way."

"Shh." Abigail wrapped her arms around the crying girl.

Jeremiah scanned the sides of the road. "Who shot your pa?"

"He was bushwhacked while working in the field. I heard the shot and found him lying on the ground with Napoleon gone. I was able to help him to the house, but then he collapsed."

Jeremiah's jaw worked. "His blood is on Fowler's hands. If he lied to us—"

"Jeremiah," Abigail pleaded. "Not now."

He slapped the horse's reins against its back. "Abigail is a good nurse, Laurel. She's seen a lot of gun wounds. And Hopkins will see that he gets his best care, too."

"Hopkins"—Laurel gulped—"Hopkins is gone, too."

"Gone?" Abigail clutched Laurel's wrist. "He's been murdered?"

"No, but he left me. We quarreled and he left. I can't ask for his help now."

Jeremiah shared the confusion that had Abigail's forehead creased. Surely Laurel was overreacting. As soon as he had Abigail settled with Hiram, he'd find the doctor. Hopkins wouldn't let a lover's spat keep him from saving Hiram's life.

After a couple of tense miles, the wagon bounced over the last rise, jangling as if it might fall apart at any moment, and sped toward the house. Narrowly escaping the wheels, Abigail bounded from her seat before Jeremiah pulled to a stop. With Laurel right behind her, they flew into the house, leaving Jeremiah to tether the horse.

He scanned the clearing around the pasture. Were they being watched even now? Would the outlaws swoop out of the trees and take this horse, too? Safest thing to do was to leave it harnessed. The wagon wouldn't make a quick getaway, as he'd just proven.

Every impulse called to him to pursue the thieves, but if they were running, they were already too far gone. If they were hiding, he'd face them soon enough.

Blood on the porch. The trail stretched out to the deeper grass before reaching the garden, but it wasn't smeared. Somehow Laurel had managed to get her father to the house, which boded well.

But she hadn't got him any farther than the doorway. The soles of his boots were visible as Jeremiah ascended the porch. Kneeling at his side, Abigail had opened his shirt and was probing beneath his rib cage, the red starkly contrasting against his white skin. Laurel cowered in the corner, her fist to her mouth.

"Two entries." Abigail pressed the heel of her hand against the lower gash. "One ball hasn't exited. We need Dr. Hopkins."

"I'll find him," Jeremiah said.

"Thank you," Hiram rasped out. "Thank you for coming."

Abigail's eyes darted between him and Laurel. "Before you go, can you help Laurel find bandages? She can't quite do it on her own, and we need to staunch the bleeding."

Poor Laurel. She was no help at all. He took her arm and dragged her to the kitchen. "Towels, Laurel. That's what we need. Or even laundry. Do you have a basket of laundry?"

"Oh, Jeremiah." She lifted her blotchy face to him. "I'm so sorry for all I put you through. I don't know how I thought Newton could take your place."

This conversation was important, Jeremiah understood that, but not as important as saving her father's life.

"We'll talk later." He threw open the doors to the cupboard. "Where are your towels?"

"But you must know before you see Newton that I rejected him. Flat out told him that I never want to see him again, because I'm marrying you."

Jeremiah stopped. "You're what?"

"I'm saying 'yes,' Jeremiah. I choose you. I wanted to tell you on a happier occasion, but now you see why you must help Pa and you mustn't send for Hopkins."

"It's too late. I'm here already." Hopkins strode into the room and practiced violence against the pump handle until water spewed. "I was coming to see you this morning, Jeremiah, to congratulate you, but Calbert sent me this way." He plunged his hands into the water and scrubbed vigorously. "Excuse me, Laurel, while I try to save your father's life." And he stormed back to Hiram's side.

Finally locating the towels, Jeremiah grabbed a handful, moving through the room, stunned. Laurel halted him.

"Pa already knows. You don't need to explain anything to him."

With heavy feet he strode away, unable to form any argument against her. Hadn't he told her that he'd wait for her? Hadn't he promised his undying devotion? Was he a man of his word, or not?

And there sat Abigail, unaware of Laurel's decision. He passed her the towels. Her eyes met his, full of adoration. She took the cloths with blood-stained fingers and reported her findings to Hopkins as she held a man's life in her hands. Jeremiah would trust his life to her. With the use of his leg, she'd already given him back his health, but would he be able to offer anything in return?

"Help me carry him to the table," Hopkins said. "Then you should take Laurel out of the house until I'm finished."

Hiram groaned as they lifted him. Blood poured from his side like thin syrup. Abigail squeezed through the doorway with them, never releasing the pressure over two of the wounds, but ordering Laurel to clear the table before they centered her pa onto the smooth boards.

"Laurel, come talk to your Pa while I get the ether from my bag," Hopkins said, then pulling Jeremiah aside he whispered, "Make sure she says what she needs to say. This could be her last chance."

But Laurel seemed to understand. Taking her father's hand she finally found the fortitude to face his injuries.

"I love you, Papa."

"I love you, too, pumpkin. And you know everything's going to be fine. You've got Jeremiah here. He's going to take care of you."

Jeremiah's vision narrowed. He couldn't bring himself to

look where Abigail labored. Laurel took his hand. "Don't worry about me. We're going to see that you get better."

This was what he wanted. For four long years of war he'd dreamt of hearing her words, but now they made him ill.

Hiram held his gaze. "If something happens to me, I'm trusting you, Jeremiah."

What could he say? He'd made too many promises already.

CHAPTER 21

If his recovery was as successful as the surgery, Hiram would survive. Abigail dropped the bloody rags into a basin and twisted her head from side to side in an attempt to work out the kinks. Before she retired for the evening she'd perform a few of Dr. Ling's gymnastics herself to relieve the tension that'd taken up residence at the base of her neck.

Hopkins dropped his probe and scalpel into the basin.

"I'm impressed," she said. "I've never seen better work."

His gray face evidenced his stress. "That was worse than anything I had to do in the war. It's a lot different operating on someone you know."

"Like your future father-in-law?"

"No, not like that." He dried his hands. "As much as I thought, but that's not the case."

"Laurel will come around. She's just upset. Once she knows—"

"He hasn't told you?" Hopkins paused from rolling his sleeves down. "I guess he hasn't had time. Laurel and I won't be seeing each other anymore. She and Jeremiah are getting married."

Abigail huffed like she'd been kicked by a mule. She didn't know what he and Laurel had fought over, but Hopkins couldn't believe that was the end. Her stomach churned.

Abigail wrung out the last of the rags as the niggling of doubt tickled the back of her throat. Was she only an option when he thought Laurel was unavailable?

No. Jeremiah wouldn't play with her. He'd kept her at arm's length for months. His actions weren't dalliances to pass the time. Yet she was eager for his reassurance.

Only then did she feel Hopkins's gaze. He sighed. "I'm sorry, Abigail. I should've thought before I spoke, but you need to know Laurel has made her choice."

Unsure whether to deny her involvement with Jeremiah or deny that he'd act so fickle, Abigail only waved away his apology, too shaken for further discussion.

"Laurel will be anxious to hear about her father," Abigail said.

He cast a nervous glance to the front door. "I'd rather not go out there just yet. Please send Jeremiah inside. We need to discuss what to do with Hiram. He's Jeremiah's responsibility now."

Abigail turned and caught her foot on the rag rug. The old injury to her ankle twinged. She straightened the crockery jar that'd almost toppled from the table, then from habit she assessed her dress before she went any farther. You never wanted to carry blood from one site to the next, but in this case she had no apron or uniform to change. The dark red spots blended with her deep plaids, so hopefully Laurel wouldn't recognize them for what they were.

Hiram rested peacefully on the kitchen table. His face was as white as Ma's doilies, but he was breathing evenly. Feeling at home in the operation room, she gathered her courage and approached the front door. With her hand on the doorknob she peered through the glass window. Jeremiah and Laurel sat on the front step, their backs to her. Laurel's arm was tucked beneath Jeremiah's, her body pressed against his.

Comforting, that's all. Their friendship stretched back to childhood. Her father had almost died. Of course Jeremiah would hold her hand and allow her head to rest against his shoulder. He was only acting as a gentleman should.

When she turned the knob, Jeremiah tensed. Laurel turned, her tear-stained face expectant. She hopped to her feet and rushed to Abigail.

"How is he?" Her eyes darted over Abigail's face, searching for a sign.

Abigail forced her worry away. "Newton removed the second ball. It doesn't appear that any organs were damaged. If we can keep him from infection, he should recover."

Laurel threw her arms around Abigail's neck. "Can I see him?"

"He's still unconscious, but you can go inside." Laurel rushed past leaving Jeremiah standing before her.

"He survived?" Jeremiah unclenched his fists. "I knew he was in good hands."

Abigail squinted up at him. Hopkins was probably mistaken. Had to be. "Hopkins needs your help deciding where to put Hiram. He'd like to have him situated before he regains consciousness."

"Of course." But no communication passed between them, not a hint of the camaraderie they'd shared as they'd worked in the field all day. Instead, he ducked his head and hurried inside.

A sickly black fear began to grow in her belly. Why wouldn't he look at her? She couldn't believe . . . couldn't . . . that the love he professed could disappear so suddenly. But why was he so distant? Should she prepare herself for the worst, or trust him?

The green valley stretched before her, ending at the wooded hills that surrounded it. Evening was on the brink of gulping down the sun. The blissful day with Jeremiah had ended too soon, and she wondered if there would ever be another.

Never before had Jeremiah noticed every rocky bump and exposed tree root along the wagon trail from the Wallace farm. By the time they reached Calhoun property, Hiram's medicine was wearing thin. From the wagon bed, Laurel murmured comfort to her father in a vain attempt to ease his suffering. It was a difficult journey, but he needed to be at the Calhouns'. He needed Abigail's care, and it wasn't safe to leave the ladies at the Wallace farm alone.

"We'll have him settled soon, and he can rest," Hopkins said.

Hopkins. He crouched in the wagon bed next to his patient. For a man who'd been spurned, he showed genuine care for Hiram. Not that Jeremiah expected anything less. His time spent with Hopkins had improved his opinion of him. If only Laurel's regard for the doctor had grown, as well.

Abigail waited on the porch for their arrival. Her plaid dress was almost lost in the busy pattern of the colorful stonework behind her, but her hair shone like a beacon. A physical response drew him toward her, a longing so strong it nearly pulled him out of the wagon and into her arms.

Home. He finally knew the meaning of the word. It wasn't a house or a property that was designated as yours. No. Home was where you longed to be. And not just with people you loved. Love was fine, but it left too much room for disappointment and pain. Love was an obligation that had to be fulfilled. Home was where your soul rested because someone waited there whom you trusted. Someone who would work at your side to fulfill all those obligations to the people you loved.

And he could rely on Abigail. Time and again she'd been faithful. She'd weathered his storms, endured his tempers, and throughout every conflict she remained true. Home: a place, a person to fall upon knowing they'd catch you and minister to you until you healed.

He'd finally found home, only to learn he could never return.

Laurel had changed her mind. She'd decided to accept his offer, and she was within her rights to do so. He was the fool. He should've never opened his heart to Abigail until he'd settled the matter with Laurel. And he'd never forgive himself for the hurt he'd cause Abigail. What would she think of him? Even worse, would she look at herself differently? Would she think she was unlovable? Would she understand it had nothing to do with what he wanted?

Rolling to the door, he set the brake.

Abigail came to the wagon and unfastened the tailgate. "I prepared your room for him."

"Thank you." He joined Hopkins at the back to lift Hiram as Laurel flitted around them. Abigail ran ahead to hold the door open. She smiled demurely as he passed, a gesture meant for him only, but he took no reassurance from it, only pain that such looks wouldn't be offered once he explained.

Abigail had already turned down his blanket. A fresh pitcher of water and a cup awaited Hiram on his bureau. Jeremiah noticed that a pile of his clothing and his pillow were stacked in a corner, ready for him to carry away. His heart twisted at the thought of Abigail going through his clothing, choosing what he'd wear tomorrow. A wife's work. His throat twisted. Laurel caught his eye.

"Papa's going to be just fine, Jeremiah. Don't worry so."

His ma appeared to announce that she'd kept supper on for them. Hopkins made his excuses and, after some basic instructions to Abigail, left without a word for him or Laurel. Did Hopkins resent his victory? If only the man knew how bitter it was.

Only when he tasted the potatoes and onions did Jeremiah realize his mother had succeeded in getting him to the table to eat. The tin plate in his lap had seemingly appeared out of nowhere. Abigail and Laurel chatted quietly, obviously unaware of any conflict the recent events had caused. The room was too little for them. The house too small. Another coy smile from Laurel and Jeremiah felt like he would choke. Abigail lowered her face over her plate, obviously displeased by the exchange. She had to know. They had to get this behind them quickly. Dragging it out was pointless once the decision had been made.

Jeremiah stood and dropped his plate in the basin.

"What is it, son?" Ma's fork clanged onto her plate.

"I've got work to do."

Laurel's chatter halted. "Do you need my help?"

He couldn't look at her. Once he returned from the barn, he'd be hers, but not yet.

"You'd better stay inside in case your pa needs you. Abigail?"

Relief washed over her face. She carried her half-eaten plate of food to the slop bucket and dumped it in without hesitation, little knowing what lay ahead. He snagged a lantern and they exited through the kitchen door.

Abigail loitered on the porch, looking over the hills that surrounded them. "It's hard to believe evil can hide in such beauty."

"Come on," he urged.

"What's your hurry?"

Not knowing what to say, he grabbed her by the arm and half-dragged her to the barn.

She kept up as he limped quickly over the rough surface. His fingers stroked the inside of her arm, wishing, praying that she would be happy for him, that he could be happy for himself. But there was no way around this, not if he kept his word. A man didn't change his mind and leave a woman without affection, which is precisely what he'd done, but of the two of them, Laurel had prior claim. He'd have to find a way back to the emotion that had kept him alive during the war, but he was afraid that the emotion had been only that. Coming home he'd finally learned that his dreams of Laurel had no real truth behind it. He'd finally found a future that suited him much better.

And it too would be destroyed.

Once inside he closed the door behind them. Too distraught to check the window for the Huckabee spies, Jeremiah set the lantern on the worktable and turned to Abigail.

As usual, her clothing bore evidence of her daily toils—this time blood mingled with the soil. She studied his face like a gunfighter watching his opponent, looking for a sign of intentions, puzzled by his hesitation to begin.

And how could he begin?

Without warning Jeremiah found himself gathering her into his arms. He pressed her head into his chest and buried his fingers in her hair. Abigail caught him in an embrace no less possessive, even if it lacked desperation.

"What are you going to do, Jeremiah?"

His arms tightened. He couldn't let her go. But he must. She had to know. With a quick prayer for forgiveness Jeremiah began. "Abigail, you must believe upon my honor that I'd never purposefully hurt you."

Her chest expanded, then released in a long sigh. Her fingers trailed across his back as she slowly pulled away. "I see." She took a step backwards, breaking his hold. Her voice wavered. "Then congratulations are in order, I suppose." Her chin quivered.

"Yes. No." He swung his arms above his head. "This is what I've wanted for years. Marrying Laurel was my goal throughout the war. The prize that awaited me after the battle."

"You don't have to explain. I knew all along."

"But at this point, it's not my decision. I can't choose between the two of you, because if I could—" He paced the length of the barn before returning. "When I told her I'd wait on her, I never thought I'd have any doubts. I didn't think it was possible. But no matter how I feel now, she broke off her relationship with Hopkins because of me. I can't go back on a promise." Jeremiah cleared his throat. "I never lied to you. Don't you doubt for a minute that I meant every word, every moment—"

"Because that's all there'll ever be?"

The pain on her face slashed through him. He reached toward her, but she stepped back.

"It's late," she whispered and wiped at her nose. "Mr. Wallace might need me."

"Wait—"

"For what?" She raised her chin, ever the brave little soldier. "What can you possibly say to make this better?"

He had nothing. He lowered his eyes and didn't lift them until she'd turned and trudged to the house, her arms wrapped tightly around her. How vulnerable she looked. How lowdown and sorry he felt. Jeremiah kicked a pail. It crashed against the stall wall, startling the horses. He'd blamed so much on his circumstances—bushwhackers inciting violence in the region, the conscription forcing them to take sides in the war, Rachel's illness leading to his bad decision with Alan—but here was a mess of his own making. No one to blame but himself.

If ever he had to retreat behind a thick skin and make the best of a disaster, it was now. He needed a backbone like never before. He'd finally achieved his quest, and he wouldn't be ungrateful. Laurel deserved a happy marriage, and that's what he was obligated to provide. And he'd be just as faithful to see that Abigail got what was coming to her. She'd be treated fairly, too, by him and his family.

He'd failed her in every other way. Taking care of her future was all he could offer.

Betrayal. Abigail lay with her back to Ma's snoring and cried silent tears. It'd happened again. When her mother and John banished her from her home, Abigail swore she'd never again be so injured. No one else could hurt her as badly because she'd never care as much. But she cared now.

She dabbed at her face with the handkerchief crumpled in her fist. She wanted to run. Wanted to be gone before the sun came up and she had to face him and had to reconcile how badly he'd broken her with how much she still loved him.

And she did. How could she not? Abigail buried her face in her pillow. If he didn't do his duty—even to Laurel—he wouldn't be the man she adored. As much as she might wish he'd leave Laurel, she couldn't help but admire his sacrifice. If only it didn't mean sacrificing her.

She had to have faith that she'd be happier without him. God could turn this for something better. And maybe Jeremiah would be happier with Laurel.

But he wouldn't. Silently Abigail sat up in bed. He loved her. He said he did, and he'd always told her the truth. He didn't want to marry Laurel. Could it be that it was up to her to see that he didn't? She'd left home instead of battling out her stepfather's accusation, but now she feared she'd walked away too quickly. Not again. Abigail wouldn't lose Jeremiah without a fight.

She gnawed on her fingernail while appraising her reflection in the dark bureau mirror. She couldn't set her wiles against Jeremiah's. He was honoring his promise, and she didn't want to oppose him.

Laurel, on the other hand . . .

CHAPTER 22

September 1865

Abigail hung her bonnet on the peg as she entered the parlor.
Two weeks had passed without any sign of the bushwhackers.
After Hiram's attack they seemed to have vanished into the
morning fog that blanketed the valleys. The men had ceased their
searches but stayed vigilant nonetheless. The ladies stayed near
the house, leaving only the Huckabee children free to wander
the hills without fear.

In the rocker Hiram sat with his shirt hanging loosely over
his wrapped torso. He scratched his sideburns as he exclaimed
over Ma's ladies' journal.

"They goodness me. I never thought to hear a firsthand account of visiting Egypt. I feel right ashamed sitting here enjoying
tales of the Orient when poor Hopkins is wearing himself thin
tending my fields, but what's a man to do?"

"You're to heal," Ma said. "That's your one objective, and
if my journals keep your mind from going soft, then so be it."

The rocker creaked as he guffawed. "While the body sleeps,

the mind leaps. Now, back to the story. What did they call that market again?"

Ma's rocker chirped merrily. "Let me see. It's a bazaar. Yes, here it says 'The bazaar itself is a perfect Babel, insufferably crowded. The salesman holds up the articles which he wishes to sell, as swords, pistols, pipes, cashmere shawls, jackets, trousers, etc. and, pushing his way through the crowd, bawls aloud the price at which he offers them.'"

Rachel glanced at Abigail from her supine position on the sofa. "Too bad you haven't been caring for Mr. Wallace all along," she said. "Ma would rather read to him than keep me company."

To Abigail's surprise, Ma didn't protest, but leaned over the arm of her rocker to point out another feature of her journal to Hiram.

Abigail lifted the teapot off its hook to check for water. "Perhaps an attempt to be agreeable would bring results."

"The only person who ever found me agreeable was sent away," Rachel said. "Besides, you might follow your own advice. Evidently Jeremiah doesn't appreciate your company, either."

Unbidden, her eyes turned to the window. From the parlor she could see Josephine grazing on the faded grasses of autumn, her sides rounded and filling with the promise of Abigail's future—a future that would someday send her from the troubled mountains she'd come to love.

The warmth of the teapot pressed through her skirt. She raised it quickly before it burned her hip. No matter what Jeremiah thought of her disposition, he had Laurel for company, and in the two weeks since she and her father had taken up residence in the Calhoun household, Jeremiah had barely spoken to Abigail. No more working together in the barn. No more fighting or teasing. It was as if she didn't exist. Every night on her voyage to the kitchen, she passed Jeremiah's sleeping form in the parlor, but he remained fast asleep. No more keeping her company as she prepared Rachel's midnight elixir.

With the teapot extended before her, she pushed through the kitchen door. Laurel spun to face her. Jeremiah tucked his chin and studied the floor.

"Sorry to interrupt." Abigail placed the pot in the basin. As she pumped, water sizzled on the hot metal surface.

"I'm glad you're here," Laurel said. "Jeremiah has been so gloomy, and I can't get him to cheer. Maybe you could coax him."

The pot overflowed and the excess gushed down the drain. Abigail should thank her lucky stars that the couple had avoided her if this was their conversation. "You'll have to solve this problem on your own. Nothing I could say would please him."

Laurel frowned comically. "Well, I have no use for a sourpuss. I might as well go visit with the elders and leave him to you."

She almost skipped from the room. Before the door closed behind her Abigail caught a glimpse of her throwing her arms around her father's neck.

"Why can't she be gentler with him?" Abigail murmured. "She's going to reopen his wounds."

Jeremiah shifted toward the back door. He took the wooden spoon from the crock that held the utensils and rubbed it between his fingers. "She's affectionate. It isn't in her nature to hold back."

Who was more uncomfortable—Jeremiah at having to defend Laurel or Abigail for being misunderstood?

"I wasn't being critical," she said. "Only worried about my patient."

"I know." He raised the wooden spoon to his nose and inhaled. "Juniper?"

Their eyes met. He thrust the spoon into the crock, upsetting it. Whisks, ladles, and knives clattered to the floor. Abigail knelt beside him to gather the errant utensils. She reached for the ladle, but his hand met hers on the cool metal handle.

She raised her eyes to his. Longing. Naked longing. Had she not looked him in the face since his decision? Only by keeping his distance had he been able to hide it from her. She drank it in, knowing she should look away but unable to do so. His eyes spoke, but he had no words for her. No promises. No hope.

Abigail would do what she could to free him, but she hadn't had much opportunity. If only Dr. Hopkins would slow down on his house calls. Couldn't he see that Laurel was hungry for his attention?

She straightened and took up the brimming teapot. "Rachel needs a cup," she said. "The warmth is good for her."

He didn't reply. Why was she explaining?

As she pushed into the parlor, Ma and Mr. Wallace jumped. They exchanged a sly glance and then chuckled. Rachel rocked a few times before getting her feet to the floor, her head upright. "Will you help me upstairs?" she asked Abigail. "I've had enough of their glee for one evening."

Abigail hung the pot over the fire and took Rachel's arm. Rachel grimaced at the pressure.

"I'm sorry," Abigail said. "Is your elbow sore?"

"Every joint is sore. I think the fever is back."

Abigail helped her up the stairs, then felt Rachel's head after she had eased herself onto her bed.

"So tell me, Nurse Abigail"—Rachel creaked back into the pillows—"is this the end?"

Abigail took her gnarled hand between her own. "Could be. How do you feel about that?"

"I stopped being a help to my family just as I was getting old enough to contribute. Instead, they've had to do everything for me. Every time I'm served a meal or helped up the stairs, I hate it. I hate myself. I'm ready for it to be over."

"If you're still here, God has something left for you to do. You aren't finished." Abigail released her hand, found a handkerchief, and dipped it into the basin on the washstand. "Did you know the last feverish patient I cooled was Alan?"

"Tell me," Rachel said.

Abigail summoned the memories—the filthy room, the hopelessness, and Alan's assurance that God was with him still. "He was my favorite patient. He wanted to get well. He fought the infection more than anyone I'd ever seen, and he made no secret of the fact that he wanted to live so he could come home to his fiancée."

Rachel smiled. "We weren't engaged. Not really."

"According to him you were. But you know, no matter how much he wanted to live, he was never desperate. He trusted God with his life . . . and with his death. He was a remarkable man. It's no wonder you fell in love with him."

Rachel was silent for a moment and then said, "I didn't want to love him. What kind of wife could I be? By the time we were honest with each other, he and Jeremiah were already gone. He had my letters. That's all he got." Her eyes sought the gilt frame that held Alan's picture. "I wouldn't say it in front of Ma, but in a way, I'm glad Alan isn't here to see me like this. Don't get me wrong. I'd give anything to have him alive. But if he were here sitting at my side, it'd be so hard to let go. As it is, well, I'm glad for it to be over. Ma will be free, and Laurel . . . well, I guess you all will have to work out that mess."

"And what about Jeremiah?" Abigail asked. "How will he feel when you die?"

Rachel's brow troubled. "I told myself I wouldn't care. He's made me miserable."

"Has he?" Abigail wove the cloth between her fingers. "You might be miserable, but I've never seen Jeremiah do anything but serve you and keep you safe."

Rachel's lips pursed. She seemed to sink even further into the pillow. "I've held him accountable for sending Alan away, but I guess I'm accountable for everything that's happened since."

"Apologize, if you'd like," Abigail said, "but even more important, he wants your forgiveness."

"It's time, I reckon." Rachel stared at the ceiling. "I'll talk to him."

"When?" Abigail couldn't allow her any time for procrastination.

"When I see him next. Don't worry, Abigail. I understand your hurry. I won't let you down."

Pulling the door closed behind her, Abigail tiptoed to the staircase. Rachel's bed creaked, giving evidence that she didn't rest soundly, but besides medicating her, Abigail feared there was little she could do to ease her discomfort. She must be hurting powerfully indeed if she finally thought she could forgive Jeremiah.

Abigail stayed on her toes to keep her boot heels from echoing on the hollow steps. She'd nearly reached the bottom when Laurel whirled around the corner and stopped her descent.

"I've been waiting on you." Laurel looked over her shoulder at Ma and her father. She lowered her voice. "Seriously, I need your help. What can I do about Jeremiah? He has been out of sorts lately. I thought you might have an idea. He never seems to misbehave around you."

If she only knew.

Abigail leaned against the stair rail and considered. "How'd you manage to keep Dr. Hopkins content?"

Laurel's eyes softened. "With Newton, I didn't have to think before I spoke or be careful what I said."

"And Jeremiah's different?" Abigail was puzzled. She'd never thought Jeremiah to be overly sensitive.

"It's just certain things, like his leg for one. If I mention that he's favoring it, he turns all sullen. If I offer to help him walk back to the house, he refuses. He's just not as fun as he used to be."

Imagine that. Abigail pitied both of them. "But you didn't have that problem with Hopkins?"

"Not until the end."

"What exactly happened between you?" Abigail asked.

Her bottom lip drooped. "He said he was plumb worn out over my hem-hawing around. He told me if I didn't make a decision, then his offer was off the table. Can you believe it? He said he'd find a woman who knew her own mind better."

"And you were surprised?"

Laurel's eyes went wide. "Of course I was surprised. I thought he loved me. How could he give me a deadline—?"

An eruption cut off her words. Gunshots, glass exploding. Laurel dove for the floor, hitting Abigail's legs and knocking her back into the stairwell. Ma's scream rent the air.

Clawing her way over Laurel, Abigail crawled into the parlor. Another window shattered and plaster dust poofed over her head as a second volley of shots rang out.

Hiram had an arm thrown over Ma's shoulders, pinning her to the floor. "Is she hurt?" she called to him.

But a voice from outside interrupted his answer.

"You'uns came hunting for us, stirring up trouble. Now we're coming after you." Cheers accompanied his boast.

Abigail raised herself enough to see through the broken window the three men who'd attacked Jeremiah and her. And the ringleader was riding Ladymare.

"You'd better watch your back, Calhoun. And tell your buddies that goes for them, too."

She covered her head as another volley ricocheted off the exterior stone wall. She scrambled to her feet as they melted away into the woods. Glass littered the floor, and Ma's table of newspaper clippings had been overturned. Sliding on the papers, Abigail all but pushed Hiram out of the way in her rush to get to Ma.

"She's fine," he said. "Maybe a few nicks from the glass."

Rachel and Laurel entered together. Laurel ran across the room and threw herself into her father's arms.

"Where's Jeremiah?" Rachel asked.

Abigail's heart dropped. If he'd been caught unaware . . . She couldn't think. Just went into motion. Rachel reached the front door before Abigail could disentangle herself from Ma.

"Don't, Rachel." Abigail commanded. "They could still be out there."

"But so is Jeremiah."

Bending, Abigail scurried across the room and took Rachel by the arm. "Go to the kitchen and stay low. Everyone is just fine, but you can't take the stress. Wait in there."

Rachel obeyed without protest, but it didn't help the sickening feeling in Abigail's chest. Where was Jeremiah?

Ignoring her own advice, she knelt at the front door and cracked it open. There he lay on the front porch, face down, arms spread over his head.

"Jeremiah." She ran outside, barely caring if the outlaws watched. But it wasn't Jeremiah stretched out flat. It was Hopkins. The doctor lifted his head. "Are they gone?" he asked.

Then Jeremiah appeared. Abigail fell on her backside next to Hopkins as Jeremiah ran out of the barn. "Get inside," he called, but Abigail couldn't move at all. She just sat on her rump, drinking in the sight of him running, uninjured.

Hopkins pushed up to his knees, wincing. "Come on." He and Jeremiah fumbled over each other, each trying to help Abigail up and get everyone inside to safety.

If enjoying Jeremiah's attention was wrong, she'd never be right again. Once everyone was inside, Jeremiah pushed the door closed behind him and locked it. Ma's cries started afresh at Jeremiah's entrance, although from relief now. One look at Hopkins and Laurel teared up, as well.

"Your back," Laurel said. "What happened?"

Abigail would much rather look at unharmed Jeremiah, but duty called. She pulled the bloodied shirt away from Hopkins's arm and ran her hand over his leather vest.

"It's just splinters," he said. "They shot the porch post and sent some chips through my shirt, but my vest caught most of them. Then I was able to get flat enough to hide on the porch. How's everyone in here?"

"I fell on my arm," Hiram said, "but I don't think I opened up any wounds."

"Just look at my parlor," Ma wailed, proving she had no real injuries.

"You might be the only one injured," Abigail said to Hopkins, a vague idea beginning to form. "But I'd better get Ma to bed before she has a conniption. Laurel can help you clean those scratches. You get that shirt off, and I'll bring down some liniment and a clean bandage."

If Jeremiah disapproved of her plans, he made no sign. He stood watch by the broken window. "Check on Rachel while you're up there," he said.

"She's in the kitchen," Abigail told him.

Broken glass crunched beneath his boots. He swung the kitchen door open and froze.

"She's not in here," he said. And at the look on Abigail's face, he rushed ahead.

Jeremiah burst into the kitchen. Rachel wasn't near the iron stove. She wasn't sitting at the table, and she wasn't under the table. She was gone, and there was only one way out other than the parlor.

The door to the outside swung on its hinges. And then he saw Rachel sprawled on the lawn.

It couldn't happen. Not on his own farm. Not home where everyone was supposed to be safe. Without thought for his safety, Jeremiah ran to her. He rolled her over.

"No," he cried. "No."

Abigail flew across the yard to kneel beside him. She tugged her shawl free and tucked it around Rachel's shoulders.

Rachel's blue lips stretched tight, trying to suppress her moans.

"Why? Why would you come out here?" he demanded.

Her strength ebbed before his eyes. Struggling for breath, she answered. "You've always taken good care of me, big brother. I wanted to take care of you for a change."

A chill ran through his body. He thought himself prepared for her passing, but not like this. He'd gone to war to keep his family safe, and here she'd given her life to save him.

Or nearly. She wasn't dead yet.

"Can I pick her up?" he asked Abigail.

Abigail already held Rachel's wrist and was monitoring her heartbeat. "How are you feeling, Rachel?" she asked. "Can we move you inside?"

"I've never died before, so I'm no expert, but I'd rather be in the house."

Gently Jeremiah slid his arms beneath her knees and shoulders. She wheezed at every step. He didn't know whether to ease along or rush her to the house as quickly as possible to end the painful transit. He settled for keeping Abigail at his side and holding a steady pace.

Rachel's eyelids fluttered. One of her slippers fell off, and her hands flopped uselessly, but she was still breathing. What had she been thinking running outside like that? She barely had the strength to move from the parlor to the kitchen. Of course she couldn't make it to the barn.

When they stepped into the parlor, Laurel froze with her hand midair over Hopkins's bare shoulder. "What happened to Rachel?"

Ma, who'd been on her knees, straightened. Her dustpan of glass fell to the ground. "Is she shot?"

"It's her heart." Abigail intercepted Ma, keeping Jeremiah free to carry Rachel up the stairs. "Stay downstairs for a while," she said. "She needs to calm down before I can assess the damage."

But Hopkins was already buttoning up his shirt. "Get my medical bag, Laurel. How's her pulse?"

Let them talk their doctor talk. Jeremiah's thoughts weren't on blood flow, valves, or rheumatism. He was worried about his sister and still furious that she put herself in danger for him. He arranged her on her bed as best as he could.

"What can I do?" he asked.

Abigail and Hopkins darted about loosening buttons, fanning, holding a candle close, and prying her eyelids open.

Rachel groaned. "Make the two of them stop. That's what you can do."

Hopkins drew back. With a slight shake of his head at Abigail, he closed his doctoring bag. "Rest is the best thing we can offer. Do you want to sit with her?"

"I will," Jeremiah said.

Abigail slid Rachel's remaining slipper off her foot and covered her with a quilt. "Just call if you need anything." She let her hand drop to his shoulder, and then with a squeeze she followed Hopkins downstairs.

The kink in his neck slowly unraveled. Maybe she'd survive after all. "I think you're going to be fine," he offered.

Rachel lay motionless on the mattress, her breath coming swift and shallow. "I'm running out of time. I can feel it."

Through her thin mottled face, Jeremiah could still make out the features of his baby sister. He sat next to her. "Are you scared?"

"Not scared. More . . . regretful? Angry? There are so many things that should've happened differently." She paused to catch her breath. "I didn't want this, and it's not getting any better. It's not fair."

A cold sweat beaded on her forehead. Not fair. Not fair. How many times had the same refrain echoed in his head? But what was fair about men lining up and shooting one another? Was there any sense as to who died when everyone stood a hair's breadth between life and death? And why did Pa and Rachel get rheumatic fever when he and Ma didn't? They'd breathed in the same dangerous vapors.

"I don't know, Rachel. Things happen to good people and bad. God works behind it all, but if your time is short, do you want to waste it asking why?"

"I do have one last why, and this one was not God's doing." She opened her eyes, the whites dulled to a sickly yellow. "Why did you keep Alan away? He wrote me and told me, you know, that you'd forbidden him to confess his love. Why would you do that? What did it hurt for us to be together?"

How he missed Alan. His best friend, loyal even when it meant giving up Rachel.

"I was wrong, Rachel. Whatever excuse I give hardly matters. I had no business meddling between you. I thought I knew best. I thought I could predict what would come of your relationship."

"And what was that?"

"Suffering. You weren't healthy enough to marry. I couldn't imagine Alan spending his youth watching you fade into an early grave. And don't forget the war. Why should you tie your heart to a man marching into almost certain death? It wasn't a safe gamble for either of you."

"But that wasn't your choice to make."

His shoulders felt heavy. "I see that now. When he told me he loved you, I was scared. I told him to wait until after the war so he wouldn't cause you more distress."

"But he couldn't hide it, even in his letters. I knew how he felt because I felt the same way. And when he denied it, I wondered what I'd done to upset him, or if there was someone else. He finally broke down and told me." A rare twinkle came into her eye. "I can be very persistent when I want something."

Although the room was cool, sweat beaded on her forehead. Jeremiah took up a cloth on the washstand.

"His last thoughts were for you. He sent Abigail to take care of you. Denied himself a tombstone, let his name disappear from the records for you."

"Don't mess up again, Jeremiah."

His eyes tightened. "What do you mean?"

She placed her swollen hand against her chest and wheezed. "You're interfering again. You chased Laurel, hounded her, begged her to accept you. Now she has and you're not happy. I know what you're up to, moping around. You can't do that. Laurel and Abigail aren't chess pieces to be moved at your will. You spoke your offer, now you need to stand by it. Stop playing with them. Send Abigail home. It's killing her to watch you with Laurel."

Guilt clogged his throat. He couldn't let Abigail go. Who would take care of her? Who would take care of him?

"I don't know what to do." He set the cloth on the stand next to Alan's picture.

"That's the problem. You keep trying to do something. You're using Abigail to heal you, to take care of me, to run the farm. You've spent your time winning Laurel, and now that you have her, you've reversed your decision and are acting like a donkey to drive her away. Do you expect her to be as fickle as you? Stop doing. Stop arranging and maneuvering and let the garden grow. It's coming up exactly how you planted it."

Exhausted, she sank further into the pillow and closed her eyes. "Now go. Just when we got the Huckabee kids to stop bothering us, we have bushwhackers shooting out the windows. I'll rest better alone."

He looked once again at his baby sister and tried to imagine her life if it hadn't been for her cursed body. "I'll try to keep everyone quiet."

He stood to leave.

"Oh, and Jeremiah," she said.

"What?"

"I risked my life to save you, but just in case you're too dense to realize it . . . I forgive you."

A very unmanly lump formed in his throat. "You're right. I might not have known for sure. Thank you for saying it." He'd heard what he needed, and rather than embarrass the both of them with more sentimental nonsense, he let the door click closed behind him.

CHAPTER 23

Because the intriguing narrow trails through the mountains held a very real threat, exercising Josephine wasn't nearly the diversion Abigail had hoped for. The only duty worse than walking each horse around the pasture for an hour would be helping Jeremiah and Laurel do whatever they were doing today. From the looks of it, Laurel's task was to meander around the property like a tipsy butterfly looking for a place to land, and while Abigail hadn't meant to note Jeremiah's whereabouts, she did notice that his leg seemed to be giving him trouble again as he chopped firewood.

If he'd ask for her help, she'd give it, but he wouldn't ask. He was keeping good on his promise to Laurel. And Abigail was doing all she could to turn Laurel from this decision. She'd hoped that having Laurel bandage up Hopkins's superficial scratches would rekindle the spark, but then Rachel's spell had interrupted their time together. For the life of her, Abigail couldn't think how to injure Hopkins again without getting caught. If only she could create a situation where Laurel had to nurse the doctor back to health. Such vignettes were especially suited to softening a woman's heart. Or that's what she'd heard, anyway.

But no one was leaving home with the bushwhackers riding brazenly. No one except Josiah and Betsy.

Josiah's pant legs only reached midcalf, and Betsy's dress was threadbare. Abigail would need to see that they had warmer clothes for winter, if she still lived there in the winter. She rode Josephine into the barn and unsaddled her while the children watched.

"Looky what I've got." Betsy cuddled a bundle up to her chest and flipped her braid behind her shoulder.

"Stay back, away from the horse," Abigail said. "Wait until I get her in her stall."

"How about we wait for you at the house," Josiah said. "Ma sent some fig preserves for Miss Rachel."

"That'd be fine." Abigail removed the saddle blanket and dried the dampness from Josephine's back and legs. She'd find the time for a full grooming that afternoon, assuming Jeremiah wasn't loitering out there.

Currently he was wrestling an armful of firewood into the house, difficult with the rough cane he'd fashioned. Back to a cane? Although she'd rather not go inside, she'd already sent the children. She might as well make over Betsy's new kitten and be done with it. She entered the parlor just as Jeremiah dumped the firewood on the hearth.

"They goodness me!" Hiram chuckled. "You trying to scare me out of here?"

Laurel popped out of her chair. "It's high time we left. I'm ready to go home."

"Sit down, Laurel." Ma looked up from her ladies' journal. "You can't leave until your pa is fit as a fiddle."

"Well, I'm on the mend, and I don't think I would've healed

nearly as fine if it weren't for your cooking." Hiram patted his stomach and winked at Ma. "Now that I'm on my feet, I'd be obliged if you'd learn me some of your secrets."

"Pshaw." Ma slapped at Hiram's arm. "If I teach you my secrets, then what reason have you to come back and eat with us again?"

From her usual spot on the sofa, Rachel groaned and covered her eyes with her arm. Hiram followed Ma into the kitchen.

"I'll find a reason to come back," he said. "Don't you worry."

The door closed on the conspirators. Josiah and Betsy stood by the entry with their backs against the wall, staring in terror at Rachel.

"I'd say he's feeling well enough," Rachel said.

"I agree." With reluctance, Laurel lowered herself into her seat. "Newton has been watching the farm for us, but now that Pa is doing better, we can't expect him to keep it up. We should go home."

"Please do, before this goes any further." Rachel grimaced as Ma's delighted laughter could be heard from the kitchen.

Doing his best to ignore the conversation, Jeremiah knelt over the hearth and swept the debris into a bin.

"Just think." Abigail waited until Laurel turned to her. "You and Jeremiah could be brother and sister one day."

Laurel's brow wrinkled as she shook her head. With a hop she turned her chair away and stared out the window. Watching the road? Waiting for Hopkins to return?

Movement caught Abigail's eye. Betsy struggled to control the bundle trying to squirm out of her arms.

"All right, Betsy," Abigail said, "show me your pet and then you better head home."

But Betsy shook her head. "On second thought, ma'am, I think I better just take it outside."

"C'mon, Betsy," Josiah said, "that's why we came. To show them your baby."

"I didn't know Miss Rachel would be in the parlor." A furry black paw emerged. Betsy tucked it back inside the dingy cheesecloth wrap. "I don't want to upset her nerves."

Rachel groaned. "Oh, what's it matter? If I survived the excitement of the bushwhackers, I don't think Betsy's kitten will do me in."

"Told you." Over Betsy's protests Josiah ripped the bundle out of her arms and dumped it on the floor.

Laurel squeaked. Rachel rolled to her side, shielding her face. And then Abigail saw it wasn't a kitten after all. They'd released a baby skunk.

"We got you, Miss Abigail," Josiah sang as Laurel scrambled out of the room.

"Josiah Huckabee!" Jeremiah brandished the fireplace poker. "You get that animal out of here right now."

The kit scurried under the sofa, right beneath Rachel. Abigail covered her mouth and nose. Should she try to capture it and risk an eruption?

Betsy boxed her brother's ear. "I told you it wasn't funny." She turned tear-filled eyes to Jeremiah. "It's just a baby. Please don't hurt it."

The baby skunk didn't seem to feel threatened by any of the goings-on. Nose to the ground, it sniffed around the sofa legs.

"Pick it up slowly," Abigail suggested, "and get it out before Ma hears."

The skunk lifted its head and its tail perked up. The sofa above it shook.

"Rachel," Abigail said, "are you having an attack?"

But Rachel cackled. "A skunk in the house? This is even better than the horses. We need to let these kids in more often."

Jeremiah stepped closer. "You won't think it's so funny if you spook the critter." He motioned to Betsy. "Go on. Pick her up."

With two hands around its belly, Betsy scooped up the curious animal. She settled it against her thin body and, with a murderous look at her brother, snatched the blanket off the floor.

Still smiling, Rachel motioned Betsy closer. "I don't know when I've had such a good laugh. Can I see your pet?" Betsy edged closer and slid the blanket away from its face. Black eyes shone above a twitching nose.

"We have a whole litter of them in the brush pile," Betsy said. "I was afeared at first, but I finally caught one to tame."

"What a brave girl you are." With one finger Rachel stroked the animal's head. "Don't ever let fear keep you from an adventure, little Miss Huckabee. Do you hear me?"

"Yes, ma'am."

Rachel smiled as the skunk sniffed her fingers. "Do you think, if it's all right with your ma and pa, you could come back and visit me again?"

Betsy squirmed. "I'd like that a heap. That is, until you're dead. I don't want to visit a dead person."

Jeremiah caught Abigail's eye. He opened his mouth, but Rachel just laughed. "I don't blame you. Dead people aren't much fun, are they? Just lying around doing nothing? If I'm alive I'll try to act like it."

"Then it's a deal."

"You'd probably better go before Ma catches that thing in her house. And as much as I hate to admit it, I do need some rest. Next time I'll try to be a better playmate."

Josiah held the door open for Betsy. He tipped his hat to Abigail, his chest puffed out in victory. "Another win for me," he said.

Abigail narrowed her eyes in what she hoped was a menacing stare. The boy was delighted, just as she'd planned.

"It's a miracle the thing didn't spray any of us." Rachel pulled the edge of the blanket over herself. She chuckled once before she closed her eyes and dozed.

But the miracle that had Jeremiah and Abigail standing speechless had nothing to do with the skunk.

In Abigail's opinion, a perfect morning would begin with working the horses. After they'd been exercised Hopkins would appear and request her help with a difficult case, but just as they would step outside, he'd decide to stay and help Laurel do . . . well, whatever it was that Laurel might want to do that morning, and Abigail would go to visit the patient without him. Oh, and Jeremiah would decide that it was too dangerous for her to go by herself, so he'd accompany her.

That would be a perfect morning.

While this morning wasn't perfect, it was close enough that Abigail couldn't protest. By the time she'd finished with the horses, Hopkins had indeed called to request her help with an expectant mother, although he didn't stay behind with Laurel—despite Abigail's suggestion—which was probably a good thing, since her experience in a prison hospital hadn't included delivering babies.

Turned out delivering a healthy baby was much easier than delivering a colt. After a full day of labor, the mother was now resting with the father attending, so Abigail and Dr. Hopkins made their cautious way back to the Calhouns'. The horses, sensing their urgency, trotted through every clearing as if feeling the eyes of the forest on them. Dr. Hopkins had complimented her on her work, but once they left the cabin, they both fell silent, unwilling to draw any attention to themselves while exposed and vulnerable.

Yet Abigail was in no hurry to return to the farm. Watching as Laurel adjusted to life at Jeremiah's side was too painful. She hadn't commented when Laurel moved Ma's spinning wheel out to the porch. She'd bitten her tongue when Laurel had cleared Jeremiah's bureau for her clothes. She'd walked away when Laurel had carelessly bumped one of Ma's bells off its shelf. No one had noticed the crack yet, and she wouldn't tattle.

The only bright spot in the situation was Rachel's change of heart. Finally Abigail had succeeded in her mission. Whether or not Rachel would survive the disease remained to be seen, but Abigail's promise to Alan had been kept. Rachel had her family and no longer needed a stranger to encourage her to do right.

If only Abigail had somewhere to go. Another opportunity. She kept telling herself that she'd only stay until the colt was born, but the colt wouldn't really change her situation.

At the sight of the Calhoun farm, Abigail urged her horse ahead. The barn door stood ajar, so she trotted into the barn and nearly trampled Laurel.

"I didn't expect you here in the dark." Abigail reined the horse to the far side and ducked beneath a low beam.

"I'm waiting on you." Laurel darted a quick look outside. "Did you return alone?"

Before she could answer, the subject of Laurel's inquiry rode into view. "I'll help you put the horse up, and then I've got to get home," Hopkins said.

Abigail dismounted. "Go on. I can certainly take care of my own horse."

Laurel bounced on her toes. "Jeremiah asked me to send you in as soon as you got here. I'll help Newton with your horse."

Even better. And what could Jeremiah want? Abigail handed the reins to Hopkins and wondered how he could miss the love-lorn gazes Laurel continued to throw his way. She hurried to the house, her feet traveling over the grass as lightly as Josephine's when she trotted.

An uncomfortable silence fell as she entered the parlor. Rachel swiped her red nose with the back of her hand and shot her a curious look. Abigail unbuttoned her cloak and hung it on the peg.

"What's a matter?" she asked. "What's happened?"

Ma left Hiram's side and came to her, bumping the center table and sending clipped articles flying. "I don't understand, dear. There must be some mistake—"

"The mistake is mine." The fire illuminated the concern on Jeremiah's face. "Abigail told me about her mother weeks ago. She probably assumed that I'd told you already."

Her mother. Abigail's stomach dropped. So much had happened since she'd told Jeremiah about her family. He'd declared his love, then rescinded it. Hiram had been shot, the house attacked, Rachel had collapsed and risen again stronger than ever. Amid all the changes Abigail hadn't thought to pull Ma aside and disclose exactly what she'd hidden.

"I'm glad you told them, Jeremiah." Abigail studied her boots. "I hadn't meant to let it go, but—"

"I didn't tell them," he said. "Hand her the letter, Ma."

A roar filled her ears. Abigail's vision narrowed to the ivory envelope in her mother's handwriting. A reply already? But what did it say?

"If I would've known that your mother was alive . . ." Ma twisted her journal into a tight cylinder. "I feel bad about you being here with us all this time. Did she know where you were?"

Abigail shook her head. "I just wrote her recently."

Ma's forehead wrinkled. "She must've been sick with worry. Why wouldn't you . . ."

But Abigail couldn't answer all their questions. Not yet. Her question held the greater urgency. The paper crinkled in her hand as she walked to the window. No matter how bad it was, she wouldn't consider it the end. She'd try again, even if they gave her no encouragement.

Abigail slid her fingernail along the ridge and broke open the seal.

> *Dear Abigail,*
> *Words cannot express our shame over our treatment of you. . . .*

Her eyes filled with tears as she read the apology. Her step-father's watch had been recovered in the possession of one of the grooms. They realized too late that Abigail was innocent. Her mother had languished for years worrying about her, sick with the thought that they'd turned Abigail out when she hadn't stolen from John. And Abigail's first letter written during the war had never reached them.

She pressed the letter against her chest. She'd do whatever she could to lessen her mother's pain, but she'd be lying if she didn't acknowledge that vindication felt good. After the accusation, she needed to hear them admit they were wrong.

And after all this time, she finally had permission to go home. The horse really didn't matter anymore. If Jeremiah wished, he could send it to her in Ohio. She trusted him to treat her fairly, but there was no reason for her to stay any longer. But could she leave? Was she ready to give up on Jeremiah?

"What's the letter say?" Ma frowned at her tears. "Is everyone well?"

"Yes, I—" Abigail couldn't imagine leaving Jeremiah. Never to see him again. Never to hear his voice, share his smile. But Laurel wasn't giving him up. How long before Abigail admitted defeat? "I need to go."

Leaving her cloak on the peg she ran outside, stumbling through the darkness.

"I can't imagine Abigail being estranged from her family," Ma said. "Whatever happened?"

Jeremiah balled his hands into fists. He hadn't meant to keep it a secret, but he didn't want it to look bad on Abigail. "Her mother is alive and remarried. Her stepfather did his best to run her off."

"Oh, poor child." Ma's hands clutched before her. "No wonder she didn't want memories so painful to be spoken of."

Someone should check on her. Not him, mind you, but someone. Jeremiah bumped his shoulder against the rock fireplace as he reached for his coat. What did the letter say? Had her mother renewed her accusations?

When he entered the barn, Hopkins and Laurel sprang apart, but he barely noticed. He threw a bridle over Lancaster's head as Laurel said good-bye and scurried to the house.

"Did you see where Abigail went?" Jeremiah asked.

"She headed up the mountain." Hopkins climbed into his saddle. "Where are you going?"

"To find her."

Hopkins raised an eyebrow. "Are you now?"

"Yes, and you're coming with me."

"Why do you need me? To keep you safe from the bushwhackers?"

It wasn't the bushwhackers Jeremiah needed guarding against. "No, but Abigail had a rough turn in there. She needs a friend." Hopkins didn't question him.

They rode in silence through the evening forest, the critters scurrying before them. Then a larger critter was heard. Rocks clattered on the hill above them. The horse swung his head toward the noise.

"She's up there," Hopkins said. "Are you going alone?"

"Yes . . . no." Jeremiah sighed. "Maybe you'd better take this one."

They both dismounted and climbed the last distance to the top of the hill. From the bald perch, the treetops below looked like dark boils of cotton swaying in the brisk wind. And there sat Abigail on the boulder overlooking the vast valley. She seemed to shrink into the rocks as they rustled toward her. Pulling her knees to her chest, she wrapped her arms around her legs and waited.

"It's cold," Hopkins said. "Why don't you come back to the house?"

Abigail ignored his suggestion. Jeremiah hated to see her shivering. He fumbled through his buttons and ripped off his coat. "Here. Give this to her."

Obediently Hopkins passed the coat to her, holding it at arm's length. Abigail pretended not to notice. With a shrug Hopkins handed it back to Jeremiah.

"I said give it to her," Jeremiah snapped.

"She won't take it."

"Then put it around her shoulders."

With a roll of his eyes Hopkins climbed the rocks, dropped the coat around her back, tugged it in the front so it wouldn't fall, then rejoined Jeremiah.

"There. She won't freeze," Hopkins said.

"We can't just leave her here. Talk to her some more."

Hopkins cleared his throat. "Abigail, Jeremiah thinks I need to talk to you some more, so why don't I ask him what I should say to you?"

Jeremiah shoved him. "Smart mouth. You know what to say. Tell her that if she wants to talk, you're ready to listen."

"Abigail, if you want to talk, I'm ready to listen."

Jeremiah shoved him again. "Are you mocking her?"

Hopkins turned and squared up to Jeremiah. "No, I'm mocking you. Why don't you go up there and say what you want? She can hear you, anyway."

Jeremiah glared at him. He longed to speak to her, but could he without breaking Laurel's trust?

"Please, Hopkins. Tell her that no matter what her mother said, it doesn't change your opinion of her. That you'll be there for her no matter what."

Abigail had turned to him. No longer hidden in the trees, Jeremiah stepped forward. "Tell her that she has a place in this family, and she's loved by us all."

Abigail's chin quivered. "Dr. Hopkins, would you please notify Jeremiah that my mother wrote to ask my forgiveness. My name was cleared and they want me to come home."

Go home? Jeremiah shook his head. She couldn't.

Her navy dress was a dark stain against the white rock. With a giant step only made possible by his healing, Jeremiah joined her on the boulder, only faintly aware that Hopkins had moved away. Jeremiah backed into its wall and slid down to sit at her side.

"I wish you would stay," he said.

"What use are wishes?" The light danced silver across her gentle face. "If it weren't for the trouble here, I might not have had the courage to write my family again. Mama never got my other letter and was sick with worry about me. They caught one of the grooms from the stable with John's watch soon after I left, and all this time she's been waiting to hear from me. I could've gone home long ago."

"How about your stepfather? Are you sure you want to live under his roof?"

"I don't know how he'll treat me, but they're my family. They're obligated to take care of me. You aren't."

Lancaster nickered. Hopkins was nowhere to be seen. Deserted him. Jeremiah rested his arms across his knees. Hopkins might go, but he wouldn't leave his friend.

The first stars twinkled at them from a clear sky. Jeremiah followed her gaze up. "In the army, I'd lie on my pallet and watch the stars travel. Before each battle I released everything into God's hands. Then, as soon as I started home I gathered up all my worries and told God I'd see to them from here. It turned out that the things I thought I could control have been a disaster. The things I'd given up on—my leg, Rachel's disposition—that's where God has worked." His hand rested next to hers on the boulder. "Looks like He smoothed your path, too."

<hr />

Yes, her path was clear. Nothing was keeping her in the Ozarks. She had to set aside her concerns over the reception she'd get from a chastened John Dennison. She didn't have to live with them forever. After the reunion she could decide from there. Maybe they'd encourage her to return to nursing. Maybe she'd meet someone who'd fill the spot vacated by the man who currently sat at her side, his coat wrapped around her shoulders. Maybe not.

"We shouldn't be alone." She pulled herself to the edge of the rock. "Is Ma terribly disappointed?"

"She loves you, Abigail. You've treated her better than her children have."

She fidgeted under his watchful gaze. Without a word he slid off the overhang, gathered Lancaster's reins, and motioned her down the hill.

She walked by his side where the trail was wide enough, until they reached the level pasture. Abigail flipped up the collar of Jeremiah's coat to protect her neck from the chilly wind. From the barn, Josephine called out her greeting to Lancaster.

"I'm going home," Abigail said. "And if I'm going, I'd better start my journey before winter sets in. About the colt—wait until it's born, and then please forward me my half. I wish I could let you keep the whole amount, but I don't know how reduced Mama's situation might be—"

He shook his head. "Don't talk like that. Go see your family. It's the right thing to do. But then come on back. We need you."

How much would she have given to hear those words that summer? But it was too late.

"I don't belong here. Not now. I'm not angry with you, Jeremiah, but you have to understand—I need more than you can give. There's nothing here for me."

He opened his mouth to argue, then his shoulders dropped. "I can't tell you what to do. I reckon you'd be the best judge of that."

He wasn't going to tell her what to do? Maybe they both had changed. And that reminded her of one last bequest she had to distribute. She pushed aside the bulky coat she wore to slip her hand inside her pocket. Her fingers grasped the cool copper penny.

"I have something for you." She stopped just short of the barn. Jeremiah turned, his face weary. "It's from my father. I've kept it all this time, but I want you to have it. I want to leave you something to remember me by."

Jeremiah's head remained bowed over her open palm. "I won't forget you, Abigail. I won't forget one moment of our time together, no matter how much I might wish I could." His fingers brushed against her palm as he gathered the coin. "I'll cherish this. I'll hold it for you with the hope that someday you'll return for it."

He pressed the coin to his lips with a wistful smile, then followed her to the house where their responsibilities awaited them.

CHAPTER 24

It was the coldest day they'd had yet—drizzly and gusty, but Abigail wouldn't be delayed. She was going home, and there was nothing any of them could do to stop her. The milk pail dug into Jeremiah's stiff fingers as he trudged from the barn to the warm kitchen. Even Rachel had pleaded her case, insisting that without Abigail she'd return to a cranky, self-absorbed tyrant, but her arguments only proved Abigail correct. Rachel had changed. Medically, Abigail couldn't help her, and emotionally her work was done.

So last night he'd stayed awake, fearful that he'd miss her evening watch. He'd squirmed on his hard pallet in the parlor waiting for her appearance, lying motionless when he heard her on the stairway. The green taffeta rustled. The floorboards barely creaked beneath her bare feet. She passed and he translated every clink of tin and drip of water he heard in the kitchen into pictures of her fixing the tea.

Then there she went again, hair tousled, eyes puffy, but at her post while the rest of the house slept. Faithful to the end.

Now he set the milk pail on the kitchen floor and scuffed his hands together to get the blood flowing. Spotting his rifle in the corner reminded him to pray for safe passage today. He'd be glad when the threat of dangerous men was behind them so he only had to worry about catamounts, bears, and razorbacks. How he wished that Abigail could've known the mountains without the hatred.

He heard someone coming down the stairs. Going to the parlor, he met Laurel lugging Abigail's valise from the upstairs.

"I can't believe she's leaving this morning," she said. "I'll miss her so."

Jeremiah's throat tightened. He took the valise. "I'll set it by the door."

Still buttoning the buttons on her wrists, Laurel followed him outside. "Jeremiah, I've been meaning to talk to you, and it really shouldn't wait." Her dark braids shone in the morning light, tight and freshly tied.

"Let's go inside. It's chilly this morning—"

"No. I'd rather talk right here." She paced across the porch. "I've been thinking about something Abigail said last week. She pointed out that if our parents were to marry, you'd be my brother." Her nose was turning rosy, her eyes bright. "I know she was just funning, but it didn't bother me like it should. In fact, it sounded right. It sounded natural. Why wouldn't you be my brother? I've always looked up to you. I've loved you like a member of my family. You tease me and watch out for me, and I'd do anything for you, just like a good sister should."

Suddenly the cold didn't bother him. "You don't mean—"

"Newton insisted that I throw you over, but I couldn't do it. I couldn't see you hurt, so I thought we should marry, but now I'm wondering if I made the right choice. I hate to be so flimsy, and if you are going to be forever heartbroken then I won't leave you." She leaned forward and grasped his hand. "I want you to be happy no matter what it costs me. I'm willing to put your feelings first."

Jeremiah fell to his knees, feeling more true emotion toward Laurel than ever before.

Laurel's eyes widened with shock. "Do you want to get married? I will if you insist—"

"No, Laurel." His smile stretched all the way to the back of his neck. "You don't need to marry me. We were both so careful with each other that we nearly made an awful mistake."

"You don't mind if I marry Newton?"

"I was jealous when I came home, but now I see that he's the better man for you. You'll make each other very happy."

Her knees buckled and she sat heavily in the rocker. "You don't know how relieved I am to hear that." She fanned her face, even though the air was frosty. "But what if he's already found someone else? I even worried about him and Abigail."

Jeremiah snatched her hand, kissed it heartily, and then hopped to his feet. "We'll just have to keep that from happening, won't we?"

His lungs fairly tingled from the cool air filling them. A huge weight had been lifted from his shoulders. Laurel was his friend, would always be his friend, but she would not be his wife. He spun to face her again. "You're sure, aren't you? You're refusing me once and for all?"

Her eyes sparkled. "I'm sure. From here on out, you're a brother to me, no matter what happens between our parents."

So happy was he that he wrapped his arms around her, picked her up, and swung her around the porch.

She squealed. "Land sakes, you don't have to act quite so relieved."

Jeremiah set her down and tried to stop grinning like a possum.

"I just don't want you to feel poorly about this. You've made the right decision."

"And Newton is coming this morning, isn't he?"

"He is." He and Calbert were stopping by to say their farewells to Abigail.

"Then I might favor him with a private word, if he'll allow it."

"See if he don't." But he didn't have time for Laurel's plans. He had to change Abigail's.

<hr />

Abigail saw the swirling skirt as she passed the parlor window. Laurel's giggles soaked through the rock walls, and Jeremiah's deep voice rang joyfully, making words unnecessary.

What a change of heart from last night's melancholy. Abigail crammed a last hairpin into her upsweep and scraped her scalp in the bargain. With her departure so near had he decided to stop pretending? If he was determined to marry Laurel, she supposed he might as well be happy about it. His misery hadn't been doing anyone good.

The kitchen chairs gathered undisturbed around the table, waiting for their owners to claim them. The cloth-covered milk pail had already been delivered. Abigail picked up the egg basket and moved the mixing bowl to the table. Breakfast would be her last meal with the family she loved. She wanted them all to be happy, but maybe she'd better appreciate their happiness from a few hundred miles away.

Jeremiah burst through the door. He rocked on his toes, grinning from ear to ear. "Good morning."

Why did he look so excited? Too bad she hadn't taken up pipe smoking, because she'd love to blow a cloud in his face at the moment.

"I found the milk," she said. "Have you already fed the stock?" With excessive force, Abigail cracked the egg against the ceramic bowl's edge. It shattered in her hand.

"I—no, I haven't. Laurel caught me on the way to the barn, and I completely forgot."

Abigail had made the right decision. For all his protesting that he was only marrying Laurel out of duty, he was doing a convincing performance. He should try the stage. She wiped her yoked hand on a dish towel. "I don't feel like cooking. Why don't I take care of the horses one last time and you fix breakfast?"

Before he could tell her how Laurel made his heart sing songs written by cupids and mermaids, Abigail snatched her cloak and fled out the back door. It'd sure been easier to appreciate his dilemma when he was miserable.

Heavy clouds blanketed the sky, making it impossible to tell where the sun was. Gray light filtered from everywhere, erasing shadows. She'd have to hurry if she wanted to be done by break-fast time. She could only hope that Laurel wasn't as addled as her beau and she'd help get the food on the table so they didn't miss the train.

The footsteps crunching behind her in the dry leaves were as familiar as her own heartbeat. When she'd started his exercises, she hadn't expected him to push himself so hard. Perhaps she shouldn't have taught him at all. Then he wouldn't be able to catch her so easily.

He passed her, unlocked the padlock, and swung the heavy barn door open for her. "Are you mad?"

She snatched the feed bucket and stalked toward the bag of oats. Equine eyes widened, stopping her in her tracks. She drew in a long breath and tried to stop bristling.

"I don't mean to snap at you." But how could she explain that his happiness made her mad?

Jeremiah closed the barn door behind him. "No apologies. You've put up with me for five months, and I reckon you're due a day of grumbling."

The gentleness of his tone left her confused. Instead of celebrating, he was treating her as carefully as she was treating the skittish horses.

"But I have no reason to grumble. You don't owe me anything. I'm not your family. I'm not tied in any way—"

He held up his hand. "We are tied, Abigail Stuart Calhoun. You can't pretend we're not."

Her eyes widened at the use of his last name. How could he be so cruel? To taunt her when he had no use for her affection? She sputtered, "Does it please you that I . . . that I foolishly gave you my heart? Don't imagine for a moment that I'm still afflicted. I made a mistake, but I've recovered."

"I hope not." At her gasp he came to her. "You should at least hear me out."

"Your time would be better spent feeding animals." She shoved the bucket into his chest, then gave an extra push for good measure.

He stepped sideways, blocking her way, uncomfortably close even with the bucket between them. "I wouldn't speak to you like this if I weren't free to do so."

Free? Hope rose like a bubble in her throat. What was he saying? "I warn you . . ."

He dropped the bucket to the ground with a clang. The horse hiccupped. Abigail took a step backwards. He stepped forward.

"Laurel and I have expressed our mutual disinterest for each other." His suspenders strained over his chest as he straightened his shoulders. "I wouldn't be surprised if she's engaged before dinner."

"She's chosen Hopkins?"

"She has, and I'm the happiest man in the world."

Was it possible? Abigail clutched a handful of her skirt. "But it's too late. I'm leaving."

"I don't believe you are." His ornery grin made her itch to smack him—whether with her fist or her lips was still to be determined. "You can't go to the train station alone, and why would I help you run away?"

"But you were so happy this morning—"

"I want you, Abigail." He held her gaze as he closed the distance between them. "When I wake up in the morning, my day doesn't begin until I see your face. While I'm out working, I'm thinking about things I want to talk to you about, how I think you'll respond, how beautiful you'll look as you argue with me." Running out of room for a retreat, Abigail bounced into the rock wall. Jeremiah took her hand. "I want you to visit your family, but not until I can go with you. I don't want you to ever be alone again." His thumb trailed over her knuckles. "Please stay with me."

Somewhere among the warm scents of the hay and horses, she caught the scent of his clean shaving soap. Whatever was going on with her heart, Abigail was sure it wasn't healthy. Her head spun in a delightful dizziness, thinking of what he might do, what she hoped he would do next. He was a fine-looking man, and he was hers. Two facts she could ignore no longer.

"Marry me," she said.

His satisfied groan turned into a chuckle. "I knew it. That dream *was* a premonition." He pushed back her loose coiffure to trace her ear. "Just for the record, I was going to ask you all proper like."

When he tugged her earlobe, he jangled some nerve all the way to her toes. To steady herself, Abigail gripped his arm and didn't even try to hide her assessment—no, appreciation—of his bicep. Definitely healthy.

"When?" he rasped.

"Today. Now."

He raised an eyebrow. "I suppose we could, but we'd have to boot someone out of a bed. Surely Hiram would move back home if we explained what we needed the room for."

"I guess I didn't think that through." She followed his gaze to her white-knuckled grip on his arm. With effort she loosened her hold. "I just meant to settle it before the sun goes down again. I'm tired of being Abigail Calhoun, married to a man who never consented. No matter what happens in the future, I want to face it as your wife and with proof no one can dispute."

"Not a bad idea. Besides, then I wouldn't feel guilty about the daydreams I'm going to have until we're hitched." Her fingers tightened again. He wrapped his arms around her and pressed a lingering kiss on her forehead. His mouth moved against her hair. "Once Calbert and Hopkins are here to guard the house, we'll go hunt down a parson and have it done by the end of the day . . . if you can wait that long."

Maybe the parson better just come to the barn, because it could take a full regiment to pry her out of Jeremiah's arms.

Or someone crashing into the barn door.

Abigail tried to look over Jeremiah's shoulder as he thrust her behind him and prepared to face the interloper. But it was only Josiah, heaving and gasping as he stumbled toward them.

"They took Pa."

CHAPTER 25

"You gotta come, Mr. Jeremiah." Josiah's words chopped short as he tried to catch his breath. "They jumped Pa on the ridge. Betsy's hiding in the hollow, but I got away."

Before he recognized a thought, Jeremiah had opened Lancaster's stall. "What'd they do to him?"

"Nothing yet. They said they was cold, and since he got them run out of their hidey hole, it was only fitting that he let them stay with us. Pa said Ma wouldn't allow it. That's when they pulled out their guns and said if she was a woman with smarts, she wouldn't mind company."

Those filthy dogs with Calbert's family? Jeremiah's neck throbbed. "Josiah, bring me my guns and my coat. And tell Hiram to meet me at your cabin. Tell him to come up quiet from the spring where he's not seen. You understand?"

Josiah took off, dirt flipping up at his heels with every stride. Across the barn, Abigail tugged the mare's bridle over her head.

"What are you doing?" Jeremiah had finished bridling Lancaster and climbed on bareback.

"I'm going to get Betsy. She must be scared to death."

He didn't like it. His Abigail should sit safely by the fire and wait for him to return, not ride against outlaws. "You find her and come back home, you hear?" Lancaster pranced toward her, itching to gallop.

"I'll hurry back," she said. "I don't want to leave everyone here unprotected."

His partner, taking care of his family. "You're a good woman. Come here."

She tugged the strap through the buckle before coming to his side. Leaning down, Jeremiah clasped the back of her head, pulled her against his knee, and imparted a kiss on her that should keep her warm on her mission. "Such a good woman."

Her hand rested on his thigh, the one that had so benefited from her touch. "Be careful, Jeremiah. I know you'll be brave. I know you'll be strong. But be careful and come home to me."

His throat tightened. In his heart, before every battle, he'd imagined Laurel saying those words. Now he realized how much better it was hearing them from Abigail. "Don't you worry. I'm coming back."

He pinched her cheek to merit a smile before he galloped out of the barn.

Hiram met him at the gate with his firearms. "Give me a minute to saddle up and I'll be there."

"I hope to get close to the cabin without them seeing us. After that, I have no idea. We can't blaze away with Mrs. Huckabee and the little ones inside." Jeremiah tucked his gun beneath his belt and rested the rifle across Lancaster's bare withers.

"Maybe we wait them out. Come to think of it, I'll bring some vittles. We could be there awhile."

Jeremiah glanced to the barn. "I pray we won't." But God often had bigger plans than his own.

Sensing his impatience, Lancaster pawed the ground. Jeremiah clicked and the horse surged onward, not even slowing when the trail narrowed. Curving his body forward, Jeremiah hugged the horse close as it left the trail and darted through the trees. Down to the spring that flowed from Calbert's house they raced. Splashes of icy water dashed against his hat and coat as he rattled the branches. Streams of smoke billowed from Lancaster's nostrils, but they reached the spring just as the horse was finding his full stride.

"Whoa." Jeremiah slid off Lancaster and tethered him out of sight. Taking his rifle, he silently followed the spring to the log cabin. From where Jeremiah crouched behind a brush pile, the cabin looked safe enough. The chimney puffed. The dogs cuddled beneath the porch. The burlap curtains were pulled to. Could this be another of Josiah's monkeyshines? But in the growing morning light, Jeremiah saw something that made his blood run cold.

Three horses were tied at the porch, one of them Ladymare. Even with Hiram, they were outnumbered.

He surveyed his cover. The branches would shield him from sight, but they wouldn't stay any bullets. Still, it offered the best view of the house. He'd have to stay hidden until time to act. He burrowed against the brush pile, making a hollow for protection from the wind, but stopped at a rustling. Some animal had already claimed the location. He hoped the critter didn't mind sharing.

Breaking a dry branch, Jeremiah situated a brace to hold the barrel of his rifle toward the only door in Calbert's house. One door made it easy enough to guard, but it didn't give the Huckabees any possibility of sneaking away. The rustling beneath the tangle of limbs started up again. A high-pitched squawking fired off. Several critters, a nest of some kind.

He hoped they didn't give away his position, but he couldn't leave Calbert and his family at the mercy of these men for long. They'd hunted down Hiram and followed Calbert back to his place. No one was safe in their hands.

But how to get them out? If he heard a gunshot, he'd charge immediately, no matter the consequences. Otherwise, he'd need to get them separated. But how? If he raised a ruckus outside, they'd leave someone behind to guard the family. He needed to get inside.

Get inside. Get inside. Quickly Jeremiah considered every possibility—the windows, the one door, the chimney. No trap door that he knew of, but if the dogs wouldn't bark, he'd go beneath to look around.

A crazed birdcall from behind alerted him that help had arrived. Hiram hid behind the smokehouse a full twenty yards away. With the hand that didn't have a gun in it, he motioned Jeremiah closer, but at that moment the cabin door opened. A stranger stepped out, one of those who'd taken Ladymare. The man scanned the area, pulled his hat down, bundled into his coat, and scurried to the outhouse. One quick look told Jeremiah that Hiram was ready. Was this his chance to get inside? If they took this man out, maybe Jeremiah could go in as a substitute. Wearing the man's coat and hat might buy him time to get between the outlaws and the Huckabees.

When would they get a better chance?

The demented bird whistled again. Jeremiah looked at Hiram. Why couldn't he just make like a hoot owl? Hiram's eyes bulged as he pointed to Jeremiah's left.

A polecat looking just like Betsy's pet only older and more cantankerous waddled through the wet grass, wanting its den after a night out. The chirping from the brush pile picked up. Jeremiah's stomach dropped. Her kits—that's who he was sharing a den with.

Mama polecat spotted him. Her nose twitched. Her babies cried.

Not since the Battle of Westport had Jeremiah been in such a dangerous position. While he could wish for a time when he wasn't sitting within firing range of a polecat marksman, this might still be his best shot.

Hiram chirped again. Jeremiah had to make a decision. He nodded toward the outhouse. Yes. They needed to capture the man before he got back inside.

The skunk eased forward. If she could make it to her furrow, she'd feel safe, but judging from her upraised tail, she didn't trust him, and the feeling was mutual.

Hiram crept toward the privy. Jeremiah was out of time.

Jeremiah held his breath as he jumped out of the brush. The skunk stomped her front feet as he rushed toward her. The outhouse door pushed open. No time to swing a wide circle around her. He just hoped she wasn't a quick trigger.

He'd never been a lucky man.

She spun and her backside burst forth with the foulest concoction an all-powerful God could create. The spray splattered just below his knee. He gagged but kept running until he tackled the outlaw. Hiram quickly crammed a rag into the man's mouth, then sprang away, his hand covering his nose.

"Help me," Jeremiah hissed as he lay atop the man's back, pressing him into the ground. "We have to get him out of sight without him making any noise."

Face crumpled, Hiram pulled out his pistol and held his fingers to his lips.

The outlaw's eyes watered and he turned his face from Jeremiah in disgust.

Hiram tossed a rope to Jeremiah, but the man didn't seem to be in a fighting mood. Jeremiah understood. Skunk spray washed the fight plumb out of him, too, but he'd have to do it anyway. There were two more men to deal with inside. If this one didn't return, they'd come looking for him.

They dragged the man into the woods and checked him for weapons. Taking handfuls of wet leaves, Jeremiah scrubbed on his pant leg, which only kicked up more stink. Could his plan still work? Would skunk stink ruin it?

"Take off your coat." Jeremiah bent over double until the wave of nausea left him. He only hoped the smell would make everyone feel just as bad.

"It's cold out here," the tough guy complained, but with the aim of Hiram's pistol he complied.

Jeremiah pulled his own coat off and tossed it to the man. "Wear this."

"No thanks. I'd rather freeze."

"Suit yourself." Jeremiah slid on the outlaw's coat and exchanged hats. Ducking his head and pulling the coat around his clothes he faced Hiram. "How do I look?"

"Better than you smell."

"Let's hope the smell keeps them away." No more talking. Every time he opened his mouth he tasted polecat brew.

He took the rope and helped Hiram tie the man to a tree. With one out of the way, they had even odds. He wouldn't mind the fight, if it weren't for the hostages.

"Get as close to the house as you can," Jeremiah said.

"Where are you going to be?" Hiram asked.

"Inside."

He buttoned what buttons weren't missing from the shabby coat and covered his face. No acting required to convince them he was sick. He stumbled to the cabin and busted in.

"What in the blazes?" The ring leader jumped out of his seat and covered his face. "Get out of here."

Calbert. He'd been roughed up a bit, but there he was, sitting on the bed with his arm around Mrs. Huckabee, who sheltered two wide-eyed toddlers.

"Skunk." Jeremiah kept his face covered and his voice muffled. "Help me."

The Huckabees didn't move. Both outlaws had pistols but didn't seem to be of a mind to use them. Jeremiah angled where the family wouldn't draw any fire when the time came.

One of the outlaws wheezed. "I ain't staying in here with him, I don't care how cold it is." He strolled out the door with a laugh, but it was cut short by a scuffle.

Before ringleader had time to respond, Jeremiah drew on him. He froze. Slowly he lifted his hands. "What do we have here?"

"Take his gun, Calbert." But Calbert didn't need the instruction. He tossed the gun aside and hogtied the man in record time.

"Been waiting all morning to do that. Where's Josiah and Betsy?"

"They should be safe at the house by now. Abigail is looking after them. I see they have her horse."

"I heard them tell of a nice herd of animals stashed away, just waiting to be taken to market and sold."

A brilliant energy coursed through Jeremiah. He had Abigail. That's what mattered most, but the outlaws had been caught, as well. If they could recover the missing horses, well, then wouldn't that be something?

For the first time in ages the weight of the world slid off his shoulders.

"There'll be a lot of people excited to hear that we found the horses." They could spread the word . . . right along with news of his and Abigail's marriage.

Abigail could've grated the pokeroot quicker without Betsy's help, but the child needed activity to draw her away from the window. In the parlor, Laurel and Hopkins had their hands full keeping an eye on Josiah, who wanted nothing more than to go to his father's rescue, a sentiment Abigail understood. If it hadn't been for the children, she probably would've sneaked over to the Huckabees' cabin herself by now, but Rachel needed her. She lay on the only sofa in the parlor, with swollen joints and the return of the rash on her torso. Abigail had never seen Rachel so bad off. She wrapped the pokeroot into the steaming poultice she'd prepared and nodded at Betsy.

"Let's see if this makes Miss Rachel feel better."

Betsy's tangled blond curls cascaded down her back and crowded her face. No smiles coming from the solemn child today. She followed Abigail into the parlor, not even acknowledging Ma pacing before the fireplace or Hopkins and Laurel showing Josiah the most exotic pictures they could find in Ma's journals.

Abigail pulled a chair to Rachel's side. "I have a poultice here. Where would you like it?"

Rachel's eyes fluttered. "Over my chest, please. My heart, it hurts." She held out her hand to Betsy and smiled when the child took it. "How's your skunk?" she asked.

Betsy sighed dramatically. "Ma made me keep it outside, and it ran back into the brush pile. I haven't seen it since."

Ever so slightly Rachel nodded. "Then it's with its family, and that's good. No one puts up with your stink like family."

Dragging himself away from Laurel, Hopkins placed a hand on Rachel's forehead. "Do you want me to get my stethoscope?"

"I think we know what's wrong with me," Rachel said. "I'm content to rest."

Laurel latched onto Hopkins's arm, and he didn't seem to mind one bit. "How about we make some gingerbread, Betsy? Do you think Josiah would help us?"

Waiting for Rachel's permission, Betsy tiptoed to the kitchen with the couple.

Abigail suppressed a smile as she arranged the poultice beneath Rachel's loose gown. "Poor Hopkins is about to burst. Until we know the Huckabees are safe, he can't let on that he's happy, but if he doesn't let some of that joy out, he's going to rupture his spleen."

"So Laurel finally decided." Rachel pulled in a short thin wheeze through her nose. "And you finally wore Jeremiah down."

"If you weren't so sick, I'd whup you," Abigail teased. "You know good and well your brother pursued me."

"Him on his cripple leg? You must run awfully slow."

Abigail didn't have the time to retort before Ma gave a small cry. Her hands flew to her heart and she pointed to the window. "They're here."

Out of the drizzly forest two men rode with their chests puffed up like bullfrogs. The kitchen door popped open as Josiah and Betsy raced by in a blur. Rachel tried to sit up.

"Do you feel like going outside?" Abigail asked.

Rachel paused. "Are they all right?"

"Yes, I think they are." No mistaking the look of accomplishment on the faces of Hiram and Calbert, but where was Jeremiah? Abigail's hand went to her throat before she remembered Rachel's fragile condition. "Why don't you stay here, Rachel? They'll come in soon enough."

As if in a trance, Abigail wandered outside. Ladymare's ears perked, but she was still tied to the back of Hiram's saddle. Calbert had his arms full of children, dispensing kisses generously.

Hiram was telling the tale of his adventures to Laurel, Hopkins, and Ma.

Ma? Was she so smitten with Hiram that she wasn't concerned with the fate of her own son? Abigail's skirt tangled between her legs as she stumbled off the porch. The gleeful activity swirling around her made her blood boil. Had they forgotten him?

Lifting two ladylike fingers to her mouth, Abigail took a deep breath and then ripped a whistle that could curl a horse's mane.

Conversations ceased, heads turned, and eyes widened.

"What's a matter, Miss Abigail?" Calbert remained on his knees with Josiah and Betsy in his arms.

She tried to keep her voice even. "Where is Jeremiah?" That's all. A simple question.

Hiram raised an eyebrow. Calbert smiled gently. "He's not here? Well, we took the bushwhackers to the county jail, and I assumed he'd beat us back. I guess he took longer than—"

"Where is he?" she asked again.

"And we got your horse back," Calbert added. "Those men had yours, Varina's, Hiram's, and a whole slew. On the way home we took back those we recognized, but there'll be some who never thought to see their animals."

"Where. Is. Jeremiah. Calhoun?" If Calbert didn't understand English she'd do a pantomime, but someone was going to answer her question.

"Oh, he got messed up something awful. He's down at the river, trying to put himself back together."

Next thing she knew she was on Ladymare's back, steam coming from her ears. How dare they leave Jeremiah to tend his own wounds?

"Now, Miss Abigail, don't you go looking for him." Calbert stood. "Considering the state he's in—"

But she spurred Ladymare before he could stop her. She was a nurse. No way in creation would she let Jeremiah suffer alone. How could they be so cruel?

Ladymare flew down the road. Up over the ridge they pushed and then descended to the river bottom. Had Abigail been cooler she might have asked exactly where on the river they left Jeremiah, but she hadn't had time. She'd just follow it toward Calbert's house. He had to be somewhere in between.

She slowed as she approached the low bank. What if he'd lost consciousness? What if she rode right past him and wasted valuable time? Why hadn't she insisted that Hopkins accompany her?

A splash sounded ahead. Ladymare's ears turned toward the disturbance. Abigail wiped her sweaty palms on her skirt, praying that the man on the other side of the undergrowth wasn't another bushwhacker.

Cautiously she eased Ladymare forward. The man turned and his smile transformed his face.

"Jeremiah!"

She dropped off the horse like an anvil down the well and ran to him. His shirt was gone, his shoes missing. In fact, the only piece of material covering him was a pair of pants that were too short and a mite too tight.

"Where are you hurt?" She grabbed his forearms and spun him in a circle. "Nothing on your chest. Is it your leg again?" Kneeling Abigail ran her hands down one leg then the other.

"What are you doing?" He stepped backwards, but she followed him.

"I can't believe those men left you alone." She didn't see any bloodstains. The only injury needing her attention was a scraped shin visible beneath his high-water trousers. "Why is this rubbed raw? Is there more?" With a tug she worked his pant leg up.

"Really, Abigail, if you'd just get up—"

"So this is your intended." At the sound of another man's voice, Abigail fell hard on her backside, making a splash in the shallow puddles of the bank. She scrambled to her feet as the young man rode out of the trees.

"Where's your gun?" she whispered to Jeremiah, spreading her arms in a vain attempt to shield him from the intruder.

Jeremiah took her by the shoulders. "This is the parson, Abigail. You asked me to fetch him. Remember?"

In Abigail's opinion, a man of the cloth shouldn't look so amused.

"I thought your request for a quick wedding was unusual, Captain Calhoun, but I think your bride is even more urgent."

Her faced burned. He'd seen the whole inspection. But then she remembered Jeremiah's injury.

"Your leg. What happened to it? And what happened to your clothes? And there's a skunk nearby. Phew. Let's get on home."

Jeremiah held her by the wrist. "Excuse me, Reverend. I need to throw the brakes on this mouth if we're going to get anything accomplished today." Then, before she could exclaim over his arrogance, he caught her and pulled her to him for a firm, hot kiss.

There her hands went again, inspecting his bare skin right in front of the preacher.

"I love interrupting you." Jeremiah's eyes smoldered and she dearly wished the parson would go away. But no, they needed him. Oh, whatever.

"Now," Jeremiah paused with a raised eyebrow, and Abigail reluctantly removed her hands from him. "Now, the skunk . . . that would be me, or rather, my clothes. Mrs. Calhoun sent me away with a pair of Calbert's old britches and lye, baking soda, a pint of tomatoes, a quart of moonshine—you can't tell anyone the parson helped carry the moonshine—and I hunkered down in this freezing river and scrubbed until my skin nearly came off because I wasn't about to go home smelling like Betsy's polecat."

Abigail wrinkled her nose. "You were sprayed?"

Jeremiah crossed his bronzed arms in front of his white chest. "Don't make that face. You're just smelling my clothes and they aren't coming home. Ever. I don't know quite what to do with my boots . . ."

"But you aren't hurt?"

"No, ma'am."

"And the parson? He's really going to marry us?"

His face lit up. "Today."

Abigail could only stare. That morning she'd packed her bags, prepared to say good-bye forever, and now . . .

"I'm glad you're not dead," she said.

"Me too."

"And that Laurel didn't mind changing her decision one last time."

"Absolutely."

"And that Rachel has decided to behave herself—"

"Um, Abigail? It's mighty cold to be standing around half dressed." As if she hadn't noticed. "Can we finish this list at home?"

The reverend had the nerve to laugh. "Come on," he said. "Let's get this over with. I can't afford to give you my whole day."

Abigail took Jeremiah's hand as they walked to their horses. She had all day. She had all the rest of her life.

EPILOGUE

"Come on. You can do it," Jeremiah encouraged. "Push one more time and you'll see your baby."

Abigail clutched his hand and squeezed. They'd waited for this day for months, but it was taking longer than she'd expected. Finally, water gushed and the last two hooves dropped. The black foal lay on its side, dazed but beautiful.

"Good girl," Abigail crooned to Josephine. "You did it."

Josephine's nostrils twitched as she tried to catch the scent of the strange beast that had just burst from her. The foal rocked, working its way closer to the warmth of her mother.

"Just what I need," Jeremiah said. "Another female around the place." But he wrapped his arm around Abigail's shoulders and pulled her against his side.

Abigail laid her head against his chest and watched as Josephine nuzzled her foal. A year ago she gave almost everything she'd had for this animal. At times she'd dreaded this day, knowing that the birth of the foal could mean the end of her welcome, but God had fashioned another plan.

"What a gift Alan gave me." She took a deep breath of Jeremiah's scent—clean cotton and pine. "If only he'd lived to see it."

"I'm sure Rachel's told him by now, if he didn't know already." Jeremiah lowered his head to rest atop hers. "I miss her," he said. "I'm glad her suffering is over, but I miss her."

Rachel's passing had been a peaceful, sacred transition. She'd had a few weeks of reprieve from her pain, during which she'd restored her relationships and made some new friends, not the least of whom was little Betsy Huckabee, who'd kept vigil at her side until the end.

Abigail wrapped her arm around his back, sliding her hand through his suspenders. "On our way to Ohio, we'll take some of Rachel's roses to leave at Alan's grave."

"Will the new tombstone be up?"

"Should be. No more Jeremiah Calhouns buried there."

He rubbed his bristly face against her forehead. "In a way, it was an honor to have my name on the grave of such a man, but Alan deserves recognition of his own."

The horse had found her way to her feet. The foal stumbled as her rickety legs discovered their purpose.

"Not too long ago I had the same trouble walking," Jeremiah said.

"You weren't quite that bad." Abigail patted his stomach. "Aren't you hungry? Let's see if Ma saved us any supper."

But he was in no hurry to leave the warm barn. He hummed a lullaby as Josephine tended her foal. "You know, when I heard it was Alan who sent you here, I thought he was trying to ruin my life."

"Sometimes the best gifts aren't convenient at the time."

"Convenient? Convenient is boring." With a laugh he swung her off her feet and into his arms. "Give me difficult any day."

He carried her outside, stealing a kiss every few steps. Their breath steamed in the cold air. The February wind rustled the bare branches above them and sped over the hills where, just on the other side of the mountain, Laurel and Hopkins were enjoying their first winter together, reveling in each other's company and the privacy the new cabin afforded them. And soon, if Abigail had to guess, Hiram would find the nerve to ask Ma for her hand so he wouldn't have an empty house any longer.

She snuggled into her husband's arms. They'd get to the supper table sooner if he'd let her walk, but he enjoyed showing his strength, and she enjoyed his being strong.

Together she and Jeremiah had seen many changes. They'd fulfilled their obligations, had completed their duties. Now their first priority was to look after the promises they'd made to each other. There'd be nothing to hide, nothing from the past to mar their present happiness or their future.

They had survived a brutal era, but with each passing season their war-torn hearts continued to mend. They wouldn't forget, but like the rest of their country, they chose to travel forward.

Regina Jennings is a graduate of Oklahoma Baptist University with a degree in English and a history minor. She has worked at *The Mustang News* and First Baptist Church of Mustang, along with time at the Oklahoma National Stockyards and various livestock shows. She now lives outside Oklahoma City with her husband and four children.

More Fiction
You May Enjoy

You May Also Like

When Eliza Cantrell arrives early to meet her absent groom, sparks unexpectedly fly between Eliza and her future husband's best friend. Could God have a different future in store for this mail-order bride?

A Bride in Store by Melissa Jagears
melissajagears.com

Brilliant but reclusive researcher Darius Thornton is not the sort of man debutante Nicole Renard could ever marry. But can she stop her heart from surging full steam ahead?

Full Steam Ahead by Karen Witemeyer
karenwitemeyer.com

Zayne Beckett and Agatha Watson have always been able to match each other in wits. But will unlikely circumstances convince them they could also be a match made in heaven?

A Match of Wits by Jen Turano
jenturano.com

✦ BETHANYHOUSE

Stay up-to-date on your favorite books and authors with our free e-newsletters. Sign up today at bethanyhouse.com.

 Find us on Facebook. facebook.com/bethanyhousepublishers

 Free exclusive resources for your book group! bethanyhouse.com/anopenbook

an open book